The Consequence of Love

Sandra Howard

**SIMON &
SCHUSTER**

London · New York · Sydney · Toronto · New Delhi

A CBS COMPANY

First published in Great Britain by Simon & Schuster UK Ltd, 2017
A CBS COMPANY

1 3 5 7 9 10 8 6 4 2

Simon & Schuster UK Ltd
1st Floor
222 Gray's Inn Road
London WC1X 8HB

www.simonandschuster.co.uk

Simon & Schuster Australia, Sydney
Simon & Schuster India, New Delhi

A CIP catalogue record for this book
is available from the British Library

Hardback ISBN: 978-1-4711-1139-6
Paperback ISBN: 978-1-4711-1141-9
eBook ISBN: 978-1-4711-1142-6

Special thanks to Faber and Faber Ltd for permission
to quote from *Four Quartets* by T.S. Eliot

Typeset by M Rules
Printed and bound by CPI Group (UK) Ltd, Croydon, CR0 4YY

To Sholto, Nick and Larissa, Louis and Tallula,
Jasper, Theo and Layla. All their babyhoods
remembered with love and pride.

To love at all is to be vulnerable. Love anything and your heart will be wrung and possibly broken. If you want to make sure of keeping it intact you must give it to no one, not even an animal. Wrap it carefully round with hobbies and little luxuries: avoid all entanglements. Lock it up safe in a casket or coffin of your selfishness. But in that casket, safe, dark, motionless, airless, it will change. It will not be broken; it will become unbreakable, impenetrable, irredeemable. To love is to be vulnerable.

CS Lewis

Two hearts have eyes and ears, no tongues to speak:
They hear and see, and sigh, and then they break.

Sir E Dyer

MAJOR TERROR ATTACK AVERTED

DEADLY NUCLEAR BOMB PLOT UNCOVERED
BY THE HEROIC ACTIONS OF A YOUNG MUSLIM

Thousands of people are alive today thanks to the fearless actions of one individual. A catastrophic disaster was averted yesterday afternoon when a hidden 'dirty' bomb was made safe with seconds to spare. The young man who tracked down the perpetrators of the most heinous terrorist plot this country has known and who faced down the mastermind behind it, cannot be named because of the threat of reprisals. He was shot, but survived. This newspaper salutes an act of exceptional bravery and regrets the shadow of danger he must live under now, at constant risk to his life ...

Continued on pages 4 & 5

Continued on pages 4 & 5

The Post, 24th December 2009.
Extract from the front-page story.

1

Absence

A lone seagull was wheeling around in the cloudless sky, swooping and diving gracefully like an accomplished pilot at an air show. Natalia Dangerfield squinted up at it idly, lazing in the baking sun and thinking of not very much. The heat was blissfully mind-numbing.

Natalia was fair-skinned and had to be careful about the sun, but had faith in factor 30 and stretched back luxuriously, lifting her arms over her head to the solid wood frame of the lounger. That was the thing about a villa like this: the sunbeds were good and sturdy with smart navy mattresses and no plastic in sight. It was a crazy rent, but her mother and stepfather, William, were paying – and they had gone home a few days early to be out of the way. Hugo had soon relaxed about piggybacking off his in-laws on their annual Algarve holiday.

It had worked out fine too, with masses of family the first week, grandparents on hand, and no major rows to speak of, which was rare. Nattie's mother and William loved to fight; it was a game to them, instinctive and fun, however hard that was for anyone in earshot to believe.

Hugo was still in the pool with Lily, their four-year-old daughter. He'd been patiently walking the widths with his hand under her tummy for ages, calling out instructions, doing his fatherly best. 'Frog's legs, Lily, it propels you forward, and don't forget the arms, no doggy-paddle now!' He was convinced she was almost there and could do without armbands, but Nattie wasn't having that. They'd taken a lot of choosing, those armbands, while she expired in a pricy little beachside store, jiggling Tubsy on her hip, trying to stop him pulling kiddies' sunhats off a stand, until the pink-kite armbands won out over the ones with yellow butterflies.

The pool was a good size, even by Quinta do Lago standards, with royal azure tiles that turned the water an astonishing reflected blue. A wiry young guy in a sweaty khaki singlet had appeared a few times to set a mini-Henry-the-Hoover-style pool-cleaner going that *putt-putted* around being a menace, with its long snaking hose ambushing any peaceful swim. His shorts doubled up as an oil rag when he cut the grass and his jet-black hair hung in clumps over his eyes. It was a job to wring a smile out of him. Was it resentment at the scale of the properties he tended? Some in Quinta do Lago were simply vast.

Nattie liked the garden, the Maritime pines that screened the next-door properties and the nasturtiums climbing the wooden fencing, prettily filling in gaps. She could smell the lavender and she enjoyed the sexy red hibiscus bushes that lifted dull corners, and the oleander in well-aged terracotta pots. The villa's owners, she decided, must be frequent visitors.

The novel that she planned to review lay face down on the spiky grass and she eyed a large black ant scurrying across its splayed covers. With tomorrow the last full day of the holiday she sensed the beginning of the wind-up, her mind on work. Nattie edited the book pages of a monthly magazine called *Girl Talk*, and her Out of Office message hadn't been entirely effective at keeping emails at bay. Her PA had been in touch. Nattie had wanted to interview a young Pakistani debut writer, Sadia Umar, for the magazine, and the publishers had called to say that was fine, but it had to take place on Nattie's first day back at work.

It was good news in one sense. Sadia Umar had written a powerful novel, and she'd be interesting to talk to, but just seeing her name in the PA's email had darkened Nattie's mood. She felt unnerved. Names spoke. They marked people out. They caused preconceptions, prejudice, erected barriers, even caused wars. Sadia's name was a small raincloud in a clear sky, a cloud heavy with past reminders and bringing treacherous thoughts.

Her own name, if she allowed it to, could be just as unsettling. Not Nattie; she liked that, she was only ever Natalia on official forms and the screen at the doctor's surgery. It was her married name, Dangerfield, that in low guilty moments caused her secret distress.

It had nothing to do with presumptions about background and lifestyle, it was the memories that could surface simply by hearing herself called by her married name. At home in London, busy and preoccupied, the anguish of the past stayed buried, but in moments of uncluttered thinking time it could rise from the depths like a drowned body. Nattie had never known what had happened to the man she loved. She couldn't let go; there'd been no closure and even seven years on she still ached and pined, wondering and fearing the worst. She held on to the love, it lived in her body, she kept it deep in her heart, but not knowing meant not being able to grieve, that was the cruelty of it; hanging on to fading hope.

She forced her mind back to the present, determined to banish the shadows. The sun felt sublime, although she'd have to stir herself soon. Tubsy still needed his afternoon nap, yet it didn't do to let him sleep on. He was fifteen months old and had just taken his first faltering steps. His grandmother had clapped him madly and Tubsy, clapping himself too, with his chubby cheeky grin, had promptly fallen backwards onto his well-padded bottom with a look of comic surprise.

'Hey, how're you doing?' Hugo splashed a few drops of water her way. 'I thought you were coming in? Aren't you burnt to a frazzle out there? Lily's been doing brilliantly, really swimming now.'

'Clever girl!' Nattie called, smiling and sitting up straighter, exaggerating the shivers as Hugo splashed her some more.

'We're just getting out so you've missed your chance to see the progress. I think the armbands aren't helping,' he added annoyingly. 'They're just in the way.'

'Can't I have one try without them, Daddy? Just one?'

'Sorry, Lily, it's time to get out. High time.'

'Shall I come and take over?' Nattie suggested half-heartedly.

Hugo shook his head and blew her a kiss. 'Don't you move a muscle. You look like an ad for Algarve holiday villas, lounging there in that white bikini, one knee raised. I'm enjoying you.' He lifted Lily out of the water and swung himself up onto the ledge. 'Chuck me that towel, though, can you, darling?'

'Lily, love, you've got goosies, you've been in that long,' Nattie said, throwing over the bulky orange beach towel that they needn't have brought; the villa was well stocked. 'You must dry yourself really well.'

Hugo squatted and gave Lily a good rub, wrapping the towel round her shoulders. 'Maybe we'll try without them tomorrow, honeybun,' he said vaguely. Then he rose from his haunches and stood staring down, his mind elsewhere.

His swimmers had slipped below the cleft and were suctioned wetly against him. He had neat, tight buttocks, straight legs with a good covering of male fair hair. Nattie gazed at him admiringly. You couldn't ignore Hugo's body. Girls stared after him on the beach; chic women eyed him up in his faded old shorts, pushing the baby buggy around the resort. He never noticed. If she teased him about it he'd look embarrassed and say painfully that he never looked further than her – and not even in a hamming-it-up way, just being dreadfully hammy.

Hugo had no self-awareness. He was in public relations and as unlike his smoothly assured colleagues as a monk from a megastar. He was a real one-off, humble, kind, understated in all but his masculinity.

Nattie sighed, her thoughts turning wistfully to afternoon siestas. She'd soon be back juggling mothering, nursery-school runs and meetings at work; the months up to Christmas were always such a hectic time. No siestas with Lily to entertain.

She sighed again and realised, feeling slightly caught out, that Hugo had turned and was studying her.

'I'll go and do that bit of shopping now,' he said, 'and we need more wine, we're right out.'

'Don't go too mad, it's only two more nights. The list's on the kitchen table.'

'Can't I come with you, Daddy?' Lily stumbled over the towel, going to hang on to his hand. 'I'm a good little shopper. You said!' She was tiny beside him in her Peppa Pig cossie, still shivering.

'But none of those gobstoppers or you won't eat your tea.' Nattie swung down her legs and felt for her flip-flops. 'Come on, let's get you dressed.'

'You stay right there.' Hugo leaned over to give her a kiss. 'I'm on the case.'

'Yes, you stay right there, Mummy,' Lily parroted. 'I can dress myself perfectly well.' She was getting far too precocious for her own good.

'Prekoshus means advanced for my years,' she'd informed them. 'Granny said.'

'No, it means getting a bit above yourself,' Hugo had told her with a firm look.

Lily had even come home from school one day saying she wanted to be a 'pallyotogist' when she grew up. 'And find lots of dinosaurs' bones!'

'Off we go then, Lily love,' Hugo said, 'and as quiet as dormice indoors, remember. Thomas is still asleep.'

Nattie watched them pick their way over the spongy, spiky grass. Thomas was Tubsy to everyone in the family, but not Hugo. He was a pompous old stick, she thought fondly, a proper old conformist now. It was nothing short of a miracle. Solid, successful, a loving father, as settled as can be ... Wasn't he?

The past reared up again. It was a quagmire; it kept her trapped, stuck fast, the memories were inescapable. Was Hugo really free of his demons? Could he ever slip back? It was in her power to see that he didn't, but there was always the hopeless ache of longing ... And Hugo knew.

They'd met when Nattie was sixteen, at a party given by one of her friends with older brothers. Hugo had been nineteen – a shy, respectable young man, just off to university. He'd had a safe country childhood, his father an Oxford architect, his mother also working in the firm. Nattie's mother, Victoria, had been all for Hugo. She'd thought him charming and good-looking, just right for her daughter, a young man from a similar background whom she could trust.

Hugo never pushed himself forward and he'd been sensitive to Nattie's teenage troubles. She'd had a bad experience and hardly said a word to him the next time they'd met, too withdrawn even to look at him.

A boy from school had forced sex on her. She hadn't let her mother report it or take any action, feeling she'd brought it on herself, but it had left her disillusioned and on her guard. Hugo had kept his distance and gradually earned her trust with his gentleness and understanding. She'd known he cared. Nattie smiled to herself. He'd always been constant, never lost faith – and to think of all they'd been through . . .

In those early days their relationship had been easy and uncomplicated. Her envious friends had said how well suited they were. That was until Shelby Tait, with his jet-black hair and electric-blue eyes, had come along. Shelby was a sexy, glamorous, no-good shit, impossible to resist. He had been at Durham, Nattie's university – not at the same time, he was three years older and had dropped out after a year – but his silky charm and numerous conquests had ensured he'd had many invitations back onto campus.

He'd spotted her at a college disco and swooped like a hawk, predatory and deadly. She'd been easy prey. She'd known he was bad news, but had ditched Hugo for him all the same. Nattie could remember her mother's sorrowful brown eyes, unspoken acknowledgement that any relationship a parent encouraged was bound to be doomed.

Shelby had sucked up to Hugo, got the measure of him and seized on his insecurities. He'd been into dealing and had started to supply Hugo, just a bit of weed at first before slyly tempting him to try more toxic highs. Nattie had been far too distracted by his insidious appeal to see what was happening. Shelby had hooked in Hugo and walked away with his girl.

No sound from the baby monitor and Hugo was still around anyway. Nattie felt free to have a swim. She did a few fast lengths, feeling a bit guilty. It was time to go in. Tubsy could work himself up into a lather so quickly.

She climbed out of the pool and allowed herself a few more minutes, stretching out again while the sun dried her fast. Tubsy was always crotchety after sleeping too long, but she was lost to the many thoughts in her head ... and the memories were powerful.

The break-up with Shelby – never much of a thing anyway, red roses and dinners, excuses and no-shows – came after she'd fallen in love elsewhere. Shelby's jealousy had been pernicious, but she'd been too much in love to care. She clung to the love even now, despite all the dramas, loss and heartache, marrying Hugo in her despair ...

Images of Hugo of seven years ago swam into her mind. Vivid images – she shivered in the heat of the sun. She could still see the syringes and used crack-pipes, sometimes improvised out of broken glass and tin foil, the evidence there in his flat, undisposed of. She would find him on his knees at times, scrabbling round for any miserable speck of crack, any fragment to rekindle the shadow of a high, a desperate attempt at recycling. She'd seen him wash out a used pipe, trying to set light to the rinse liquid for a pathetic last gasp.

Nattie had sometimes arrived only minutes after his crack experience, which he once described as like a golden light shooting up into his brain, his heart, coursing through every vein in his body. It was an orgasm on the moon, he'd said, indescribable joy. That was before the plummeting down, the paranoid panic, which she'd witnessed too often at first hand. She remembered Hugo whimpering, showing the whites of his petrified eyes, swearing he could hear voices, feel cats' claws, and that the devil people were coming to take him away.

She could still recall the sense of hopelessness, letting herself into his Hammersmith flat; still smell the sweet sickly stench, the mould in his fridge, the unwashed sheets; still see the empty bottles, ruined designer jackets and jeans. She'd felt revulsion and had to resist a burning urge to back right out of the door.

Once when his parents were coming to London, she'd cleaned up his flat in a frenzy and stayed till the last minute, determined to get him through. Showers helped to distract him. His body was so raw, Hugo said, that the water had felt like the Victoria Falls raining down, while the force and sensation helped to blot out his mind. Nattie had given him a Valium and urged him to tell his parents that he had a stomach bug and was feeling below par.

Had his parents known? Hugo thought not, but Nattie suspected they'd had some idea. Unless perhaps, she wondered, that to imagine their son a crack-heroin addict had been a step too far. Nattie had been anxious to keep Hugo's condition dark for reasons of her own, not least because her mother had been Home Secretary at the time and the press would have had a field day.

She had lived through it all, the detox, the rehab, pleading, begging him to find the will. It was only when helping Hugo to get clean that she realised the depth of his feelings for her and in her heart she felt a deep sense of responsibility.

He'd hung on to his job with the prestigious public relations firm, Tyler Consulting, by his fingernails, the grace of God and the chairman. It had been an immense relief to Hugo, never having to tell his parents that he'd lost his job.

He had been junior in the firm, expendable, and the moment had come when his haggard looks, lateness and unexplained absences could be tolerated no longer. Other guys were coke-heads, but they handled it. His line manager's ultimatum had been curt. 'Shape up or you're out.'

Would Hugo have made it through without the enormous generosity of the chairman of the firm, Brady Tyler?

Hugo had told Nattie every word of that pivotal meeting. Brady, who must have seen it all before, had obviously a soft spot for him. He still did. It was Hugo's extraordinary good luck that his chairman had been prepared to give him a second chance. Brady had told him, after a meeting that was clearly seared on Hugo's mind for life, to take a six-month paid sabbatical, sort it, and report back for work.

Clients appreciated his reticence, Brady had told Nattie at one of the client events that were now part of her life. They liked Hugo's self-effacing temperament, his reliability and quiet intelligence.

When she'd relayed that back to Hugo he'd guffawed, but at the time of the meeting he'd been on his knees. 'What I owe Brady, Nattie! I mean, he was just a-mazing, a fucking saint no less. Anyone else would have kicked me out on my arse, all the way down from the seventh-floor window. But Christ, what an interrogation. Brady had looked so remote behind that vast glass desk of his – it's like some Tate Modern sculpture, three great cubes, grey, black and white – and the office is all glass and white leather. He'd started on about how only I could do it, how I had to want to be helped and prove I had it in me.

'He even talked about you,' Hugo confessed, looking sheepish, 'he prodded that deep. He droned on and on about putting his faith in me ... God, it was hard. I was screaming for a hit.'

'But you did it,' she said. 'Brady's faith wasn't misplaced.'

Nattie leaned over the cot – provided by the rental agency – whose acid-drop yellow hideousness caused her to wonder; the pink and blue dancing teddies covered both bases at least. Tubsy was stirring, grizzling, drawing up his knees, raising his bottom high into the air; his buttery curls were damp and plastered close to his head. 'Time to wake up, little love,' she murmured.

He was heavy with sleep as she lifted him out, lighter when cuddled, hot and sweaty, smelling of cot bedding, his baby self and a very wet nappy. Her heart swelled. Was any woman luckier? Two beautiful children and a husband – who could turn heads – who truly loved her. A job she enjoyed, cool, fun friends, Hugo's friends too. She had a good home, a full life, so much to be grateful for . . .

'My precious little Tubs,' she whispered, settling him on the changing mat.

He was wide-awake now, saying, 'Dad, dad, dad . . .' with a smiley grin.

'Mum, mum, mum,' she said, smiling too, 'and Dad, dad, dad. Daddy and Lily will be back soon, we'd better go down and make tea.'

2

Ahmed

Twenty minutes to landing. After a long overnight flight the cabin staff were collecting up rubbish and bringing the Business Class passengers their jackets and coats. Ahmed Khan took delivery of his linen jacket. He had a window seat and gazed down as the plane flew in low over a long-missed, long-remembered landscape. It was mid-morning, a cloudless late-summer's day; he could see the harvested fields – squares of yellow and bronze – copses, villages and southern towns. England. His homeland.

Was it a good omen to be arriving back in sunshine? His skin pricked with fear and anticipation. He hadn't set foot on British soil for seven years.

The moment of leaving was still starkly resonant, the agony of the parting on that cold January day in 2010. Nattie's beautiful face had been wet with silent tears. Saying goodbye to his family too, seeing them for what could be the last ever time.

They had come to London the week before, his father, mother and sisters, his little nephews and nieces, all formally dressed – the girls in coloured abayas, the boys in salwar kameezes – and dragooned into silence. His family had stood round his hospital bed looking awkward and ill at ease, regretting his actions that were going to make life so difficult for them back in Leeds. Actions that were bringing the loss of him too: his parents' only son, their boy.

His head had been so full of Nattie. He'd felt claustrophobic, coping with his family in that stifling, ammonia-smelling cubicle room, in pain from his gunshot wound, stressed out and deeply resentful of their muted accusations while he tried to make stunted chat. They'd been out of context in that London hospital with a police protection officer in the passage outside. Ahmed had almost wanted them gone. Until they had gone. And then the reality had set in.

His father had stayed in London overnight and met Nattie at the hospital next day. His tension had showed and he'd transmitted a wrongly held suspicion that *she* was the cause of his son's wretched plight. Yet when his father warmed to her, despite all, Ahmed's heart had overflowed.

Thinking of him as landing neared brought fresh twists of the dagger; his father was dead now and the pain never lessened. It got worse.

Seven years. Ahmed had total recall of his emotions as the plane had lifted off, bearing him away with a great surge of power and setting course for New York. He'd felt a surge of his own, not of power but self-belief, fiery determination to succeed in his new identity in a new world, and be worthy of Nattie. Everything he achieved would be for her.

He'd never been west before. A stimulating new job had been lined up. His editor on the *Post*, William Osborne, had arranged a transfer to the New York desk for him, and his pulse had been racing like it was set to win Olympic gold. The authorities had tried to veto the job – too obvious and easy to trace, they said – but Ahmed had argued that his enemies would instinctively look further afield. A knot of fear had been tightening all the same. Staying alive had mattered; he was in love.

One day, he remembered dreaming, he would return to marry her . . .

Those emotions had sat uncomfortably alongside an engulfing sense of loneliness. The homesickness had been immediate, attacking even before the plane was clear of England's shores. He was exiled, denied the freedom to come and go or contact his family and friends; cut off from the girl he would have given his life for – and almost had.

People wanted him dead. Going away was all for his own safety, but it had felt like being banished.

Nattie had begged to come with him to America, but the danger had been immediate and immense. And she was young; he'd wanted her to finish her exams and be really sure. She'd still been in touch with her first love, Hugo, who had seemed beyond hope, a crack-heroin addict, and Ahmed had suggested she try to save him. Hugo had seemed a safe mission for her soft heart. Why had he done that? In a kind of reverse jealousy? Hoping to keep her out of non-junkie arms?

It was a question he would go on asking till his dying day. Seeing a press photograph, Hugo and Nattie on their wedding day, had made him wonder if staying alive was worth the struggle. He'd felt broken, disbelieving, cut to his core, but still savagely in love.

It was a lost cause, risking a return. She was married. She'd moved on.

'Five minutes to landing. Cabin staff, take your seats.'

Ahmed felt his gut tighten and he concentrated his mind on the instructions from his old flatmate, Jake Wright.

'The keys are with my lawyer, Don Maxwell, in Holborn, the

car keys too, and sheaves of crap about boilers and stopcocks. I'll text the address. You can take a cab from Heathrow, since you seem so fucking flush these days, you old sod. At least you've saved me from having to sell or garage the car for the duration. It's right outside the house in a permit bay. A black Mazda hardtop and my great, five-year-old love – just make the fuck sure you don't lay a scratch.'

Calling Jake, the years had melted away like snow on hot coals. Jake was his closest friend, close as a blood brother, yet they'd been out of contact until last month when Ahmed couldn't stand his feeling of holding life at arm's length, living outside all he cared about, a moment longer. Whatever the rights and wrongs, his guilt about the risk to Nattie, he'd had to return. It was high stakes, emotional life and death, but he'd picked up the phone to Jake that day and cast the die.

Jake was married now, a qualified architect and going places. Literally. He'd just left for Australia, hoping to broaden his experience. It was a stroke of luck, sad as Ahmed felt at not seeing him, that Jake's house in South London was sitting empty and he needed a private place to stay. Jake hadn't given a thought to letting the house – nor had his wife, Sylvia, who sounded a bit of a depressive – and he'd even fought against accepting rent. 'You'll be keeping it warm; just pay for the upkeep, you bugger, that'll do.'

Ahmed smiled. It wasn't often you had to argue the toss upwards, but he'd been determined to pay the going rate and not feel beholden. He'd taken the house for three months and paid upfront.

Jake had never been into money. Art, architecture, music, poetry, anything but dosh; when sharing the flat, he'd always been strapped, moaning that his academic parents never factored in landlords and their poor student son's need to eat.

He and Jake had met conventionally enough at a party. One of those bring-a-bottle, sex-the-objective dos, with loud tuneless pop and stale crisps. Ahmed hadn't known a soul there; only the guy from work – a colleague in his research department at the BBC – who'd asked in a slightly bored, patronising way whether he'd care to come along. Ahmed had got to the BBC via Manchester University and an internship, which had happily translated into a proper job.

They'd been a cliquey crowd at the party, earnest young leftie graduates, talking politics, eyeing-up, trying to slough off their parents' prejudices. But you never know what happens in life as that evening had proved. He'd got talking to a lanky architecture student, they'd hit it off and become firm friends.

Jake had suggested the flat-share and Ahmed had leapt at the idea. He'd been going stir crazy, living with his mother's cousin in Dagenham, putting up with her snooping, poking her long nose into his life and belongings. And he'd just landed a great new job on a national newspaper, the *Post*; he could afford the rent.

He and Jake found a top and attic floor in a small Victorian terraced house in Brixton. They'd closed their minds to the peeling hall wallpaper and stink of stale beer, the mouldy carpet and lethal stair rods; they'd painted their new pad white and never looked back.

They were down, landed. The Business Class passengers were off first. Ahmed was swiftly through Passport Control and into the baggage hall. He'd planned ahead, anxious not to linger in taxi queues, and ordered a car to meet him. He soon spotted a man holding up a card with *Mr Bashaar* written on it.

He was Daniel Bashaar on his passport now. Ahmed Khan was lost to the mists of time – along with so much else. He'd acquired a new backstory, which he'd had to memorise before leaving the country, a dispiriting, hurtful process. He was born in Lahore, not Leeds; his father was now an Islamabad bureaucrat, not the civil engineer from Peshawar, a Pashtun who'd immigrated to the UK in the sixties, who'd ended up jobless, reduced to driving a minicab – the father he'd loved. Ahmed felt a renewed stab of pain.

He'd changed his appearance too. Crewed his hair and taken to wearing glasses – a non-prescription pair he'd been allocated that didn't look like plain glass. He'd swapped his jeans, sweatshirts and scuffed leather jacket for button-down white shirts and a dark suit, shiny black shoes with discreetly raised heels; a look that had seemed more appropriate for Mr Bashaar.

Nattie had seen the crew cut in the days before he left – she'd hated it.

He'd kept his hair short for the first few months in New York before growing it back, thinking of Nattie, missing her as wretchedly as he did. He was seven years older now, but felt he looked much as he had done, much as she would remember him.

He knew the wrongness of returning, even without all the risks. But just to see her again, to have the chance to explain ... And if it didn't happen? How would he feel, alone here in London? But he would see her, he was certain of it.

Ahmed followed the card-holding driver out of the airport feeling travel-worn and sweaty in the hot, late-August sun, and as he climbed into the car his nerves were raw. The car was a smooth-running Lexus. He was glad of its darkened windows, the backseat privacy, and forgave the driver his sickly aftershave, which smelled like coconut-oil sun cream, for his ability to know not to chat.

The M4, Cromwell Road, everything was so familiar. Ahmed stared out, but introspection soon had hold and he sank further back into the seat. What was he doing, making this journey, renting Jake's house, staking his emotional all?

Nattie had two children, Lily and Thomas. Lily had been born five months into the marriage . . . Easy research, he'd been a journalist, but whatever the circumstances, however she felt in her heart about Hugo, she was married. And Hugo cared – he loved her deeply, he always had – whether or not his love was returned.

Nattie wouldn't want to see him. The thought of how he'd messed up plagued Ahmed night and day. He imagined how bitterly resentful she must feel after the years of non-contact, not even knowing whether he was still alive. She wouldn't realise that he'd known she was married either; he'd been incapable of getting in touch after that, hurting to the marrow of his bones.

They were outside the Holborn office. Don, Jake's lawyer, was cautious, asking to see his passport, but was soon twinkling away behind his red-leather-topped desk, saying he was always there to help. A useful contact.

Arriving in Lambeth, Ahmed soon spotted Jake's car. It was a mean machine, but covered in sticky from an over-hanging lime tree and attracting layers of dust – not looking its best. The house, by contrast, looked beautiful; early Victorian at a guess, with a charming yellow-brick front wall topped with trellis and a tumbling rose.

It wasn't that far from their old Brixton flat, closer into town, quite close to where Nattie's mother and William lived. Ahmed, like everyone else on the *Post*, had lived in fear of his editor, but he and William had been on first-name terms by the time he'd had to leave the country with his new identity.

He opened an elegant wrought-iron gate onto a small paved area with camellia bushes, lavender and some grey-leafed shrubs. He wasn't good on plants. He hefted his two bags up several steep steps to a porch set with exquisite little chequered black and white tiles, and was relieved when one of the keys in the envelope he'd been given fitted the lock on the discreet black-painted front door.

Jake had described the house as typical South London, four-storey and terraced, and Ahmed had checked out the market rate for similar properties. He could see at once that he'd underdone Jake and felt a warm rush. Jake was a hopeless case.

But a highly talented architect. Ahmed dealt with the alarm and looked about him. The hall was opened up and the living room had the run of the whole ground floor. It was a brilliant use of space and when he folded back the front window shutters and sunlight streamed in, the light, easy-living feel of the room lifted his heart and spirits.

He sat down on a long grey sofa that had its back to what remained of the hall wall and put his feet up on a sturdy glass coffee table. He took in a classy rug in shades of corn and barley, tall china reading lamps on either side of the sofa. He imagined Nattie sitting with him here while he held her hand and tried to explain. He wanted her to know that he'd never stopped loving her, through his disasters and failings, her marriage, his bitterness; he'd loved her obsessively through it all.

He had to decide the best way to get in touch. He could email her at her office. He knew she edited the book pages of *Girl Talk*; the blurb with the wedding picture had mentioned her working on the magazine. He could call her there, but hearing his voice would unnerve her, he feared, and if she put the phone down in a fluster, to call her back would seem like pestering.

What gave him a ray of hope was that she'd never closed their joint email account. The authorities had warned against keeping in email contact, but he'd hit on the idea of opening a joint account in a fake name. He and Nattie could save messages to Drafts, since they both had access, and no email ever need be sent.

They'd decided to write in code as well, although they'd chosen one that a child could have worked out.

He got his laptop from the hall, sat with it on his knees and clicked onto the account. His heart gave a lurch as he brought up a few of their old messages and read the coded words of love and caring, longing and missing. Nattie had written briefly of Hugo's condition while Ahmed himself had avoided any mention of his job and life in New York; it was safer that way.

Would she ever understand why he'd cut off all contact? Her messages had kept coming. *Where are you? What's happened? Oh God, please say you're alive. I'm here for you – always. Love you for ever – ever and always.*

She'd sent messages for months, though they'd all gone unanswered. Ahmed hadn't seen them at the time, he'd been incapable of looking. He clenched his fists; he was finding it hard not to cry.

He fought the bleakness and worked out what to say. Using their old code seemed a bit silly and unnecessary, laborious too, but he decided to end with a sentence in code. It felt a better way to put across his feelings.

Hello, Nattie,

I'm in London! Very much hoping we can meet, and that you still look in our old account once in a while. I've put the sentence below in code just for old times' sake, but don't you bother with that. Any word back from you in any form would be wonderful.

In Namibia elephants exercise, dippy things, otherwise sane, expressive, engaging. Young ones uppity – babies are darling little yawners.

Please, please see this. I'm holding my breath. Love, as ever, Ahmed.

The number beside Drafts in the mailbox list was 267. That had been the last message she'd written, five and a half years ago. Would she notice the new number? Did she ever look any more? Was there the slightest chance he was still in her thoughts? Unlikely. Keeping the account open was probably an oversight on her part and didn't mean a thing.

He would give it two days and if there had been no word by end of play on Thursday, he would email her at the office. But a return message in their account would speak volumes. It would be connection and fill his heart with hope.

3

Hugo

Hugo was lingering by the door in Lily's darkened room. She'd fallen asleep instantly and he was in need of a drink, but hesitating to go down in his present mood. He felt on the edge of a row. Seeing the misty, distant look in Nattie's eyes that afternoon, all too familiar in her unguarded moments, had got to him more than usual, really touched him on the raw. He knew there was nothing to be gained by bringing up the past; even talking around it would be upsetting and counter-productive – but the way he was feeling, something had to give.

Nattie cared and she understood him, probably better than he did himself. She genuinely wanted him to feel loved and central to her life, but he wasn't central to her heart – that was the truth of it. Down by the pool, seeing her distracted gaze ... she hadn't been thinking and caring about him then.

The last thing she wanted to do was to hurt him, he was sure, but did she have any idea of the torment within him, the loneliness, even sense of rejection? Hugo felt a cruel alien need for her to have a taste of the pain. They were living in the now, for God's sake, married, with a home, jobs, children. Wasn't it about fucking time she binned the past, kicked it out of touch and moved on? Christ, how many years was it – seven, eight?

They seldom rowed, he and Nattie, just a few mini-snipes, the usual marital junk. She got at him over nit-pickiness and pomposity, he nagged her about her coats and jackets piling up on chair-backs – God forbid she'd ever hang them up in the hall cupboard – and leaving her jeans just where she'd stepped out of them, subsided but still with form. He minded her damp bras and pants decorating every radiator. Her untidiness drove him mad.

But did he really want to bring up Ahmed, the shadowy elephant in the room, the stalking ghost, and ruin the cosy promise of the last evening of the holiday? Less elephant more Loch Ness monster, Hugo thought morosely, since the mystery of Ahmed seemed destined never to be resolved. The man had probably met his end and his maker by now – some retributive killing that the authorities had chosen to play close – or else he was married with three little Ahmeds, fuck it, and living in Pittsburgh, Preston or Pakistan. But would it even help if Nattie knew?

Hugo stayed in Lily's room cursing quietly and trying to contain his corrosive burn of resentment about the past. His regret at his own past too, whose horrors never left him; he still woke shivering in the darkest hours of night, reliving the pulsating headaches and screeching pain in his bones, the agonies of paranoid psychosis. Women were supposed to forget the pain of childbirth, but the memories of his torment were like a tic in his mind, always there.

Would he ever have made it through without Nattie? He had clung to a fervent hope that surviving the throes of detox and rehab would seal their relationship somehow and be the glue, the bright blue sky of their future together.

He'd known deep in his heart that there was no magical solution; he'd needed her on any terms, yet handling his feelings was becoming harder than ever and never more so than tonight. Perhaps it was the effect of two weeks in the Algarve – weren't holidays traditionally supposed to exacerbate emotional troubles and rows? He felt spineless, useless, longing for more self-confidence, to have the sort of forceful personality that women seemed to go for – though Nattie had lost her heart to someone not at all like that. Ahmed had been unassuming, selfless, quixotic, quick-minded – qualities that were hard to beat.

Hugo sighed and, squaring his shoulders, had a last look back at Lily. She had her precious woolly kangaroo, but the room had an unfamiliar feel. It was a typical holiday-villa spare, with twin beds, a pair of antiseptic landscapes and short floral curtains over mosquito-netted windows. The child looked lost in one of the adult twin beds. He and Nattie had pushed it against the wall, put cushions in front in case she rolled out in the night and shut down the noisy air-conditioning.

Lily had chosen the story then fallen asleep a few pages in and even that was making him feel inadequate – he'd minded being denied his good-night kiss. She usually flung her arms round his neck and hugged him before burrowing down and cuddling her kangy.

'Sleep tight, angel,' he mouthed, going over to the bed and fondly touching her cheek. He lifted away a long wisp of spun-silk hair, just like her mother's, and she gave an irritated little mumble.

Crossing to the door, he went out and pulled it quietly to behind him, and turning to go, almost bumped into Nattie. She was barefoot and he hadn't heard her come upstairs.

'Oops!' she laughed. 'You must have got through a lot of stories. I was waiting for you to give me a shout. Has she gone off?'

'Yes. I'm going down for a drink. Glass of wine? Pink or white?'

'I'm ahead of you,' she said, giving one of her heart-stopping smiles. 'I've opened the pink, but the white's nicely cold and it's got to be drunk, we can't take it back on easyJet. I thought we'd eat outside. There's no wind and the lemony candle bowls do seem to work.'

'Whatever,' he muttered, pushing on past, conscious of Nattie's hurt, questioning look.

'I'll just have a peep at Lily,' she murmured, looking back. 'You've plugged in one of the mozzie disks?' He nodded without turning and carried on.

Delicious smells were coming from the kitchen. Nattie had been making some sort of fish stew, a huge pan of it, he saw, with the crayfish, squid and some white fish or other that they'd bought on a companionable trip to the market – a child-free one, since Victoria and William had still been there to take charge. Nattie had frozen the fish, promising it would be fine, and it certainly smelled as good as fresh. She'd done a vast bowl of lettuce and avocado, basil-strewn mozzarella and tomatoes. She never stinted over food.

Hugo poured himself a glass of the Portuguese white, downed half of it and went out to the terrace with the bottle in a Thermos cooler. He pulled out a chair at the wrought-iron table and sat down. He'd taken down the covering sunshade after tea, liking the feeling of the terrace being open to the night, not overhung with a huge square canvas shield. The terrace was set in large pinkish tiles with steps down to the garden and he sat looking out into the shady dark.

Nattie had brought out dishes of crisps and immense shiny olives. She'd laid the table with rush mats and decorative pottery plates, the lemon candle bowls, and put a few sprigs of bougain-villea in a small round vase. Hugo palmed a mouthful of crisps. He sipped the cold white wine, drinking steadily, and refilled his glass. He felt as strung up as a plucked chicken.

Nattie came out to join him. She kissed the top of his head before sitting down and he smelled her scent, which was honey-ish, like jasmine or rose, he thought, and freshly applied. It was distracting and alluring, he was trying to get a grip.

'You're making fast work of that bottle,' she said cheerfully, reaching over him for an olive. She bit into it and held it half-eaten between her fingers as if about to speak. Hugo could see her small teeth-marks in the flesh round the stone. He wanted to grab her wrist and make her drop the stone, kiss her mouth, taste the piquant saltiness of the olive.

'We saw a little hedgehog in the garden this evening,' Nattie said, finishing the olive in tiny bites, 'when we were bringing in the toys. Lily was over the moon! It was snuffling in the grass near the pines. I called, but I think you were in the shower. We put out a saucer of milk, though I've brought it back in now – don't tell Lily. I was worried about rats and things.'

'I'll get your wine.' Hugo rose abruptly and went inside. He came back with the bottle of rosé and Nattie's glass, which he topped up without speaking. He was feeling ridiculously put out. Lily told him everything and she hadn't breathed a word about the hedgehog. He knew how stupid it was to let it upset him, but it did.

'Lily fell asleep after three pages of *Tim to the Lighthouse*,' he said levelly, making a conscious effort.

'Done in with all that swimming, I expect. You were up there such ages, I thought she must be getting her way as usual, winding you round her little finger.'

Hugo gripped the stem of his empty glass. With his over-sensitivity about Lily he was in no mood for Nattie's trite chat and smiles. 'Far from it,' he said curtly. 'I had things on my mind, I was in no hurry to come down.'

'What like?'

He stared back at her. She looked exquisite. She was wearing a flimsy, greenish sundress with shoestring straps. The colour showed off her tan, and her nipples, standing out against the fabric, were hard to ignore.

'I was actually wondering,' he said, 'looking at Lily, peacefully asleep, whether she'd grow up and fall in love with a Muslim reporter from Leeds.'

Nattie visibly flinched. She looked away, then bringing her eyes back, found some fight. 'That's a silly thing to say and you know it. What's got into you, darling? What on earth is the point of harking back to something so long ago in the past? We've had a cool holiday, just us, with the place to ourselves these last days. It's been great; don't spoil it now.' She pushed back her chair. 'I'll get the food. Then can we start over? Calm down and relax a bit, love. Please let's just enjoy tonight.'

'Not so sure about that,' Hugo muttered as she left, probably out of hearing. He emptied what was left of the bottle into his glass. He'd been off alcohol ever since getting clean, but had started again the previous year. It had been a conscious decision, a rare feeling of certainty that he could drink purely for pleasure and socially, without ever letting it lead to a relapse. Never again the tyranny of that absolute need of a hit; he'd come through.

He unscrewed the second bottle feeling well in control. The food would help as well. The wine was shoring up his determination to spell out his grievances before they spread like suffocating weeds and strangled his ability to cope.

Nattie was subdued and said nothing as they ate. The crickets made their symphony. The garden below the terrace was ink-dark, but the stars were out and the air as warm and soft as a woman's touch. She caught his eye finally, with a rather frail, uneasy smile.

'The fish isn't bad, is it,' she asked, 'cooked this way?'

'No, it's good. Tasty.' He felt unable to maintain a total freeze-up, though it was hard to suppress his urge to put her through it and make her aware of his bitter mood.

She watched while he made inroads into the second bottle, but didn't raise her eyebrows. Then she pushed back her chair. 'I'll get the peaches and there's all that cheese left as well. Coffee ice cream in the freezer.'

'No, stay for a moment. I want to ask you something.' Hugo wasn't about to be deflected. He stared at her, determined to shake her up and inflict pain. 'Here's a question. What would you do if, say, the doorbell rang one day and you opened the door to Ahmed?'

Nattie's eyes filled with tears. She still cared that fucking much? He felt chilled to the pit of his stomach. She brushed at her eyes impatiently with the back of her hand, sat up straight and faced him. 'How can you do this, love? Why keep obsessing about something that's history now, long over and done with.'

No, Hugo thought, it wasn't over and done with. Ahmed had control of her heart, he owned it – he still would even if he was buried and below ground.

'We have so much,' Nattie pleaded, more in control, doing her irritating best to soothe and placate him. 'I love you, I treasure our life, I love our children, I'm wildly proud of you, my tall handsome guy. Can't you just be glad of what we have and be happy like me?'

'You haven't answered my question.' Hugo stared stubbornly; his hands were shaking and he pressed down hard on his thighs, fingers splayed. Sure she loved him, just not as much ... He felt the pain tear into him. 'Well?' he demanded, leaning forward, still gripping his thighs. 'What would you do? And don't say it's hypothetical; don't fob me off. I need to know. '

'But it is hypothetical, probably impossible – I doubt he's still alive. And even if he was back in England and managed to track us down, he'd know by the same token that we were married. It would be a social call. Darling, it's been nearly eight years! Don't be such a gloopy loon, you know how much you're loved.'

Hugo had a barely containable urge to swipe at everything on the table, send plates, glasses flying. Nattie couldn't spit it out, couldn't bring herself to say that it wouldn't matter if Ahmed turned up, it wouldn't mean a thing. He froze when she reached for one of his trembling hands and entwined fingers. 'I love you,' she repeated uselessly, resting her head on his shoulder. 'And always will.'

Hugo could feel the heat of his fury ebb away. 'It was the look in your eyes,' he mumbled, still sitting rigidly upright, unyielding and unresponsive. Retrieving his hand he rose and stood with his back to her a moment, trying to regain his composure. 'I'll get the bloody cheese,' he said over his shoulder, going into the villa, pushing open the sliding glass doors.

There was no release, nothing gained. She couldn't love him in the way he wanted. He'd married her knowing that, though, and challenging her tonight had been a stupid unwinnable battle, even tanked up with two bottles of wine. He loved and needed her; without her he wouldn't survive – the addictive need would surface. Living on crumbs was better than starvation.

He returned with the fruit bowl and some pungent black-rinded cheese. Nattie hacked at it and put a piece on his plate, reaching for the bread basket with a cautious smile. She always did it to him, the way she looked. It wasn't the flickering candlelight, she looked like it in the early morning, in bright sun. Her long fair hair – too straight, she always complained absurdly – golden eyes, the teasing, wicked upturn of her smile . . .

She was his wife. The disbelief never left him. Nor the acid fear of losing her, the wild thoughts that haunted him, the bitter frustrations of the night; resentment hung around like the smell of charred remains, but he never ceased to be transfixed by her face with its velvety bloom.

She got her fair hair from her father, Barney, who'd been a blond charmer in his day – a heavy, sometimes violent drinker as well. Her parents' divorce had surprised no one. Barney had lost his looks and it was shocking to see him now, a bloated, fumbling alcoholic. He'd taken up with June, the ex-wife of an old drinking crony who'd seemed able to handle the situation, his ex-wife and his friend, Barney, in a relationship – so well, in fact, that he'd even moved in with them. They made a weird drunken threesome, Nattie had said, laughing. Hugo knew she couldn't stand June, but she loved her father through it all.

Nattie touched his arm. 'One more day. I hate to think it's back to work again so soon. Has Christine been on at you today? I bet she's back at her desk already, with the Bank Holiday so early this year.'

Hugo stared at the ripe yellow peaches in the bowl. Three emails from the woman that evening. Christine was Head of Communications at Palmers and a hard-nosed, hyperactive cow; she never left him alone. He cursed internally. The trouble with a world-famous, upmarket department store was its many departments. Palmers was always revamping its food counters, opening a cupcake-and-coffee corner, exciting itself over some unexciting new line, the start of the sales, seasonal displays. And he had to deal with the lot, magic up big-name celebs to give endorsements and bite into a cupcake – Victoria Beckham at the very least to satisfy Christine. He enjoyed his other clients, but Palmers and Christine ground him down.

'You're right. She's been peppering me endlessly, up her arse about some new Japanese designer, Hiroki, who's opening a shop within the store. Christine only wants coverage in every bloody national. It's a bit of luck, but the *Post*'s fashion editor is free the day after we're back – not sure what I've done to deserve that! Hiroki's this-season stuff is punky black leather, very S&M, so what do you think if I push that slant?'

'It's still Beverly, isn't it, who's fashion editor? With your charm you can't fail to win her round, but I'd try to keep it more up-market – family newspaper and all that. "Black leather punk, the new chic", more that sort of thing.'

She touched his cheek and brushed over his lips with her fingers. 'I think it's bedtime. Let's go up, the holiday isn't quite over . . .'

Hugo's gut churned. He lusted after her, but felt mentally unable as yet to unwind. Nattie's overtures felt too effortful and forced; he wanted passionate abandonment, though knew it was rather a tall order that night.

She started to clear the table, then sat down again and took his hand. 'I can't bear this. Can't we just cuddle up in bed and find our wavelength? I want to be close to you, more than anything.' Her eyes were glistening, her fingers kneading his palm. As so often his love formed a knot, a tightening sensation in his chest. It was physical, constricted his breathing. It made Hugo fear for his life; he wouldn't have one without her.

She'd been pregnant with Lily. Would she have married him otherwise? He never stopped asking himself that, knowing at heart she'd have held off and he'd never have felt able to push it. Nattie had come out with it herself one evening after discovering she was pregnant. 'Let's get married,' she said, with sparkling eyes, 'and have an instant family!' She'd heard nothing from Ahmed, not a word for well over a year by then, and had been at the height of her disillusionment – as well as being pregnant.

'Better clear up, I suppose,' Hugo said now, battling with the tensions of the evening and leaving her invitation unanswered, holding in his desire. 'It won't take long.' It did. When Nattie started wiping kitchen surfaces he lost it completely. 'For Christ's sake, can't you ever stop?' he snapped, grabbing the cloth and hurling it at the sink. 'I thought you wanted to be close.'

He took hold of her upper arms and kissed her hard on the mouth, her soft, lovely mouth, feeling the heat charge through him with roaring speed. He dropped the thin straps from her shoulders and lowered his head, excited to distraction by her body's arching response.

She led him by the hand upstairs with her eyes never leaving his, even as they fell on the bed together, even as she hooked him in with her legs. He felt deluged, intoxicated as he sank into her, engulfed by an obliterating passion. She was filling his senses, blocking all thought. At that moment everything and nothing mattered. He'd ride any storm while he had Nattie. She was his everything, his wife, his Nattie. With her hand holding his he would survive.

4

Nattie and Sadia

Nattie was pleased to have secured an interview with a writer whose first novel was causing such a stir. She arrived early and the restaurant, which was a red-check-tablecloth bistro, probably more of an evening place really, was a sea of empty tables. An elderly man in tweeds was eating alone at a corner table with his broadsheet newspaper folded into three, and two women in suits, who looked like senior executives, were coming in. Marks & Spencer's head office was just up the road. Otherwise the place was deserted.

It suited Nattie. She'd have her audio recorder running and didn't want Sadia Umar's voice drowned out by the rowdy din of some on-trend place that was humming. She chose a table at the rear, checked the machine was working, ordered water, looked at her watch and sat back.

She had to calm down about Hugo. He never normally went on the attack like that, letting out such bitter resentment over Ahmed, and it had left her feeling emotionally bloodied. She could so easily have said it wouldn't matter if Ahmed miraculously reappeared, that it wouldn't affect their happiness and never could. Why hadn't she lied?

She could have found it in her. She kept questioning herself over and over while the answer, which she knew in her heart, kept advancing and receding like a distant African drumbeat. Hugo would probably have only half believed her, but to hear her say it would have made him feel comforted and more secure. Lying didn't come easily to her, but it wouldn't have taken much. Telling a white lie would have kept the peace and laid the thing to rest. Yet it would have felt like a death knell on hope, that was the truth of it, cutting the last threads. Disappearance left untied ends, the door a whisper ajar . . .

She couldn't stop thinking about it, even while talking to Jasmine that morning, catching up after the holiday. Jasmine was her wonderful daytime help, a big, bosomy, loving girl with a frizz of bleached hair; she had the patience of ten mothers and the children adored her. She took over on the days when Nattie was at the office, two or three a week, depending on meetings and her workload, which Jasmine, who was always easy-going, seemed not to mind. They'd agreed a minimum amount so a third day or lateness was extra.

Nattie glanced at her watch. Sadia would be here any minute. Nattie resolved there and then – as a way of making private amends to Hugo – to close down the old email account she shared with Ahmed. No more sneaking forlorn looks in Drafts; it was seven years, for God's sake, and the moment had come to call time.

Looking over to the door she saw a girl coming in who had to be Sadia. She was small, delicately built, and wearing Western clothes, a flowered shirt and blue skirt. She stayed near the door, looking hesitant, peering round cautiously. Nattie rose, but a waiter had stepped in to help and was pointing over to her. Sadia negotiated a way through the empty tables, glancing warily from side to side, almost as if expecting a pair of heavies to emerge from the shadows and strong-arm her off the premises. Her nervousness was disconcerting; Nattie wasn't in too great shape herself.

'It's good to meet you,' she said with a warm smile as Sadia sat down opposite. 'Lovely you could make it. I hope you're okay with Italian? I chose this place as it looked quiet and your publishers suggested somewhere near Baker Street.'

'Thanks, yes, it's good for the Jubilee Line. I'm in North London.' Sadia gave a frightened return smile while constantly twisting a jade ring on her little finger to and fro with quick, flicking movements. She wore her dark hair parted in the centre, loosely looped back and fastened at the nape of her neck. Her face was elliptic, a perfect oval.

'Shall we order before we start to chat?' Nattie said, as a waiter came up with menus. Sadia lowered her head to read hers and the way her long curling eyelashes shadowed her cheeks caused a disconcerting flurry of memories. Nattie let out a breath slowly.

'Perhaps some pasta,' Sadia said uncertainly, looking up.

'The spinach and ricotta cannelloni sounds good – I'm going for that, I think.'

'Yes, I'd like that too,' Sadia agreed, with obvious relief at a decision made, and Nattie caught the waiter's eye.

'I've got masses to ask about the book,' she said. 'It's strongly drawn, and the title too – *Help Me to Flee* is very emotive.' It was the sort of novel that brought visceral engagement, beautifully crafted. Simple opening pages about a little girl wanting to sprout wings and fly over foreign lands where seas and lakes gleamed like jewels, where streets smelled of dew-bathed fruits and new dawns, where people lifted up faces lit from within. The storyline had stayed with Nattie, the child growing up, yearning to flee from her cruel brother and, later, from an arranged marriage to a tyrant who took Sharia law to extremes. It was a predictable theme for a Pakistani novelist, but no less heart-wrenching.

'I'd love to know what inspired you, your involvement with the characters, that sort of thing,' Nattie said, 'but first can I ask a little about you? You left Pakistan in your teens, didn't you, and came to live here with your parents?'

'Yes, I was sixteen – there's nothing much more to tell.' Sadia seemed desperate not to talk about anything personal. She hadn't begun to relax and Nattie wondered if something more than the interview was troubling her.

'Don't be anxious. I really don't want to pry, just set the scene for our readers so they can have more of an image and place you. Please feel you can talk freely and share any concerns. I can let you see the copy, if you like. I won't print anything you don't want, I do understand . . .' She wasn't at all sure she did, though, but was trying to be as encouraging as possible.

'I'd love to know, for instance, if it was a wrench to leave your home in Pakistan,' she went on. 'You describe the garden and birds exquisitely. Did you mind coming to England and settling here?'

'Not at all. My father had the offer of a good job – he's a doctor, well qualified – and we'd spoken English at home. I loved our house in Lahore, which is a cultural, sophisticated city, unlike how Pakistan is often depicted, but I wanted to get away, to be educated in England and hopefully go to university here.'

'Which you did. Your parents must be very proud.' Sadia looked down, those long lashes again . . . 'Is your mother working? And is she in medicine, too? By now she will have settled in well and made friends, I expect.'

'No, she went back,' Sadia said flatly, making clear a need not to elaborate. Her lower lip was trembling; whatever the problem, it was unsettling her badly.

The waiter chose that moment to bring their food, fussing around as he served them. 'That's fine,' Nattie snapped, impatient and frustrated. 'We can pour the water ourselves.' He was an ingratiating type, still hovering, and Sadia seemed distressed.

The restaurant had become slightly busier, but there was still no one at the nearby tables. Was it some emotional difficulty with her mother? Nattie asked herself. Her questions had been very mild. She wondered if Sadia would, in fact, find it a comfort to talk to someone unconnected – an impartial, sympathetic ear – and she ploughed on, hoping to break through the girl's reserve.

'Your mother didn't feel at home here then? But your father had to stay, of course. He had his job. Does she come over regularly to visit?'

'No. She left him and went back to Pakistan. She married again out there.'

Nattie felt she was getting nowhere. 'Have you any brothers and sisters?' she tried, hoping that was safer territory.

'Yes, a sister.' Sadia bent her head low over her plate, hands in her lap, and her shoulders began to shake very slightly, lifting up and down.

'Would it help to talk? I'm turning off the recorder ... I, um, was in love once with someone whose parents were from Pakistan.' Sadia looked up with her wet eyes, caught by surprise. Nattie was deeply embarrassed. It had just slipped out; Ahmed was so much in her thoughts. 'I know that's quite irrelevant,' she said, feeling a blood-rush. 'It's just that it is sometimes easier to share something emotionally difficult with a comparative stranger.'

Sadia raised her head further and sat up straighter, looking startled, yet more reassured, less like a fluttering bird at a windowpane. 'My sister's six years younger,' she began, dabbing at the corners of her eyes. 'She was only ten and had to return to Pakistan with my mother. There were terrible rows over whether I should go too, but I'd started my first year of A levels and my father wasn't having it. He sent me to a friend's house, telling me to lie low. We're very close,' Sadia said, which her smile confirmed.

'But why, if your father came to a good job with excellent prospects and your mother came too, would she want to go back? I mean, even if the marriage broke up she could have stayed. Was it our way of life? This is nothing to do with the interview, I promise. As I said, I've turned off the recorder.'

'She'd become much more observant and my father much less so. The man my mother is now married to is extremely religious; he could accept her previous relationship, because he was "bringing her back into the fold". She got a Khul divorce via the religious law of Pakistan, which wouldn't be law here. The word *Khul* means termination, you see. The wife has to pay back a dowry – though my father didn't demand that – wait through one menstrual cycle and then she's free.'

'Tell me about your sister. Can you talk about it, why you feel so upset?'

'It's the whole problem. It's terrible. I'm so sorry for my poor sister, Alesha. She's trapped in that closed society and has no freedom at all. My mother wears the burka now, she's gone very religious, all to do with her husband's extremist views. But Alesha's seventeen now, with all that that means.' Sadia bent her small tidy head and fumbled for another tissue.

Nattie stared. 'What does it mean exactly?'

Sadia looked up, sniffing a bit, and blew her nose. 'She's about to be married off, you see, to a first cousin on our mother's side. Cousins can marry in Pakistan, there's none of the outrage about it like here. His family and elders came to the house to formally propose – to the parents, not the bride; the girl doesn't have anything to do with it. He's not a cousin my sister knows, but she's seen him and says he looks revolting, pot-bellied and at least twenty years older.

'My father and I are British citizens now and I'm not sure what Alesha's situation is, only having lived here that short time, years ago. It would help if she had her passport, of course, and could try to get a visa, but there's no chance of that. They'll keep it under lock and key, you can be sure, and hand it over to the husband when she marries. Alesha is desperate to escape before the wedding and come back to England. She's in touch online whenever possible, begging me for any help I can give.'

Nattie sympathised. 'It's difficult to see what you can do from here,' she said, wishing she could offer comfort. 'And I'm not sure what kind of visa she'd be eligible for, even if she had her passport and could get to the British High Commission.'

'I'm flying out tomorrow. I've written to my mother, saying it's been too long, that sort of thing, but she hasn't replied. I thought I'd go to the British High Commission in Islamabad and ask for help – do anything I can on the spot.'

The situation seemed very fraught, given that the sister wasn't a UK citizen.

Nattie looked down at her laden plate. 'We'd better eat, you'll need to keep your strength up. And I should really turn my recorder back on now and ask more about the book. Is it being published in Pakistan as well?' She knew its UK publication day was that week.

'I don't believe that's decided yet, but it wouldn't make things easy for Alesha.'

They picked at their food and ordered nothing more. Nattie asked a few innocuous questions – about Sadia's childhood in Pakistan, so vividly described in the novel, her writing routine, favourite authors, her part-time job teaching English as a foreign language. Then, with just about enough material for the piece she had to write, she switched off the tape again.

'Has your father any advice?' she queried, as Sadia prepared to leave. 'Has he been out to see your sister?'

'He visited a couple of years ago. He was allowed to see her, but he'd have had to go to court to see her away from the home. It would have been hard for him to fight for right of access out there, though; it's not like in the British courts. And if the judge were religiously conservative he'd certainly have found against my dad. He was powerless really. He's against me going – he doesn't trust my mother and stepfather one little bit.'

'You'll stay at a hotel? I'd leave your passport with reception at all times.'

Sadia seemed grateful for that tiny bit of advice. She looked anxious, as if unsure whether to ask something, and Nattie waited expectantly. 'What happened to the man you were in love with?' Sadia came out with eventually, twisting her ring round.

'He had to go abroad – it was a bit of a life-threatening situation. We kept in touch, but then after a year he disappeared, vanished, and I heard nothing more. It broke my heart, but it's all in the past. I'm married now, with two small children.'

'Don't you wonder what happened to him just the same?'

Nattie smiled with her eyes, pressing her lips tight together in a can't-answer-that sort of way. It was a disturbing note to part on. She got out a card and handed it over. 'Call just whenever you need to, please do, and definitely when you come back. I'd love to hear how you got on. And good luck!'

'Thanks,' Sadia said. 'I feel better for talking about it. Braver now too, about flying out with all the tensions to come.'

Nattie stayed to pay the bill. Ahmed was more in her thoughts than ever and she was feeling proud. No one had been braver. He'd saved her life, the lives of her mother, stepfather and brother, and countless other people in that public place when he'd faced down the ringleader of a nuclear bomb plot. He'd averted an unspeakable atrocity.

She recalled the horror of a bomb going off in Leicester Square, the many lives lost. That had been just before she and Ahmed had met, but she knew he'd feared that there could be more terrorist attacks and had asked her stepfather William, his editor on the *Post*, if he could go undercover in his hometown to see what he could find out. He'd gone with his editor's blessing, yet MI5, the Home Office and the Counter Terrorism Unit hadn't known whether to trust him. Nattie fumed to think of it. And her own mother too, who'd been Home Secretary at the time, had authorised the bugging of Ahmed's phone – that had been hard to take. She loved her mother, but their relationship had come under a lot of strain. It still had its shaky moments where Ahmed was concerned.

The email account had to go. She remembered being at his Brixton flat just before he left, and choosing a name for the account together: *Vera Lysawe,* an anagram of *ever always.* They'd been laughing and crying as they thought it up, clinging together for one last time. Ahmed had flown to America the next day.

Nattie heaved a sigh. It was insane, keeping that account going after all these years. She was heading into the office and would close it down there – better there than at home – and try to finally draw a line.

She had a busy afternoon ahead, making a start on the Sadia piece, preparing for a general ideas meeting next morning, which involved scouring newspapers and magazines for cuttings, anything that sparked new ideas. News stories, celebrity gossip, real-life weepies; all the features staff would come well armed. Nattie had work to put in. She would take the lead with her book pages, but was expected to contribute more widely as well.

As she left the restaurant, the sun was out and she crossed the street to feel it on her bare arms. She wanted to hang on to her holiday tan. It was a hot spell, in the high 20s that day. London smelled of melting tarmac, petrol fumes and dust, rotting food too, as she passed a split bag of rubbish. On the way to the tube station she checked her mobile and found a text from her mother – she and William wanted to see the children at the weekend – and a voicemail from Hugo too.

He sounded ebullient. 'Just had lunch with Bev on the *Post*, who was singing your praises like mad – but then you are her boss's stepdaughter! Anyway, she really liked "Punk Chic", so thanks for that idea. It's solved my problems over the Japanese designer – a fashion spread in the *Post* is the Holy Grail to Christine. She does my head in, that woman. Who'd have Palmers as a client with a Head of Communications like bloody Christine? Oh, nearly forgot: tomorrow night, we've got Maudie's dinner party, remember, for her heavy-duty art buyers. She can't open a tin, let alone cook, but we said we'd go. Just checking you've fixed a babysitter, darling. Want me to try if not? Love you. Kiss, kiss.'

It was a timely reminder, but Hugo knew her weak spots. He seemed to do Nattie's thinking for her these days. He'd never gone much on her old schoolfriend, Maudie, who worked in a chic West End art gallery. She was a toughie, no question, but she and Maudie went back a long way. Nattie phoned Jasmine first, who was free to babysit, which was a relief. She'd forgotten all about the dinner. It had been arranged before their holiday and she'd been preoccupied and distracted since being home, hadn't even looked at the diary.

Texting back Hugo she had a smile on her face. She quite depended on him now, a real reversal of roles.

Jasmine's okay for tomorrow – thanks for the prod. Why should Maudie's clients be heavy-duty, you old stick-in-the-mud? They're all sorts. Could even put work way of Tyler Consultancy. And Maudie's sure to get in ready cooked, so you'll live! xxxxx

The reversal of roles only went so far, though. Hugo was still insecure and vulnerable, he never believed in his own abilities. He leaned on her, she was his steadying hand and prop.

Nattie was thinking fondly of Hugo as she pushed on the revolving doors of Buckley Building. *Girl Talk*'s offices were on the sixth floor, open-plan and bright, flooded with daylight in summer, less kindly lit in winter with unforgiving neon strips. It was one of the Buckley Group's more successful magazines, glossy, aimed at working girls and young marrieds. Going in, Nattie enjoyed the familiar sense of clutter, the piled-up past issues, overflowing in-trays, cosmetic samples, knitwear samples, the perennial packed rail of clothes for fashion shoots, wilting pot plants, polystyrene food containers, lipsticked mugs.

On the way to her desk space – she sat opposite Ian, a keen young fashion-features writer, a Scot with a well-developed bitchy streak – friends hugged her and asked after the holiday. It felt good to be back.

She was soon stuck in, dealing with the most urgent of her emails. She sifted through new books for review, which took time, and wrote the bones of the interview with Sadia while it was fresh in her mind. It flowed easily. Nattie wanted to do the girl proud.

She knew the moment had come. It was hard, she was clenching and unclenching her fists. Bringing up the address for the very last time, she had a strange telepathic anticipation of finding something unexpected, some weird personal connection or contact in the predictable trickle of spam.

There was nothing out of the ordinary in her in-box – offers from estate agents, airlines – Viagra sellers and money fraudsters in Trash. She scanned further down the list of mailboxes, past VIPs, Flagged, as far as Drafts.

Nattie stared at the number beside Drafts in a disbelieving fog.

It couldn't be, she was seeing things . . . The number of messages had been stuck on 267 for six years. Today it read 268.

It couldn't be. She felt dazed, almost too scared to look; in a state of suspended panic, like being alone in the house, hearing footfall on the stairs and heavy breathing. Only it was her own loud heart she was hearing, her own raggedy breath.

She clicked on Drafts and brought up the new message, tingling to the tips of her fingers.

Hello, Nattie, I'm in London! Very much hoping we can meet.

Her eyes were blurring as she read through Ahmed's message. She worked out their old easy-to-decipher code and read the short sentence the letters made.

I need to see you badly.

There it was, the message she'd hoped and dreamed of seeing one day. Ahmed was alive; he'd made contact. Her heart was loud, pumping at a great pace, and she had to swallow hard.

The message was two days old. Nattie was poised to respond right away; she had a thousand questions to ask and couldn't rest now, without answers. But to see him again . . . and with the message making his feelings clear – or did it? *I need to see you badly,* that could be for a variety of reasons. Who was she kidding? The passion was there in the message, loud and clear.

Where would it lead? She was in another life now, but just to meet, to hear what had happened, to explain her situation . . . He could be married too. Her stomach contracted at the thought. 'Don't be married,' she mouthed silently. 'I couldn't bear it.'

She had to make contact, but did she tell Hugo? It upset her to think of seeing Ahmed behind his back, lying and keeping secrets. It was of such fundamental enormity to their relationship. Suppose Hugo found out? Yet if she did tell him, he'd beg her not to see Ahmed again, certainly not alone. He'd do everything in his power, he would plead and cajole, say it would jeopardise five happy years of marriage; everything they had. No, she couldn't tell Hugo.

She had no idea how long she'd sat gazing at her screen, but began to absorb the shouts of goodbye, people packing it in. It was time to go home. She imagined the evening ahead with Hugo, trying with every fibre to act normally, however hard, and to resist constant looks at her laptop. It was going to be a test.

Nothing compared to the test it would be to see Ahmed again, knowing what she'd have to say. She'd never stopped loving him and never would, but she was committed now, tied, married to Hugo and with two children.

'Nattie? Are you okay?' Ian was staring, pausing as he prepared to go. 'Is there something on your mind?' He looked quite hopeful; other people's predicaments were his meat and drink. 'All set for tomorrow's meeting? You can't have had much prep time, I'm sure, with being away. Anything I can help with?'

The forward planning meeting had gone clean out of her head. Shit, she should have been online for the past hour, hunting out ideas, poring over newspapers and magazines, foreign ones too. 'Not really, thanks, Ian. I'll gen up at home later. I've been a bit distracted, thinking about this girl I interviewed at lunch; her novel is so powerful. It really stays with you.' Nattie smiled, as unsure as ever of how far to trust her colleague. He had chin-length gingery-brown hair and was all bones – they stuck out in every direction; his cheeks were hollow and his thin nose twitched as it scented advantage.

Ian lost interest and shuffled off.

Nattie looked at the clock and phoned Jasmine. 'I'll be a bit late back, sorry.'

'No rush, don't you worry, just whenever.' Jasmine was pure gold. Nattie felt so emotionally overloaded she had to wipe her eyes.

She wrote a return email to save in Drafts, feeling tremors in her spine. It wasn't easy to hit the right holding-back note.

After a lot of backspacing and with shivering anticipation, she wrote, *I can't believe this is really you and I'm seeing this message after six years of no contact! I've been staring at my screen, stunned. There's so much to ask and tell. Meet Tues or Wed next week – just for a catch-up? Coffee? Drink? Or I know a quiet Italian bistro near Baker St.*

She added a last sentence in code with her heart battering at her ribcage.

Infants never exactly easy, do tumble often, such effortful exhausting young obstinate upstarts, toppling over obstacles!

That was showing her feelings too much. Her finger hovered over the delete button, but she couldn't bring herself to press it. He was here and she had to see him, she'd be in pieces otherwise, unable to function. But either way, seeing him or not, it could only end in tears.

5

A Dinner Party and Family Tea

Jasmine was always relaxed about being kept late. Half-running home from the tube station Nattie found that far from being whingey and scratchily impatient for their supper, the children had almost finished it. Lily was asking to get down, Tubsy being fed a last few spoonfuls. He was wading through them with steady determination like a glutton putting away a seven-course meal.

'I got on with their tea,' Jasmine said. 'Pasta with tomato and grated cheese, if that's okay?'

'Brilliant! Such a help, thanks. One of Tubsy's favourites – but then, what isn't.'

'Well, I'd best be off,' Jasmine said. 'Just get me things.'

She collected a straw-basket handbag with a pink heart on the side, and a red cardigan, despite temperatures still being in the high 20s, before squatting down on the floor. 'Bye, bye, my lovelies, give us a hug then.' Lily ran into her arms, happy to be squashed against Jasmine's vast cushiony boobs. 'And you too, angel boy, show Mum how many steps you can take.' Tubsy wobbled to his feet, tottered like one of the Lego towers he was learning to build while they held their breath, but he made it. 'See you tomorrow, honeybuns,' Jasmine said, kissing their cheeks. 'Be good for your mummy.'

Nattie went with her to the door. 'Thanks for helping out with the babysitting tomorrow. We won't be late, Hugo will see to that.'

It was twenty minutes to bath time, which was when he usually made it home. Nattie burned to open her laptop, but she played with the children and cleared up toys while Lily prattled on. 'Jasmine's got a new boyfriend. He's called Pete. She showed us a photo and he's got a little beard and sticky-out ears and he's a meccaneec.' Lily stamped her foot, making Nattie jump. 'Mummy! I'm telling you things. You've got to listen. And your face is gone all pink.'

'I heard you very well, cheeky thing.' Blushing in front of Lily, how bad could that be? 'Do you know what mechanics do, Lily?' she asked, still feeling red in the face.

'They mend cars, Jasmine said, and vans – and nee-naws.'

'Yes, it's very important that nee-naws don't break down,' Nattie said. 'People need ambulances when they're sick. It's bath time now, upstairs we go.'

Their living space was on one level, great for the children, though the stairs up to the first floor were very steep. The house was in Queen's Park, inherited from one of Hugo's aunts. His father, Adam, was the youngest of six and with five sisters had been smothered with girly love all through his childhood. Adam's eldest sister, the only one to leave Oxfordshire, had joined the Civil Service and moved to London. She'd never married, bought the Queen's Park house in the late sixties and lived in it till she died.

She'd always doted on Hugo, her only brother's only child. Her will, Hugo said, had come as a shock and surprise; the estate had been divided between her siblings, but not the house, which she'd stipulated wasn't to be touched for death duties. A couple of the sisters had grumbled bitterly, sorely put out as they had children too, but not to the extent of contesting the will.

Nattie had grown to love the house. It had a long, thin back garden, a small patch in front, and was late-Victorian, very late, quite gothic-looking. They'd taken it over in grim nick, untouched for decades. Hugo's aunt had been neither domesticated nor a gardener, she'd never even got round to putting in central heating. The house had been as damp as to have patches of mould, and smelled of cabbage and mouse droppings.

Hugo's savings had gone on rehab and Nattie, who was earning little anyway, was on maternity leave. They were newly married, living in his one-bed, rented Hammersmith flat, though, and only too glad to move in. Hugo had painted, put up shelves, dug the garden, and with his growing income, a mortgage and parental help, they'd rewired the place and put in central heating, a new kitchen and bathroom too, and, thanks to William who was a naturally expansive and big-hearted stepfather, the garden had been extensively landscaped.

Nattie loved the way the pergola – covered with wisteria, climbing roses and evergreen clematis – disguised the garden's long skinniness. Flowering shrubs and successfully transplanted small trees gave added form. Roses – Iceberg and sweet-smelling New Dawn – climbed up the back wall, lovely to look at from the garden in summer, their winter leaflessness unseen. She'd felt the pair of immense urns William had bought them was OTT, more for the middle-aged rich, but Hugo had been ecstatic. 'Think of the resale value! They'd reach parts of prospective buyers nothing else could. Not that we'd ever want to sell . . .'

She heard his key in the door, despite the noise the children were making, Lily complaining, Tubsy splashing in the bath,

50 *Sandra Howard*

and felt her tension rise. Hugo sprinted upstairs calling out, 'Hi, darling!' and as he came into the bathroom to squeals of 'Daddy, Daddy!' she hoped he'd be distracted enough not to sense any stiffness or see wariness in her smile.

He asked after her day, pulling off his tie and rolling up his sleeves. 'I can take over here,' he said, 'if you want to go down to do Tubsy's bottle?'

'Thanks. Tubsy still needs soaping. I'll be up in five.' Darting downstairs, she couldn't help flipping open her laptop while the bottle warmed. No new message in Drafts. God, the strain ...

After supper Nattie tried to get her head round the ideas meeting next day. She brought her laptop to the kitchen table, which had cream-painted legs and a scrubbed top, while Hugo washed up the saucepans. There was a refectory table at the garden end of the room where they entertained friends.

'We have all the newspapers and mags at the office,' Hugo said, turning from the sink. 'Tell me next time and I'll bring some home.' Drying his hands on a tea towel, he leaned over her and gave her a kiss. 'I'm done here. I'm going through to catch the news. You'll come soon?'

'Sure, but I must do a bit more yet.' She listened for the sound of the television with her cursor hovering over Mailbox. She held back; he was only in the sitting room, could pop back any time and she'd hate to be seen to be acting furtively.

Her good intentions lasted no time. She clicked on Mail, her heart beating loudly against her ribs, and saw a new number beside Drafts. She opened it up, shivering with trepidation, and was visibly trembling, reading Ahmed's message.

Quiet Italian bistro — perfect! Very glad about the code. Meet at 12.30? Can it be Tuesday? Message me address. And, for God's sake, come!

She deleted Ahmed's message and all previous messages from

years ago, deleted them from Trash as well. She quickly typed the restaurant's name, Bella Cucina, the address and telephone, but with no signing-off message, no word from her. She had to cool it. Keeping Ahmed's return a secret was forgivable, she believed, and meeting him a single time was too. She had to know what had happened, what he'd been through. But that had to be that; any suggestion of seeing him again would be like sailing where there was no lighthouse and without a rudder or guide. What chance would there be of survival?

Nattie didn't do well in the meeting the following day. She managed when her book pages were being discussed, enthusing about Sadia's and other new novels, and her suggestion of a Reader's Column that could be largely ghosted went down well. The editor, who didn't often attend, looked interested – to Nattie's relief. She was a tricky woman, the editor, easy to rub up the wrong way. Tall, with a thick white streak in her dark bobbed hair, she had an in-charge, don't-mess-with-me manner, barking out orders like a baton-twirling majorette. Someone had once called her the Badgerette, which had stuck.

Ian, true to form, had kept asking Nattie for her opinion whenever her attention wandered, which was often. She was high on anticipation, finding it impossible to concentrate, and had floundered more than once.

She came out of the meeting shaking, but had been incapable of shaping up. She could have done without Ian enjoying himself so much at her expense, though, and stared at him truculently across their facing desks, spoiling for a fight. She contained the urge, however, and began to fill her book bag, preparing to go.

'Well, that's me done for today,' she said, softening her look more diplomatically. 'I'm off! See you Tuesday, Ian. Have a great weekend.'

She'd decided to get her hair done; it badly needed some TLC after two weeks of sea and searing Portuguese sun. She didn't trust herself to be at her sparkiest at Maudie's dinner party; it would help to have tried to look her best.

'Oooh, Mummy, you're all dressed up, you look very pretty!'

'Thanks, Lily, love. Sleep sweet. Daddy and I really have to go now.' They blew kisses and slipped away and downstairs, where Jasmine wished them a grand time.

'I can do better than "very pretty",' Hugo murmured, nuzzling her neck on the front path. 'You've never looked more beautiful.' He saw her into the car; it was a nearly new silver BMW, bought after a recent pay rise. 'I'll be staring across at you all evening at this wretched dinner. I can't wait to get you home.'

'You never know what bit-of-all-right you could be sitting next to,' Nattie said. 'Maudie will get in the glamour, she knows what her rich old clients want.'

'Who says they'll be old?' Hugo raised an eyebrow before revving up and setting off down the quiet, tree-lined street. 'They'll be chatting you up whatever their age.'

The last thing Nattie wanted was Hugo keeping his eyes trained. She'd avoided sex the previous night, hyper-tense, inhibited, Ahmed filling her heart and mind, but it would be harder tonight. Four more days before she saw him and the pressure was getting to her, her nerves and need spilling out of her like an over-filled kettle. Perhaps if Hugo knocked back the drink he wouldn't pick up on any unresponsiveness. And he probably would drink, since he wasn't into Maudie's slick crowd; he was guarded with Maudie, whom he saw as a bad influence and sure to lead Nattie down decadent paths.

Maudie was a tough go-getter, self-centred and mercenary, but she was Nattie's best friend. She'd been a rebel at school, often in trouble, fun to be around; she was loyal in her way too, and always gave a straight answer. If a dress didn't suit you she'd say so; if you asked a favour, she'd say openly that she couldn't be bothered – and, anyway, old friendships died hard.

She lived in a south-of-the-Thames penthouse, typically minimalist and white-walled with sumptuous views up and down the river. It belonged to her married lover, who'd bought it as an investment and let it to her for a peppercorn rent. Maudie had said it was a proper arrangement, but paying such minimal rent she'd be laughing if she wanted to break the contract and move on. She always fell on her feet. Nattie wondered if the lover's wife was even aware that he owned an apartment. Perhaps she was – perhaps she had a lover herself. Who knew?

Maudie had walked out on Nattie's stepbrother, Tom, though, which was hard to forgive. Tom had been hopelessly in love with her and shattered when she left; he still wasn't over it, three years on. He was an artist, successful and sought-after, up to a point, and had taught Maudie everything she knew. She'd taken it all in, got into the art world, used him and dumped him with no apparent regrets.

Tom was no blood relation, but Nattie adored him; he was like a twin to her, sensitive and talented, always there for her, and he'd been a good friend to Ahmed too. They'd hit it off from the start. Tubsy was named after Tom. Hugo had been keener on Adam, his father's name, but he'd soon been persuaded, as long as it could be Thomas; Nattie had her way.

Tom had been there for her the day of her wedding. He'd known what she was going through, the trauma, the sense of finality and loss, the immense control she'd needed to manage her conflicting emotions; fondness for Hugo fighting with a burning urge to flunk it, to pick up her wedding skirts and run. Tom had transmitted his support even as she'd walked down the aisle. Nattie had known how much he understood and cared. She couldn't have borne to do it to Hugo, though, and had gone through the ceremony with her head held high.

Her mother still had a house in the part of Hampshire where she'd been the MP. She was no longer in politics, yet she and William loved the area and went as often as they could. Nattie and Hugo's wedding had taken place there, in the tiny church in the local village. A simple, conventional wedding, but it had felt surreal; a day of swirling emotions, contrasts, rainy, yet with a symbolic, optimistic ray of sunshine when they stood for the photographs. The lump in Nattie's throat as she spoke her vows, struggling for volume, yet so aware of what it meant to Hugo and happy for him. He'd had tears in his eyes, walking back up the aisle, a married man.

Barney, her alcoholic father, had given Nattie away; he'd swayed a bit and she'd felt that they were propping each other up. Bystanders wouldn't have known; the church, the traditional service, the profusion of fragrant flowers, family and friends being boisterous and warm, Victoria looking truly beautiful, feted and admired as the mother of the bride. Her wide brown eyes with their flecks of gold had glistened with proud happiness. Those joyful tears, though, had pierced Nattie's heart like the point of a sharp knife. Victoria's euphoria had been as much about relief that her daughter wasn't marrying Ahmed.

William hadn't felt the same way. He'd known the depth of Nattie's love for Ahmed, respected her feelings, and believed in his bright young reporter, while others – advisers to Victoria, the head of MI5 particularly – had been suspicious and mistrustful, unsure whether Ahmed was genuine or playing a double game. Nattie tried not to harbour past feelings of bitterness; she loved her mother through it all.

*

It was Thursday, late closing, and as they tried to cross Oxford Street the backed-up buses and blasting horns were getting to Hugo. Being late anywhere always really bugged him. 'It's as noisy as fucking Cairo! You know how I hate being the last to arrive. It makes it harder to be first to go – which I'll certainly want to do.'

When they finally arrived, bursting out of the lift on the uppermost floor, Hugo couldn't stop apologising. 'Traffic, traffic! So sorry, Maudie,' he said, kissing her upturned cheek. 'It was truly awful.'

'Stop, stop, Hugo, who cares?' The domestic small print, the fine timing of a dinner-party meal, meant nothing to her – nor was she flustered on anyone else's behalf. She was petite, gamine, her pert face prettily framed by feathery dark hair, wearing a skimpy, figure-hugging electric-blue dress and eight-inch heels. She had a smooth coil of gold round her neck and her scarlet lipstick was perfectly applied; she looked cool, polished and confident.

'I must have a girly minute with my old friend,' she said. 'Hugo, go grab a drink from Stefan over there and mingle. He's a gem, Stefan, serves at all our gallery previews.' Hugo trailed off and with Nattie to herself Maudie studied her, cocking her neat head to one side. 'You've really got it together tonight, Nats. That dress is great with the tan. I love the netting midriff, I'm madly jealous! So spill then, I want to know what's going on; there has to be something, you look far too fab – anyone would think you had a new lover. My God, I really think you have! You're blushing like you used to at school.'

'Come off it, Maudie, you know me. How's Harold?' Nattie asked, desperate to shift the focus. 'Is he around? Any more exotic little "business trips" coming up?'

'He's being Daddy in the South of France right now, then we're off to New York. I shop and give him the tab, he does his Goldman Sachs bit and takes me clubbing.'

'Will he leave his wife, do you think?'

'God, I hope not! Harold's okay in small doses, but I certainly don't want him cramping my style. I mean, my date tonight is a dish.' She took Nattie's arm. 'We should eat, I'm getting glances, but come and say hi to a few people first. Hugo needs rescuing, by the look of it.'

He was talking to a lanky man with a droopy, yellowing moustache and looked relieved to see them. 'This is my wife, Nattie,' he said with pride as they came up.

Droopy Moustache squeezed her fingers till she winced. 'Great to meet you, Naty.' He sounded South African. 'Your man's a lucky fella! Pieter's the name, and that's my missus yonder, Earnestine.' He nodded towards a tall woman across the room.

Yonder? Nattie's lips twitched and she caught Hugo's eye as Maudie moved them on. Earnestine towered, even over Hugo who was six foot. She was an avid collector of British twentieth-century art, it transpired, and Pieter owned extensive vineyards.

Maudie's date, Miguel, with his haughty chiselled features, was magnificent. He looked like a Spanish bullfighter, but turned out to be a ballet star. He kissed Nattie's hand and his eyes were molten and smouldering as he gazed into hers.

They met Walt next, a nattily dressed American whose wife was a languorous brunette. 'Walt and Gloria are health freaks,' Maudie said, 'but I can forgive them anything for their amazing eye – except that they always buy the one painting I can't bear to let go!'

She introduced them to a couple of women, Sophia, a silken redhead in a white toga, and Helen, handsome, high-boned, wearing magnificent diamond earrings.

Maudie summoned everyone and they settled in at a glass table in the dining alcove, which was glass-walled with arresting views of the river to take the place of paintings. Nattie was between Walt, the health freak, and Helen Longman who, she remembered, hearing her surname, was a highly regarded film director.

Helen was a fascinating dinner neighbour. They talked books, ones that were filmable, and some they'd both loved that weren't.

Stefan cleared the first course, slightly greasy smoked salmon, and served the main dish. 'It's a recipe called Chicken Alexander,' Maudie said. 'I haven't done it before, so apologies in advance.' Nattie knew it was from the frozen food company, Cook; she'd served it herself once, but owned up to it.

She retreated. Ahmed was in London somewhere; it seemed unimaginable. What was he doing at that moment? Was he working here? Was he safe? She prayed he wasn't looking down the barrels of any guns. Four whole days and four long nights ... the waiting was intolerable. She flicked her eyes to Hugo, hoping he hadn't been picking up vibes. He was on the opposite side of the table next to the silken-haired Sophia and hanging on her every word. After all he'd said! Nattie was more irritated and jealous than amused. Men were so predictably susceptible.

She was ignoring Walt, on her other side, and he touched her arm.

'I've been waiting my turn to talk to the loveliest girl in the room.'

Nattie shook her head with a self-deprecating smile. 'I'm very far from that.' She could have done without the chat-up line; he'd managed to sound as obsequious as a social climber and self-satisfied at the same time.

'Tell me, Nattie,' he said, facing her full on while his foot strayed to touch hers, 'what do you do? I want to know all about you.' His American-accented voice carried and Hugo looked across, his attention momentarily diverted from the silken red-head. It was small comfort.

Nattie knew from long experience that the last thing a man like Walt wanted was to 'know all about her'; he'd far rather talk about himself. Shifting her foot, she took her cue from Maudie and admired his physique.

'You're in great physical shape, Walt,' she said, beaming with an admiration she didn't feel. 'You must be doing something right! Tell me about your regime.'

He beamed back. 'Well, diet is important, of course. I can recommend the bloodless diet, it's excellent.' Nattie resisted asking whether it didn't make him feel a little light on the corpuscles. 'And I have a superb personal trainer who promised me a whittled-down waistline and rock-hard thighs in no time.'

She smiled warmly, hoping that would keep Walt going while she indulged herself, thinking of Ahmed – his body and thighs meant rather more to her than Walt's – the clean male scent of his skin, his way of wrapping her up in his arms very protectively after sex. Everything about him was still so vivid. They had fitted. His outflow of energy, love and enthusiasm had lifted the levels of hers. Suppose she had closed down the account a month or even a week earlier? Would he have still got in touch? Would her world have stayed righted while the kernel of sadness in her heart remained?

'I work out real hard every day,' Walt was saying, 'though one has to be careful. I actually had some breathing issues recently, just while I was doing a big presentation. Had to see a cardiologist. He put the ultrasound scanner on my heart and sticky pads with wires all round my chest. He watched and listened and it seems I have a very calm heartbeat. He kept time like slowly, saying, "Ba-boom . . . ba-boom . . . ba-boom," then he said, "You have a beautiful heart."'

Nattie couldn't decide whether Walt was being entirely serious, but suspected he was. 'You must have felt very proud of

those fine regular ba-booms,' she said. 'I'm terrifically impressed
with your dedication.'

Walt was on a roll after that, detailing how most people rigged
up with sticky-pad wires in hospital rooms would have elevated
heart rates – unlike his own tranquil organ, she presumed. She
switched off again, feeling agitated. The waiting was unendurable;
she was buckling under the strain. Hugo's eyes were trained on
her now, too. The weekend loomed – it wasn't going to be easy.

'Do you run, Nattie?'

She stared at Walt blankly. 'Only after my children.' She
laughed, managing a comeback just in time. He said she couldn't
possibly be old enough to have any.

The evening dragged on. Hugo seemed in no hurry to leave.

'Well, that wasn't so bad,' he conceded, when they were finally
on the way home. Nattie was driving; he'd moved on to single
malt whisky after various wines and was very mellow. 'They were
an okay lot, after all – apart from that slime-bag, Walt.'

'He was in great physical shape, though.' Nattie said. 'You have
to give him that.'

She drove on, feeling full of angst and irritation. 'So was the
beautiful copper-haired Sophia,' she threw out. 'She seemed to
cheer up your evening no end.' Hugo looked so infuriatingly
pleased with himself that Nattie couldn't help having a bitch. 'I
would say that Walt wasn't the only one round that table trying
his hand . . .'

The hot sunny spell was over. It poured on Sunday morning,
steady rain, the sky sagging under solid pewter clouds. Nattie
was glad that her mother and William were coming to tea; it
would fill the afternoon. She and Lily made flapjacks and fairy
cakes with much tasting of the mixture while Hugo spent most
of the morning on his knees, building a wooden train circuit. It

involved linking bits of track that had to rise over wobbly bridges to make slopes for the train to shoot down – a task that took infinite patience, since every time he achieved it Tubsy would stumble against one of the bridges and cause a concertina-ing scene of destruction.

It was the last day of Lily's school holidays and they went out to lunch at a local pizzeria. It was busy, full of other young couples with children and buggies, all steaming and smelling of wet clothes. They got the last table, although squeezing in Tubsy's buggy alongside others took a feat of precision parking.

With Hugo preoccupied trying to attract a waiter and Lily spelling out phonetically the few words she recognised on the menu, Nattie struggled with a great worry on her mind. She'd been wrestling with it all weekend, a particular problem about her mother and William coming to tea. Suppose William, as editor-in-chief of the *Post* and Ahmed's old boss, knew Ahmed was back in the country? Would he keep shtoom?

He'd be sensitive to Hugo's feelings – he knew how things were – but would even William really imagine that she, married now, with children, would keep Ahmed's return a secret? Nattie prayed he didn't know. A corner of her longed to share the news, talk to him and be advised. She couldn't and wouldn't, but it was a comfort to know that William would be understanding; he knew how things had been and what Ahmed meant to her.

'They're here, Mummy!' Lily was standing on a seat at the window and jumped down. 'Granny and Grampsy are here.' She raced to the front door, standing on tiptoe to unlatch it. 'Granny, we've made fairy cakes!' she exclaimed, before they'd stepped over the threshold. 'Yours is the one with the pink heart. And Grampsy, yours has blue icing with a silver ball. But you can have two if you want.'

'Two silver balls or two fairy cakes? Come and give me a big hug.' William swung her up in the air, golden hair flying, kissing her head as he returned her to the ground.

Victoria kissed her next. 'I love your T-shirt, Lily, with that enormous *Hello*, and the biking shorts too! I had to wear frilly frocks when I was little. And look at you, Tubsy, getting so big – Thomas, I should say, or Daddy will be cross. Have you got a kiss for Granny, darling?'

Tubsy hadn't. He clung to his mother, he wasn't long up from his nap. Lily tugged on her grandmother's hand, pulling her towards the kitchen.

'It's a bit early for tea,' Hugo said, 'and the television's on for Gramps's match . . .'

It was a four o'clock kick-off, the game just starting, and they went into the sitting room. William's football team was Liverpool and he sat as motionless as a cat in front of a mouse hole, watching them play, his concentration total, his eyes never straying. Nattie began to relax a little. If he knew about Ahmed being back in the country he was hiding it well.

Her mother was into football too, although since her team was Southampton she wasn't as keen to watch a rival game, especially with Tubsy ready to be sociable. He enjoyed being clapped when he took a few hesitant steps and allowed himself to be hugged. 'Come and see Tubsy's train circuit, Mum,' Nattie said. 'Hugo spent all morning building it.'

Victoria was soon on her hands and knees in the kitchen, pushing the wooden engine round the track. 'You're a lot more patient with these two, Mum, than you ever were with me,' Nattie complained, only half lightly.

'Don't tell me you have memories of being fifteen months old!' Victoria laughed, but she looked quite got-at. 'I wasn't in Parliament back then,' she said, 'and I was always on my knees with you, so there. You were the very round little apple of my eye.'

'Does that mean Mummy was a fat baby, Granny?'

'Chubbier even than Tubsy! Can you go to get Gramps for tea, Lily? I'm longing for my heart cake and it's half time, tell him – he won't miss any of the match.'

Lily shot off, and alone with her smiling mother, Nattie felt on the defensive.

'How's everything?' Victoria asked. 'It seems ages since the holiday already. Why don't we have lunch out somewhere, without the children? We never do and I'd love it. You seem a bit on edge, to be honest, but who wouldn't be, working and running after a fifteen-month and four-year-old!'

She kept up her warm smile. She had a lovely face, wide-eyed and individual; she was over fifty and timelessly beautiful. William still gazed at her with the kind of adoration few would have credited him with being capable of feeling. He was a hard newspaperman; they didn't come tougher than William Osborne.

'Be great, Mum, I'd love that. Not least to say extra thanks for our glorious holiday. I shouldn't be the slightest bit stressed after that, no way, but the autumn's such a frantic time at work.'

'How's Tuesday? That's a Jasmine day, isn't it?'

'No can do,' Nattie said, too quickly, with a fluttering heart. 'It's a day of meetings, not the best.' They settled on Thursday. She would know where she was with Ahmed by then. Her nerves spiralled off in a coil; she felt spirited away to some never-never land of dreams and the blood galloped in her veins.

After tea Nattie had a moment alone with William. He had slipped back into the sitting room for the second half of his match and she took him in another cup. 'Thanks, I need that,' he said. 'We're losing!' He patted the sofa beside him. 'Everything okay, love? I kind of feel you've got something on your mind. You're like your mother; it shows upfront. All fine at home?'

'Sure. I'm having a few small issues with a guy at work, though, and a brilliant young Pakistani writer I interviewed the other day is on my mind too. She's got family problems and I wish there was a way someone could help. Her younger sister's still in Pakistan, being forced to marry a much older cousin who she can't bear the sight of, and this young writer, Sadia, has gone out there to try to help her escape. I can't see she has a hope, though.'

'Send me the details, I'll see if there's anything to be done. I suppose she made you think of Ahmed? It's tough, I know. It doesn't go away.' William smiled. 'But that's just how life is.'

Nattie was glad of his comforting squeeze.

6

Tuesday Morning

Hugo was in a fluster. Worse, he was in a real state, dropping his papers as he stuffed his briefcase, in a great rush. Nattie felt sympathetic, but relieved that his mind was elsewhere and impatient to have him gone. She was in a frenzy of anticipation. To be seeing Ahmed in hours . . .

'I've done Lily's lunch box,' she said, trying not to sound too pressuring. 'She's out in the garden, I'll just get her in. She's feeding Moppet an entire salad drawer.'

'That guinea pig's going to need treatment for obesity soon,' Hugo remarked, though he was only half tuned-in. He gazed at Nattie with the sort of pained, helpless look that usually meant he was about to ask a favour. She steeled herself, wary, in no mood for helping with anything that took time.

He had a press launch that morning for one of his clients, the bed people, SleepSweet, who were bringing out a new made-to-measure luxury range. They'd always been an easy client to handle, he'd got on well with the chief executive, but the man had just been headhunted and his successor, so it seemed, was all attitude and had it in for Hugo. He sounded a real box of nails.

Nattie hoped Hugo would calm down and not worry, but she feared he'd let his nerves show.

'What is it?' She smiled, hardly focusing.

'I hate to ask when you're going in today, but can you take Lily just this once? It's getting harder to park anywhere near the school these days, which means quite a walk to the tube. Be a real help if I can go straight from here. It's getting late . . .'

'Okay, I've just got time.' Nattie forced a smile. Hugo didn't have to bundle Tubsy into the baby-seat, do a round trip in rush-hour traffic and miss the chance of precious minutes alone. Lily's school was on the way for him.

'Thanks,' Hugo said with a heartfelt smile. 'Sorry I'm a bit uptight, but this new CE, Murray Beard, is after my guts. I bet he's got a pet PR firm of his own, the fucker, and wants me out.'

Nattie frowned. Lily was still outside, but she didn't want Tubsy swearing before he could walk.

Tubsy was clinging to her knees and she lifted him up. 'Forget Beard,' she said, settling Tubsy on her hip. 'Just be your special self and you'll do fine.' She shouted for Lily. 'Time for school! I'm taking you; Daddy's got late. Come and say goodbye to him.'

Lily raced in from the garden and into her father's arms. Nattie caught a whiff of Moppet and despaired of the mud that Lily had managed to get on her clean white socks, a grass stain too on her pink-and-white-striped uniform dress.

Hugo set his daughter down and kissed Nattie, even as she gently propelled him towards the door. 'I wish I knew what's eating you,' he said. 'You're very wound up.'

'No, I'm not – *you* are! Good luck today, but hadn't you better get going now?'

The moment he'd gone she felt ashamed of feeling so resentful. Taking Lily was the least she could do. It scared her how Hugo, with all his own panics and preoccupations, could read her so well. He'd been watchful all weekend and had started asking questions. She would need to have some very believable answers at the ready for later.

She couldn't go on with excuses and evasion, guilt piling on top of guilt like a stack of pancakes. She wasn't built for deception, couldn't cope. One lunch.

To be seeing Ahmed in hours seemed unimaginable. Seven years. He was a lost world. What was she going to find? Strong pillars standing tall? Crumbling buildings that echoed faintly of old ecstasies? Or nothing but a few haunting memories carried on a sighing wind?

Tuesday morning. Ahmed gave up on work. He sat back in his chair and tried to dissect his motives for coming. Why now? What was he doing here? Why take the risk? There were no safe havens in any country, least of all here in Britain.

He'd risked coming simply because he had to see Nattie. His feelings for her had become impossible to contain. He'd saved her life and the lives of those thousands of people – small beer really, instinct took over, you rode the fear when you knew what you had to do – only to have to flee the country for his own safety.

Now, years later, he wanted her to know that loving her had propelled him to make something of himself; his small achievements were all for her. Not to make her feel wretched – he'd done with bitterness – but to share the years, explain, talk to her and see her lovely face.

It was no good, he had to accept how selfish and irresponsible he was being by coming; he had to spell out the reality of the risk to Nattie and say he couldn't let her take it. But was it really so terrible to want to meet a couple of times, to have the chance to say what was in his head and heart? To spill out the feelings he had carried round for seven years? He knew there could never be closure while she was married; she couldn't bear to hurt Hugo. She'd saved the man, brought him back from the abyss, and the fear of a relapse would always be there. She'd feel duty bound as well as feeling a great fondness. She always had. That was the fucking rub. Ahmed felt an intense, impassioned frustration; those very qualities, her soft nature and strength of character, were at the heart of his love for her.

He thought back to the beginning of it all, reliving yet again the past and pain of leaving. He'd found his niche on the *Post*, loved his job, revelled in the stimulation, the excitement of breaking news, working to deadlines. He remembered the thrill of leaving his childhood home in the Harehills district of inner-city Leeds, the dark terraced house in a steep sunless street. Top of the street was the wide white mosque with its vast mint-green cupola. He'd felt trapped in that closed community, desperately longing to grow his horizons and be off to cosmopolitan London. Leaving Harehills had been a high day.

A junior reporter was as lowly as a washer-up at the Ritz, but he could go places, he'd known. He had a quick mind and could write – although he'd feared his editor with the rest of them. Every last wanker in the building had held William Osborne in terrified awe. He strode the desks, barking out orders, slagging off, singing praises while having unexpected laughing fits and genius ideas. Ahmed had felt about to be sacked any time the man was near, yet his first real encounter had been seminal, branded forever on his psyche and soul.

He could vividly remember his shock and shaking knees, ordered back to the paper one night by the news editor, Desmond Wallis. 'Better leg it back here and fast, laddie. Summons from on high.'

Ahmed had heard a blast on his way home to Brixton, smelled cordite, and turning on the television, he'd had his worst fear confirmed. A bomb had gone off at the entrance to the Leicester Square cinema where a film première was taking place. A Royal had been minutes away, about to step onto the red carpet. She must have tasted acid fear, drawing up in time to see the explosion. Eleven dead, others critically injured, it had been a horror scene of utter destruction.

The Home Secretary, Victoria Osborne, had come on air to make a statement, and since she was married to his editor, Ahmed had stayed glued to the set. She'd been a hate figure to many in his home community – people who'd actually believed 9/11 had been a conspiracy and that Bush and Blair had plotted the 7/7 bombings – yet watching her closely that night, he'd admired her fierce determination. He remembered being more aware of her as a person too, sensing her sensitivity, appreciating her delicacy and wide eyes. He had yet to meet her daughter, Nattie, and be on first-name terms ...

Taxiing back to the paper that night in a great rush and panic, Ahmed had felt sure that Osborne must have had the television on in his office and been watching his wife too. Why summon back one of his most junior reporters at such a time? He'd decided that Osborne must simply want a Muslim slant.

Ahmed recalled with amusement his timid knock on the partly open door and Osborne's peremptory command. 'Come in, come in!' It was his first time in the editor's tenth-floor office and the view from its vast windows was awesome. All London was out there and at its heart, a hollowed-out cinema where lives and limbs had just been lost at the hands of a suicide bomber.

Osborne pointed to the grim scene on the television screen. 'What do you feel?'

'Anger.'

'British anger, Muslim anger?'

'British anger and Muslim shame.'

'Why didn't you become a suicide bomber?'

'That doesn't deserve an answer,' Ahmed had snapped in fury, instantly cursing himself and expecting to be out on his ear.

Not so. They'd talked and he'd been given leave to spend time in his home community. He'd been picking up some disturbing signs on weekends home. Certain people, guys he'd known since school, were manipulating susceptible students; he'd had his suspicions and fears and been proved right.

Ahmed had given evidence in court, put those same guys inside; they had brothers, fathers, relations who were friends of his family. His seven-year absence felt like an eternity but it wasn't, and the need for revenge could be infinite. He'd discovered too, having checked it out before leaving, that a couple of the lesser players involved in the foiled bomb plot could soon be up for parole. He had to tell Nattie he couldn't let her take the risk.

Eleven o'clock, two hours to go. He'd already been out to buy flowers. After two days of prowling round the house, brooding, catching up on British news, having brief bursts of creativity at his desk, he'd had enough.

He'd decided over the weekend that trips to the local shops wearing his glasses – not supermarkets, you never knew where anyone's second cousin worked – driving to shops further away, varying his routes, was a minimal risk. He was sick of takeaways and anyway, what could peering at the blurry monitor screen in the house tell you about the delivery boy on the doorstep with his cast-down face? Still, it had been a good precaution, having a televisual entry system fitted in advance. Jake's trustworthy old cleaner, Mrs Cruikshank, who Ahmed knew – she'd looked after them years ago at the flat – had helped. She'd been at the house to receive the technicians and keep an eye during the installation.

Mrs Cruikshank, Nattie and Jake were the only people who knew he was in the country. He was simply Mr Bashaar to Jake's lawyer, just a friend. He trusted Tom, Nattie's stepbrother, and wanted to make contact with him, but that could wait. Nattie first, she came before everything else.

He kept seeing her smile, the wicked lift at the corners, the teasing warmth in her eyes, and wondered if she still chewed on her lip. Better she didn't ... The flowers he'd bought earlier looked fresh on the coffee table and mantelpiece. The shop girl had been keen on dahlias, but they were too bright and showy, kind of fake. The lilies and pink roses softened the look of the room. Nattie wouldn't get to see them, she'd be going back to her office and there'd probably never be another time.

He went down the short flight of stairs that led to the kitchen; it was a bit too 'cool school' for his taste, too many bald surfaces and shades of white and grey, everything tidied away in shiny handle-free cupboards. He would have liked more clutter, a message board, books, herbs and bottles of oil. He approved of the long white table in a sky-lit extension that had sliding glass doors to the back garden. It was laid to lawn and there was an apple tree bursting with fruit.

He got a bottle of water from the fridge, took a few swigs, put it down. Looked at his watch again. Taking the tube would be best, head buried in a copy of the *Post*. He was used to the tension of fear, but his adrenalin had really invaded; it was buzzing like bees, speeding up his heart. Anticipation was overtaking his sanity.

He studied his hands, holding them steady. He remembered Nattie making the first move, slipping her hand into his, her slim white hand. Would she have changed? Become more self-confident and sophisticated? Have a slightly harder edge?

He locked up and set out for the tube station, thinking of her sentence in code. *Infants never exactly easy, do tumble often, such effortful exhausting young obstinate upstarts, toppling over obstacles!* He mustn't take comfort from it. *I need to see you too.* She probably just wanted to say she was married and it was time to draw a line, but somehow he sensed her vulnerability coming through.

7

Tuesday's Lunch

Nattie left the office at noon. The weather had turned hot and humid again, summer stretching into September. She walked slowly to the tube station, far too nervous to stride out. Everything around her seemed in sharper focus, images to be recorded in a new file in her mind. Gauzy sunlight was glancing off the glass-sheeted blocks that had sprouted in South London while the huddled, narrow Victorian back streets, with their small terraces and dingy shopfronts, were shadowed in grey. The streets seemed less grimy than of old, despite the clusters of blown litter round the tube station entrance. They seemed to belong; it was how London was.

Waiting on the platform she rehearsed what to say. 'I never imagined ... I can't believe this is happening ... I'm married now, you know – to Hugo ... You must come to supper, catch up with him again.' No, not that. Hugo would want to believe it was a hopeful sign, yet in truth feel his world was imploding. One lunch.

At Baker Street Station she paused to comb her hair. It was shoulder-length, a little shorter than in Ahmed's day. She had chosen to wear a sleeveless, belted shirt-dress, a pale apricot colour, and had been told all morning at work how fab she looked, that she had such a radiant glow.

Nearing the bistro her legs felt weighted, her steps slowing while her heart shot ahead: a thousand beats to one cautious step. Who did she ask for? Ahmed had messaged that he would book the table, but he had a new name. She would find him; the restaurant had been virtually empty last time. Bella Cucina was hardly the Ritz. Suppose he wasn't there? She would wait till about one-fifteen – or one-thirty. Two at the latest.

She pushed on the glass entry door and saw him. He was by the bar just inside, leaning against a barstool, his back to the bar, keeping an eye on the door. He was leaning on the heel of his hand in a familiar pose. It was disorientating. The shock of seeing him was like a physical collision, the rocks of her life upheaving like an orogeny; she felt herself buckle.

He came up and looked about to kiss her, but didn't. He simply touched her arm with one finger, resting it a moment, causing a burning sensation, as though heat was being concentrated through the small pouring end of a funnel.

'I was watching for you out of the window as well as guarding the door,' he said, staring as intently as always. 'Covering all the bases. Hello, Nattie.'

'Hello, Ahmed.'

'Let's get to a table,' he said. 'Can we sit anywhere?' he asked a waiter, looking round at the desert of red-check vacancies.

The waiter gave a sort of Italian shrug of the eyes. 'Sure. Some tables is reserved.' He followed with menus as Ahmed, his hand lightly under Nattie's elbow, went purposefully towards a table at the back.

The menus were lengthy and the waiter, different from the one at her lunch with Sadia, was another hoverer. 'You like some drinks?' Nattie longed to be shot of him.

'Just a bottle of still water, and we'd like some time,' Ahmed said impatiently, sharing her need for him to be gone.

'Let's just have some pasta,' she said, raising her eyebrows for Ahmed's approval. 'I can't face choosing.' She smiled up at the waiter. 'Can we go with whichever pasta you recommend? Your choice!' That went down well. He looked delighted and hurried away.

He was back quickly with the water and a basket of bread, then they were alone.

'You've made a friend there,' Ahmed said, 'as always. You made his day.'

It was a curiously awkward moment, sitting opposite him, feeling the strangeness and tension that was all-enveloping, yet completely at one with him as well. There was a sense of time-lessness and compatibility as well as the physical pull, but they didn't belong any more, as she'd always felt they had done; she had to remember that. She sat stiffly upright, eyeing him fixedly across the small table. She was in a slew of needs and feelings, thick as honey.

'You haven't changed,' she said, fingering her wedding ring, her words floating off and fading like smoke rings, disappearing like the last seven years. 'Except . . .' He stared at her quizzically, his eyes amused. 'You look smartened up, better turned-out.' She gave a small grin. He was in a light blue, faint-stripe shirt, and had hung a good-looking charcoal linen jacket over the chair-back.

He was holding her eyes and kept on staring. It was hard, sitting opposite at the small square table, trying to keep their knees from touching. Ahmed reached over. holding out his hand, open-palmed. 'Give me yours,' he said. She uncurled the small clenched fist in her lap and rested her hand on his. 'You broke my heart when you got married,' he said, parcelling up her fingers.

Nattie said nothing. She was close to drowning, thinking about her own heart being broken. This was no good; she had to stay afloat. 'What about you?' she said finally, her voice squeaky with emotion, dreading his reply. 'Are you married?'

'No.'

She couldn't take away her hand; she wanted more of its transmitted warmth, the feel of his thumb gently massaging. She should leave now, go home, back to the office, anywhere, stopping in some dark alley to cry a river of tears.

'I haven't got two children either, no Thomas who's fifteen months, no Lily who's nearly five.' She couldn't hide her surprise and he smiled. 'I was a reporter once, remember?' She'd forgotten how much of his smile was in the eyes, never broad and hearty, always genuine and warm. 'I was actually a fully-fledged journalist for a time, while I was still on the New York foreign desk.'

'What are you now?'

'In love with you.'

'Shut up,' she said, snapping, pulling away her hand. 'You cut off all contact with no thought for the pain it would cause – what kind of love is that? Not a word to William who'd supported you all down the line, seen you right with a good job in the New York office. No thought for the gap you left to be filled; think of the guys on the paper spending valuable hours trying to find you when you went missing. And do you really have any idea of how it was for me? Sick with worry, having visions of you dead, kidnapped, being tortured, knocked about in some unspeakable hellhole. You've got some explaining to do,' she muttered, blinking away hot tears.

The waiter arrived with two oval plates piled mountainously high with some creamy, glutinous-looking mush and a salad that would have fed six. 'Seafood pasta,' he said. ''S'nice.' It smelled of a freezer cabinet and floury white sauce.

'Shades of *Fawlty Towers*?' Ahmed muttered.

'I will tell you everything,' he said, when the waiter had gone, 'but it's a long saga and painfully difficult to explain. And you're going to say you've got to go any minute, when you've eaten two mouthfuls of your friend's seafood special. And anyway you've got plenty of explaining to do yourself. You think you had a monopoly on living through agonies of pain? What about the question I've had in my head night and day: *why?* Why did you have to marry him? I couldn't believe you'd done it. Seeing that wedding picture in the newspaper, I was a wreck, unable to cope. I'd trusted in you, Nattie. I'd been convinced you'd hang on and keep the faith you had in me.

'Why did you have to marry him?' he repeated. 'Why couldn't you have had the baby and stayed living together? Think of the numbers of people who do. It was only a year after we'd been out of contact, for God's sake. But you had to go and get married. Don't you see how impossible it was for me to get back in touch after that – once I'd seen that photograph? You in a white wedding dress – you think I was going to send a message and say, "Hi! It's me – congratulations! Oh, and by the way, I actually happened to have loved you for life. But I hope you'll be gloriously happy and have lots of children, dogs, cats and summer holidays."'

'No dogs and cats, only a guinea pig. Lily has a guinea pig called Moppet.'

Nattie's tears were flowing more freely. Wiping her eyes, she saw that Ahmed's head was turned; he was emotionally wound up too. It made her feel glad, moved that he should feel strongly enough for an outburst, while burning up with the unfairness of such a monstrously one-sided attack. She was conscious of the dangerous potency; they were talking and fighting as if they'd never been apart.

He'd given no explanation, not a word; the opposite, in fact, since everything that had happened – certainly in her eyes, from her perspective – had stemmed from the moment he'd cut off all communication and vanished. He had a lot to answer for. A year of silence, nothingness, not a word; was it any wonder that her loyalty had wavered? If she hadn't found herself pregnant ... The shock, the realisation of what that had meant, responsibility, the bond with Hugo who was a good, decent man. It was a marriage born of genuine affection, not from her sad sense of defeat when thirteen months on with no word, no sighting, despair had set in.

Her anger spilled over. 'Aren't you forgetting something? You'd disappeared off the face of the earth, remember? Left everyone high and dry. Let me down, sure, but others too – William, your colleagues – and you talk about believing in people? I'd been faithful, "loyal", pure as a nun all the while we were in contact, and for months afterwards, living in hope, however wretchedly bleak the chance that all was well. Blindly believing in you ... I'd been helping Hugo, as you'd suggested, and he'd come through. He'd managed to lick his demons with all that took. I'd given him something to live for. And *still* no word from you.

'So I got drunk one night and went to bed with him. I'd kept taking the pill on and off when I remembered and was pretty certain I had done that night. But a month later I was pregnant. So what do I do? You're nowhere, a ghost. And what about Hugo? It was his child. I'd spent most of my time hiding my tears from him, as I've gone on doing over the years. Marrying was an impulsive decision, yes, but I had Hugo to think about too.

'And don't tell me *you've* been nowhere near a woman in all this time.' Ahmed started smiling, which made her feel completely incensed, almost about to hurl something at him. 'I'm glad you think it's funny,' she said, through clenched teeth, sticking out her jaw. 'I don't.'

'I can't help it; it's you. I was terrified you'd have become someone else, cooler and more sophisticated, just as beautiful obviously, but more worldly and closed off. You've grown into your loveliness, Nattie, like a true swan; you're still the soft, fantastic, unique woman I fell in love with and was absolutely determined to marry one day. As I still am.'

With those four words hanging loose, giving off vapours like a genie out of the bottle, he leaned forward on his elbows and buried his head in his hands. He was as aware as she was of the enormity of those words. But he hadn't said them challengingly, more as if there was a humility underlying his declared intention. He wasn't a selfish man and Nattie wondered if he'd been thinking of Hugo in all this. There were three people's feelings to consider.

Ahmed lifted up his head. 'You've got just as much fight, all the same instincts; you're everything I've always loved – it's like we've never been out of touch.'

'But that's just it!' she exclaimed, in an agony of frustration. 'We *have* been – for seven years. All that time I've thought you dead or married. You owe it to me to tell me every single bit of what happened. You've been asking why. Well, I have to know why too, why you vanished and not a word. Don't you see?'

She was quivering, feeling in desperate need of physical contact. She fought it, turned her knees sideways, picked up her fork and gripped the table edge with her other hand. She wanted him to prise away her fingers and bite on them lightly as he used to. It was all she could do not to reach out to him.

He was distant for a moment and she was too, thinking about him, loving his eyes, dark chestnut with infinite depth, his hair, straight and black with a shank of it falling forward. It was tidy and well cut and from his clothes, all outward signs, Ahmed was far from the penniless reporter of seven years ago, always desperate to have his expenses paid on time. Yet he'd made it onto the

Post, no mean achievement. William had seen his star quality, and it was through the paper that she and Ahmed had met. She'd gone to a party to celebrate William's ten years as editor. People were seeds blowing in the wind, settling where they could, and she clung to the wonder of everything turning on chance.

Ahmed had outgrown Harehills, that small inward-looking community in a corner of Leeds, and blossomed. He had ability and knew it; there was no false modesty on his part, but no cockiness either, he didn't strut about. The love she felt clawed at her heart, which was pounding so fast and loudly she wanted to cry out.

She had a sense of his pain too. Not just for the wretched situation they were in, but for his lack of freedom; not even able to see his own family – not in that tight-closed community where people wanted him dead. She could only imagine his heartache and sense of deprivation, how lonely he must have felt, cut off from the unfettered love of family, his life in London, his close friends. His need for contact must have intensified over the years.

Nattie wondered if he'd find a way to see his father – secretly in London, perhaps. She'd met him once, a small bald man with bright wary eyes, and seen at first hand the fierce love, pride and affection that flowed between father and son. It had been just before Ahmed left for New York and she'd sensed his father holding her to blame in some way for his son putting his life on the line. But those wary eyes had softened and she'd felt his father warming to her, despite all. It had given her hope for a future that wasn't to be.

Ahmed was looking at her again, back from his thoughts.

'Well?' she demanded, still feeling miserably thwarted and forestalled. 'You owe me a whole continent of explanations. You owe me and I have to know.'

'Of course. I'll tell you everything, but it will take time and it will be a struggle for me. It's not for now. The food's getting cold too – you should eat something or you'll hurt your new friend's feelings. And any minute now you're going to look at your watch and cut me off, say you have to go.'

Did her panic about having to leave show that much? Her feelings were seeping out fast. It was nearly two; would take half an hour to get back to the office – she had a meeting at three . . .

A restaurant nearer the office would have allowed more time, but there was always the risk of being seen by colleagues. Word got around and she worried about Ahmed's safety. Hugo too, was often in her part of the world, lunching with journalists; nothing could cause him more pain than if he happened to see her or if anyone else did, for that matter, and it got back. Bella Cucina had felt the safest bet.

'Telling you is going to be impossibly difficult,' Ahmed repeated. 'And I have to hold out a bit, don't you see? You've made it clear enough that you feel our meeting again like this is a bad, dangerous idea and would have to be kept secret from Hugo. You've deleted every single message from the past. I see our account too.'

'So this holding out is by way of a bribe? To get me to agree to see you again?'

'Call it what you like, it's my only hope. You have to, Nattie. You know that. I had to wait this long before coming to London – any sooner would have been an even more irresponsible risk and the authorities wouldn't have been pleased. They wouldn't be now if they knew. I had to think of that, but I'd reached a point, however guilty I feel about Hugo, which I certainly do, where I couldn't last another day. Maybe it's wrong and selfish of me and I should have stayed away, but we belong, Nattie, you and me. Our lives were passing us by and my need of you was desperate.'

He smiled. 'We'd better eat something. Race you through the seafood special!'

'No contest, you'd win.'

'I'm going to.'

She looked down.

'Tomorrow?' he said, leaning across to lift up her chin. 'Thursday? Anywhere, any time, any place. You say.'

'I'm working from home tomorrow, looking after Tubsy – Thomas. And I've got lunch with Mum on Thursday. It would be hard to put her off without an inquisition, which is not what I want right now.'

'After work on Thursday then if you can't do lunch?' he asked. She nodded cautiously. 'How are your mother and William? Does your mother miss politics?'

'Not in the slightest. She says she's glad to have got out when she did. They're both fine, in fighting form. You haven't been in touch with William then?' Nattie looked at him nervously.

'How could I, before seeing you? Jake's about the only person who knows I'm here. I got in touch with him before coming. Have you kept up with him?'

'Of course! You know how keen I was on him; I always said if I'd met him first you'd never have had a look in. He's doing great,' Nattie said, 'exams behind him, an architect who's going to go far. I've seen him with Hugo, we've been to his place for supper – his house is very state of the art. But he's been so busy and as I expect you know if you've been in touch, he's just left for Australia. He emailed saying how sorry he was not to say goodbye. It was quite a shock. I still haven't told Hugo. I'd love to have seen Jake before he left,' she said, sounding wistful. 'I've missed him in my life, but to be honest I'm not that gone on his wife.'

'I haven't met her obviously. But she must have something going for her. Thursday then. Can you get away by half four? Meet by the Millennium Bridge, Tate Modern side?'

Nattie's thin words of resistance were never said; she was still hesitating when the waiter reappeared. 'You no like? No good?' He stared at their little-touched plates with soulful eyes. 'You like some tiramisu? Very nice,' he said doubtfully.

'Nothing more, thanks. Delicious pasta! Sorry, we just weren't very hungry.'

'Two double espressos and the bill, please,' Ahmed said, less disingenuously.

The waiter cleared their plates and left with an audible sigh.

Ahmed paid the bill with a shiny American Express card and left a large tip. He walked with her to Baker Street Station, close enough for his arm and the back of his hand to brush against hers, but no hand–holding. Nattie was grateful. Walking in the street left her feeling very exposed.

He looked sideways at her. 'You're chewing on your lip.' That was too intimate and Nattie looked away. 'What about *my* lip?' he used to say. '*I* want your bite.'

She couldn't respond, the effort of keeping control was more than she could handle. She wanted to be wrapped in his arms, feeling the contours of him; the longing was infinite pain.

He came with her on the tube, sitting close. They walked together down deserted back streets, south of the Thames; then they were in the vicinity of her office, which felt dangerous. Both of them were keeping their eyes skinned, but there wasn't a soul about.

'Your scent is just how I remember,' Ahmed said. 'I've hung on to the memory for years. It's you, Nattie, everything about you is the same, my Nattie . . .'

She was Hugo's, though – and Lily's and Tubsy's. She couldn't be his.

'I should carry on alone from here,' she said.

'You'll look in Drafts?'

'Why, what for? In case you can't make it on Thursday – either of us can't?'

'For love letters,' he said. They were standing close. He traced over her lips and kissed them. It was a sweet, fleeting touch, featherlight, like a passing cloud-shadow that caused a small shiver, a breath of wind that presaged a coming storm.

Nattie turned away and rounded a corner. The Buckley Building and *Girl Talk*'s offices were right ahead.

8

A Mother's Instinct

Victoria was annoyed about having a tight schedule on the day she and Nattie were having lunch. Her Women in Health board meetings often overran, but as Chair of the Trustees she could hurry it up that morning. She couldn't be late for her afternoon meeting, though, which was important and likely to be fraught. Victoria was a non-executive director of a drugs company, Haverstock, which she considered impressive, ethical and responsible and she approved of how it was run, but the *Post* was sniffing about, making mischief, something everyone could do without. Being married to the editor of a national newspaper was no breeze; their jobs were often clashing – all the more so during her time in government – and William seemed to take positive delight in provoking his wife.

Nearly midnight. She and William were still up, enjoying their big, comfortable, book-laden sitting room. They often let time slide. The room had wonderful symmetry, fine cornices, full-length sash windows with creaky shutters and heavy cream curtains on fat rosewood poles. They never drew the curtains, preferred the look of the shutters. The room was mainly William's doing. The soft glow from the table lamps was soothing and he'd made reading a positive joy with two huge swooping chrome arcs that had cost a bomb. They harmonised well with their mix of modern and antique tables, the Chesterfield sofa and old armchairs.

He'd found the house, an unmodernised wreck on a main road in Kennington, when he'd been newly divorced and far from flush, but it was Georgian, set well back from the road with windows that could be double-glazed. Victoria had been Home Secretary back then, battling with suicide-bomber terrorist attacks and only too glad to hand over the house-hunting. She'd fallen for the house just as William had and it was only a stone's throw from Parliament too, just over Lambeth Bridge.

It was time for bed, but she wanted to talk. 'It's my lunch with Nattie tomorrow,' she said, partly to herself. 'Probably silly of me to be worried, but she did seem rather nervy on Sunday.'

No response, but Victoria knew William would have taken it in – in some compartment of his brain at least. He was sprawled on the sofa, peering at smudgy newsprint through his stern new tortoiseshell-framed glasses.

'I'm taking her to the Savoy Grill,' she carried on. 'It's close to where I'll be and she only has to walk over Waterloo Bridge.'

'She was a bit restless,' William agreed, 'acting a bit artificially. I suppose it could be something to do with Hugo, though I doubt he's playing around. I asked if anything was up, but she fobbed me off. It's so unlike her, keeping something close; if it weren't so fanciful I'd have said it could be connected with Ahmed. It must be tough for her, living with the unsolved mystery. My advice, for what it's worth, is talk about him at lunch. Don't start saying how hard it is on Hugo, that's not the point. Tell her that you do understand – though I don't believe you do really, do you?'

William eyed her, taking off his glasses and reaching for their case.

'Not entirely, not seven years on. She and Hugo seem such a good match, easy in each other's company, and he does love her so. It was the happiest day for me when they got married.' Silly thing to say, it would only irritate William. He'd been very unconfident that it would work out. Nattie wasn't enough in love with Hugo, he said.

For a hardened newspaperman William had a sentimental side. He'd been swept up by Nattie's love and loyalty for Ahmed, trusting of his reporter himself, hurtfully so, as far as Victoria was concerned, considering all the pressures and responsibilities of her job. William and Nattie had been proved right, of course, Ahmed had been on the level; he'd saved theirs and the lives of many others.

'She was particularly tense with Hugo,' Victoria said, 'which seemed odd. I will bring up Ahmed if you're convinced it's a good idea. But why should she be pining for him more than usual? It has to be something else.'

'I suppose her feelings for Ahmed just get the better of her at times, and it makes her feel extra guilty about Hugo. You should try harder to understand. Think of us, the risks you took. There was Nattie, my children, our two marriages, you even risked losing your brand-new government job! I like to kid myself that you once had those same powerful feelings as Nattie.'

'And I still do, you crusty old curmudgeon. But it's no comparison. True, you and I took the risks, but our situations and the state of our marriages, particularly mine to Barney, were very different. You're always unreasonably unfair to him, don't be unfair to Hugo too! Come on, this is getting us nowhere and that was a big fat yawn – time for bed.'

William was more often right than not, but Victoria wasn't at all sure about raising the subject of Ahmed at lunch. And should she really try harder to understand? She'd genuinely believed her only daughter had a better chance of a safe, practical, lasting marriage with Hugo than a leap into the dark with Ahmed. Was it so terrible to have felt so happy and secretly relieved on the day? She prayed that the marriage wasn't beginning to fall apart; nothing could be worse.

William put his arm round her as they rose and she leaned up to kiss his cheek. He was dark-haired, greying now, and had a strong beard; his cheek was rough and bristly at that late hour. She could tell the time by his stubble.

She felt incredibly close to him, warmed by the memories and the love they'd found. His making comparisons, though, and reminding her of the depth of Nattie and Ahmed's love, was unsettling. She kept her sighs to herself and reached to smooth William's hand. He gave her a kiss.

'You smell of print ink,' she said, 'but the scent in this room is gorgeous. It's your roses, isn't it, you man of hidden talents.' Growing the lovely fragrant, blowsy old shrub varieties was one of William's many passions. The back garden was a bower, a triumph, though how he found the time ... She was no gardener; politics had taken up every spare minute, in Parliament till all hours.

'I thought those wonderfully scented shrub roses only flowered once,' she said. 'Aren't they all over by now?'

'It's jasmine you're smelling, and even that should be over but it's still doing its thing; it's in the vase with some late climbers. I'd stick to cooking and your questionable business interests if I were you!'

Victoria was first at the restaurant and watching Nattie weave her way over to the table, she felt moved to tears. She wanted to hug the breath out of her daughter, smother her in a storm of maternal love. She'd always felt overprotective; Nattie's beautiful open face made her too vulnerable, defenceless as a sleeping child. Men had taken advantage in the past. Not Hugo, though. With his patience and steadfastness, he was a truly decent young man.

Nattie was making slow progress, held up by a chic woman with steel-grey hair swept up in ivory combs. She was talking to Nattie, using her hands expressively, but detaining her for too long. There were a few other women dotted about, but the Grill with its sleek black furniture and glass, watermark-effect crimson walls, was a largely male domain. Bullish-looking businessmen in broad-shouldered, hand-tailored suits were leaning forward over the tables, busily pursuing and probably clinching their various deals. They looked up as Nattie went by, easily distracted, though she appeared oblivious to the interested stares.

Nattie came up, smiling. 'Hi, Mum, sorry. I tried to hurry up that woman who called me over. She's a literary agent, very excited about a new author – she wouldn't stop! It's great this, way above my pay grade.' She glanced around as she pulled out a chair. Her smile was as sweet as birdsong and she'd never looked more glowing. Sexy too, in a discreet navy button-through dress with short sleeves. Victoria eyed the dip of cleavage as Nattie leaned over with a kiss, feeling, as always, ever so slightly envious.

She reached out and touched Nattie's arm. 'It's lovely to have you all to myself for once. It gets harder, but we must try to do it when we can.'

'Sure thing, Mum. Best sometime when I'm looking after Tubsy and I need to fill his day. It will have to be a pizza place, though. He does love munching his way through bits of pizza with his splendid new teeth.'

An elderly waiter came to take their order. They chose a hake dish and agreed to have just one course. The waiter hesitated before going, then addressed Victoria: 'I was sad when you left Parliament,' he said. 'You were a great Home Secretary. When I think of this lot . . .'

Victoria thanked him and said 'this lot' were doing a good job in tough times.

Nattie was grinning. 'Still got your fans, eh, Mum? I remember William once said there was always a right time to go, but then when you did, he tried to stop you.'

'Much better to go before you're pushed. How's work, darling? I loved the September issue. You had a really good spread.'

'It's a frantic time with the Christmas book pages. I suppose it's as well, though, that we work quite far in advance and I'm not doing all the extra along with Christmas shopping.'

'So what should I be reading? The last book you recommended was a triumph. I couldn't imagine a novel tackling dementia being such a good witty read. I've seen rave reviews for a book called *Help Me to Flee* – by Sadia Umar, I think. Have you read it?'

'Yes, I've done an interview with the author. The book is piercing, very poignant, but extremely depressing in its way. I'm not sure if it's quite your thing.'

'I don't see why not. It's basically about a forced marriage, isn't it? Why are you blushing, Nattie? Because of the connection with Pakistan?'

'Possibly – I don't know, Mum. I wish I didn't blush so easily. It's so mean! Let me tell you about the children, how well Lily's doing at school. Her reading's way ahead, so her teacher told Jasmine yesterday. Hugo thinks she gets it from you.'

Nattie was looking like a hedgehog in the middle of a motorway, prickly and bristling, and at the mercy of fate. She seemed to be on her guard, anxious not to discuss Sadia Umar's novel. Since it was fairly obvious why, Victoria decided to go with William's advice.

'That Pakistani author, she's not related to Ahmed, is she? From your reaction I wondered if she could be connected in some way.'

'I'm sure she's not related,' Nattie said, fingering her bread roll. 'She certainly didn't say anything when we had lunch. Don't get at me like this, Mum. I blushed, that's all – we can talk about the book as much as you like.'

'I just wondered. You seem on edge and I can't help worrying. You must still really want to know what happened, I'm sure.'

'Mum, do you have to go on? You know I hate being made to talk about Ahmed. It hurts more than anything.'

'Everything's okay with Hugo? All good with you both?'

'Of course, why ever not?' Nattie snapped, flushing again and sounding defensive. 'He's got a few work problems; he looks likely to lose an account, SleepSweet, the bed people, and he's as fed up as ever with that nightmare woman at Palmers, Christine, the Head of Communications. I do worry about him; he's surprisingly lacking in confidence for someone in that job. Sorry if I wasn't at my best on Sunday.'

Victoria had always thought Hugo was in the wrong job. He was nobody's fool, but not a natural for the communications world, too charmingly reticent. It was hard to know where he'd flourish best. Nattie had spoken warmly of him, though. Wouldn't she have sounded more spiky if they were falling out? Interviewing a Pakistani author had probably put Ahmed in the front of her mind, but it was a tenuous link to have caused such edginess.

Victoria sighed inwardly and tried to move things on. 'We had supper with Uncle Robert, Katie and the boys last night,' she said.

'Joe's following in your footsteps and off to Durham next week and he was lording it over his brothers. Pity you don't see a bit more of your cousins, darling, they're good fun.'

'Mum, they're ten years younger! Tell me about Granny and Grandpa, how are they? I'd love to see them and take the children, if it weren't so busy between now and Christmas.'

'They're actually coming to London this weekend, staying with Uncle Robert. I heard last night. They want to see Joe before he goes. I know they'd love to see you all. Saturday would be best. They'll want to leave straight after Sunday lunch to be back before it's completely dark.'

Nattie stared, looking intensely frustrated. 'That's such sod's law!' she exclaimed. 'We're at Hugo's parents this weekend. He's taken Friday afternoon off and keeps saying how much they're looking forward to it. But I'd really hate not to see Granny and Grandpa the one time they're here.' She hesitated and seemed to be giving it a lot of thought. She adored her grandparents; she'd often stayed with them when Victoria had been up against it, and was especially close to her grandfather, John. He'd been someone she could turn to, through her difficult teens, her parents' divorce, and he'd taken to Ahmed wholeheartedly. For that reason if no other he could do no wrong in Nattie's eyes.

'I could come back Sunday morning,' she said, 'and see them then. I'll talk to Hugo about it. I'm sure his parents wouldn't mind, as long as he and the children stay on for lunch.'

'Let's try for that. Look, I'll have to go in a minute. I've got a board meeting with Haverstock, which is bound to be fraught. It's all the fault of your stepfather too, and the wretched *Post*. They're trying to lay something on a drugs company whose record I know to be as unsullied as snowdrops. I sometimes think William starts poking around simply to wind me up.'

'Mum! You can't seriously think that.'

'Whose side are you on?' Victoria laughed, catching a waiter's eye. Then she stared at her daughter, her heart reaching out. 'I'm sure nothing's wrong, love, but don't ever feel you can't turn to me, even with the smallest niggles. It can sometimes help. We've always been able to talk. Don't let's lose that.'

Nattie gave one of her glorious smiles. 'You've got to go. I have too. Thanks for saying what you did, it means a lot.'

William called. Newspapers being what they were he seldom got away much before ten, but he and Victoria spoke often during the evening. 'How was it at lunch?' he asked. 'Did Nattie open up? Are you any the wiser?'

'No,' Victoria replied. 'And feeling no less concerned. Something's definitely up, but whatever it is she couldn't have been less keen to tell me. What was slightly odd was that she seemed on a high; maybe there'd been some turn of events she wasn't expecting, something she'd wanted to happen. Who knows? And despite all the edginess she was looking terrific, that way she has of looking lit from within.'

'It could be to do with Ahmed, but I'd be surprised if he's back in the country,' William said. 'I'm sure we'd have had a sniff of it at the paper; my guys are pretty much on the ball. By the way, I guess I have to eat humble pie over Haverstock. They're not so easy to pin down. I still don't approve of these dubious drugs companies one little bit; "ethical" in their book always seems a very elastic word.'

Victoria snorted. 'But it isn't an elastic word in *my* book. Remember that cartoon of me you once printed in the *Post*, "The Schoolgirl Who Always Did Her Homework"? I think you can trust me to know the good guys from the bad.'

She ended the call smiling, enjoying having won that small battle. William had only momentarily taken her mind off Nattie, though. Instinct told her that her daughter had something going on in her life that was difficult to resolve. As well as the aura of tension about her, she seemed high on adrenalin, which gave conflicting signals. One thing Nattie couldn't have made clearer, though, was that whatever the problem, it wasn't one she was prepared to share with her mother.

9

A Second Meeting

Nattie had urgent copy to finish. She was trying to clear the decks before leaving to keep a date that she knew now, more than ever, was a terrible mistake. It was impossible to concentrate, and she cringed to think of her mother's shrewdly penetrating questions at lunch. Fending them off had been both painful and embarrassing. Had it simply been intuition, she asked herself, or had William's sleuth reporters got wind of Ahmed's return and were busy tracking him down? If so, his detractors could be doing the same. Was he safe? And was she at risk too, going to meet him? Would she be seen?

If only she'd been calmer and more together with her mother. It was one thing, managing not to tell a bald lie, but wasn't deliberate omission just as bad? Nattie knew she wasn't built for liaisons and evasion; she felt incapable of not giving herself away. Yet here she was, dementedly impatient to run to another illicit meeting with the man she loved – and nothing, barring breaking both legs, was going to stop her.

She needn't have kept his return a secret. She could have told her mother, William, Hugo, and it would have gone no further, put Ahmed at no extra risk. He'd have been safe with his new identity that she still didn't know. Nattie had felt justified in seeing him alone the first time, given the pain it would cause Hugo, but now, with the floodgates reopened on her longing, it was another matter.

She couldn't focus on her work. Her fingers were poised over the keyboard while her mind raced. She was disapproving of Ahmed's tactics, holding back from telling her a single thing, but wouldn't it be inhuman not to need to know? And then? What then?

Her world was tilting, but her copy was overdue. It had to be handed in that day. She was almost grateful to have the deadline; it screened out the question that overrode all others, that pressed down on her like the lid of a coffin; that scared her to death. How was she going to find the will, whatever his story, whatever the truth of it, to wave a cheery goodbye then and never see Ahmed again?

'Leaving early?' Ian looked up over his screen with raised gingery eyebrows.

Nattie gave him a huge wide smile. 'It's one of the few perks of being a part-timer. I've just banged off my copy too. Good feeling!' She filled her bag with reading and rose, wobbly at the knees with anticipation. 'God, this lot are heavy, they'll sort me out over the weekend. Have a good one, Ian – see you next week.'

It was no distance to the Millennium Bridge, but Nattie had left it late. She'd held back slightly for appearances' sake, usually doing a full day, but it helped to be in a rush and have no time to think. She couldn't call her emotions to order like troops on parade. Nor could she control them. She felt faint with need.

Hurrying away from the building and down the street, her

head was full of Ahmed's emails of the last few days. His words were living passion, the past in the present, yet she was married now. He'd talked of constancy, of love's ability to ride fear, partings, failings, misery and now, at last, its reward of reunion and rediscovery. Words couldn't bear the burden, though, he said, not any more. Nothing he'd written to Nattie had ever jarred, neither these nor his words in the distant past; they'd always leached into her heart.

She quickened her step with the bridge in sight. Ahmed was there, in T-shirt and jeans, hair lifting in the warm September breeze. He was mingling with the milling tourists who were out enjoying London and the pale afternoon sun, but he stood out for Nattie and her stomach contracted as he saw her and came swiftly to her side.

'You had me worried,' he said, touching her cheek and reaching for her bag. 'God, this is heavy! You shouldn't be carrying this much weight around. Let's go and find a taxi quick.'

'Where are we going?'

'Jake's house – it's where I'm staying.'

'Oh, I see. You didn't say . . .'

'I didn't want to fill you in too much at lunch. I'm really sad not to see him, but he says it's good to gain experience elsewhere and he is very focused on his career. I think it's got a bit to do with Sylvia as well, he says she's up and down. They've gone to Melbourne, where her mother lives. She remarried and settled there apparently, and when the new husband died she stayed and started a nursery school. Jake thinks Sylvia would be happier with her mother nearby and she could help in the school. I hope he's right. Anyway, I'm keeping the house warm in the meantime, so it's my gain. I've rented it and it's fine for three months at least.'

'It's a great house,' Nattie said. 'I love it being so near your old Brixton flat.'

'Very close to your mother and William, of course. I'm taking good care not to bump into them!'

Her cheeks flamed. Jake's house suddenly felt risky; Victoria's meeting could easily be over and, more to the point, Nattie didn't trust herself one bit. 'Wouldn't it be better if we went to a café?' she said. 'Some quiet place where we can talk?'

'Why, Nattie? We won't see them, I guarantee.' He smiled, not letting her off the hook, while keeping an eye out for a cab. 'There's one.' He raised his arm and as it drew up alongside, his hand touched hers before he helped her in.

They didn't speak in the cab, which dropped them right outside the lovely old front wall of Jake's house. Ahmed clicked open the wrought-iron gate and closed it carefully behind him. Nattie shivered a little as the front door sprang open to his key.

Alone in the house they looked at each other for a whole minute before he kissed her lips lightly, just as he had done saying goodbye after lunch. She knew how he was feeling, everything was there in the look.

'Come to the kitchen with me while I get us a drink,' he said. 'I'm afraid I've spread a bit. I like the place looking less sleek and streamlined – well, that's my excuse!'

He'd set up a small television on a worktop, left books splayed open on the island unit; there was a huge bowl of fruit, a breadboard with half a loaf and plenty of crumbs. The kitchen, which had looked immaculate even when Jake and Sylvia were cooking and talking to friends, looked more homely now.

Ahmed went to the fridge and took out a pretty pottery jug. 'Have some home-made lemonade. I even squeezed the lemons – all my own work.'

'And this is the guy who said his mother never let him lift a finger? That sounds a bit keen. I'm sure there's a juicer in this state-of-the-art kitchen ...'

He held the jug to the icemaker and clunked in some cubes. He made room for the jug on a tray that he'd put ready with glasses and a plate of shortbread, picked it up and went to the door. 'Let's go up to the sitting room and settle in.'

Nattie followed him upstairs. Ahmed rested the tray on the coffee table in front of the sofa and sat down. She stayed standing, noticing he'd bought flowers, how they freshened the room, while looking for a chair to pull up. It took an effort of will not to sit down beside him, close, hoping for the brush of his arm, bare in his T-shirt, against hers. She wanted his hand to stray to hers, to feel his physical warmth.

'I'll sit in that chair,' she said, as he patted the sofa and smiled.

'I'd much rather you were here beside me. I need to be able to reach you – mentally, I mean. Come and sit down! I feel nervous. Don't make this even harder.' He rose and steered her carefully to the sofa as though she were blind, kissing her cheek as they sat down. She couldn't turn to look at him, didn't trust herself even to turn and smile.

'Have some lemonade,' he offered. 'And the shortbread's good. Two young girls have set up locally and make all their own stuff.'

He knew she loved shortbread. Nattie sipped from her glass and set it down. She was feeling oddly cocooned from harm and reality, despite her extreme tension as she sat beside him. She was fighting her every instinct to lean into his side, yearning to have his arm round her, his fingers lightly stroking as he talked.

She sensed his own extreme tension. He was struggling to find the words, unsure how to begin, and her heart filled as she shared the strain.

10

Ahmed's Story

Ahmed felt almost too emotional to speak. His throat was constricted. He was trying to handle Nattie's nearness, the overwhelming sense of physicality. He was intensely aware also of the fragility of the moment, convinced that she'd react badly, feel miserably let down and disbelieving. He imagined her walking out of his life, leaving him to drown in a well of loss and sadness, while a corner of him dared to hope she'd be forgiving and even understand.

His fingers were trailing her arm, he realised, and lifted his hand away self-consciously – only to take hold of hers and clench it. He needed physical contact.

'Sorry,' he said with a smile. 'I've been trying to find the courage to begin. I guess I should start with my name. It's Daniel Bashaar, which I'm still getting used to, even seven years on – and having a whole different backstory as well.'

'Daniel Bashaar,' Natttie smiled. 'I like it. It has a nice biblical feel.'

'I was Dan to everyone in the New York office, which was fine. I was keen to fit in.'

'Was anyone else from the London office out there too?' Nattie asked. 'Wouldn't that have been a bit of a problem?'

'Good question.' He tightened his hold on her hand, moved by her anxious gaze. 'Only one who I knew and she never gave a hint of recognition. She'd have been a good recruit for MI6, William must have laid the ground well. So how about I start with New York, which you don't really know very much about. I was missing you, which goes without saying, lonely, but on a high as well that first year, loving the new job and Manhattan. It's such a frenetic, energising place. I went about with the two guys I worked with mainly, Matthew and Charley. They were fun, rowdy and out for a good time; keen to show me the city's underside as well as the glitz. I'd thought I knew it all, working on the *Post*, but I was wrong. I wasn't into dope, but they had me doing most else, certainly drinking and I'm not a great boozer, as you know, with that upbringing of mine.'

'And girls?' Nattie raised her eyebrows.

'They featured. There was plenty of ... availability.' He grinned, hoping she'd handle that, though she could never hide a lack of coolness where girls were concerned. He had no wish to talk about the meaningless one-night stands with the brittle savvy girls he'd met in New York. And it had just been sex, a release, a man's approach; a way of rounding off a boozy night out.

He carried on. 'These two guys, Charley and Matthew, played the field, they had a kind of rota, but the girls I met through work and out drinking with the guys weren't for me. They were tough pushy career girls, not into relationships. I used to wonder, in fact, if they'd be capable of falling in love. But then of course,' he touched Nattie's cheek, 'I'd wondered about your true feelings at first. You hadn't exactly held back. I can remember worrying a bit about that! It was the sweetest moment when it dawned on me that you were serious.'

'Something tells me you're being a touch evasive here,' Nattie said.

'I was in love with you, then and always. But you can't imagine how isolating and bleak it feels, being someone else in another country. You weren't alone, remember, you had Hugo.'

Nattie looked down. 'I was trying to save him, that was different.'

She had eased away her hand, now slipped it back into his.

Ahmed held it tight. 'I worked hard in New York,' he said, 'and did fine. The drinking helped actually, as it turned out. I met useful people, made contacts. I wrote articles for mags, a short story or two, made a bit of spending money. You need bucks on tap in Manhattan. Everything costs, and it's like there's a pall of go-getting hanging over the entire city, an atmosphere of obsessive money-making, whatever it takes.'

'That's not unique to New York.'

'No, and I'm not being entirely fair. We all want to make money, but it seems so much the culture there.'

'And the bit I have to know about, the crux, why you did a bunk and vanished and broke my heart?'

She was looking him straight in the eye and he flinched. He took a sip from his glass and put it down again; he rested his forehead on his hands. She'd never understand. 'Bear with me,' he said. 'I will get there, but it'll take a little time.

'The CIA had a go at recruiting me while I was in New York. It was a direct approach – a cold one, they call it. Someone bumped into me in the subway and I found a card in my pocket. We had some meetings. They wanted me to infiltrate certain groups, people they suspected, and build up relationships much as I'd done in Leeds. I wasn't having it. It's one thing, saving the girl I love and her family, her Home Secretary mother, but I'd had enough of double-life deception and making enemies; I had no wish to live with any greater fear than I was feeling already. Fear had me in its clutches, you see, Nattie. It had a lot to do with why I went to ground.' He stared hard at her, wanting his look to reach in. 'Fear was at the heart of what it was all about.'

She didn't blink, but she'd gone quite pale. 'What sort of fear?' she said. 'What happened?'

'My father died.'

Her face softened and she brought up their linked hands to her cheek. 'I'm so sorry. I know how much he meant to you. Words are always inadequate.'

'It came as a most terrible shock. I saw it on my sisters' Facebook pages; I know their passwords. It was, still is, my only source of news of the family. Unknown to them, of course, and I can't make contact even now. They'd never keep it secret and I'd be done for. But you'll be wondering about the relevance . . .'

'Yes, tell me about the fear.'

'I'm dreading telling you. I'm very glad you're here beside me and I can plead.' Ahmed smiled and she gave him a melting look in return. Her scent was filling the space between them. He wanted her badly and tried not to squeeze her hand too tight.

She'd retreat after hearing him out, he thought, climb back into the hard protective shell of her marriage. How could he possibly expect her to understand why he'd made such a mess of his life if he couldn't fathom it himself? He had to get on with it.

'I was overwhelmed with grief over Dad, coping with the shock of not knowing and not being able to be at his side through his illness. My every instinct was to be on the first plane home and make the funeral — it's always straight away, traditionally. And as well as my agony of loss, there was the family honour. It matters, being seen to be there, paying one's respects, mourning for a prescribed length of time. It's a ritual, however remote from the religion and unobservant you may be, of fundamental importance. Even if I hadn't ached to be at the funeral and able to mourn my father, it was my duty to be there, especially as the only son. But I stayed in New York, too pathetically frightened to get on that plane and show my face at home.'

'You can't blame yourself,' Nattie said. 'You couldn't have gone. There was no way. It would have been like taking your own life – *and* endangering others, don't forget, people in the crossfire.'

He fought it, but his eyes misted. She really cared. He touched her sweet anxious face.

'True. I doubt I'd have survived, turning up in Harehills only a year on. Everyone knows me there and word would have got round faster than a bullet out of a gun. Not everyone involved was rounded up and they want revenge – it's justice in their eyes. It's why I was given a new identity, after all. Someone would have "accidentally" pushed into me as a bus went by. I'd have been rubbed out one way or another, knifed in an alley, beaten to a pulp – there's no shortage of ways to do people in.

'But the point was, Nattie, I was shit-scared, awash with guilt and shame. Hating myself for the cowardice, fucked to bits frankly. I'd wanted to live, very badly. I was determined to marry you. Not for a while, you were still so young and I hadn't made the money I felt was needed; I hadn't saved a dime with all the drinking and sloshing round the bucks, out with Matthew and Charley in New York. That played into it. My revulsion at myself grew until it became a mammoth, the sense of failure and self-loathing.'

'Your fear was a delayed reaction,' Nattie said. 'You'd been so incredibly brave, it was going to hit you sometime.'

'But not to have been there for Dad ... and I can't tell you the hurt and shame my mother must have felt, the dishonour my absence had brought on the family. Her only son not there to support her, not praying for his father and being dutiful. She wouldn't have been able to look a single person in that tight community in the eye.

'I flipped, Nattie, I went into a complete decline. I could think of nothing but how saddened by my New York life my father would have been. It was irrational to say the least. My life in London before you were in it hadn't been all that different. But most of all I felt unworthy of you. New York felt alien and brash. I just knew I had to get away and lick my wounds.'

'Why couldn't you have told me about your father and let me share your pain?' Nattie had taken back her hand and she faced him square on with hurt eyes. 'And nothing you've said really explains why you cut off contact. No word of where you went, what you did. I need to know. I need answers to the seven years of questions I've carried around in my heart and head.'

Ahmed looked over to the window, where the sunlight was pouring in.

'You could have told the office you needed time to grieve,' Nattie persisted. 'You could have asked for a sabbatical. They wouldn't have denied you that. Please, look at me.' He turned towards her. Her lower lip was trembling. 'I care about what happened to you,' she said. 'I've been pining and worrying all these years. You've never been out of my thoughts.'

'Nor you out of mine. But I couldn't have borne to talk to anyone in the New York office about my father dying. No one would have understood. Anyone else would have been on the first plane home, after all. I could have lied about the timing, asked to go home for the funeral, but that could have led to complicated questions, which would have got me in deep. The last thing I wanted anyway was casual commiserations and meaningless sympathy.

'My father was dead and I felt beneath contempt. It was all about you, which is the hard bit. I couldn't face getting in touch.

I needed to get away, see what I could salvage of myself. And the other thing was, you see, I was as certain of anything in my own heart that I wouldn't have given my safety a second's thought had I not passionately wanted to stay alive for you. I knew I'd have found the courage, gone home and taken my chances.'

'Then I'm selfishly very glad you didn't, very glad indeed.' She rested her hand on his arm.

'But having *not* flown home, I was completely fucked up, feeling a snivelling coward, hating myself with a vengeance. And constantly scared, scurrying past dark entrances and alleys, heart thudding. America wasn't so far away, people could track me down . . . It wasn't exactly a breakdown, but I was in that sort of paranoid state where I could have persuaded myself of almost anything – like that it was almost more your fault than mine, my need to stay alive for you.'

He looked at her, feeling gutted; she'd never understand. 'And having wrapped myself up in a scratchy blanket of blame-gaming I kept putting off getting in touch. It's beyond my comprehension now,' he said wryly, managing a small helpless smile. 'In the pantheon of screwing-up I did pretty good.'

Nattie didn't know what to think. She felt deep sympathy, yet Ahmed hadn't fully explained, all he'd said was like the first wash of a watercolour and she wanted the whole painting. She could understand his desperate state, but a single word or message from him and her life would have been so different; she wouldn't be married to Hugo.

She was feeling too hurt and confused to get her head round any of it and in her misery and frustration she couldn't help a spurt of rage.

'So you packed up your apartment and cut loose? You were together enough for that?' She faced him quivering, seeing the pain in his eyes and hating to hear her own bitter tone. She didn't feel bitter. She was straining for contact, as in love with him as ever. The years had melted away.

'Where did you go?' she asked in a level tone.

The tension was intolerable. Nattie gazed distractedly around the room. The light was streaming in through the far window, dust motes dancing in the beams. The fight went out of her and she spilled over with tears.

She felt her head being turned. Ahmed held her face, wiping away the tears with the back of his hand, leaning in to kiss the wetness. He picked up her hand again, rubbing with his fingers, with his thumb on her palm. It was as though there'd been no absence, she was feeling it ever more acutely, no missing seven years. His nearness, his smell, clean and natural, like her grandfather's fresh-cut logs, was vividly recalling for her past togetherness, lying in his arms with her face pressed close to his skin.

He brought her hand to his lips. 'If only you knew what I went through. The longer I left it, the harder it got. I kept funking it, drafting messages, deleting them; I didn't know how to explain. William, the New York office, everyone was looking for me. I knew the trouble I'd caused by going to ground and I'd felt somehow that getting in touch with you would start a whole chain of events. You'd naturally have wanted to know where I was; I could have kept shtoom, but I wasn't seeing straight, had this nonsensical notion that it would have led to the paper finding me. It seemed so . . . complicated.'

'I don't see how a message in Drafts could have led to the paper finding you. You could have explained. I'd have understood the torment you were feeling.'

'You don't know what it was like, the guilt, the fear, my mental confusion. I'd thought somehow, you see, darling Nattie, that I didn't have to do anything, that you'd believe in me, wait for me, be there for me – that I could work through my agonies and feel strong again. But it couldn't have gone more wrong.' He smiled, his eyes full of contrition.

She touched his face and felt a charge, felt it travel all through her body. She had to go. She should be out of the door, running to the tube station, thinking of Hugo and her children . . .

'I need to know more,' she said. 'Where were you – where had you gone?'

'Vancouver. I'd met a man once, in one of the Manhattan clubs I used to drink in, a Californian, he was in the film business. He'd talked about Canada – Hollywood makes quite a few films there. I remembered him describing the plight of the native Canadians – aboriginals or First Nation they're called there – saying it was particularly acute in Vancouver. I thought that was somewhere to lose myself. I could work for a charity helping those people.

'It was easy to get into Canada as a visitor with my UK passport and I didn't need a permit to work as a volunteer. The charity paid my day-to-day expenses; it was virtually nothing, but I got by.'

Nattie was thankful his disappearance had nothing to do with the FBI or CIA, or Islamist extremists tracking him down, but found it hard to digest everything, to handle her bruised feelings, and her list of questions kept growing. What else had he done? How long had he stayed?

'What was the charity? What did it do?' she asked, worrying about how late it was getting. She'd told Jasmine she'd be back by seven. How could she leave with one rushed goodbye, never to see him again? It was impossible. She had to go.

'It was a charity for homeless aboriginals called ARC, the Aboriginal Relief Centre. The city draws them down south from British Columbia's boreal forests, but the jobs aren't there. The drug, alcohol and homelessness problems are huge. Down in the Gastown area of the city you'll see all the people settled into cardboard-box houses on the streets. Groups of tough-man cops circling round.'

Ahmed's smile arrowed itself straight into Nattie's heart; it would stay there, she knew, leaving her bleeding. She had to go home . . .

'I was Daniel in Canada. Nobody persisted with questions and I gradually eased up on furtive looks over my shoulder and expecting to be left dying in a ditch. It was a rewarding, restoring year, that year in Vancouver. But then, seeing those photographs of your wedding, it turned out to have been nothing short of catastrophic. I didn't go into another decline once I knew. I was too bitter. I stewed in my own juice for a few months, cursing the world. Eventually, though, I calmed down and my life took another turn. But there's no time for that now, you have to go, I know. And we need to find times and make plans.'

'No. I can't – *we* can't. We're where we are and there's nothing to be done. We can't undo it. I got pregnant, I took an impulsive wrong turn, but Hugo's a good kind man and I can't—'

'See me again? Don't say it, Nattie, not that.' She was on her feet, trying to find the strength to leave him, and made a move towards the door. Ahmed had risen too. He stopped her going, turning her to face him, holding her arms. 'There's so much more to explain. I'd been living in limbo for so long, then a few weeks ago I snapped, gave in, persuaded myself that enough time had gone by for any risk to you to be minimal. And now I'm here I can hardly bear to look at you, for the need I feel. Don't say you can't see me again. You can, there'll be times. Tomorrow? Lily will be in school. Can you bring Thomas here?'

Nattie shook her head. They were standing close. His hands were on her bare arms which made her shiver. She knew there was no not-seeing him again, no pure, sane, sensible course of action, not the way she felt. 'Tomorrow's not possible.' The words seemed to stick in her throat. 'Hugo's taken the afternoon off. We're going to his parents in Oxford for the weekend.'

'When? Monday? Can you come with Thomas on Monday?'

He held her arms more tightly; they were both shaking. 'My grandparents are going to be in London this weekend, seeing my uncle,' Nattie said slowly. 'I'd be so sad to miss them, you know what they mean to me.'

'And to me,' Ahmed said. 'I owe John and Bridget so much. Think what could have happened if I hadn't been able to hide out with them in Worcestershire. Fahad might have tracked me down before I'd worked out where he'd planted the bomb.'

'I'd been thinking of coming back early Sunday morning, leaving Hugo with the children.' Nattie smiled hesitantly. 'I'm sure his parents won't mind. They'd love a day of having him to themselves.'

'You'd see your grandparents first then come here?'

'It may not work out. Mum only told me today they were coming. I don't know how it will go down with Hugo, but I'll try.'

'Sunday afternoon with you, worth waiting seven years for . . .' Ahmed's kiss was tender, but his body was taut with the strain. Nattie clung to him a moment before breaking away and edging towards the door. They were struggling to stay within bounds.

'I have a car,' he said, breathless. 'I'm driving Jake's till he knows his plans. I'll drop you at the tube station; you won't be late. And I'll pick you up,' he said, kissing her, 'at whichever tube on Sunday.'

He picked up his car keys and hurried her away.

11

A Weekend in Oxford

Hugo was seeing out the morning in his Covent Garden office. It was a dank, grey Friday and he wished they were staying in London for the weekend. He longed for time alone with Nattie. He sensed a distance between them and was desperate to reconnect. What chance was there, staying with his parents, which could anyway be a bit of a strain? He had looked forward to going, but not now; any sense of anticipation had drained away.

His relationship with his parents had never been easy. As an only child he'd felt in the way, an intrusion into their golfing lives, more bother than he was worth. He'd seen little of them; a weekly boarder at school, he'd had many weekends and spells in the holidays with his close friend, Patrick, at his home in Staffordshire, which was a vast mansion on a private estate. Hugo had begun to feel self-conscious about his background, too middle-class, neither one thing nor the other; his parents had begun to embarrass him too. He'd avoided going home whenever possible.

Their pride when he got into Cambridge had been gratifying, yet Hugo felt that had been a fluke and with a mediocre degree in History of Art, choosing to go into public relations which they didn't rate or understand, the awkwardness had continued.

Looking back, he could see how much the time he'd spent in Staffordshire must have hurt his parents; he'd been almost more part of Patrick's large aristocratic family than his own. He and Patrick had needed each other, though; two shy teenagers, one overwhelmed by the weight of family expectations – Patrick's father had been a government minister, coincidentally Victoria's boss at the time – and he by his innate feelings of inadequacy.

Nowadays he was fine about going home to Oxford, seeing his parents; Nattie had been the glue, they adored her. But not this weekend.

He had to find out what was wrong. Nattie was distracted and distant, hardly absorbing a word he said, and the times she did pay him any attention, her interest felt somehow effortful. Her mind seemed constantly elsewhere. Warning bells had rung too, when she'd sprung her plan to see her grandparents on Sunday. He felt suspicious and uncomfortable about the way she'd pressed so hard, saying how much his mother and father would love having him to themselves. Her smile hadn't masked the look of trepidation in her eyes, almost as though her very survival depended on his consent. She said Victoria had only just told her at lunch about her grandparents' visit, but she could have easily explained the weekend clash. After all, she'd see them at Christmas.

Hugo stared out of his office window at the sullen sky. Maybe they could leave the children with his parents and go for a long walk. Except that it was forecast to piss with rain all weekend and was looking that way already. He cursed, minding deeply about Nattie leaving early on Sunday. It felt wrong, impolite, standing up one set of grandparents for the other. He'd have to explain, remind his mother and father of the circumstances; Victoria's overworked government minister days and Nattie spending large chunks of the school holidays with her maternal grandparents. It wasn't surprising that she had formed such a bond with them. At times she'd confided in her grandfather John before her mother, Hugo knew, especially when Ahmed was being hounded by the authorities and even having his telephone tapped.

Hugo felt waves of jealousy imagining the private intimate conversations between Nattie and Ahmed. And to know they'd been recorded, listened to by spooks in their shirtsleeves in stuffy office rooms, hurt even more. He sighed. Ahmed had been vindicated, he was the brave fucking saviour of them all.

He forced his mind back. Jeanie, his PA, had come in. 'When do you want the B-list invites to go out, Hugs? They're all done.' She parked herself on a corner of his desk and studied her nails – newly painted from the strong smell of the varnish.

'Maybe hang on a bit,' he said coolly, irritated about the nails. 'How we doing with the As? What are we up to?'

''Bout ninety – not bad.'

'Cupcake Corner opens November one,' Hugo said, trying to keep the impatience out of his voice. 'We'd better not wait with the Bs. Can you send them out Monday?'

He cast an eye at his watch, anxious to be off, home for lunch with the children before setting off for Oxford. 'Anything else?' he asked tersely, wanting her gone.

She was almost out of the door when she stopped dead. 'I nearly forgot. Christine called while you were on the other line – I said you'd give her a bell right back. You're off then, are you? Have a cool weekend.'

'And you,' Hugo muttered ungraciously as the door closed, frustrated at having to deal with yet another of Christine's not-so-bright ideas. The cursed Palmers department store, his great bugbear, with its endless demands on his time.

Hugo cursed all the way home, feeling put-upon and under-valued. Christine had only expected him to drop everything for an 'impromptu meeting'; nagging on in that squeaky little voice of hers like a mouse on steroids. He'd had to lie through his teeth about back-to-back sessions all afternoon.

He felt wretchedly low. They'd lost the SleepSweet account. He wasn't undervalued, he was a complete fucking failure, a no-hoper, a joke. Brady had said 'Lose one, win one' with an easy, understanding smile. He was a decent chairman, good to Hugo, but it wasn't good for Tyler Consulting. He can't have been pleased.

A wash-out at work, unloved at home ... Nattie had always been great at sensing when he was down and being positive, but not this week, not lately. Something was going on in her life and he didn't feature. He felt desperately out in the cold.

He hadn't told her about losing SleepSweet, hadn't been able to face it, not after hearing her Sunday plans. She hadn't even asked after the press launch when he'd been in such a frantic state. It would have helped to tell her what a fiasco it had been. A key home editor not showing up and Murray Beard poncing around, acting like he was a hard-pressed chief executive, let down by his useless public relations firm, the jerk. Pissing himself with excitement at being given just the thin ammunition needed to 'let Tyler's go'. Beard had his pet agency, the writing had been on the wall, but Nattie would have said helpful things and had some bright ideas.

Hugo walked tiredly up to the front door, keys in hand. He could hear Lily squealing with delight on the other side, on tiptoe, probably, unlatching the door for him. She stumbled as it opened in on her, righted herself and jumped up and down. His heart swelled. She was his beloved angel child, as golden as Nattie.

'You're late, Daddy! We've had lunch. Mummy said you'd be home in time.'

'Have you saved me any?' He dropped his briefcase and swung her up for a kiss. 'How was school?'

'I got another star! It was for tidying up.'

'Not sure you'd get one of those round here, my girl.'

Nattie kissed him and asked rather mechanically after his morning. 'There's some ham and salad and the Cheddar needs finishing.' She smiled. Her smile lit up her face; it was lovelier than any smile in the world, heart-piercing, the core of his devotion. He carried it with him night and day, dreamed of reaching out to touch it. But he never could; he had no foothold, was never on solid ground.

'You seem a bit down,' Nattie said. 'Is it Christine, just for a change, or that Murray Beard joker?'

'Both. Other stuff too, but this isn't the time. Are you lot quite ready? I'm keen not to be stuck in traffic when I've only got you for half a weekend.'

'Don't be sarky. I'm sorry, love, but you said last night you were okay with it.' Her eyes were pleading, willing him to play along. 'You even said you'd get me to that early train on Sunday, which is as saintly as they come.'

They made it out of London with comparative ease only for the Oxford rush-hour traffic to do them in. 'Must be an accident surely?' Nattie said, as they crawled along.

Lily had been driving them mad with her constant questions. 'When are we there? Are we there yet?' Thomas had a screaming fit, which must have punctured eardrums all down the line.

Hugo jollied them along, containing his irritation, and when they finally drew up outside the house he turned back to the pair of them with a tired grin. 'Phew, made it at last.'

Out of the car he eased his shoulders and stretched, glad to have changed into jeans, badly in need of a drink, then tackled the unloading. 'Buck up, old man!' he coaxed, leaning in to unstrap Thomas. 'Grandma and Grandpops would love to see a smiling face.'

'Tubsy won't do one,' Lily said with satisfaction. 'He wants his tea.'

Nattie held out her arms for Thomas, leaving Hugo to sweet-talk his daughter into a better mood. He squatted down. 'Grandma and Grandpops hardly get to see you both and it means a lot to them. Will you give them a big hug, just for me? You're very special to them, you two, their only grandchildren.'

'We're Granny's only grandchildren too.'

'But she sees you more often, angel. Be a good girl this weekend.'

The front door opened and Adam and Claudia came out to help them with the paraphernalia. 'Sorry we're late,' Hugo said, kissing his mother's cheek, 'lousy traffic. Good to see you both.' He hugged his father awkwardly in an embarrassed, British sort of way. His parents had aged; it was a few months since he'd seen them. Their golf-players' tans belied an underlying pallor, a more faded, slack-skinned look. His mother, in lavender cut-offs and a lacy lemon top, had gained a pound or two and her hair that had been richly dark and glossy, much admired, was now uniformly grey. His father had lost most of his. And he'd developed quite a little pot belly too, which sat oddly with his height and basic leanness.

'Lily, you've grown, you're such a big girl!' Claudia crouched down with cricking knees and held out her arms. Lily hung back a moment then stiffly accepted the embrace. Thomas flung his head away dramatically, rejecting any suggestion of contact, and burrowed deeper into Nattie's chest, clutching on to her left breast with his little fingers.

'Give him time, Mum,' Hugo urged. 'He sleeps in the car and wakes up in such a grump. How have you been?'

'We're fine, darling,' his mother said.

The children behaved better at tea. Thomas chomped through chipolatas, peas and mash, followed by a banana forked up with brown sugar and cream. Lily wanted black cherry yoghurt, about the only flavour Claudia hadn't got in for her.

The kitchen was lower-ground, a large living space transformed by his architect parents from a warren of sculleries, cellars and storage. A front window onto a stairwell let in light, as did a big modern window at the back and a side door out to the garden.

There was no time to be alone with Nattie. Lily refused to believe that her room was a spider-free zone and had to be coddled and read to for hours. Thomas was slow over his bedtime bottle, and as soon as he was tucked up in his sleeping bag – in Hugo's old cot, retrieved from the attic – Nattie disappeared to help Claudia in the kitchen.

She did her best at supper, was almost her old lively self again. Warm with her in-laws, helpful, appreciative, enthusing about the garden flowers, the chicken dish. 'It's so tasty with the olives and peppers, I'd love the recipe if it isn't too guarded a secret.' His mother promised to photocopy it for her.

Hugo drank his wine feeling little involved, tired and depressed.

'How's work?' Adam asked predictably. 'Not great, I take it, since you're putting back the vino like water. You can't sit with that empty glass. Help yourself and look after Nattie's glass too.'

'Not the best,' Hugo said. 'We lost an account yesterday, one of mine, but as the chairman said, you lose some, win some. It could be worse.' There seemed no point in prevaricating and pretending, flannelling along; no point in saving it up to throw at Nattie either. What the fuck?

He flicked his eyes her way. She looked mortified, guessing it was SleepSweet, probably, and feeling hurt not to be told. Guilty too, if she remembered that she hadn't even asked after the launch. She'd be full of sympathy later, which might help with a little togetherness, but what use of that if it wasn't from the heart? It wouldn't fill the void. Hugo felt himself sinking deeper into a mood of self-pitying desolation.

Claudia was looking maternally anxious. 'I'm sure something else will come along,' she said, with a need to console, though it was just the sort of anodyne remark guaranteed to irritate. 'You won't let it get you down, will you, Hugo dear?'

'Anything you say, Mum,' he grinned, humouring her with effort. Much as his parents tried to hide it, they didn't care for his job. How much did they even really care for him?

Claudia made a game effort to move things on. 'We went to a dinner with the Wrights last weekend,' she said, with a bright informing smile, 'in that gorgeous house of theirs. It was very civilised and intellectual, the full academia with all those dons.' The name didn't mean a thing to him; Hugo couldn't think who the hell she was talking about. 'Don't look so blank, dear,' she said, with slight impatience. 'You know, the Wrights – your friend Jake's parents. You and Nattie went over there once when Jake was down the same weekend. They asked after you very warmly. They're really sad to have lost Jake to Australia. I expect you're both going to miss him quite a lot too.'

'Jake's gone to live in Oz? Never! Has he won some great architect's competition or something? Some jammy project Down

Under?' Hugo continued to stare, feeling another solar punch to his system. Jake was the egghead architect his parents would have loved their son to be – following in their footsteps, overtaking them. To have his mother twittering on about Jake just at that moment was all he needed. Jake had only been Ahmed's fucking flatmate and best friend.

He'd become one of Nattie's best friends too, naturally; she'd kept up with him – with all the constant reminders of Ahmed it must bring. Hugo didn't dislike Jake, nor even his sour-faced wife, Sylvia, but having them in their circle of friends only under-lined the feeling he had of living life in Ahmed's shadow.

He glanced at Nattie who must have been as surprised as he was and was amazed to see she'd blushed to the roots of her hair. She often did, she embarrassed easily, but he couldn't see why, over this. He felt even more suspicious and quite unnerved. 'Did *you* know Jake had taken off for Oz?' he demanded in an accusing tone, forgetting himself. 'Did he call to say goodbye? You might have told me!'

His mother threw him a cross look and Nattie reddened even more. 'I had no idea he'd gone,' she said, speaking pleasantly in front of his parents. 'It's an age since we've seen them. I've felt a bit guilty, if truth be told, about not being in touch.'

'They've gone to Melbourne,' Claudia explained. 'Jake's mother-in-law lives there, and he's joining a practice, staying for a year or so to broaden his experience, Ruth said. He's only rented his house out, not sold it; she was relieved about that.'

'It's good to see how they do it in other countries,' Adam remarked, 'but from what I hear in the trade Jake is quite a high-flyer already, going places himself.'

'Yes, Dad, yeah, okay. Sorry I'm not Jake Wright.'

It was a churlish outburst, which caused a small shock like a stone hitting the windscreen, leaving its imprint if not shattering the glass. Hugo regretted it immediately. He saw flickers of emotion flit into his father's face; there was truth in it, they both knew, though Adam was quick to swipe it away.

'That's the wine talking,' he said crisply, in a vain attempt at damage limitation. 'Winning and losing accounts must go on all the time in PR. Hardly something to lose sleep over, I'd have thought.'

'Sure, Dad, it's just a bit frustrating, that's all.'

Claudia went to the fridge and brought out a mounded summer pudding and a dish of crème brûlée. Nattie was at her most effusive. 'Hugo's fave, as I'm sure you must know. Mine too. Summer pudding's a perfect treat.'

Hugo sipped his wine and assumed the role of smiling onlooker, quietly brooding on life's disappointments and his woes. He wondered if his father, both parents, felt a bit unfulfilled themselves. Theirs was a provincial architects' firm, thriving as far as he knew, yet they'd never branched out and expanded, never moved from the inconvenient Victorian semi they'd lived in all their married life. It was on five floors, handsome in its way, but you'd think they'd have moved to somewhere detached, more practical and on fewer floors. Still, the house was in Oxford's quiet Victorian conservation area and they seemed happy enough in their chosen rut, playing golf, seeing friends, pottering on pleasantly towards old age. He was probably their only worry.

'We loved Lily's postcard from Portugal,' Claudia said, handing Nattie a heaped plate, 'and in her own writing too.'

'One or two backwards letters, you mean,' Nattie prattled on and the tame tenor of the evening was restored.

They were alone upstairs at last. Nattie unpacked their few things and handed Hugo his washbag. She looked at him with pained, questioning eyes. 'Why ever didn't you say about losing an account? I'd always want to know. It's SleepSweet, I suppose. I feel dreadful, I should have asked about the launch, but there's been such a lot going on, I just never thought—'

'No, you haven't been doing much of that lately, where I'm concerned.'

'Don't, love – don't be in a sulk. I only wish you'd come home and told me straight out.' She smiled anxiously and gave a slightly affected little sigh. 'Well, better get to bed, I guess. I'm pretty tired. You must be too. But, darling, we've always shared every little setback, you know that.'

'You're not sharing anything right now, not a bloody thing,' he muttered, though her back was turned as she made for the bathroom and she either didn't or chose not to hear. 'And anyway,' he said, catching up and swinging her round. She looked shocked and he let go of her arms. Her scent was reaching him, which ignited hot rods of need. His body strained, he ached for her. 'You'd sprung this Sunday plan of yours,' he went on. 'You were full of that. It hardly seemed like a good time.'

'I'm truly sorry, love. It's been full on at work. And you did say you were okay about Sunday.'

She looked away, she'd sounded agonised. He stood by as she brushed her teeth, head bent, not wanting to look him in the eye. What was going on in her life? It was as though she was on the far bank of a fast-flowing river, a distant figure, walking away. Was it anything to do with Jake? Had they been seeing each other and now he'd gone to Australia? Had she been attracted by the link to Ahmed? She'd anyway always said how much she liked Jake. Surely not Jake, Hugo couldn't seriously believe it. And the gulf between them was recent – wouldn't he have sensed an affair from day one? He felt angry, disorientated, broken and alone.

Nattie cleaned off her face with lotion and covered herself in night cream. The smell, like custard and marshmallows, masked her own intoxicating scent. She gave another coy awkward smile and left the bathroom. The night cream lived on her bedside table at home; she put it on after sex.

Hugo burned with frustrated need; all he craved was a little togetherness, was that so much to ask? Was she going to let him near her? He tried to calm down. Better give it a few minutes if there was to be any hope of making up. He looked round the new ensuite, grey-tiled bathroom that his mother had shown off earlier with such pride. 'Finished just in time for you!' He'd admired the use of space; it was cool and spare, typical architect's style.

He went into the bedroom. Nattie was out of the red dress she'd been wearing, a demure, in-law-appropriate number with rounded collars and little pearl buttons. He wasn't mad on it, but it came out every year.

'Pity about the weather,' she said, draping the dress over a chair; why couldn't she ever use a hanger? 'Your mum suggested the Museum of Natural History, which Lily would love, of course – remember her saying she wanted to be a "pallyotogist"! Or there's Oxford Castle if the rain holds off. Be good to get out if we can.'

She was in a black bra and pants, her nightie ready on the bed. He wanted to hold her, reach for the bra clasp, bury himself in her magnificent boobs. He felt knotted up with desire, hungering to make love to the woman he'd married, to feel her warm and responsive in his arms, his Nattie, all the tension and distance forgotten.

He went close up to her, wanting her eyes, and felt badly jolted, seeing the nervous, almost hunted look they held. She glanced away, sending a signal. It brought an icy sense of rejection – she'd been finding excuses all week. He longed for even a kiss and turned her face back, smiling, bending to kiss her mouth, gently, cautiously. His need was overwhelming, hot and coursing, yet it was as much a need for togetherness, to be reunited again in bed. Nattie flinched visibly; she backed away, putting up her hands in smiling apology, repulsed by even a kiss.

He stared at her in disbelief. Nattie's remoteness was unbearable; she'd always been warm, genuine and caring, loving in her own way. They had good sex too. The times she didn't want it, she'd always tell him in a friendly, happy-to-be-kissed sort of way. She'd never once, in all their five years, shuddered and shrunk back from his touch.

Hugo undressed in silence. Nattie was already in bed, the alien, guest-room bed, watching as he climbed in on the other side, stiff and ungainly with tension.

She touched his bare shoulder. He hadn't brought pyjamas and wished he had. A cold anger was building up within; he wanted love, warmth, sex, not empty guilty gestures. He felt strung up and chilled, unloved. Sick about SleepSweet too, useless as ever.

'I've been thinking,' Nattie said, 'about the chief executive at SleepSweet – Brian, the one who was headhunted and who you got on so well with. Would it be a good idea to ask him to supper – with his wife or whatever, if he's got one? You said he had a great new job with a furniture chain, and I'm sure he'll have heard about the turnaround at SleepSweet. He'd probably like to have the lowdown on his shit replacement and it would put you back in his mind. It's always good to keep in touch with people who know your worth.'

Hugo kept silent. He got what she was saying. PYA, Putting Yourself About, being pro-active. He heaved a sigh and turned on his back, hands behind his head, staring out into the darkness. He felt defeated, inadequate and pathetic. PYA just happened to be yet another of the endless things he was fucking useless at.

The anger in his system burned and he felt a need to go on the attack, to wound and fight. How could she start talking about such mundane things at such a time, when she'd just rejected him in the cruellest way imaginable?

'Why did you blush bright red when my mother talked about Jake and Australia? Did you know already and not let on? Have you been seeing him without me? A few cosy lunches?'

'You don't seriously think that? I blush the whole time, as you well know – and how much I hate it. The last time I saw Jake was with you. It was just a bit embarrassing, your mother telling us and her surprise that we didn't know.'

Hugo brooded in silence. He was stressed-out with testosterone tension and had the acid taste of rejection on his tongue. Did he keep up a freeze? Try to get some sleep? Some hope. 'I think you should tell me what's going on,' he said finally. 'You're on a knife-edge, you wouldn't even let me kiss you. Do you know what that's like?' he raged. 'Do you? Do I smell? Not make enough money for you?'

He heard Nattie's intake of breath. 'That's a shocking thing to say. Have I ever moaned to you about money? We're doing fine – if you had to go on the dole we'd cut our cloth and sort it. You should never, ever undersell yourself the way you do. I'm intensely proud of you. Sorry if I'm edgy. I hate that it's upsetting you, more than words can say, and I love you just as much as always.'

Something didn't add up. Hugo couldn't get a handle on it and stayed silent.

'I think what's best, darling,' Nattie continued, speaking so slowly and quietly that he had to turn to hear. He could see her profile in the dark, achingly beautiful; he felt shrunken now, though, no pumping organs, heart drained, blood frozen. 'I know it's not what you want to hear,' she said, 'but if you could just give me a little space, just a week or two. I've been doing my head in, I've had so much to think about at work, Ian being bitchy as well ... It's impossible to explain, but there can come a point – with a woman certainly, and I'm sure men too – when you yearn to be alone with your thoughts and less pressured. It's not fair on a partner, I know, but I need to sift out what's good and what's bad with myself to try to find some calm and know where I'm going.'

She moved closer, close enough for him to see the gentle look on her face. He longed to pull her into his arms then, a fresh coil of desire overtaking him, held down and compressed like a spring. It had to stay that way. He'd lose her if he lost control; lose everything.

'I know you're pressured too,' Nattie said, 'but can you understand? Can you live with allowing me a little space?'

'You're not giving me much option, are you?' What the hell did she expect him to say? That he wanted to fuck her then and there if he had any choice in the matter? 'I hate this,' he burst out. 'I want to hold you and be close, just as always. I've got a lot on my plate as well, but it doesn't change any of that. But if it's what you feel you need ...'

He stared into her eyes and his anger drained with the way she was looking at him. He was always putty in her hands.

Her smile became teasing, more of a grin. 'But I'll say one thing, my love, you don't smell. You never have, no bad breath ...' She leaned and kissed him chastely. 'Sweet as roses. Night then, sleep well.' She was already turning on her side.

Hugo turned away too. They were back to back and he was an unhappy man – the unhappiest, he thought, he'd ever been.

12

A Brixton Reunion

On Sunday morning Ahmed paced the kitchen slowly, one foot in front of the other, as though gauging the room's dimensions. He was marking time and his thoughts were all over the place, skittering about like hailstones on a pavement. He was wildly impatient and sexually hyped-up, but also brooding and deeply concerned. He thought of the day he'd looked down the barrel of Fahad's gun. He'd known the rightness of what he was doing then – unlike today.

He'd had to come back. He was going against the strongest advice: the chance of a reprisal was shorter odds than Russian roulette, so the authorities had said, laying it on. Leaving England hadn't been from choice.

He tried to rationalise, genuinely believing that slipping into London, taking every precaution, in fact made the risk pretty slight. It didn't lessen the guilt, but all that time away, those seven long years, he'd been obsessed with his love of Nattie, unable to cut loose and get on with his life, certainly not marry and settle down. Was it really so surprising that he'd reached a point where he could stand it no longer?

He dreaded any sound from his phone. Her plans would go wrong; she wouldn't come. Hugo would be deeply disbelieving – and let her know it, most likely. He'd try to touch her conscience, and who could really blame him? Nattie was soft-hearted and serious-natured, she'd care about hurting Hugo and wouldn't be able to hide her guilt either. There was no shortage of girls who would play it cool and lie with ease, but Nattie wasn't one of them.

Ahmed tried to blot out his images of her lovemaking with Hugo. He had no right to such feelings of jealousy, yet his skin crawled and his fists were clenched. He couldn't expect her to turn away, but now that he believed she still loved him, he passionately wanted her to have avoided any weekend sex. They'd both known why she was coming to London. There'd been no prevaricating, no misgivings; nothing needed to be said. He couldn't quite imagine her sleeping with two men in the space of hours, but could hardly ask about that. He just had to suffer the thought.

The morning stretched ahead. He felt caged, pacing Jake's kitchen, and decided to go out for the Sunday papers. They weren't the best online, too weighty, and he needed milk and a few staples too. The nearest shops were the ones most likely to be open on Sundays, but it was risky, getting too known in the area. Still, wearing his glasses helped and different people worked the mini-mart tills at weekends; it should be okay.

It was a relief to be out of the house. The weather had turned. No more sunshine and clear skies, it was almost tropically hot, oppressively humid and with heavy, threatening clouds. Were the gods trying to tell him something? Ahmed thought about his route, which he regularly varied, and set off, chancing the rain, glancing casually up and down the street, trying not to look furtive. A man in beige chinos, he looked like a barrister or City type – a number of them lived locally – was coming towards him, walking a yappy terrier and with his pooper-scooper ostentatiously on display. He nodded civilly as they passed.

Ahmed walked on, fretting guiltily about the risk to Nattie. If she were with him she wouldn't be spared; the thought made him draw in his stomach. Suppose his movements were being watched. The house opposite seemed to be multi-occupancy, not well maintained. Anyone living there could have absorbed that the owners over the road were away and there was a new arrival.

Suppose someone renting one of those bedsits was from Leeds, Manchester University, any of the places where he was known – someone who suspected him and spread the word that a man who looked like Ahmed Khan was living locally. He was a hero to the majority of British Muslims, most of whom hadn't known his identity, but as well as those directly involved in the bomb plot there was a hard core of sympathisers and extremists who would go to any lengths.

Nattie had been to the house once already. If she started being seen here more often ... He felt fear pricking, lifting the hairs at the back of his neck. To have to part again now would corrode his soul. His small achievements would lose all meaning, his life feel like a dead-end street, going nowhere. But she'd probably find the resistance and say she couldn't see him again after today. She had Hugo, her children, their safety to worry about. And her feelings couldn't be as powerful as his after an absence of seven years – could they?

He was back at the house without mishap, unpacked his shopping and prepared a tray with tea things. He read the Sunday papers, which were full of another terrorist atrocity and calls for 'moderate' Muslims to show a lead. He resented the tag 'moderate'. What did it mean – moderately violent? There were extremists and sympathisers and the rest. Muslims should show a lead.

At one thirty, excessively early, he left the house without setting the alarm, wanting no distractions on the return, and drove Jake's throaty car to South Kensington. He parked up by the side entrance to the tube station as planned. He waited with butter-flies in his stomach, lust on his mind, and when Nattie finally came out of the station, saw the car and her face lit up, he was done for. He switched on the engine and revved it, hardly able to contain his impatience. She ran across the street and climbed in. 'Let's go, quick,' she said, and he roared off with hardly a kiss. No lingering. Not till they were behind a latched and locked door.

'I died with every ping on my phone,' he said, putting the back of his hand to her cheek as the traffic slowed them down. 'No one knows I'm here, but with all the calls and emails I've done a lot of dying! And I've shared the strain, worried endlessly about how things were with you and Hugo. I actually dreamed of him last night; he was sitting at a kitchen table with us and wiped at his eyes with a hankie that came away covered in blood.'

'That's hardly sharing the strain, making me handle that image. It's cruel.'

'I needed to tell you. It's what I've yearned for most of all, being able to tell you things, every needling little aggro, the good bits and all the rest.'

Nattie smoothed his hand on the wheel and his blood raced. 'What are we going to do?' she said. 'I feel in despair.' Ahmed glanced and her eyes on him were helpless, as though willing him to whistle up some magic solution. She smiled wanly. 'You used to be so jealous of Hugo, even knowing how I felt about you. The trouble is he's always known it too, that's what's so infinitely sad. We have to talk seriously. You do know that?'

'I've been psyching myself up all morning to say the same thing, hard as it will be. But just for now, this afternoon . . .'

She gave him a sideways look. 'Everything on hold?'

He couldn't contain the lust he was feeling. God, why wouldn't the traffic move?

'I know you as well as if I were married to you,' he said, struggling to hold on, shifting about in his seat. 'I know you'd have dressed in that pink shirt and jeans so as not to give Hugo cause for concern and suspicion.'

'No black lacy bras today,' she said.

She was looking straight ahead, lips twitching, and Ahmed stopped the car abruptly. They were almost opposite the Imperial War Museum. Her mother and William lived just up the road. Nattie turned and they stared at each other unflinchingly. It was lust in its purest form, making love in a look. He was the first to look away; the air in the car was hazy with lust and the dust from it was blurring his eyes.

Outside the house with its protective wall and rose-covered trellis he switched off the engine. 'We're here, Nattie. The bedroom's a flight and a half up, at the front of the house; twee net curtains, not Sylvia's finest, but they'll keep out the world.'

'No sipping tea in the sitting room?'

'Not first off.'

They stumbled up the couple of front steps, his arm round her, seaming her to his side while he fumbled urgently, one-handedly, with the key, stabbing at the lock. She took the key from him and turned it the right way up. The door closed behind them and he shot home an enormous white-painted bolt. No more lusting, only a frenzy of passion, seven lost years of it, where they stood in the narrow hall. Were they even going to make it upstairs?

*

Nattie had been living for this moment ever since the shock of seeing his message in the account she had been about to close. In some subconscious corner of her frenzied brain she felt the pain of having failed in her resolve, the first time of coming here, to have made it her last – though any hope of that had been a deep self-deception, she knew. It hadn't been in her to stay loyal to Hugo and resist. Her feelings were too powerful; they were too long held.

Climbing the stairs she felt weightless. There was no gravity, no world, no thoughts, only the giving of herself to the man she loved.

'This won't be the best,' Ahmed mumbled, mouths locked as he reached for her bra clasp. 'I'm out of control.'

He stared at her body and kept staring as she rode him. 'Two babies later,' she mumbled self-consciously, before her breath was taken away and her consciousness floated up to another level. She was in another life, an old familiar country, swept along on an avalanche of undisciplined sensations, whole squads of them. Could any living, feeling human being have called them to order? Two people in love, in their own private bubble of oblivion. Hard landings were for later.

'How long have we got?' Ahmed's head was buried in her neck, his arm loosely flung over her breasts. She could feel and hear his heart beat, still at a great rate.

She turned on her side to be facing him. 'Another hour or so, not much more. I must be back by four, just in case.'

He hitched up and stared at her. 'We've got a lot of talking to do. This weekend has been pure hell, Nattie, thinking of you and Hugo, living with images . . .'

'I haven't been able to let him near me and he's going to erupt sooner or later. He's confused and suspicious already, unhappy about me coming to London. We can't go on – well, not for long. Even if I wasn't so scared for you.' She bit her lip, looking up at

Ahmed. He would be safer back out of the country, far from the hostile home shores, but how could she not see him again now?

Ahmed pulled her into his arms and kissed her. 'It's not my safety that matters, Nattie. I can take my chances; it's yours. And your children's. God, this is wretched, even to think of saying this, but I can't let you take the risk of coming to see me here. Even if I stayed in the house twenty-four-seven I could arouse the suspicions of someone over the road. What I said at lunch in the bistro stands. I want to marry you and I'm going to one day, but being here now, back in South London, when I was given a new identity and expected to stay away . . .'

'Why can't you have full protection like Salman Rushdie?' Nattie said, feeling the injustice of it all with bitter indignation.

'He was known worldwide. It's different with me. I'd given vital evidence, my identity was protected as far as possible and the authorities feel they've done their bit. Gratitude can be an ephemeral thing where the courts and officials are concerned.'

'But that's so unfair! Think of what you did!'

'Life *is* unfair. Bomb disaster averted, job done. And, if we see each other often, Nattie darling, Hugo's going to find out soon enough. You'd have to face that or be prepared to tell him with all that that means.'

'I feel physically sick at the thought. He's desperately easy to hurt, insecure and vulnerable at the best of times. I never told you the full scene in our coded messages that first year, since you knew I was trying to help him, but Hugo almost died. No more snorting office coke, it was snowballs and worse.' Chilling to remember that lethal mix of heroin and cocaine, killer chemicals, used needles everywhere. 'Most days I found him curled up in agony on the floor,' she said.

'And you nursed him back? He owes you a lot, Nattie, you shouldn't forget that.'

It wasn't easy to explain. It hadn't been her dutiful nursing, Hugo had only found the immense reserves of will he'd needed to draw on for the detox and rehab because of his love for her. And her deepest, darkest fear now was that learning about Ahmed would cause Hugo to relapse.

'Time for that cup of tea,' Ahmed said, climbing off the bed, 'and I've years to unload – if you really want to hear more about my loveless life.'

'But not sexless?'

'Well, not quite. Come downstairs, just as you are. I'll get us a couple of wraps.'

She looked round the bedroom while he was gone. It still had the original fireplace with an antique ornamental fireguard and a fine bare mantelpiece, presumably cleared of Jake and Sylvia's personal stuff. It was a handsome room decorated in neutral tones; the two full-length sash windows were draped with mud-coloured curtains and the offending nets.

'I've ordered some shutter-blinds,' Ahmed said, returning from the bathroom in a summer-weight white dressing gown, bringing one for her too. He held it out with a smile, his soft familiar smile that had always melted her into a liquid pool. The dressing gown with its raised basket-weave texture felt crisp and freshly laundered, cool and good against her skin. She thought about the fine-cotton blue check shirt he'd had on earlier, the discreet Rolex wristwatch; he could never look flash, but he had a quiet assurance about him now. There was so much she wanted to know.

She felt a kaleidoscope of emotions, staring at Ahmed, but her heart sang. She wanted to be with him every second of every day. She loved him. Was there a way? Coming here, just once in a while? Surely the risk of being seen was infinitesimal? She could take a long lunch-hour. Her office was south of the Thames, not far, and she could be doing an interview . . .

Some days she took Tubsy with her to see friends. Most, like Maudie, were still furthering careers – Nattie was young to have two children – but those on their first babies loved to chat over coffee and ask advice.

Tubsy usually slept from one to two-thirty, which was useful time to catch up with her reading. He wouldn't need looking after if she brought him here at that time. No – she couldn't let in such thoughts, they weren't allowed. Ahmed was watching her – was he reading her mind? He had hold of her hand and linked fingers in an encouraging way then they went downstairs.

13

The Next Instalment

They took their tea into the sitting room and sat together on the sofa. 'On with my lonely life then,' Ahmed said, settling a hand between Nattie's thighs.

'The day I saw you'd got married, I flipped. I went straight out to get drunk – first alcohol for a year – which was all part of being so messed up and guilty,' he added, not wanting her to think he was having a go. 'And being flat broke as well. I'd been thinking of ways to make money, though – for when I could come back for you – but instead I stayed on with the charity, ARC.'

Ahmed kissed her mouth, wanting more and wishing there was time. 'I did begin a relationship while I was at ARC,' he admitted. 'It was with a native Canadian girl whose brother had come to Vancouver and found no work. He was sleeping on the streets, spaced out. She and I helped him over the worst and she persuaded him to go back with her to their small home community in the forest up in north-east British Columbia. She'd worked in a hairdresser's in Vancouver, but jacked it in. She and her brother were very close.

'I went too. She'd fallen for me, I knew. It helped to have someone adoring and needing me, but she wasn't you.'

'What was her name?'

'Alyana.'

'I know I shouldn't mind about her,' Nattie said, looking like she did mind, very much. 'Were you together a long time?'

'About a year – I'd got sucked into all the problems and issues her people faced. It was weird, living in that community. I soon got mighty sick of acorn pancakes, buffalo and fish-head stew – which I can cook you any time, by the way. It's made with various bits of a salmon, not only the head.'

'No, thanks.'

'The big issue for the aboriginals was fracking. It's a real concern. They live by hunting and fishing, tourism, forest products, and if the fracking's done by cowboys and the wells aren't properly capped, bad greenhouse gases like methane can cause contamination. It's a minimal risk and I won't bore you with the detail, but it's vital that everything's regulated and tied up tight.

'Quebec and Nova Scotia had imposed moratoriums and Alyana's community wanted one for their province. Things were getting going, hearings underway, so I joined in and fought the aboriginal cause. I was living from hand to mouth, but still had my New York sharp suits, I could look the part at the hearings. Having worked on the *Post* I knew how the media works. I could maximise the coverage, feed stories to lazy reporters and punchier angles to the more serious press. I began to get noticed, which I didn't really want. I'd become a bit of a liability, in fact, in terms of fighting the community's cause. Trouble was, I could see both sides.'

'And you were with Alyana all this time?'

'Mostly. But I'd started to have itchy feet. Ideas come into your head when you're sitting on a log in the forest or pathetically trying to fish. I'd reached the point of wanting to move on.' He stroked her cheek. 'Another cup of tea, or shall I keep going?'

Nattie was looking at her watch when her mobile rang. She paled. They'd both jumped, hearing the tone, and she shot out of the door as if her phone was a starting gun. 'My bag's in the hall,' she called back. 'I'll never get to it in time.'

Ahmed cursed inwardly. It was sure to be Hugo, home early, or with some problem or other to cause stress. He went to the door to listen to her side of the conversation, tense to the tips of his fingernails.

'Hi, darling! You okay?' Nattie asked brightly, a bit artificially. 'Sounds like you're still there. You're not still going with lunch, surely? . . . So when do you think you'll leave?

'No, I'm not actually there yet,' she continued, after a long pause. 'I, um, decided to come into town. I'm rather out of clothes and it's always such a rush, trying to shop in my lunch hour or trailing Tubsy round in the buggy.'

Ahmed smiled to himself. He'd thought she might need an excuse and had taken care of it. He was burning to know how much time they had, though, and Hugo seemed to be talking for an age.

'Okay,' Nattie said, getting a word in at last, glancing his way with a hopeful smile in her eyes. 'Yes, darling, me too. Drive safely. Kiss to Lils and Tubs.'

She clicked off and Ahmed, seeing the look in those beautiful amber eyes, felt ready to swoon. She was naked under the wrap. He went up close and took the phone, dropped it back into her handbag, which was on the floor by the door – they'd been oblivious, coming in. He slipped his arms inside the wrap and round her waist. 'How long have we got?' He found her mouth, not waiting for an answer

'Couple of hours, max. I must be home first.' She drew back and stared at him, her mood flipping, tears brimming in her eyes. He kissed each of them in turn.

'What's wrong? Tell me,' he said, fondling her hair. 'What did Hugo talk about for so long?'

'Two of his aunts who'd come to lunch, which slowed things up to our advantage.' She gave a forlorn half-smile. 'His aunts still resent his being left the house; they feel entitled to use it as a pit stop on London visits. One's coming tomorrow. I'll have to do lunch, but it's not that. It's just . . .' Nattie looked away and back again. 'He'd called the house phone first, you see. He knew I wasn't home. I can't bear this deception and lies.'

'But you managed a neat little sidestep.' Ahmed smiled, touching her face. 'It was hardly an outright lie. "I'm rather out of clothes"! Quite accurate, really.'

She pulled away. 'Don't make light of it,' she said huffily. 'I can't cope.'

'It's no good getting too heavy either,' he said, leading her back to the sofa where she sat stiffly forwards with her head bent. 'It's not going to help. I swore to myself this morning I was going to say – even if there hadn't been Hugo to worry about – that I couldn't let you take even a minimal risk. But God, it's hard!'

She lifted her head and stared, wide-eyed. 'I don't rate this business about the house opposite,' she said, with a determined expression. 'I can't not see you again, I just can't.' She started to cry, shoulders heaving.

'Suppose we take it very slowly,' Ahmed said, gathering her up, feeling the full weight of responsibility – and the weight of his guilt. 'I'll try to check out the house opposite, get the measure of who's going in and out. There's a family next door on one side, with twin girls who have lots of giggling friends, and an elderly couple on the other. The immediate neighbours seem fine,' he said, releasing her, 'but, Nattie darling, suppose Hugo found out? He could do, you'd have to be prepared for that. I want to be with you now, tomorrow, for life, but as well as the risk of word getting back to my enemies and anyone tracking me down, you do have to face up to what coming here would mean. Skirting round things, evasion, even telling outright lies . . .'

'Do you think I haven't been facing up to what it means – every which way, every second since you got in touch?'

She was staring at him, tight with tension, and Ahmed held her gaze. 'We had to have this conversation,' he said. 'I've been planning to touch base with Tom, now I'm back – if you'd be happy for me to do so. He's a good friend, the best, along with Jake, and I'd trust him with my life. Tom's this side of London, so you could always have been seeing him if you needed somewhere to have been. He'd be prepared to help, I'm sure, and cover for us if need be.' Ahmed knew how much Nattie adored her stepbrother and he didn't believe Tom would let anything slip to his father – nor to Victoria, which was more to the point.

'It would help hugely to share it with Tom,' Nattie said. 'He'll understand more than anyone. He knows what it's like – he's still in love with Maudie. Will you tell him, though, and explain?' She gave a shy smile. 'I'd find it a bit hard.'

'Why don't I ask him round at a time you can be here – a detour on your way home from the office. We can tell him together.'

Nattie leaned against him. 'I love you so very much,' she sighed. 'You know what's best, you do it right.'

He kissed her purposefully, laying her backwards, and his hand that had gravitated back between her thighs after Hugo's call began stroking her, feeling its way to a point where she couldn't hold in her moans. 'There're no nets on these windows,' she mumbled, making space for him on the narrow sofa, 'somebody might look in.'

'They'd need to be very tall. Of all our worries . . .'

14

A Fuller Picture

Ahmed made more tea. Nattie ate three pieces of shortbread as she'd had no food all day, but now that they were settled on the sofa again, she was impatient to know more.

'We've got less than an hour,' she said, 'and there's so much I still need to know. About other loves, for instance, and how you got from being skint in Canada to being this new groomed you. You must have either swum with the sharks or done something very clever.'

He smiled and set down the chipped Leeds Football Club mug he'd been nursing in both hands. Had he carried that mug everywhere with him over all that time? Nattie felt moved. She imagined how much he must have needed tangible reminders, though, banished from his homeland and everything comforting and familiar.

'I'm not sure what you're going to think about it all.' Ahmed looked sheepish, almost shy.

She gazed at him, treasuring every short-lived moment. In less than an hour she'd be a wife and mother again, smiling at Hugo and dissembling, shedding her cloak of happiness and dressing herself in shame. How long would it be before he suspected something and asked her outright? She was already causing him pain. How could she bear the far greater agony he'd feel when he discovered about Ahmed's return? As he surely would. How could she bear to lose Ahmed, now that they'd found each other again?

She thought of his strength of character and the exceptional bravery that had cost him his family, his identity, his peace of mind. She thought of his shock and grief on hearing the news of his father's death, and she tried to imagine the fear he'd described. She was beginning to understand the insidiousness of its iron grip, how it could have eaten into him the way it had and taken such obsessive hold, depriving him of reason, filling his head with crazy notions of cowardice, impotence and self-loathing. The sadness of it all carved a notch in her heart.

It explained so much. His flight to Canada, his need to do good works; it wasn't difficult to understand his bitterness, desperate loneliness – and Alyana.

'Tell me more. You admitted to some questionable ambivalence about fracking when you were in Canada . . .'

Ahmed wrinkled his forehead. 'Yes, well, that was rather awkward. I didn't change sides, just rode two horses – and only as far as saying I could see the pros before punching in with the cons. I didn't hold back with those. There's a real gold rush on the province's water; fracking gobbles up billions of litres and there's always the fear of some disaster, bad old human error. The aboriginals are understandably terrified of water contamination. There'd been a recent small gas leak into the Peace River; it was easy to push their case.

'Away from the hearings I tried to explain the remoteness of any really dramatic risk. The wells are drilled so deep, you see, that the chemicals would have to seep through two metres of solid rock—'

'Can we shelve the fine detail? We're not getting on very fast.'

Ahmed kissed her. 'Sorry! Anyway I persevered at the hearings, making clear that I wasn't opposed to fracking at any price – unlike the loons who never stopped yelling "Frack off". Some of these environmentalists are off the wall, so radical and extreme – this is leading somewhere, I promise!

'My ambivalence got noticed eventually, and after an interminably long meeting one day, a guy from one of the smaller chemical companies asked me out for a drink. I needed one, I was back drinking by then and I liked this guy, Jeff. He was fair-minded, even prepared to admit there were minimal risks. We got quite friendly over time and Jeff picked up that I was ready to move on. He said I should think of heading back to Vancouver, get myself some temporary job and tag along with him to a few events and parties. In other words put myself about.' Nattie's thoughts flitted to Hugo, longing for him to do a bit more of that.

'I knew Jeff was right,' Ahmed continued. 'You were married, but it was impossible to shake off my dreams of being with you again and somehow making something of myself. They spurred me on.

'It wasn't easy, being back in Vancouver. I was fresh out of money and on borrowed time too; my Canadian visa was up. No one had come after me or seemed to give much of a toss, but I went to see the authorities just in case. I told a small lie about being "in negotiations" with an American sponsor and asked to stay a few more months, doing volunteer work for ARC. The charity backed me up; they were glad to have me back, and I was granted a six-month extension.

'I needed a bit more going for me than working with homeless aboriginals, though, if I was to make any sort of mark at Jeff's parties. No one rates worthy do-gooders, I'm afraid, when it comes to getting yourself noticed.'

'How *did* you make your mark?' Nattie was fascinated to know. 'And where was Alyana in all this? Did she return to Vancouver with you?'

'Yes, she insisted on coming. I'd tried to stop her, said it was time, that happy as I'd been ... that sort of thing, but she clung on. It was awful. In the end all I could do was to tell Alyana I was in love with someone in England and always had been. That rang as true as it was and I had to live through her pain. I felt brutal, abject. There's nothing worse than the bodies that love can leave strewn in its path.'

'Don't. Don't say that, don't make me think about it.' Her head was against his shoulder and she sat up and stared miserably into his eyes.

'But it's the case,' he said. 'It's a fact you have to face. How's our time? I can drop you somewhere close to home, which gives us a bit longer.'

Nattie felt nervous about that, but she wanted every minute going. 'I shouldn't really chance it.'

Ahmed kissed her lips. His bare feet were up on the coffee table, ankles crossed. She loved his neat toes, legs with the right amount of hair, his sinewy body, the aura of energy that lifted off it like a shimmer of summer heat; she loved the male scent of his skin. Her stomach curdled with longing and the acid truths of being married to another man.

'So I shacked up with ARC again, helped out there, and set about making a few bob from scribbling. I'd made useful contacts and ensured that anything I fed the press was professional and snappy, reporter-on-the-*Post* style – which I could do falling off a kayak – and a provincial newspaper ran a few pieces. One of the nationals took an article on living in the wild and I ended up doing a weekly column bylined *The Forest Walker*. I'd done quite a bit of that!

'It was good pocket money. I could buy clothes and repay Jeff with a few drinks. I wrote a couple of short stories for magazines, sent a piece on the plight of First Nation Canadians to the *New Yorker*, calling myself I.D. Newel – which felt vaguely appropriate, my third identity – and they ran it. I'd got myself better set up.'

'I'm panicking a bit, we've got to go,' Nattie said, swinging her legs down. Ahmed stood up. He lifted her into his arms, carried her to the foot of the stairs. 'Can't make it any further – and anyway, we're in a rush!'

They dressed at speed and were racing out of the bedroom when Nattie noticed Ahmed's two bags. It was a prompt. 'You still haven't let on what you're doing now,' she complained. 'Obviously quite a lot, it would seem, from those Business Class labels on your luggage.'

'I'll give you the gist in the car,' Ahmed said, smiling.

Downstairs they clung hard and left. Nattie gave an involuntary shiver as the front door clicked closed behind them. They held hands as far as the gate, on the paved path through the scented front-garden shrubs. Ahmed had taken charge of her book bag, along with a carrier bag he'd picked up that was by the front door.

He did an efficient three-point turn in the road, talking all the while. 'I'd had an idea for a television series and mentioned it to an old boy I'd been stuck with at a do that my new friend, Jeff, had taken me to – a lunch party at his chairman's house, all very lavish. The old boy, an astute businessman, in fact, who knew half Vancouver, had seemed interested and given me his card, saying he had friends in the film business and to call up if I ever had a finished script. As I said before, Hollywood makes loads of its films in Canada, especially around Vancouver; I knew that. It short-circuits American union problems and saves them a packet.

'I'd worked on my idea after that, fitting it in between articles and helping out at ARC. It was hard graft and I didn't hold out much hope, but I still dug out the businessman's card and called him up on the off-chance.'

'And something came of it?"

'Yes. Amazingly. He asked me to a drinks party. Someone was coming, he said, who'd just finished making a film for television and was off back to Hollywood, but I could meet him at least. Talk about coincidence! He actually turned out to be the guy I'd met in a New York bar when I was drinking my way round the city, living the life with Matthew and Charley – before Dad died.'

'And the film man liked your idea? Wasn't it a bit tricky, though, explaining yourself? I mean, he'd have known you worked on the *Post*. Didn't you have to tell him about dropping out and why you were in Canada?'

'He's had an edited version of why I'd left my job on the *Post*'s foreign desk. I had to swear him to secrecy and promise I hadn't done anything he wouldn't want. I also insisted on using the name I'd been writing under, I.D. Newel. He had a wobbly moment, thinking I could be a terrorist, but he remembered my New York drinking, which seemed to mollify him, and he was hooked on the script. He's called Hank Patzer and we get on great.

'My time at ARC had given me the idea, working with all the sad dropouts, the homeless and abused. They're mostly spaced out on drugs, lives ruined by the drug dealers. I didn't want to write about them directly – for *Homeland* read *Homeless,* that kind of thing. I was keener to be into the big timers. People are endlessly fascinated by the bad guys – they're better box-office, to be crude about it. So I wrote about the shipping business, which seemed to have possibilities. The drugs have to get into Vancouver somehow and the cruise ships travel up from Mexico to begin popular trips up north. I had good captains, bad people, unwitting handlers, loud-mouthed tourists and little old ladies who wouldn't have wanted to know what had been sewn into their padded winter coats.'

'But that's exactly like *Shorelands*!' Nattie exclaimed. 'You're not telling me that's you?' She stared at him in wonder and he flashed her a proud smile.

'Yes, I write the scripts. I've been living in California for the last couple of years. I'm working away on Season Four, upstairs in the study I've made for myself on the top floor.'

She was astounded. 'I can't believe this. I don't know what I'd thought. You'd obviously written something brill, but a whole, ongoing series? You're famous, you clever old stick.'

'I am, after a fashion, but it's complicated. Everyone wants to interview me and I always refuse, which makes the media all the more curious. Hank's been complaining that it's hard to hold the line.' Ahmed lifted his hand off the steering wheel and put it to her cheek. 'We're only just going to make it by half five, Nattie, darling, with this traffic.'

'Best drop me near the tube station so I'm walking from the right direction.' She was past worrying, too bemused and full of wonder. 'Famous twice in your life, that's some going – my small-screen genius and Hollywood recluse.'

'Forget that. When can you come again?'

'Not tomorrow with Hugo's aunt to entertain,' Nattie said, frustrated.

'Tuesday – straight from the office?'

'Lunchtime would be best. I haven't negotiated a late pass with Jasmine. It won't be easy to find times.'

'Call me as you leave the office and I'll be outside with the car.' He gave her a quick glance. 'I love you, Nattie.'

She leaned close, but then straightened up again in a panic. 'Shit! I've just remembered I'm supposed to have been shopping all afternoon. I'll just have to say I couldn't find a thing.' She smiled, while feeling guilt settling in for the duration like heavy rain. It wasn't going to let up either. Hugo needed her; the children needed her. And Ahmed's words of love would be filling her brain; his touch would be warm on her skin.

'I can solve the shopping problem,' he said. 'It's a bit of serendipity, but I've been longing to buy you a present and it felt precautionary too, I thought you might need an excuse. I bought a dress online, but I think it'll fit; it's a blueberry colour. It wasn't expensive, you could have bought it yourself.'

He pulled up short of the tube station, reached behind his seat and handed over her bag and the carrier he'd picked up in the hall.

'Don't get out, better not.' She gave his cheek a quick brush, trying to avoid tears. 'And I want to rush home and try on my new dress. Thank you! Tuesday it is then,' she said, damp-eyed, with her hand on the door handle, before tearing herself away.

Hugo's car wasn't outside the house. Nattie unlocked the door, turned off the alarm and tried to de-tense her shoulders. It was muggy outside, but the hall felt chill and the house had an eerie stillness about it. She stood shivering a little before forcing herself into action. She went upstairs, her thoughts chasing each other, and into the bathroom to wash away her sins. She was married to Hugo – married to the kind, handsome, loving, wrong man and sleeping with the right one.

The blueberry stretch-velvet dress fitted. It had a low cowl neck, clung in the right places and was perfect for winter parties. She longed for Ahmed to see her in it. There was a pair of shoes in the bag as well, strappy sandals that encased the ankle. How did Ahmed know her shoe size? Nattie absorbed the labels to know where she'd been shopping, carefully laid out the dress on the bed and went downstairs.

She got supper ready for the children. Hugo rang. He was about fifteen minutes away; he and Lily were trying to keep Thomas awake, he said, or he'd never settle to bed. They'd sung a lot of songs, 'Old MacDonald' more times than Hugo cared to say. She thanked him for coping so manfully and told him to hurry home.

She made a mug of tea and wandered into the sitting room with it. The room felt airless and smelled of stale flower water. The shaggy garden roses in a jug vase on the mantelpiece had drooped and shed papery petals. They made her sad. Nattie brushed the ones around the vase into a wastebasket, bent down for others in the hearth and went to tip out the smelly water in the sink.

She texted Ahmed to say the dress and shoes fitted perfectly, miraculously. How could he have known? The text he sent back brought a misty inward smile. She deleted the texts, unlocked the back door and went out into the drizzly garden to pick fresh roses.

She sat at the kitchen table with a Sunday paper in front of her, the culture section, and peered at the week's television programmes. *Shorelands* was on Thursdays, she knew that, but needed to see it there in print. It was hard to get her head round that little bombshell, though Ahmed always was full of surprises. She smiled to herself again then dropped her head into her hands and wept.

15

Hopes and Fears

It was Wednesday, nearly two weeks since Nattie's painful rejection. Hugo knew it was best to stand back and let her be, but he couldn't hack it. He felt adrift, like a lost child in a department store, separated from all that was familiar and comforting. It was so unlike her and he had to find out what was going on. Some couples had sex-lite relationships and seemed to handle it, but he and Nattie had always got it together. The sex made everything possible – it helped to make up for her absent heart. It would break him to go on this way.

Should he talk to Victoria? She was always sensitive to any nuances, but it was a delicate area. Not easy to explain that Nattie could be cooking, chatting, involved in his doings, right beside him and as far away as Tasmania. She smiled a lot, was warm, friendly and obliging, but not in bed; she was still frozen and backing off. And to think of her reaction that Friday night at his parents' made Hugo shrink in his skin. Not the easiest thing to get across to her mother.

He was on his way home and the tube train was swaying, making him feel slightly sick. The heat wasn't helping, nor was the fug, the heaving crush and the stink of the Mexican, Thai, or whatever people were eating out of cartons, fucking anti-social on a packed train. It was October, for Christ's sake, who needed an Indian summer? Hugo longed for some cooler autumnal weather.

The train lurched and clanked to a stop with such a jerk that he nearly threw up. He felt better out in the open, striding down the leafy streets for home, glad to have got away early. He went in the door, heart lifting in anticipation. However full of tension, fearful and depressed he felt, seeing Nattie always brought a tingling rush.

'Hi, Daddy,' Lily said, looking up from her macaroni. 'You're first back.'

'Why? Where's Mum then?' Lily shrugged and Hugo turned to Jasmine who was with her at the kitchen table, feeding Thomas. 'Do you know where she is, Jasmine?' he asked, with the feeling of nausea creeping back.

'Not sure. She just said she'd be late today, back about seven, I think,' Jasmine offered cheerfully while wiping Thomas's mouth with a smelly-looking J-cloth.

'Oh. Well, I wasn't expecting to be home early,' Hugo said, feeling defensive and annoyed to be making it so clear he hadn't known. 'I can take over now, Jasmine, you go on home. Keep the extra, of course, just whatever was arranged.'

'No worries 'bout that. I'll just shove this last mouthful into Tubsy then and be off. You'll see to his afters? A chopped-up pear always goes down well and Lily will have a yoghurt – she knows which one she wants.' Jasmine pushed in her chair. 'Bye then, me lovelies,' she said, planting kisses on their preoccupied heads. 'Be good for your dad now, won't you?'

Hugo walked her to the door, hardly able to contain his urge for her to be gone. Where the hell was Nattie? It was irrational to be suspicious, he knew. There was probably a perfectly good reason. She'd told Jasmine she'd be late.

'I wonder what's keeping Mummy,' he said vaguely, taking a pear from the fruit bowl. 'Does Thomas have his pear with the skin off or on, do you know, Lily?'

'Dunno. He eats anything, he's a greedy pig. He'd eat a worm if you put it in his bowl. I want a raspberry yoghurt, Daddy.'

'That's no way to ask. What should you say?'

'*Pleeese* may I have and thank youuu . . .'

Hugo frowned. 'Not good, Lily. They should teach you some manners at that school – and that means being polite and respectful to grown-ups, my girl.'

Lily ignored him and concentrated on her yoghurt that smelled rather artificial, like the revolting dried raspberries in her morning cereal. Hugo washed the pear and left the skin on; he'd read somewhere that all the goodness in fruit and veg was just under the skin.

'Can I have a carrot for Moppet – pleeese, Daddy?' Lily asked, getting down. 'Mummy says Tubsy should have a run-around after his dinner; she plays football with him on the grass.'

The image brought a pang. 'Okay, let's go,' Hugo said, opening the glass doors to the garden.

The fragrances on the evening air were refreshing and helped to clear his head. He dribbled a few balls to his small toddling son, lost to his introspection, absorbing eventually, though, which played into his growing nervous rage, that dusk was closing in and he should start the bath. 'That's it, guys,' he said, picking up Thomas and the ball. 'Close up the hutch door, Lily, and come in now. It's bath time.'

He locked up behind them and was down on his knees in the kitchen, easing Thomas's pudgy little feet out of his first pair of proper sturdy shoes when he heard the sound of Nattie's key in the front door.

'Hi, Jasmine!' she called. 'Sorry if I'm just a bit later than ...'
She came into the kitchen, saw Hugo and her startled look said it
all. He got up from his knees and faced her; she had gone as pale
as if he were an intruder. 'Hi, darling! Gosh, I wasn't expecting
you back so early. Jasmine's gone? Nothing wrong, is there?' She
smiled, making a thin attempt to recover. 'You'd said seven-
thirty, though, or I could have planned things differently.'

What 'things'? What plans could she have changed?

'You're late, Mummy. Jasmine's been gone ages,' Lily admon-
ished, as Nattie bent to kiss her. 'I've fed Moppet, but dunno if
the hutch is proply locked.'

'I'll check it out in a minute, love – or perhaps Daddy can,'
Nattie said, raising her eyebrows at him, 'while we start the bath.'
She picked up Thomas who was clinging to her legs and made to
leave, but Hugo stared at her coldly. He was tense, heart thudding, mentally forming the questions he wanted to put.

'Where have you been?' he queried slowly. 'Why didn't you
tell me you'd asked Jasmine to stay on? Then I could have let her
know that I was on my way.'

'She's easy about timing, we had it sorted, there was no need
to bother you.' Nattie sounded cooler, more in control. 'I must
get this show on the road now,' she said firmly. 'Upstairs we go,
kiddos. How was school, Lily? Did you do sums?'

'Yes, and drawing and singing. Daddy gave Tubsy his pear with
the skin on, Mummy.'

'It was washed,' Hugo protested. 'And he ate it all up, didn't
he, cheeky girl?'

Nattie was silent, preparing the supper. Hugo put a couple of mats
on the kitchen table, cutlery and glasses, and opened a bottle of
red Bordeaux. It was bargain-basement stuff, but drinkable, he'd
bought a dozen bottles. He poured himself a large glass. Nattie

didn't want one. 'Later,' she said, filling a saucepan. He watched as she put on the rice to cook, sipping his wine, wanting her to feel his eyes on her, to know how hurt, suspicious and full of misgivings he felt.

She chopped onions, tomatoes, peppers with concentrated briskness. 'It won't be the best supper,' she said, without looking up. 'I'll do some shopping tomorrow.'

'Where were you earlier? What kept you till seven?'

She carried on chopping, didn't look up. 'I went to see Tom. He'd called yesterday, wanting an address, and he sounded a bit down; I do worry about him. I went round after work to have a cuppa and a catch-up.'

Nattie slid the onions from the chopping board into a non-stick pan, shushing them round intently, adding the tomatoes and peppers and a handful of chilli flakes. Hugo was sure she'd flushed, talking about Tom; her discomfiture had been palpable. 'Is Tom still living in Brixton and working out of that crap studio?' he asked. 'I can't imagine many prospective clients making the trip.'

'Don't be so snobbish! It's fabulous, with a perfect north light, and Tom has exhibitions in the West End. He's doing fine. I just wish he'd find the right girl.' Nattie turned, wooden spoon in hand, and looked Hugo in the eye. 'Have you had a rotten old day or something? You seem in a bad mood.'

'No, I'm not. But it wasn't such a good day. Jeanie fucked up, just for a change; got the timing wrong for an important strategy meeting with the leisure people out in Staines. I'd ordered a car and was just leaving when they called, apologising if I was almost there, saying the chairman was delayed and the meeting pushed back till twelve. Jeanie got away with that one, but she's a bloody liability.'

'It happens,' Nattie said vaguely. 'Everyone makes the odd slip.'

'Some more than others. Oh, I knew I had something to tell you. I ran into Brian, ex of SleepSweet, yesterday on Piccadilly and invited him round to supper.' He had an acid taste, recalling Nattie suggesting it, that sickening night at his parents'. 'Brian called back today with a couple of dates so I've gone ahead and asked him round. We fixed on Wednesday week. Hope that's okay? We haven't anything on.'

'It's fine,' she said. 'You never know, something might come of it. He sounded a good guy from all you said and he can't have approved of the new CE arbitrarily shafting you.'

'He's coming on his own. They live out in the sticks, I think. How about asking Maudie? And Tom too, with that odd woman he's seeing, which would make us six?'

'I'm really not keen to have Tom and Maudie together. He's never got over her, it would be very unfair.'

Hugo felt impatient. 'It's years since she ditched him, for God's sake! Tom sees her around and I don't know who else we could ask who would be as easy to fill in about Brian, he's hardly a close friend of ours.' Any lingering sensitivities of Tom's were the least of his worries. He wanted to check out Nattie's story as well. He hated to feel so mistrustful, but his suspicions were octopus-like now, putting out feelers in all directions.

'Well, let's see if they can come first,' she said mildly, 'and take it from there.'

They got on with the evening. She'd done her best with leftover chicken and the wine slipped down, the bottle finished in no time, though Nattie had no more than a glass. Hugo resisted opening another; the way she looked, her still golden tan in her white shirt, so easy to unbutton, her soft skin and exquisite glow, he didn't trust himself. He had to play it cool, had to go along with it. What other fucking choice did he have?

Nattie broke into his reverie. 'Can you finish off the lemon tart, love?'

Hugo stared at her. 'If you want me to. I'm not sure what you do want. You're in another place, somewhere I'd rather you weren't.'

'Sorry, I did try to explain. Bear with me, darling, just for a while, can you? Life catches up sometimes.' She smiled. Which bit of life had caught up with her, he wanted to know. He opened a second bottle of wine.

The lemon tart, which was home-made, reminded him of Sunday teas with Victoria and William. The children loved seeing them. Hugo wished his own parents made more of an effort to see Lily and Thomas at this special stage. They never came to London, never put themselves out and took an interest. He called home sometimes, but the contact was always one-way. He felt lonely and unloved. Nattie's relationship with her mother had its sensitive moments, but the love was there. And with William. Hugo slightly resented their closeness – unfairly, he knew. William was more of a father to her than her own, but he'd also been Ahmed's boss and mentor, which was hard to forget.

Nattie was clearing plates and he caught a yawn – as he was probably meant to. He felt randy and frustrated, despairing and harsh. 'You needn't yawn.' He glared at her. 'I know you'll be off to bed any minute, you don't have to advertise it.'

'It's very early,' she said, grinning back at him. 'I quite want to watch a bit of television.'

He washed the saucepans and turned from the sink. Nattie was standing near the kitchen table, glancing at her phone, and he moved close.

'Just a kiss,' he said. She gave a cautious half-smile. He drew her into his arms and kissed her full-on, which she allowed while giving nothing. He could feel the force of his own physicality, not just his hard-on and wine-loosened urgency, the overt sexuality, but his height and strength as well, the maleness of his straining body that she'd always responded to in the past. Why couldn't she be just a little less wooden and give him a crumb of hope? The fight went out of him suddenly. 'Oh, forget it,' he said, his hands making fists. He turned away feeling racked with bitterness and anguish.

The questions buzzed in his head. Why? What had gone so badly wrong? She'd always responded so warmly and instinctively; what had turned her? Could she be having an affair? Surely not, it couldn't be, she wasn't like that ... but the signs were there. In fact, the more he thought about her reactions, the more it seemed the most likely explanation.

The fault line had always been there — Nattie's love for Ahmed — but it had been a fissure in the rock of their marriage, not a chasm. But had her sense of loss reached a point where she could no longer bear to be touched by her own husband? Was she feeling trapped — was that it?

A shiver of premonition shook him to his roots like a gale ripping out a tree. Ahmed was only missing and Nattie had never given up hope. Could she have heard from him in some way? The possibility of his return had always lurked in the wings, shadowing Hugo, dangling like a noose over his head. Suppose it had happened? What would he do? Nattie held him together, he'd disintegrate without her.

A couple of lines from T.S Eliot's *Four Quartets* came into his head, about things that might have been remaining forever a possibility. His pulse pounded; he could feel and hear its thud. He couldn't bear Nattie's distance, didn't trust himself to keep his cool. He'd have to do something, see someone, talk to Victoria: there was no one else.

Nattie went upstairs first. Hugo followed slowly, feeling

morbid and slightly drunk. She'd taken to wearing a long white nightie, despite how warm it was. Cool autumn nights were nowhere in sight. She was drawing it over her head as he entered the bedroom and bundled herself quickly into bed and was glued to a book when he joined her. She turned, leaning over to give him a chaste kiss on his cheek before settling back on her side and returning to her book.

In the office next day Jeanie put her head round the door. He was wanted upstairs, the chairman's PA had just called. A summons from Brady Tyler. Hugo felt his world was collapsing about his ears. First Nattie's rejection and now Brady about to tell him he wasn't cutting it, not quite the man for the job.

He felt a pricking sensation, the beginnings of an old rash that used to attack painfully between his fingers, a form of eczema that was stress-related, unsightly and liable to spread. It itched to distraction and he felt nauseous again. Hugo swallowed back the sour-tasting bile, hoping it wasn't giving him bad breath, and picked up the phone to the chairman's PA. 'I'll be right up, Alison.'

'Come in, come in,' Brady said, leaving his desk and indicating the long white leather sofa. 'Come and sit down.'

Hugo concentrated on trying to relax. 'How can I help?' he said, attempting to sound eager and on the ball.

'With a bit of potential new business,' Brady smiled. 'We're in the running for Bosphor Air, the new Turkish budget airline company, and I'd like you along. You do well at presentations, Hugo, nicely restrained, very much the classy Brit. I'm sure the Turks who know all about pushiness would find it a refreshing change. They're after our British know-how as well as our tourists and provincial airports, I expect. I'd need you to fly out to Istanbul with me. It's all happening third week of October. We'd fly out Wednesday, pitch on Thursday, give the guys who got us in the door, our local contacts, a slap-up dinner, and fly back the next day. I don't think it should run over. Can you clear those couple of days? It's three weeks away.'

It was an unexpected vote of confidence, a much-needed boost, except that Hugo felt it misplaced. He had no faith in his own ability and was sure the Turks would be a lot more impressed by punchy go-getting than old-fashioned British understatement. Brady would do the upfront stuff, but he'd expect some smooth elegant talking from Hugo, and backup. What chance of that? How could he perform with his head full of Nattie, his problems blurring his vision and sapping what little poise and verve he could have summoned up?

Brady was waiting. Hugo beamed and tried to sound positive and game. 'Sure thing, I'll get going on it right away. Great stuff!' he enthused, knowing he'd have to get on with it all himself; Jeanie wasn't to be trusted.

Hugo left his chairman's office feeling slightly amazed by the turn of events, but little better. Between his nerves and misery, the frustrations of Jeanie, the rash between his fingers, he was in need of a stiff drink. There was a bottle of vodka in his office cupboard; no ice, better not get any from the machine in the busy corridor, someone would suss him out. Vodka and flat tonic – the mixers in the cupboard were old and flat as cowpats – would get by as a glass of water. Anything to tide him over; he wouldn't make a habit of it.

He decided to hold up telling Nattie the news about Bosphor Air and his travels till the weekend. He'd do it with William and her mother there as well. The new airline company could be a point of discussion and he'd be interested to hear their take; William might even do something on it editorially, for which Hugo could claim the credit. And, Hugo thought, if he managed to talk to Victoria privately before going he could possibly suggest she looked in on Nattie while he was away.

He'd still be giving her a clear run, which was almost certainly what she wanted. Perhaps a little break was for the best, though, and could possibly even help her to sort herself out. He could be reading the signs wrong. There was always hope. If only his every instinct wasn't telling him otherwise.

16

Talking to Tom

Nattie left the office at three o'clock and walked quickly to the narrow side street where Ahmed could stop on a yellow line. It was a depressingly sunless street full of warehouses, yet when she saw the Mazda her heart sang. Whatever the agonies of the future, the joy and promise of the now were incontestable. She climbed into the car and Ahmed pulled her into his arms. Nattie felt drunk on his kissing, his nearness, the seductive smells of leather, heat and dust in the airless car, the smell of the man she loved.

She sat up abruptly and brushed back her hair. 'We can't be late for Tom. I'm so ashamed; I hate not having told him. I know I went bright red with Hugo too, which won't have helped his suspicions. If only Tom hadn't been in Somerset last week. He hardly ever goes to see his mother!'

'He's coming at half three. We'll be in time.' Ahmed revved the engine. 'Can you stay on afterwards for a bit? There's nothing worse than these extended Thursday to Tuesday weekends.'

'Jasmine knows I may be late again,' Nattie said, feeling cautious all the same.

She was with Ahmed and ecstatic, but on edge worrying about

the office. Ian had been looking a bit sniffy as she left; his pale eyes had narrowed with his resentment of her freedom. Most of all, though, she felt raging guilt about implicating Tom, who might actually mind quite a lot. When Ahmed had suggested getting in touch, asking him round and explaining together, Nattie was grateful. Tom was a good friend to both of them and sensitive to the situation, but he knew Hugo. She had no right to be burdening Tom.

He was a few minutes early. Nattie hung back while Ahmed went to get the door. She felt wretched with nerves and stayed listening from the kitchen doorway as Tom came in.

He sounded overwhelmed. 'Ahmed – God, this is amazing! It is really you again, the man himself, you old fucker! How're you doing? Great to have you back. We thought you were a goner, pushing up roses or mud slime.'

Nattie ventured out and saw Tom and Ahmed having a spontaneous back-patting hug. She felt less abashed and self-conscious as Tom gave her one too, then reached for her hand, which he held tight. 'So isn't this something, having him back? What you must have felt, hearing from him again out of the blue! I can hardly imagine it, except that I can – I can see it in your eyes.'

She felt the tears spring into them and laughed, brushing them away.

'Come and have some tea, Tom – and I hope you can eat a bunch too. There's plenty of food. Ahmed's got a good line in shortbread and fancy cakes.'

'And fizz,' said Ahmed. 'I'll get a bottle. Tom needs a drop with his afternoon tea and we have to celebrate this little reunion. You're the only two people in the whole of London who know I'm here.'

'What about Jake?' Tom interjected. 'You're renting his house, this cool pad.'

'He's in Oz. I was being literal.'

'Got an answer for everything, hasn't he?' Tom smiled at Nattie and followed her into the sitting room. 'So spill then,' he said, squeezing her hand again as they sat down on the sofa, 'as much or as little as you want. And don't worry, I know to keep everything under wraps.'

It struck Nattie afresh how like his father Tom was: they both had the same dark colouring and height, the same raw-boned look to their faces, strong, well-drawn features. Tom was rangy and loose-limbed, always wrapping his arms round his long legs in chairs, and he was a dreamer with none of his father's dynamic newspaperman's drive. He and William were close, but Nattie sensed William's frustration; he felt his son was too easily walked over and needed to be more assertive.

She explained that Ahmed was living in California and that *Shorelands* was his brainchild, although he wrote the scripts under an assumed name.

'Wow, Nattie, that's a lot to take in. Some success you've had there, clever bastard.' Tom grinned, looking up as Ahmed returned. 'But how did you get from going missing to taking over Hollywood?'

'That's a long and emotionally draining saga,' said Nattie, 'for another time.'

She chewed on her lip, pressed her linked hands together under her thighs. Ahmed raised a slightly impatient eyebrow in an aren't-you-going-to-get-on-with-it sort of way, then took over himself.

'Nattie's putting off telling you, Tom,' he said. 'She was a bit late home from work the other day and used you as an alibi.'

'I'm truly sorry, Tom, I feel really bad about it, but you see I told Hugo I'd looked in on you after work. I'd wanted to ask you in advance, but you were down in Somerset and it wasn't something for the phone. I'll quite understand if you want me to set the record straight, if you don't want to be dragged into any of this . . .'

Tom looked from her to Ahmed and back again. 'You love each other, Nattie, you always have, right from day one. Somebody's going to get hurt and I know all too well what that's like, but you two belong. Don't worry, I'll tell Hugo, if he asks, how good it was to see you the other day. I have now, after all!'

'Thanks, really. I'm aware it's a lot to ask. He'll have to know soon, but I just need a window of time.'

She was causing Tom discomfort, going on about it; he needed to close that door.

'You should come round,' he said, turning to Ahmed. 'I'm only down the road. The studio's a real tip, but I'm out of the old basement flat – out from under my father so to speak. I live with Imogen, a psychiatrist. She's away this weekend so come round – if you can stand the mess.'

'Love to. I don't get out much for obvious reasons. It's good for cracking on with Season Four, but lonely as hell.' He gave Nattie a look that said it all. Great as it was to see Tom, they were craving a few leftover minutes alone.

'How's Imogen?' Nattie asked, trying to picture the two of them together. Not easy. Imogen was a fierce, intense woman, a high-powered professional, intellectually demanding – attractive, though, with heavy, piled-up auburn hair.

'She's fine,' Tom said, 'all good. But she's not Maudie.' He turned pained eyes on Nattie. 'We were a good team. Maudie loved my art, the art world, and she had to go off with that paunchy turd of a dealer and break my heart. It didn't last, nor with the next one – she even still works in his gallery too. It's all so cynical. I still love her.'

Nattie was beside Tom on the sofa and touched his arm, a

helpless gesture. 'You have to try to move on. I know how hard it is, having mutual friends and seeing Maudie around. She's hooked on the fast life and playing the field, but think how successful you are now, Tom. Focus on your art. She'll see how you're doing and can't fail to be impressed and you'll have that satisfaction.'

They were empty words, useless; it was like trying to comfort a teenager, embarrassingly dumped. Nothing Nattie could say would ease the pain.

She remembered about the Brian evening. 'I've got a boring ask, Tom. Hugo lost a client when the chief executive he got on with left the company. We've asked the guy round for supper – I had this long-shot notion that he might know of an opening or at least put the word about. It's next Wednesday, bit short notice. Can you and Imogen join us?'

Tom thought they could.

He sipped his champagne, staying a while. 'I'm on a new set of paintings, abstracts, working in neutrals – layering the paint then whipping the canvas onto its side or rotating it. The effects are like shifting reflections on a pond, calming, and you sort of feel the ripples. Or at least that's the idea.' Nattie smiled fixedly as he chatted, feeling Ahmed's needs as her own. She sensed Tom's needs as well, though; as Maudie's oldest friend, she knew she helped him to feel connected.

When he left, his eyes were hooded with sad envy. 'You're lucky buggers,' he said. 'Got it sorted.' It carved Nattie up.

Alone together at last, Ahmed was tender and caring, and when they lay intertwined afterwards, Nattie couldn't drag herself away. She was where she wanted to be. She felt the pumping in her chest, the unquenchable physical yearning, but there was more; shared instincts, the meeting of minds. How could he reach so deep into her psyche and pull her into his own? How could she feel such overpowering passion and easy compatibility as well? All that was missing was selflessness and restraint.

'I've got to go.'

'Don't. Not yet, we still have some time.'

Nattie looked at the bedside clock. 'Not much. Just enough for you to say more about the missing years.' She turned side on to face him. 'You've skipped a bit – like who came after Alyana? Like, for instance, who you met partying with your friend, Jeff, in Vancouver. There must have been someone and I need to know.'

Ahmed grinned. 'Sure you want to? Okay, here goes. Remember I told you about a summer lunch party at Jeff's chairman's house? It was where I made the contact that eventually led to *Shorelands*. Jeff had sold me to his chairman as a voice of reason on the anti-fracking side and suggested asking me along to keep me sweet. It hadn't seemed to occur to either of them that being on the side of the disadvantaged, the lavishness of the chairman's home might have made me rather more inclined to sourness!

'The house was in an area of Vancouver called the British Estates, one of those vast, stately mansions with rolling manicured lawns like you see in American films about the super-rich – usually the home of a mastermind baddie with a spoiled pretty daughter.'

'And Jeff's chairman had one of those?'

'Yep. Danielle fitted the bill, though her father wasn't a baddie. She was a slightly zestless, chocolate-boxy blonde in her mid-twenties, very much the opposite of Alyana, which had a certain attraction. She had her own mates at the lunch, rich boys and girls, and they'd completely ignored me. I was stuck with her parents' generation, dry businessmen with plump, heavily perfumed wives.' He grinned. 'The mint juleps were good at least.'

'But if you were stuck with the older lot, how did you get off with Danielle? Wouldn't she have been seeing someone anyway, who'd have been at the lunch?'

'Yes, she was in a relationship with a deeply suitable budding banker. She'd hardly spoken to me that day, but Jeff gave me her email later on, saying she wanted me to get in touch. She was no career girl, but she worked on the fashion pages of a Vancouver freebee and thought her mag might take one of my pieces. She'd noticed me, after all.'

Nattie wasn't surprised. Women did. Ahmed had that quality about him. He was good-looking in an unobvious way, but his eyes drew you in and it was hard not to feed on his energy and sparkling intelligence. She felt the familiar hollowing of her insides, gazing at him, then mentally shook herself and gazed at the clock instead.

Ahmed kissed her. 'There's not much more. The Danielle thing didn't happen in a hurry. She was with her uppish banker and I wasn't pushing it. We eventually got it together and it lasted a couple of years, but it was a superficial relationship in many ways, very on and off.'

Two years didn't sound so off to Nattie.

'She was a very material girl,' Ahmed remarked. 'It fascinated me how designer labels could matter so much, how she had to be seen in all the right places and could always suss out anyone's exact degree of wealth.'

'She sounds charming,' Nattie said, loathing Danielle with every fibre. 'But you were hardly in her financial league. How did you get round that?'

'She seemed to assume I was slumming it at ARC from choice. Once I'd sold my idea to Hank Patzer and been paid an embarrassing amount to tie me in, my finances spoke for themselves. There you are, that's my non-love-life.'

Nattie felt cleaner for knowing. 'I'm glad Danielle sounds so unlikeable,' she said.

'It's a sad fact of life, though,' Ahmed said, with a sheepish look on his face, 'that her father's lunch party got me to the right people. It's all about getting a foot in the door. I could have written a book, but even if it had been published and the film rights sold, the whole process would have taken an age. I was impatient, I needed to prove something. It was all about you, Nattie, then and now.'

They had to go. There was never a chance, and she had no right anyway to relax and just be with him. The clock was her slave master, the whip-cracking breaker of the spell. And as well as the rush and panic, she had to face an instinctive tightening of her gut, leaving the house. Were they being seen, Ahmed recognised? The media had honoured their promise not to use his photograph, but his enemies knew what he looked like all right.

She felt quivers of fear and avoided looking round, climbing into the car. Ahmed drove off smartly. 'If I can't see you till Tuesday,' he said, looking ahead, 'how am I going to survive?' He threw her a quick glance. 'No Friday, no Monday, is there really no way?'

She'd been secretly wondering about bringing Tubsy on non-office days, timing it with his midday kip. It would mean bringing the travel cot . . . She forced herself not to voice the thought.

'One day I'd love you to meet the children,' she said guiltily, voicing it tangentially. 'Trouble is, Lily would chatter away about seeing you.' Nattie coloured, knowing that what she'd just said anticipated the possibility of separation. The thought was in her mind now – and after only a few snatched meetings over a few short weeks. She couldn't do it to Hugo. He needed her, he'd go to pieces, relapse, start using again. But how could they go on as they were?

'Suppose,' said Ahmed, bringing her back and holding her eyes, 'you brought Thomas here when Lily's in school? Is that a possibility? Perhaps even tomorrow?' Did he always know the thoughts in her head?

Hugo sometimes got away early on Fridays. Would it matter? She'd go straight to pick up Lily, and Tubsy always had to come with her in the car anyway. They could have been to the park. Rain was forecast. And what about the cot?

'It is a possibility,' she said, 'but I'd rather leave it for this weekend and think it through. We need to take this slowly, step by step.'

Nattie hurried in the door. Hugo didn't seem to be home. 'Sorry, I've kept you again, Jasmine. There's just such a lot going on. It's that time of year.'

'No worries, all good, they've been little darlings – better than sometimes, eh, young Lily?' Jasmine rose from the kitchen table. 'Bye then, my precious ones, see you both Tuesday.'

Jasmine had given her an odd look, Nattie felt. Walking with her to the door, she wondered if she'd blushed slightly, making her excuses, and laid bare her guilt.

'Hugo called,' Jasmine remembered, as she was half out of the house. 'He said to tell you he was running a bit late, he'd be home after seven-thirty.'

'Thanks. *And* for doing supper. We can have a nice bit of play-time now, before bath.' Nattie smiled, warmly, anxiously, and was rewarded with a rather knowing smile in return. But it was also, in a funny way, shaded with understanding.

Hugo made it home in time to read to a sleepy Lily, which allowed Nattie to get on with supper. He kissed her cheek as he came back downstairs, and asked after her day. She smelled the whisky on his breath.

'I called earlier,' he said. 'You're certainly working all hours of the day, but you'll say it's that time of year.'

'Certainly is. The December issue's out in a month, panic stations all round. I've heard back from Tom, by the way; he and Imogen are fine to come, but I'm not asking Maudie. I couldn't do that to Tom.'

'You'd made that clear enough. Anyway,' Hugo said, pouring himself a brim-full glass of Bordeaux, 'I want to ask Amber. She's good fun, she'll liven things up.'

'Yes, I suppose she will. She's loud, at least,' Nattie added, feeling irrationally irritated. She dished up and handed Hugo his chops. Amber wasn't one of her favourite people.

He topped up his glass. 'It was a good find, this wine,' he said, slightly defiantly, feeling her watchful eyes. 'It'll do for the Brian evening. I've bought another case.'

He continued to drink steadily, but Nattie felt in no position to nag or complain. Amber was such a pain. She was another Tyler's executive, a pushy ginger blonde, blatant and full-on; she carried a little extra weight, but had neat sexy ankles and knew how to flaunt her assets. Nattie had met her a couple of times at office dos where Amber had made no secret of having the hots for Hugo. She'd made a beeline for him, drooling over him like he was a screen hero, and Hugo, who couldn't handle that sort of thing, had squirmed. But women went for him. He'd been mistaken for Tom Hiddleston in his day – there was a passing resemblance. Amber's attentions had turned him off in the past, but was Hugo trying to prove something now? Make his wife jealous or have it off with Amber? She'd be an easy lay.

He'd finished the bottle of wine and started another – Nattie had had half a glass – but he was more mellow than morose and helped her to clear the dishes.

'*Shorelands*,' he said suddenly, making her almost drop a plate. 'It's on in ten minutes, it's good stuff, I'm really into it. I should do a few emails, but will you come and watch with me then?'

'Sure,' Nattie said, hoping she hadn't gone a deeper shade of pink. 'Thanks for the reminder.'

They brought their laptops to the kitchen table. Nattie clicked onto her work email, since she'd left so early that afternoon. A tediously large batch had come in. They could all wait, but there was one from Sadia Umar that caught her eye.

Sadia had emailed on arrival in Pakistan thanking for the lunch at Bella Cucina, and for Nattie's stiffening of her backbone. That email had been bright and positive, Sadia full of excitement about a plan she'd worked out on the plane, but the tone of this latest email was the opposite. All the fight seemed to have gone out of her. Sadia sounded low and defeatist, frightened for her sister's life.

Dear Nattie,

I'm sorry to trouble you and be a bother, but you asked me to let you know how I was getting on and I'm afraid I'm really depressed and in a quandary. My dad thinks I should come home, that I'm putting us both at risk, but I can't desert my sister. There's nothing to be done, unless she can steal away her passport, but I dread to think what our stepfather would do to her if he caught her or found out. Even if she succeeded, there's the near insurmountable problem of the visa. That's down to me, persuading the British High Commission in Islamabad, and time is running out. Alesha is eighteen in three weeks and has no chance of a visa then. I can't bear to think of her being forced to marry that fat, middle-aged man and he's a first cousin, but how can I allow her to endanger her life, trying to escape? It's such a terrible responsibility. I'd be so grateful for any advice.

Apologies again for bothering you,
Sadia Umar

Nattie sat back with a heavy heart. She could only tell Sadia what her own instinct would be, which was by no means the right course of action. And the thought of the punishment meted out, if Alesha were caught . . .

She sent a quick return email.

My very hesitant advice would be to risk it. Your sister's whole
life's happiness is at stake. If your plan fails, the violence
done to her would, I'm sure, be appalling, but your mother and
stepfather have entered a contract, remember: they'd want the
marriage to go through. Wouldn't that be a point of honour as
well? Whatever the risk of physical suffering, I don't believe
you'd be risking Alesha's life.

Nattie prayed she was right. Wasn't the prize of freedom worth going through any number of dangerous hoops for, however remote the chance of success? Perhaps William would have some off-the-wall ideas. Better William; her ex-Home Secretary mother would feel she had to go by the book. Nattie texted him, saying that the situation with the young writer she'd told him about was more urgent, the girl feared for her sister's life. There was probably little he could do, but just in case . . .

'You coming?' Hugo had closed down the lid of his laptop and was on his feet. 'Mustn't miss the start. Come and snuggle up on the sofa,' he called over his shoulder, going out of the door. 'If you can bear to . . .'

17

Hugo and Victoria

'Those two are for Granny and Gramps and Tubsy can have that one, Mummy.' Lily's sticky fingers were hovering over the gingerbread men on the baking tray.

'No, Lily,' Hugo said, 'you must give your brother a good one and have the no-arms one yourself. That's what cooks do, give other people the best.'

'But I want the man with the Smartie red nose. Mummy, you said I could!'

'I did, actually,' Nattie admitted with an apologetic smile. 'Don't worry, Lil, I'll have the one who's lost his arms, it's not a problem.'

'No, Mummy, *that* one's yours.' Lily stamped her foot. 'Tubsy can have it. He doesn't know it's got no arms, he's just a stupid fat baby.'

Hugo faced his daughter, getting angry. 'We'll have no stamping, Lily, do you hear? And that's no way to talk about your brother. Say sorry, right now.'

'No.' She stuck out her little jaw, grabbed the broken biscuit and bolted out of the open doors into the garden.

Hugo chased after her. 'Come and say sorry, Lily, or no ginger-bread man for you and I'll tell Granny and Grampsy why!' She was by the guinea-pig hutch and threw the biscuit into the run when he reached her, screwing up her face and starting to cry. Hugo marched her back indoors, fed up to his teeth. Why did it always have to be him? The doorbell was ringing. 'They're here now! Say sorry – quickly!'

Lily mumbled something unintelligible that just about saved the day and raced to get the door. Nattie followed after her, looking back at Hugo with a wry smile that didn't help his mood. He hung back a moment feeling jagged. He needed to calm down if he was to use the afternoon to get things across. He wanted a quiet word with Victoria and to talk about Bosphor Air and his trip to Turkey – which was going to come as news to Nattie.

William would know about the Bosphor start-up, though; trying to interest him in it was pointless, especially since they had yet to win the account. A cat's chance in hell of doing that. Hugo felt as braced for failure as ever.

He stared abstractedly at Thomas, criss-crossing the kitchen on his walker, happily chatting away to himself in baby talk. 'One, two, see, Daddee.' Thomas stopped, hearing voices in the hall, Lily's excited hellos, and let go of the walker. He took a few steps towards the door, stumbled over a toy car and fell flat on his face.

Hugo rushed to pick him up. 'There, there, Thomas, not hurting, brave boy now.' Thomas gazed at him with huge, solemn gold-brown eyes, his mouth in a comical turndown, but he held in the tears. It was a tiny precious moment and Hugo's heart overflowed. He smoothed back his son's buttery curls, kissed him and went out with him into the hall, hugging him close.

'Hi, good to see you both,' he said, relinquishing Thomas to Nattie and greeting his in-laws, kissing Victoria's cheek and catching her scent. She was still an extremely attractive woman.

'Come on through. We thought we'd have tea in the garden. With this crazy weather, you'd think it was Midsummer's Day!'

Lily was bursting with excitement, tugging on William's hand. 'Okay, okay,' he said, allowing her to pull him into the kitchen. 'Let's see what's cooking then.'

'It's gingerbread and it's cooked already, Grampsy, silly. We made a cake as well.'

Nattie and Victoria ferried plates out into the garden and Hugo, taking Thomas's high chair out too, noticed Victoria's anxious glances. Nattie was radiating tension; his wife was like an animal sensing danger, a child facing the school bully.

Hugo left them and went to join William who was up the garden, peering at plants with a proprietary air. 'Looking good,' he said, without sounding condescending. 'Your plumbago's still flowering and the roses keep going with this weather. I'm keen on that hydrangea too. Annabelle, isn't it? I like the way the white flower heads go that lovely lime green in September time.'

'Yes, it's less obvious, and I think it goes well with the Solomon's seal.' They could talk gardens at least. Hugo had never been entirely comfortable with William, feeling awkward and inadequate, however easy that was with the powerful editor of the *Post*.

'Tea's up!' Nattie called.

The wrought-iron table needed repainting, but she'd spread an embroidered cloth from Madeira, a present from his parents, over it and put a few late roses in a vase. It was a proper Sunday tea, with cucumber sandwiches, Marmite soldiers, lemon cake; the gingerbread men had pride of place, all with their limbs intact.

Lily apportioned them, avoiding her father's eyes. 'This is yours, Granny,' she said, proudly picking up one with orange buttons – only to drop it and burst into tears.

'We'll stick him together with jam,' Victoria said, 'and he'll taste extra good.'

'How's trade, Hugo?' William queried. 'Any new accounts?'

'We're about to pitch for something juicy, but the competition will be tough.'

'Can we know what it is?' Nattie asked. Hugo knew she was struggling to think what she could have missed; she was so fucking off in her head the whole time . . .

He took a small perverse pleasure in carrying on talking to William. 'It's Turkey's new budget airline, Bosphor Air. An interesting challenge, breaking into the market. What do you think, William? Can they pull it off?'

'It's a volatile part of the world. They're a bit vulnerable, but what country isn't these days? They should do okay, the tourists pour in,' he said. 'They're based in Istanbul, aren't they. Will you have to go out?'

'Yes, for the pitch, which doesn't help any. I'd rather be on home turf.'

Nattie was registering the significance of a trip to Turkey, it was written all over her face. She'd be storing up questions, burning to know. How soon? How long for? He was almost amused. 'Sorry, darling, it does mean a couple of nights away.' He tried not to lace his words with sarcasm, bitter as he felt. 'You'll be okay?'

'Of course. How exciting, though. Let's hope for good things."

Victoria's eyes had flickered anxiously to William, which made Hugo feel guilty. Had he sounded that cold and derisive? Surely Victoria hadn't imagined that he'd been callously trying to score points. She knew he cared . . . He felt the cracks in his marriage widening, new ones forming and letting in more pain.

'Best of luck. I'm sure you'll pull it off.' Victoria was clearly trying to sound encouraging and positive. 'How soon do you go?'

'Some time the week after next. Just a quick in and out, we're cramming everything in.'

'Can I get down?' Lily said, seeming to sense the strain. 'Can we play Pelmanism?'

William had taught her, so he had no out. Nattie played as well, with Thomas shushing the cards about and causing chaos. Hugo carried him off into the garden.

He'd cut the grass that morning, its last cut most likely, and it smelled fresh and new-mown. He sighed, just as Victoria came out to join him and play with Thomas. She sat on the pocket-handkerchief lawn in her neat navy jeans, hugging her knees, freeing a hand now and then to roll a beach ball to her chubby smiling grandson. Hugo helped to roll it back, psyching himself up to ask about coming to see her.

'I'm worried about Nattie,' Victoria said, when Thomas had tired of the ball game and tottered off to his sit-in car. 'I feel very diffident asking this, Hugo, but I just wondered if you knew what was wrong. Tell me off if I'm interfering.'

'The opposite,' he said, extremely glad to have his opening. 'Things have been a bit difficult. I've, um, wondered if I could come over, ask your advice. I know how busy you are, though, and I hate to bother you.'

'Of course, do come, I'm pleased you asked. Let's find a time right now.' Victoria reached into a back pocket for her phone, which she consulted with a frown. 'How's Wednesday? I'm working from home till two.'

Hugo had no lunch date, he was sure. 'I could be with you by half twelve or a bit after. But please don't do anything about food, certainly not on my account.'

On Tuesday Victoria decided to walk home from a meeting in the House of Lords; it was too beautiful an afternoon to take the bus. She started off over Westminster Bridge, enjoying the view of the London Eye with its lightness and delicacy of construction.

She walked beside the river in the other direction feeling cheered and less worried, and turned down Lambeth Road.

She crossed at traffic lights and waited to cross again to the far side of Kennington Road, which was more open and sunny. As the Lambeth Road traffic started up she happened to notice a couple in a black car in the slow flow of vehicles going into town. The car moved on, she'd only had a fleeting look, but the girl had been Nattie for sure. She'd been in profile, leaning forward, making it hard to see the driver, but Victoria was in no doubt. She knew her own daughter.

She felt shivery and disturbed. The man had been dark-haired. It could have been anyone: a colleague at work, an author Nattie was interviewing – even Tom, whose studio was only down the road. But Tom had a Mini Cooper. Could it possibly have been Ahmed? Surely not.

Should she say anything about it to Nattie? A casual mention, a comment about seeing a girl in a car who was Nattie's absolute image? Or be more upfront and say she'd happened to catch a glimpse of her on Tuesday late afternoon – at traffic lights on Lambeth Road? If it had been Ahmed, Nattie would almost certainly give herself away. Victoria couldn't bear to think of the fallout; to be setting traps, putting her daughter on the spot like the cross-examining barrister she once was. There were sensitivities enough, it could only add to them.

Reaching home she went inside, feeling in urgent need of a cup of tea. Standing in her big bright kitchen, she felt calmer; and with a mug of tea in her hands, sipping it as she looked out into the back garden, at the climber-clad frames, the tumbling cottage-garden profusion, all William's clever planting, she felt she had things more in perspective.

Hugo was coming the next day. Best not to say anything about seeing Nattie. Let him do the talking, ask questions and give gentle prompts. It must have taken a lot for him to pluck up the courage to ask to see her, which was worrying enough. Victoria hoped it was all making a storm out of a breeze, but the odds on that weren't looking good.

William would have his usual strong ideas and whether or not she agreed with them she always valued his input. She hadn't got round to mentioning Hugo's visit; he wasn't good at seeing things from her son-in-law's point of view and there had seemed no great rush. Now, however, she was desperate to tell William all, most especially about seeing Nattie. She longed to hear him snort and say the idea of the man in the car being Ahmed was as far-fetched as they came, but much as he'd kept quiet about it she knew he had always anticipated Ahmed's return.

William was late back and they had to rush out to a fundraising dinner. It was for a colleague's charity; she was doing a favour and felt guilty, dragging William along. The evening turned out to be as heavy duty as she had feared. Victoria could see how crotchety and irritable William was getting and felt that any serious discussion would have to wait till morning.

They always tried to have breakfast together, to talk and share plans and she knew that after his Weetabix and toast he'd be clear-headed and in a more receptive mood.

And so he was. He listened keenly. 'Ask Hugo straight out if he thinks Nattie's having an affair. If he does, I'd be willing to bet the house on it being Ahmed in that car. Bad news for poor old Hugo.'

'Don't sound so bloody cheerful about it then, will you!' Victoria felt furious.

She pushed back her chair and clomped about, clearing away the breakfast in silence. Not only cheerful, bloody callous, she thought. How could he toss off an aside like that when there was a marriage at stake? Ahmed had been incredibly brave and they owed him their lives; her movements as Home Secretary had been known, she the primary target of a bomb designed to cause maximum devastation. He and Nattie had been deeply in love, no question – but that was in the past. Fate hadn't worked out for them.

William rose and came to make amends. 'Look, sorry, don't get excited. It's all surmise anyway right now. We don't *know* it was Ahmed in that car. But, darling, you have to face it, Nattie's fine with Hugo, loving, very fond of him, but it's a different sort of relationship. She was always going to be vulnerable. She may even have fallen for someone else. Who knows? But if Ahmed's back she'll be torn apart and finding it unbelievably hard to cope.'

He touched Victoria's cheek. 'I must be off. Find out what you can from Hugo and I'll talk to Nattie if you like – probably better coming from me. I'm sure if I ask her straight out, she'll tell me honestly. It's the way she's built.'

William kissed her. 'Good luck with Hugo. Call any time.'

'Thanks – and about talking to Nattie.'

Victoria watched him out of the gate and went back indoors. The emails were piling in, files of papers on her desk to be tackled. What would Nattie do? Surely not walk out on Hugo who loved her so much, who'd always been so good and kind. And what about Lily and Thomas? Victoria felt in despair. A child could bring such wonderful sunlight, but at that moment Nattie's sun seemed to be in total eclipse. She wanted only happiness for her beloved child.

Hugo walked briskly from the tube station to Kennington Road feeling harassed by the traffic, the petrol and diesel fumes, all the inner-city grime. His nausea was back, sickly bile swilling into his mouth that he had to swallow down. Should he see a doctor? It was lowering enough to be on his way to cry on his mother-in-law's shoulder without feeling physically debilitated.

He was in a state of panic about what to say. And what could Victoria give back other than platitudes? Wouldn't she instinctively want to defend Nattie? But he had no one else to talk to, no one as sensitive, no one who knew about Ahmed. Hugo's oldest and closest friend, the only other person he could have trusted, was living in America. They'd taken different paths, Patrick to Harvard, New York and moneymaking; he, the road of coke, heroin and near destruction. But he hadn't needed to confide in anyone before now; he'd had Nattie.

Hugo walked on, lost in his dark emotions. It was a whole month since that night at his parents'. Nattie had been friendly, never sarky, but never once had she let him near her. Was he about to lose her completely? He felt powerless, atrophied, encased in ice. He couldn't wield sexual power like Shelby, who'd walked off with her in those long-ago days before Ahmed. She'd been infatuated with Shelby, but that hadn't lasted, not like her love for Ahmed.

Shelby had a lot to answer for, not least weaning Hugo onto drugs, yet they'd weirdly hit it off. Shelby buttering him up, as lavishly flattering as a chancer, but Hugo had needed that. The sweet-talking had been as comforting as a hot-water bottle, balm for his ills. Weirdly, Shelby had called up the other day – how he'd had Hugo's mobile number was hard to know – and said they must meet. 'You've got my number now, and I'll text you an email address. Give me a bell sometime. Let's have a drink.'

Shelby had done time for his dealing; he'd be out of all that, not pressing drugs, surely. Hugo was tempted to take him up on the offer.

*

Victoria opened the door, smiling and welcoming. 'Come on in. Come and have a glass of something – wine, elderflower, Perrier?'

Hugo relaxed a little. 'That last sounds good. I've just walked at a fair trot from the tube.' His mother-in-law was dressed for her afternoon meetings: cream shirt, dove-grey skirt, her suit jacket ready on a hall chair. 'It's really kind of you to spare the time,' he said, staying by the kitchen door while she got a bottle of Perrier. He followed as she led the way into the sitting room. 'I've just been feeling so worried.'

'So have I. I'm glad to have this chat. I felt anxious when Nattie and I had lunch a couple of weeks ago, I felt she was holding something back then. It's hard to know what, though.'

Victoria sat down on the sofa. Hugo sat opposite, grateful for the glass of water she handed over. It would help with his nausea. There was a dish of sandwiches on the glass coffee table; side plates, napkins. 'Smoked salmon,' she said, following his glance. 'We have to eat.'

She took a sip of water and sat back. 'Where do we start? Do you know what's the trouble?'

'I think Nattie's seeing someone,' Hugo said, not quite believing he'd come right out with it, his worst fears exposed. Saying it out loud brought a momentary sense of release before the full significance hit home. It couldn't be true, please God.

He looked down at his knees, rubbing his forehead, before straightening up and battling on. 'It's terribly difficult this, but we're living under a sort of cloud. She won't let me near her and my obvious suspicion isn't helping. She's been late back more than once. I've called, spoken to Jasmine, and the other evening when I was home early, Nattie seemed alarmed when she returned. She was out when I called her on the office phone too, and the guy she sits opposite was kind of furtive about where he thought she'd gone. I don't know whether to ask her outright or let things ride.'

He looked at Victoria with pleading eyes. 'I know there's really nothing you can do,' he added, feeling a sudden, overwhelming sense of disloyalty to his wife.

'I suppose,' Victoria said, considering, taking her time, 'I should ask if you've any real proof – but then, when you love someone as I know you do Nattie, it's impossible not to have a strong sense of these things. My advice, for what it's worth, is not to ask her straight out. There's no going back after that. You don't want to bounce her into saying or doing anything you'd both regret. Just suppose you're right and she is in some ... emotional situation, it could be that all she needs is the time to try to resolve things. Or it could run its course. I'm sure she'd tell me if she were about to take any fundamental step. There's only one area where we don't—'

'Ahmed?' Hugo cut in. He couldn't help himself.

Victoria shot him a glance. 'Well, yes. If by any chance she's in touch again or has some link to Ahmed, she wouldn't find it easy to talk to me – as I think you know.'

Hugo felt he'd put her on the defensive. She was right, he was well aware of the tensions over Ahmed, but too preoccupied and self-obsessed to try to help with her embarrassment over it. Victoria's relationship with her daughter was her own affair.

'Perhaps,' she said, 'William could have a word. Nattie would never lie to him, and if there has been any development or um, contact, it might help her to talk. Nattie's close to William, she'd trust him with a confidence.'

Hugo swallowed and had to look away. Victoria must know something. He blinked, found some control and turned back.

She met his eyes with a steady, understanding gaze. 'William could advise Nattie if she needs advice. She may be in some difficulty and not sure who to tell, what to do.'

Hugo stared. No softening of the pill. His heart was thundering, like as a galloping horse with the panic he was in. 'You'd tell me . . . any news?'

'Of course – as long as I'm told myself!' She smiled, though it was clear she was still deeply pained by Nattie's continued resentment. She must yearn for her daughter to forgive her misgivings over Ahmed during the bomb-plot threat in her Home Secretary days.

Victoria's smile lit up her face just as Nattie's smiles did. 'We should eat,' she said. 'Have a couple of sandwiches, Hugo; I'm going to. And what we need, I think, is a nice glass of cold white wine.'

She went to a bar fridge behind a cupboard door and came back with a chilled bottle of Sancerre. He was grateful; he badly needed a drink.

'It's next week you're going away, isn't it?' she said, 'Bosphor Air? Good luck with that. I'll look in on Nattie and be around. She mentioned at the weekend that you're having a little dinner party this week and that Tom's coming. Pair him up with someone nice, Hugo. He's a worry of mine, too.'

He wasn't one of Hugo's, but he knew how close she was to Tom; he was her stepson, but she thought of him almost as her own. 'It's that girl in his life, that doctor, Imogen,' Victoria confessed. 'She's not right for him, he doesn't truly love her.'

Was she trying to take his mind off his own worries? She wasn't succeeding. Victoria looked at her watch. Hugo had already looked at his; he was feeling a desperate need to go, to be alone, get away, curl up and die.

She came to the door with him, waving aside his effusive thanks. Looking at her, seeing the caring in her wide beautiful eyes, he wanted to cling, bury his head in her chest and sob. He hovered a minute on the step. 'You'll let me know if William . . . if there are any developments?'

'Of course. I have your mobile number and you can call me any time.'

He thanked her again, brushed her cheek and left.

He walked to the street corner to hail a cab. He needed back-seat solitariness. He climbed in, glad of the familiarity of a black London cab; it smelled of shoe polish and faintly of garlic, almost strong enough to mask the scent of some distantly lingering perfume. Hugo sank back and tried to focus on his busy afternoon ahead.

18

William Has a Word

Everyone arrived at once, the way it sometimes happened; answering the bell, Nattie found all four guests on the doorstep, making their own introductions with awkward smiles. Amber, with her carroty-blonde bob fluffed out and backcombed, had a pussycat smile for Nattie, which made her feel weary; she sensed battle lines being drawn. A corner of her felt natural feline jealousy, but wouldn't it actually help a bit to have Hugo looking Amber's way?

Brian, she'd noticed, opening the door, had been doing just that, eyeing up Amber on the steps. So he was one of those. It was hard to see him being altruistically interested in helping Hugo and the evening suddenly seemed much less of a good idea.

'Hi! Come on in, all of you,' she said with her best welcoming face, 'out of this miserable wind. Delighted to meet you, Brian.' He was a small plump man with close-cropped dark hair, smelling of aftershave and wearing a donkey-brown jacket, button-down shirt and skinny blue tie. Nattie shook his hand, feeling his eyes boring into her too, and she turned quickly to kiss Tom and Imogen hello and greet Amber.

Hugo came up behind her to say hi and take coats. He kissed Imogen's cheek – Amber's too. 'Hello, handsome,' she said, like some games-show hostess with a line in trite quips. 'Long time no see. We were only sat round a table like an hour ago,' she explained, laughing her head off.

She was slightly stocky and short-necked, but had smooth, attractively plump shoulders, shown to advantage in the low-cut black dress she was wearing, along with scarlet high heels to draw the eye to those sexy ankles of hers. Nattie had to concede she had chutzpah in spades. Amber was a lot more suited to public relations than Hugo.

She led the way into the sitting room with Brian hard behind her. 'I must say,' he murmured, 'Hugo's got a lot to answer for, keeping *you* under wraps.'

Nattie felt free to ignore that. She settled everyone and took round cheese straws while Hugo dealt with drinks. 'I gather you and Nattie had tea the other day,' she heard him say to Tom, handing him a glass of Bordeaux. Hugo was wasting no time in checking that out.

'Yes, it was great seeing her,' Tom said loyally, which was adaptably true enough. 'We talked about old times.'

Imogen shot him a hurt look. That meant Maudie to her: she knew that Maudie was Nattie's close friend. Imogen was wearing a burgundy suit and looked ill at ease, which the severe suit only seemed to emphasise. It wasn't her sort of evening. Media people – lightweights in her eyes – were far from her scene. Nattie could imagine her coming alight and being vivacious in the company of academics and scions of her psychiatric world.

She stayed chatting lamely to Imogen, but soon slipped away to see to the food.

Thick cream candles in white china holders, blue-and-white-striped mats, white cyclamen plants in dark blue pots, she liked the look of the table. She'd asked Ian's advice about what to have for dinner, smiling over the desks and sipping coffee. She often did that; he was a keen cook and always looked pleased. It helped to keep relations friendly. His suggested first course, roasted peach with Parma ham and salad leaves, was ready on the plates and she called people in.

Sitting between Brian and Tom and dutifully turning to Brian first, Nattie realised she hadn't a clue about his interests. Perhaps he was a keen cook too.

'Hugo missed you at SleepSweet when you left,' she said, still hoping for something out of the evening, 'especially when your successor brought in his own pet PR consultants. That seemed a bit unfair to me.' Brian said nothing about Hugo deserving better or about any help he could give; he said nothing at all, just gazed at her. She ploughed on. 'I hope you're enjoying your great new job. So much responsibility – Ambiance Furniture is huge! But that must mean long hours, of course. Do you have an easy commute?'

'Not so bad,' Brian said. 'I often stay up in London anyway.'

'Still, I hope you'll be able to get home tonight,' she said. 'It's lovely you could come, we were just sorry your wife couldn't make it.' That was a bit pointed and Nattie hurried on. 'I don't know if paintings are your thing, Brian, but Tom's the most brilliant artist – even allowing he's my stepbrother.' She'd needed to bring Tom in, he was looking down at his plate; Amber on his other side was all eyes for Hugo.

'Yes, I'm into contemporary art,' Brian said, mildly surprisingly, sounding genuinely keen. 'I'd be interested to see his work. Perhaps you'd come with me?'

Nattie attempted a Delphic smile. 'Sorry, must just leave you for a minute to see to the food. Do have a chat to Tom while I'm gone.'

Hugo brought plates over to the draining board and kissed the back of her neck. 'All okay?' he murmured.

She turned with warm eyes. 'Hope so.' He stared a moment, unsmiling, and began carving the meat. Had she stiffened when he kissed her? She'd tried hard not to.

Brian and Tom were talking art. 'I'm a great fan of Charles Willmott,' Brian was saying, as Nattie brought over their plates and offered veg. 'I love his obsession with ballet and form. And Ed Chapman too. Sad he's beyond my—'

'Isn't Ed Chapman the tights tycoon with the wife who's always boozed out of her mind?' Amber threw in. 'Too legless to wear his tights, they say!'

'That's Ed Champner, I think,' said Nattie with a neutral smile. If battle lines were being drawn . . . 'Ed Chapman's the artist. He does beautiful portraits in mosaic.'

'Whoops, silly me!' Amber roared with laughter. She didn't embarrass easily.

The meal went down well; the Béarnaise sauce looked a bit weird, but tasted okay. People said so, and Amber called across the table, 'Delicious! Aren't you a clever little cook.' Patronising cow.

The summer fruits tart was popular too, and taking people into the sitting room for coffee, Nattie felt the end of the evening was in sight.

She handed round cups of coffee and herbal tea. Amber lifted a cup of coffee off Nattie's tray, without even troubling to look up. She was still latched on to Hugo, laughing like a clown with every second breath and talking loudly about Bosphor Air. 'I'm coming too now,' another cackle of laughter. 'What an opportunity!'

She was brazen, wanting Nattie to hear. And Hugo was smiling, going along with it. He was certainly trying to make her jealous, or was it just a desperate need for a bit of the sex he was being denied? With Amber – who'd always made him squirm? Nattie had no leg to stand on, no business to feel peeved and disbelieving.

What would happen when she told him what she planned to do, when she flicked the switch on life as he knew it? She imagined the past repeating itself, Hugo sinking into self-destruction, submerged, and felt a shiver of premonition. It wouldn't take much. A match could start a forest fire; a low moment and line of coke could do the same. Would he really go there again, knowing the horrors of what he'd been through?

Tom touched her arm. 'Here, let me take the coffee pot.'

'Thanks,' she smiled. 'I was far away. I've forgotten the chocolates too – I'll just get them from the kitchen.'

She quickly checked her phone, read a text from Ahmed, which she deleted instantly. Her heart had started up and she tried to control her inward smiles. William had sent a text too. Nattie was pleased. He'd promised to put his mind to the Sadia situation and she'd been waiting to hear back. She stared down, reading the text. *I've had a thought about your young friend's problem, which I'll pass on, but I need to have a word on another matter that's closer to home. I know you're busy now, but can you call tomorrow? Mid-morning if possible; we need to talk.* She could guess what about and her heart pumped faster.

'What are you doing?' Hugo was in the doorway, white in the face.

'Just looking at a text from William.'

'Can I see what it says?' She gave him the phone. Did he really think she'd lie about that? He would never trust her again. 'I was just curious,' he said in an unflustered way, handing it back. 'But why did you come out here?'

'I forgot the chocolates.'

'Who's your young friend with a problem?'

'Oh, just an author with an immigration issue. Nothing important. I'd mentioned it to William on the off-chance.'

Hugo hadn't asked what William could want a word about, but he'd be able to guess as well as she could. She felt the walls closing in. Yet, for all her panic, the chance to talk to William was calming. She had a sense of the knots of stress being massaged away and eased back her shoulders, unwinding slightly.

Tom and Imogen soon made a move to go. Nattie pressed another drink with such obvious half-heartedness that the others stood up too – even Amber. Seeing them all out, standing on the front step with Hugo, Nattie wondered how glaring were the strains. Did they show at all? Did everyone think that they looked such a lovely well-suited couple?

She closed the door and switched off the outside light. Hugo rolled up his sleeves and they soon had the kitchen looking ship-shape again. He was quite chatty, less caustic and bitter than of late; was it the Amber effect? William's text? It was hardly likely to have much to do with Brian whom she couldn't see being any use to Hugo – though he'd redeemed himself slightly and hadn't been as bad as she'd first feared. She'd wondered how on earth Hugo could have got on with him. It was lucky she'd asked Brian about art instead of cooking. Tom might even make a sale.

She called William mid-morning. 'I don't want to talk over the phone,' he said, 'but I'm free for lunch. Can you make it?' She would have to change her plans with Ahmed. She hadn't seen him since last Thursday.

'Thanks, I'd love that,' Nattie said, 'but I wouldn't have much more than an hour.'

'We'll go to Wilton's and make it quick. Can you walk round to the *Post*? I'll meet you in Reception at one and we'll go in my car.'

'How the other half lives,' Nattie laughed, hiding her nerves. 'Editors certainly!'

William made small talk in the car; his driver was no slouch. But immediately he and Nattie were seated – opposite each other in a wood-panelled booth with green velour banquettes where, William assured her, they wouldn't be overheard – he launched in.

'Is Ahmed back?' he asked, picking up a glass of water and eyeing Nattie over the rim.

'Yes.'

'Want to tell me about it?'

'Does everyone know? Your reporters?' A clutch of panic skewed her thoughts. If William knew, surely that meant her mother did too.

'Only me – no one else at the paper.' Was that a qualified answer? It seemed carefully crafted. 'I won't blow his cover,' William said, 'you can trust me on that. And it won't go any further if you'd like to talk things over and want it to be between us alone.'

He was watching, waiting on her answer, and while her adrenalin pounded, she also felt the tension drain. It was a release.

'If you want any help or advice,' William said, patiently edging her on, 'I'll do my best. How about starting with how you suddenly came to be in contact again?'

Nattie told him.

'And you didn't say anything to Hugo?'

'No.'

Nattie had to answer more fully, she knew. William still wasn't hurrying her, instead, commenting on the excellent fish. He looked as dishevelled as ever. A hard man with soft eyes, the

ravines in his face looked carved with a scalpel; he'd started on
newspapers in the hard-drinking, sleep-deprived days. Nattie
adored him. No stepfather could have been more loving or put
himself out for her more.

'No, I didn't tell Hugo,' she said. 'I should have, of course, but
I knew what a shock it would be, hearing Ahmed was back, how
destabilised he would feel, however much I tried to reassure him.
I was in shock myself. After seven years I needed time to adjust.
I was angry as well. He'd left me high and dry and desolate, after
all, but I had to find out what had happened before giving vent,
as I'm sure you'd understand. Ahmed knew that I was married,
he knew all about me, as it turned out. I said we could only meet
once then never again – for Hugo's sake.'

'But he persuaded you otherwise?'

'He's not to blame. I am. I'm the one who's married, I have
a will of my own. He left me on a cliff-edge all the same. His
story took a lot of telling.' Nattie felt her colour rise. Talking
about Ahmed was like stepping into the warm out of a raging
snowstorm.

'You haven't stayed angry with him, clearly,' William said.
'There are stars in your eyes, but it's hardly straightforward, is it?'

Pushing away his plate, he leaned forward and held her gaze.
'You don't need me to tell you how much you're hurting Hugo.
You've shown the strain, and your mum's been worrying herself
sick. You'll have to take some decisions soon and let Hugo know
where he stands. You must see that?'

'Of course I must tell Hugo, but everything unravels so fast
then and it's like a spool of film; you can't wind it back neatly if
at all.'

William kept up his concentrated gaze, yet his expression was
sympathetic. 'Did Ahmed have a very hard time of it in that long
absence?'

It was a distracting switch away from Hugo. Was William simply allowing her a breathing space? It was more likely just his incorrigible curiosity. He was a newspaperman to his boots.

'It's long and complicated,' Nattie said. 'It would take forever to tell you and I need to talk more about Hugo. It's still very early days, you see. I've been terrified of acting too hastily. I tried not to see Ahmed again, but it was kind of inevitable with our feelings as strong as ever. The trouble is, Hugo's wired very physically and when I asked for space, he couldn't handle it. I hoped he'd accept a sort of marital sabbatical and give me time, but it wasn't to be.

'I only want to wait till Hugo's back from his trip to Istanbul. I feel he'd cope better out there, not knowing, wretched as he is, and have more chance to help secure the account. Winning new business would be good for his self-esteem. I'd like the children to have met Ahmed too,' Nattie explained, knowing that spoke volumes.

'Have you come to a decision? Are you going to leave Hugo?'

She looked at her nails, picked at one of them. Was she? She lifted her head finally and faced William's steady eyes. 'What I'm hoping and praying for is a friendly trial separation. Everything's happened in such a rush, so compressed and emotional. Separation feels the best solution; time to let the dust settle and just see.'

'But what's really behind that is seeing how Hugo copes, isn't it, Nattie? I know about his past problems, how bad it got; we'd exposed Shelby as a pusher, remember, when Ahmed was still one of my reporters. Your mum knows about Shelby, what was in the papers, but not about him supplying Hugo in those early days. When you said you were getting married, I felt it was best to keep things that way.'

'Can you hold off telling her about Ahmed and any possible separation?' Nattie pleaded. 'I'll talk to her very soon, I promise, and before I tell Hugo, but I dread it almost as much. She'll be so shocked and heartbroken, and feel I've let her down. Which I have.'

Nattie sighed and carried on. 'Ahmed's rented a house. I could move straight in with the children. Hugo would still be in his own home, able to see them and have them at weekends.'

'Is the house in South London?'

'Yes, actually – what makes you ask that?'

'Just an educated guess, it's familiar territory. What's Ahmed doing now?' William asked, signalling for the waitress. 'What about money?'

'Not a problem. He's been living in California for a couple of years, writing the scripts for a television series, a big one, which was all his own idea. He's cooped up working hard on a fourth series.'

William was the only person, other than Nattie herself, who knew Ahmed's new identity. He'd had to be in the picture, despite the considerable reservations of the authorities, if Ahmed was going to be working for him on the New York desk. Nattie regretted mentioning the television series, however, even as she spoke. She worried about William's irrepressible curiosity; he would want to know the series and start ferreting about.

'Ahmed's given himself a third identity for his scriptwriting,' she carried on quickly. 'He writes under another name, which I'd rather not tell you as I think you'll understand.'

'He's done the scripts for three series already? That's going some.' William grinned. 'He's quite a guy. Here's the "but", Nattie, love. I know more than anyone how much you love him and I'm certainly in no position to lecture you, but there'll be a lot of hurdles. Not least the very real concern about Ahmed's enemies; even seven years on and with a new identity his cover could be blown. He'll always be at risk.' William stared at her gravely.

'And not only Ahmed, you would be too – and the children. You'd have to live abroad.'

'As if I didn't think about that every waking hour.' Nattie wanted to cry out loud. What did you do when you loved someone to distraction, with every cell in your body? Tears prickled and welled in her eyes, which William sensitively chose not to notice.

She'd recovered by the time he'd ordered coffee and asked for the bill.

'I've had a few thoughts about your young writer's sister out in Pakistan,' he said, making clear that the subject of Ahmed was closed – and also managing to intimate, Nattie felt, that everything discussed had been strictly between themselves.

'Forced marriages are a serious problem here in the UK too, British Muslim girls being packed off to relations in Pakistan to be "dealt with". A unit has been set up to help rescue them. Your friend's sister may not be a UK citizen, but she has strong British connections, so there's a chance something can be done.' William smiled. 'I know the head of the unit, I'll have a word if you like. He's out in Pakistan a lot and if your friend, Sadia, contacts the unit it's just possible he'll be around and able to press her sister's case. No promises, but that's her only hope, I'd say.'

'Thanks, it would be a huge help,' Nattie said, 'and a relief to have something to pass on.' Alesha still had to get hold of her passport, though. The situation was no less fraught.

Nattie was glad of William's arm round her shoulders as they left the restaurant. It was a comfort. He asked after the children in the car and wished Hugo luck in Istanbul.

She thanked William again as he dropped her off at the Buckley Building, and kissed his cheek. 'And for being able to talk; it really means so much to me.'

She wiped at her eyes and hurried up to the seventh floor with her emotions in turmoil. Few people would trust a newspaper-man, even a respected editor like William, but she trusted him from the bottom of her heart. He hadn't condemned her, called her heartless and selfish, but others would. They'd be censorious, scathing, reproachful, all of which she could handle; it wouldn't mean much, it couldn't break her. Only Hugo's pain could do that.

19

Meeting Thomas

Ahmed fondled Nattie's hair, lost to his thoughts. They were having a quick cup of coffee in the kitchen before he gave her a lift to the office, sitting on stools at the island unit, and she leaned her head against him. He knew she was thinking too.

Tomorrow was set to be a pivotal day. She was bringing Thomas. Ahmed had seen photographs of the children, golden and glowing with happy smiles, but he imagined them giving him cold stares, sensing, with that instinct of the innocent, that he was a threat to the equilibrium of their young lives in some unknown way.

Nattie lifted her head and swung her legs down from the stool. 'I've got to go.'

It was becoming a mantra, almost a joke between them, but no less painful. She stared at him, looking frightened, unable to hide the conflict, the pull of loyalties. It was written all over her face.

'Hugo must know what you're going through,' Ahmed said, putting the back of his hand to her velvety cheek. 'He knows how much you care. You've helped him so much.'

'There's nothing I can do for him.' She looked away.

He stood down from his stool and held her face in his hands. She was trying to confront the moment of truth about separation. Ahmed had an urge to press her. He had needs too. How did you equate two people's intense happiness with three people's unfulfilled lives? But he couldn't push it, wasn't in his nature. It had to be Nattie's choice, her decision, and her eyes had to be wide open to the enormity of the risk. Did he even have a right to ask her to take it?

'I want to talk about the safety risk for a moment,' he said. 'I can't be sure, but I'm fairly confident that it's slight while we're tucked away in Jake's house and that you and the children will be secure here. I've checked out everywhere round about, got the feel of the neighbourhood, and I wouldn't be easily recognised except by people who know me. There was only that one photograph in the *Courier*, when Shelby was making his mischief, and that was seven years ago, after all. I worry about you coming and going, Nattie, ferrying the children, but I wouldn't be with you and you'd be in your own car.'

He took a deep breath; he had to say it. 'I still can't ask you to take the risk. I can go away, go back to California without you, if you think that's for the best and feel it's right. It's the only way you can be truly safe.'

She met his eyes. His insides curdled when she seemed to hesitate, trying to frame her words.

'Don't go away and leave me,' she said. 'You've done that once already. You're my one certainty in all this, whatever else.'

'Well, that's cleared the air.' He laughed, but the thorny issues of 'whatever else' still loomed large. 'Better get you to the office now then,' he said. 'Whatever else.'

They stood together and he held her arms. 'I don't want you humping a travel cot about. Why don't I just buy a cot and high chair? I can have them here for tomorrow.'

'Fancy you thinking of a high chair,' she grinned. 'Very domesticated – but buying them? I don't know. It feels a bit extravagant somehow.'

'It's hardly a big spend. I'm paid this silly amount of money. Are you worrying about changes of heart or being still undecided, that sort of thing?'

'A bit,' she said honestly. 'It would be a help, though, so thanks. Keep pressing on my arms like that, will you, with your thumbs? It speaks to me and gives me hope. It helps me bear the pain I'm causing Hugo.'

Ahmed felt as if he was on probation, meeting Thomas. The child was only sixteen months, but out of babyhood and he could make his feelings known. It would be one less hurdle if they hit it off, but Ahmed knew it would be difficult, striking the right note between father figure and friend, no easy balancing act. He watched from the front window as Nattie came up the path with Thomas settled on her hip and marvelled at how well they fitted together, how perfectly she was designed.

He let them in and closing the door behind them, put up a hand. 'Hi, Thomas, I'm Mummy's friend, Dan. It's good to meet you. Can you do high-fives? Like this?' Nattie put up her free hand to help demonstrate and Ahmed said, 'High-five!'

Two deep amber eyes stared solemnly back at him and he felt himself being assessed with a healthy degree of caution.

'Do you want to have a try?' he said.

He had Thomas's attention at least, and was mildly gratified when the child lifted a chubby little hand. Ahmed grinned, swinging up his hand to meet it. 'High-five!'

''Gain.'

'How do you ask, Tubsy?' Nattie hitched him more onto her hip.

''Gain, pees.'

Ahmed met hands a couple more times, enjoying the child's sunny beams. 'We'll go downstairs now,' he said. 'There are a few toys in the kitchen you can play with, although I think,' he said, glancing at Nattie, 'it's nearly time for your nap.'

She stood Thomas down on his feet and he toddled off as if he owned the place. 'He's very independent,' she said, 'learning to take the stairs backwards too, which is a bit hairy at times. Lily was more agile at his age. Still, he's not doing badly for seventeen months, and the words are coming fast.'

'It's okay about the toys?' Ahmed queried, as they stood close together watching Thomas. 'Only a couple of stacker-ring things and building blocks, and a little car.'

Nattie nodded. 'You did well with the car,' she said, as Thomas homed straight in on it, fervently clutching a tiny blue toy Mercedes as though no one, but no one, was going to prise it from his hand. 'Blue cars are Tubsy's absolute passion.'

'You know what mine is,' Ahmed murmured. 'Isn't it time for his rest?'

Tubsy was soon settled in the new cot – erected late that morning with much cursing – and burbling quietly to himself, mumbling, 'Hih, hih fff . . . Hih ff,' to Nattie's amusement. There was a convenient half-landing box room for the cot, probably a bathroom in its day, but space had been found for one on the bedroom floor.

Thomas drifted off to sleep quite quickly to Ahmed's immense relief.

'I'm glad about the cot,' Nattie said, locking eyes. 'I'd feel a lot more anxious about what you have in mind if Tubsy wasn't peacefully penned in.'

Ahmed took her in his arms, overcome with his need. The passion poured out of him as he pulled off her shirt, her jeans, laid her back on the bed and felt the soft silkiness of her. He was groaning with exquisite joy as he slid into the body he knew so well.

'Shush. No noise, two little mice . . .'

'Making squeaks of delirium.'

Lying back recovering, half listening for any stirrings from the cot, Ahmed dared to dream. He wanted married life with Nattie, a family, Nattie having his child . . . No sound from Thomas. It was a rare day when she didn't have to rush off, a luxury to be savoured. Ahmed settled his arm round her and lifted the hair from her eyes. He wanted to broach what was being left unsaid, but of such critical importance, vital to know. He'd been back in the UK for six weeks already and something had to give. They were in limbo, all three of them.

'What are you going to do, Nattie? William knows now and Hugo must too, more or less. I've been determined not to push you, but it's hard, living this way.'

'I'm going to tell Hugo as soon as he's back from Istanbul. I'm going to suggest we have a trial separation, say I'd be the one moving out, that he'd be in his own home. He goes next Wednesday, back Friday. I'm only hanging on till you've met Lily; it'll help so much if you're a friendly face and both children have been here before. They'll be confused and unsettled whatever happens. I'm paralysed with dread about telling him and what sort of upheaval we'll be in, but I will do it.'

Ahmed pulled her close for a moment then sat up, elbows on knees. Nattie sat up beside him and he reached absently for her hand. He couldn't let in euphoria, however electrically charged he felt at hearing her say it; there'd be mishaps, obstacles, blind alleys, Hugo's vulnerability and the agony of how he'd cope. The way ahead was strewn with boulders. Nothing was for sure.

'The car's a bit of a problem, isn't it?' he wondered, trying to think practically. 'It would be best if you leave it for Hugo. I'll get one for you, something unremarkable and routine and kit it out with baby seats.' Nattie looked at him with alarm in her eyes, her predictable anxiety about accepting such an offer. 'It'll be mine,' Ahmed assured her. 'I need a basic little run-around while I'm here, after all. It'll just be in your name.'

'You do think of things,' she said, leaning close with a kiss. 'Whatever would I do without you? I can't bring Lily till Friday week, though. Bringing her any sooner, she'd be too full of coming here and tell Hugo all about it. "We saw Mummy's friend today, Daddy. He's called Dan and he has a fridge in his house that shoots out ice cubes into your glass and he's a very nice man, lots of fun."'

Nattie kissed him again. 'In all sorts of ways.'

'Tell me more.'

Ahmed grinned, fighting a sense of disbelief. It was huge, what Nattie was doing to be with him, but she was taking it in stages. A trial separation left Hugo with hope, which had its downside. He wouldn't believe there was hope; it would seem like a lost cause to him, very likely, a foregone conclusion. And if Hugo couldn't hack her going, the empty house, the misery, and took the road to relapse, what then? Wouldn't Nattie feel less and less sure of what she was doing? Hugo was already drinking heavily, she said.

Ahmed banished his unwanted thoughts and scrunched her hand.

'Come on! We'd better get a move on and get Tubsy's lunch on the go. I've been hearing a few grunts and groans.'

'Keen ears,' Nattie said. 'I suppose that really means you're ready for yours. I should warn you, though, Tubsy gets his first and he eats slowly, savouring every mouthful, like one of those judges on *MasterChef*. Don't go expecting a peaceful orderly pattern of life with children around.'

20

A Mother's Advice

Hugo was going to Turkey next day. One more evening together, possibly not quite the last if he was back too late on Friday, but the last in this suspended bubble of faux-normality. He'd probably be late on Friday, Nattie anticipated, and tired and hung-over. Suppose he was early? There would be no postponing it then. He could even try for the first plane out, either to surprise her or clinging to the hope of some miracle. What miracle? That he could walk in and gather up his loving family in his arms, take his wife to bed and be reunited?

Nattie shivered. How could she feel such an ache of deep affection when she was completely in love with another man? She clenched her fists. She was only going to suggest a friendly trial separation. They weren't uncommon; it was a way forward. She couldn't live with Hugo, couldn't give him what he wanted. There'd be no tug of love over the children, neither of them would want that, she was sure.

He was late that evening; usually he was home before seven-thirty. She'd just finished reading to Lily and had come downstairs. If he made it home in minutes he could catch a sleepy goodnight, Lily's arms around his neck, which he loved.

Nattie heard his key turning in the door right then, telepathy at work, and stayed in the hall to greet him. He kissed her cheek, coolly, whisky on his breath, and dashed upstairs to see his daughter.

Nattie went into the sitting room and stood by the window. A chill wind had swept in that morning – she'd felt it deep in her bones. Her fingers were white and numb when she reached the office, and people had been hurrying along with their heads bowed. She looked out at the leaves swirling where streetlight shone down, pooling between parked cars. The two woody hydrangeas in the patch of front garden looked about to snap, bending to the wind's bitter will. Hugo had been complaining for weeks about the heat and humidity; he at least had welcomed the sharp drop in temperature. 'Finally, some proper autumn weather.' How could she bear to tell him?

'I've done Moroccan chicken and polenta,' she said as he came back downstairs, 'kind of to get you in the mood for Turkey. Long day?'

'Usual pre-pitch panics. Drinks for someone leaving too – why I was late. People told jokes, they were having fun,' Hugo muttered, with icy emphasis. 'The joke was they actually expected me to join in.'

'Good jokes?' Nattie asked lightly, struggling to keep the show afloat. She thought how often Hugo had come home from work, full of some wisecrack or other. They were a quick-witted bunch at Tyler's, in the business of being on the button.

'You want me to tell you jokes?' Hugo sneered, but the hurt showed in his eyes. He took out the ice tray, held it under the cold tap, put a single lump in a glass and filled it to the brim with neat Scotch. 'Okay,' he said, fastening his pained eyes on her, 'since you seem to want to make believe you still have the slightest interest in my life, I'll tell you how Miss Li, the Chinese girl at the office, raised a laugh. It's fucking appropriate as it happens. She's just back from the States and was full of a health-product commercial showing a corny older-age couple, all happy and crooning.' Hugo glowered. 'They have to reel off the whole gamut of side effects in the US, and Miss Li started giggling, telling us about one of them on the list. "If you have an election lasting more than four hours,"' Hugo mimicked her accent, '"consult your doctor." We didn't get it until Brady asked what the product was for. "Electile dysfunction," Miss Li said, and we got it then.'

Nattie couldn't help smiling. Hugo scowled. 'It could be a fucking metaphor for our marriage, that. Erectile dysfunction – bloody marital dysfunction, more like.' He sipped his whisky morosely, nursing a bitterness that seared her heart.

She talked about the children over the meal, a one-way conversation. 'Lily was impossibly precocious tonight.' No spark of interest. Hugo kept drinking steadily, his eyes watchful over his glass. Nattie pressed on. 'She'd pushed Tubsy over backwards, and I screamed at her furiously that I never wanted to see her do that again. So what do you think she said, sticking out her cheeky chin?' Hugo shrugged, radiating misery. '"Well, you can close your eyes then, Mummy, can't you?" I didn't know whether to laugh or send her to bed.'

Nattie kept up the chat, doing her best, being warmly affectionate, desperate for any sign of softening. They had to stay friends. Hugo gave a sigh from the depth of his soul, but he finally reached across the table for her hand.

How could she bear to tell him?

'I'll take you to the airport tomorrow,' she offered.

He frowned. 'I can get a cab; it goes on the office. Don't do things out of bloody guilt. You've got better things to do with your time.'

'I'd like to. Jasmine's here all day. It's more difficult to come to pick you up with all the Friday traffic. Of course, it would depend on the time of your flight,' Nattie carried on hurriedly, keen to close off any sardonic response. 'Do you know when you're likely to be back?'

'I have no idea. Nor what will happen – there or here.'

They said goodbye outside the terminal. Nattie squeezed Hugo's hand and smiled, feeling winded, unable to speak. He stared at her fixedly, kissed her unexpectedly hard on the lips, before breaking off abruptly and wheeling his bag briskly towards Departures. He didn't look back.

She stayed rooted to the spot, only moving when the driver of a car wanting the parking space leaned on his horn. Tears had gathered; she let them slide down her cheeks and dry of their own accord.

She didn't go to see Ahmed, but returned home to relieve Jasmine and get the children's tea. She waited to phone him too, till they were in bed and the house was quiet. He understood why she didn't want to ask him over. It was Hugo's house and that was important; nothing of her passionate rekindled relationship had felt sordid, adulterous as it was, but lovemaking in the home she shared with Hugo would.

Their call was interrupted. The house phone was ringing. 'I expect it's Mum,' Nattie said, 'so few people have the number. Call you back later.'

'Hello?' she said cautiously, lifting the receiver.

'It's only me, darling. William's going to be as late as ever and I wondered if I could pop round. I know Hugo's only gone for two days, but I told him I'd look in.'

'Be great, Mum. Of course – have you eaten? I haven't. I'll make something.'

'Don't think of it! I'll call up a takeaway and be with you in half an hour.'

A gum-chewing boy with a Rasta ponytail and baseball cap rang the bell, opened the large square box on his motorbike and handed over a Thai dinner for two. Nattie tipped him and put the food to keep warm in a slow oven. Her knees were wobbly. She poured herself a glass of white wine. Her mother arrived and they had a hug. Victoria's scent, the Calèche she always wore, was potent in the narrow hall. Nattie got the bottle of wine from the fridge and they sat at the kitchen table.

She was close to breaking down, desperate, suddenly, to pour everything out and cling to her mother.

'Tell me what's going on, darling,' Victoria said. 'I understand more than you think.'

'I hope you do, Mum. I need to talk to you, but I'm so dreading explaining, or trying to. It's a mess and it's all my fault.'

'You know, love, I saw you last week. You were with a man in a car in Lambeth Road. And Hugo came to ask my advice, worrying you were having an affair.'

'Did you see who I was with in the car?'

'I guess it must have been Ahmed. Is he really back?'

'Yes, hard as it is to believe. He's right here in London, renting Jake's house. Jake's having a year in Australia.'

'I can't imagine what it must have felt like, seeing Ahmed after so long,' Victoria said. 'It can't have been easy for Hugo – and not only these last few weeks.'

'That doesn't need saying, Mum.' Nattie felt frustrated. Her years of yearning for Ahmed were in the past, not what this was about, and she got up to unpack the meal. Peeling back the tin foil released the spicy aromas, chilli, lemongrass, lime and ginger.

They picked at the food, the chicken pieces and peppers in the perfumed sauce, not saying much, both of them postponing, Nattie felt, all the awkward questions, the search for solutions. There were no easy answers to be had.

'Is Ahmed back for long?' Victoria asked finally. 'Has he got plans?'

'Nothing that's set in stone. But not seeing him now, Mum – whatever the wrongs of having got in this deep – would be no solution. Hugo's trust in me is blown to bits. Our relationship would always be uneasy now, in the future. Whatever we've had in the past, things could never be the same.'

She took a breath, holding it in; she had to say it, her mother had to know. 'I'm going to suggest having a friendly trial separation, Mum. I'll do everything in my power to ease Hugo's load, but we can't go on as we are. The children are young, resilient, at an age when it's easy to adjust,' she felt her words were overdone, cloying and sticky, like overcooked rice. 'They can see lots of their father. You loved William enough to leave Dad,' she pleaded, hearing the guilty whine in her voice.

'You know that wasn't comparable, how things were with Dad. He had no control, I'd have had to leave in any event. Hugo's kind and good to you, he has none of Dad's violent, addictive weaknesses. He's a decent, genuine man.'

'And a wonderful father too. But Hugo was an addict, years ago, Mum. I helped him through.' Should she have said that? It felt a little self-serving and disloyal.

Victoria didn't look particularly shocked. 'I knew about Hugo's habit, more or less,' she said. 'I saw the weight loss, the look of him at times, but he had a far harder struggle than Dad and still found the will. He did that for you, he loved you that much.'

Nattie couldn't help herself. 'What about Ahmed and what he did, averting an unspeakable catastrophe and losing his freedom?

He's waited this long for me to minimise the risk, and he would have done so even if he hadn't known I was married. He "did that for me" too, Mum, he "loved me that much".' Couldn't her mother even acknowledge what Ahmed had been through, how much he'd sacrificed of his life?

Victoria sighed. 'You know, I never believed he'd come back. I felt sure he would carve out a new future for himself in the States. If I'd ever thought he would, I'd have tried to stop you marrying Hugo.'

'What you mean,' Nattie said angrily, 'is you didn't *want* Ahmed to come back. You didn't want me to marry him, deep down. You never felt he was suitable, did you? Be honest! You had smiles of relief the day I married Hugo. Sorry,' she mumbled, feeling ashamed. 'Water under the bridge.'

'But you're wrong anyway. Ahmed is exceptional.' Victoria looked at her watch and looked up again, squarely at Nattie. 'I should go, but there's something I really have to say before I do. I hope it makes you understand better and see why I felt as I did. Any relief or happiness you saw on my face on your wedding day had nothing whatever to do with suitability. I knew you loved Ahmed and the conflict you must have been feeling that day. You were pregnant, there was that, but my relief had been entirely about your safety.

'You must understand, surely, that had it been Ahmed you were marrying, how desperately worried I'd have been, the panic I'd have felt about the risk to you and any future grandchildren? Surely you can understand how concerned I'm feeling for all the same reasons now.'

Nattie felt put on the defensive. What could she say? She was about to bring the children into contact with Ahmed. He'd been reassuring about Jake's house, which had the feel of a protective bubble, but they wouldn't always be able to be so sheltered and shielded and not seen together. If they were married and living a proper life, they'd want to be out and about, going places as a family. They'd have to live abroad.

'I'm well aware of the risks, Mum,' she said, more humbly. 'It's a trial separation, nothing final. I just badly need some space, time to think, to see the way ahead. Living as Hugo and I are, in this limbo land . . . my whole world feels like it's a blur.'

'I can understand that, darling, but never forget that the threat would always be hanging over you. As Home Secretary I saw all the intelligence, I knew what went on, how Ahmed's enemies' minds work and the lengths they'll go to.'

Her mother had tears in her eyes. Nattie felt in despair, wretched but unbowed, however deeply chastened.

Victoria stood up and managed a smile. 'There, I've said all I can, got that off my chest. I'd better make a move. It's late – William will be back. Promise, though, you'll always remember your happiness is everything to me, yours and the children's. I'm here for you always.'

21

Meeting Lily

Meeting Thomas had been one thing, but Lily ... Ahmed felt more nervous than he could remember. Meeting Lily was a minefield, with all the potential for getting it wrong, and he wanted to make a good first impression. Fixed in his head was Nattie saying that Lily could be a right little madam. She looked angelic in her photograph ... Being natural and normal was best, but it wasn't an entirely natural situation.

Her school finished at twelve on Fridays; they'd be with him in half an hour. It was time to order in something for lunch. Pizzas, he decided, should be fine. Nattie hadn't mentioned food. If she brought it all with her they'd have a feast. Ahmed clicked onto an online delivery service. He'd been living on takeaways for weeks. He was no cook – did Nattie know that? Did Hugo regularly share the load and knock up trendy foody meals?

His phone pinged with a text from her. *Shall I pick up some lunch?*

Pizzas on the way. I'm scared I'll look like an ogre to Lily.

Ogres have a certain fascination. Pizza, spot on!

*

'Hello, Lily. I'm Dan, your mummy's friend. It's good to meet you. Mummy's told me lots, so I know you're a clever, precocious girl and you've got a guinea pig called Moppet.'

'I know what precoshus means,' she said suspiciously, fixing Ahmed with uncertain eyes. She was absorbing, wondering – probably where he fitted in.

'That's a smart red puffa,' he said. 'Shall I hang it up? Is it your school uniform colour?' She nodded solemnly. 'Lucky you. I remember ours being a sort of muddy brown and we had horrible orange-and-brown-striped ties.'

The pizzas were warming in the oven, a cheesy smell coming up from the kitchen.

'What are we having for lunch?' Lily asked, looking hopeful, glancing back at her mother for reassurance.

'I got in some pizzas, Margherita, quattro formaggi and pepperoni. The Margherita ones have basil leaves on them, but you can pick them off.'

'Mummy says they're like salad, but I don't like the taste.'

Thomas was holding up a chubby palm, jigging up and down on Nattie's hip.

'High-five!' Ahmed met palms with an upward swipe and a smile.

''Gain,' Thomas said, more than once. He didn't do things by halves.

'Lunchtime now,' Ahmed said crisply, calling a halt, 'and I know a young man who likes his food. I hope you're hungry too, Lily, they're big pizzas.' She'd been looking a bit huffy, peeved at Thomas's show-stealing. 'Would you like apple juice to drink?'

'Yes,' she said, adding, 'thank you', with a prompt. 'Margherita is my best pizza and I like apple juice too. Mummy puts water in it.'

She held on to Nattie's hand and Ahmed led the way down, taking over Thomas and carrying him in his arms. He set him down at the foot of the stairs. The kitchen, despite its supra-modernity, looked welcoming, he felt. The light was streaming in through the sky-lit extension, even on a cold dull windy day.

Tubsy made straight for the toy box, tipped it up and extracted the blue car.

'You've got toys here,' Lily stated, gazing up at Ahmed accusingly. She had a delicate face with a high forehead and meltingly appealing gold-brown eyes. Her hair, which was primrose pale, silky fine, she tossed about like a young colt shaking his mane. She was, as Nattie said, quite a little madam, but completely irresistible.

She stayed beside her mother, watching while Thomas pulled out various toys. She was unrelaxed, treading with care.

'Yes, it's nice to have a few toys when people come. Are you into books, Lily? There's one or two over on that chair you might like, and a puzzle peg-board that's quite fun.'

'I'm doing well in my reading at school.'

'Have a look at what's there. We can read one after lunch if you like and you can show me all the words you know.'

Lily went over and stood in front of the chair, picking out one of the easy-read books. Ahmed touched Nattie's hand unobserved and raised his eyebrows, lusting for her as always. He had a job to hide it. She slipped him a teasing smile.

'It's time to wash hands, Lily,' she said, sharpening up, 'time for lunch.'

'I'll see to Tubsy,' Ahmed suggested, 'and strap him into his chair.'

Nattie took Lily off to the loo and she was bouncier coming back, beginning to relax. 'Tubsy should have tidied away the toys,' she announced bossily. 'He has to at home. Mummy and Jasmine make him.'

'He is meant to,' Nattie said, fitting round his blue plastic bib.

'He's good at doing it all by himself too, he makes lots of little trips to the toy box.'

Ahmed put up a hand. '*Mea culpa!* But I'm learning, I'll see he does next time.'

'What does mayaculpa mean?'

'That I'm the one to blame. It's Latin, which is a very old language. It would be good to learn it when you're older, Lily. Lots of words we use come from Latin.'

'What like?' She bit into a wedge of Margherita pizza.

He had to think for a moment. 'Did you stay in a villa on holiday, Lily? Villa is Latin for house. There, that's your first Latin word. What did you do in school today?'

'We learned the capital of France. And we did writing and stories.'

'Let me see, does the capital of France begin with P?' He said the P phonetically.

'It's Paris! And in America it's, um . . .. Mummy, Tubsy's dribbling bits of pizza out of his mouth, it's disgusting!'

'That'll do, Lily, none of that.'

After lunch Nattie wiped Thomas's mouth and lifted him out of his chair. 'Tubsy's off for his nap now. Will you and Lily sort out some pudding between you?'

'Where does Tubsy sleep?'

Lily wasn't quite ready to be left alone with him, Ahmed sensed, and it seemed a good chance to show her round the house. If all went to plan – and it had to, it must – she'd be sleeping in the room he'd got ready for her as soon as Monday night.

'Come and see,' he said. 'He's got a cot in a very small room on a half-landing.'

Tubsy's box room, which Sylvia seemed to have used as an ironing room, was hardly bigger than the cot. Ahmed and Lily watched from the doorway while Nattie changed Tubsy's nappy on the mat on top of a tall white stack of drawers. When he was snug in his sleeping bag, murmuring quietly to himself and about to drop off, Ahmed turned to Lily. 'Would you like to see round a bit?' She lifted her head slowly up and down and reached for her mother's hand.

The master bedroom looked out to the front and a very pretty bedroom at the rear overlooked the back garden. Lily stood looking into the room, taking it all in, taking her time. Ahmed had sought Nattie's advice and bought a child-size bed, little and low to the ground. He'd also bought a small blackboard on an easel, a mini-armchair, navy blinds decorated with moons and stars, a doll's house and more easy-read books that he'd arranged on a low shelf beside the bed.

'Whose room is this?' Lily asked. 'Does a little girl live here?'

'No, it's for you. Mummy may possibly come to stay here for a bit, you see, so I thought you'd like a room of your own.'

Lily looked at her mother. 'Would Daddy come too? What about Moppet?' She looked worried, uncertain – not very happy while loving the room.

It was never going to be easy, but it was a starting point. Nattie had looked a bit panicky, but he'd had to pave the way.

'We'd bring Moppet, of course,' Nattie said, skipping the Daddy question, 'he can come too. Let's go down now and we must try to be quiet and let Tubsy sleep or he'll be all whingey. There are the books and the peg-board, but Dan had an idea. He writes stories for television, Lily, and he said he'd help you write a story of your own while Tubsy had his sleep.'

'Would you like that, Lily? We can do it on the computer downstairs in the kitchen. I've got a way to draw pictures on the screen too. It's a graphic design app,' he said, for Nattie's benefit. 'So we can do a story with pictures and print it out afterwards for you to keep. You can colour in the pictures then too.'

'What can the story be about? Can it be about a guinea pig?'

'That's just what I was thinking myself!'

Nattie told Lily to go to the bathroom before settling in and Ahmed grabbed the moment for a kiss. 'I got the car,' he said. 'It's right outside, a Ford Focus. Baby seats are in and I've seen to the parking permit. It's all ready for you on Monday. Have a peek at it as you leave. It's blue!' Nattie gave him an alarmed smile, which got him worried. 'You'll get through the weekend,' he urged, 'as long as your mind's made up and you're really sure. But you'll need some steel and bravery. There'll be no worse agony than breaking it to Hugo – you do want to go ahead?' Ahmed wished he felt more certain of that. She cared about Hugo, dreaded how he'd cope, and she had the worry of the children, even without the enormity of the risk. And he, Ahmed thought, had to bear the guilt of being prepared to let her take it.

'It helps me to face telling him, saying it's a trial separation, nothing final, and he can see the children plenty, every other weekend. I'm—'

Lily danced back into the kitchen and Nattie broke off. Ahmed got the show on the road. He pulled up a second chair at the far end of the long table, where he had his laptop, found a cushion to make Lily higher and lifted her up onto it. He knocked out the start of a story about a guinea pig escaping from his hutch and ending up in a cage in a zoo.

'What's going to happen next?' Lily's eyes were round and wide, full of anxiety. 'Wouldn't his family be very upset and looking for him everywhere? I love how he looks in the drawing!'

'His owner is a little girl who's five, called Poppy, and she is very upset. She thinks he's lost and cries for days, but she goes to the zoo one day and sees him. The zookeeper's a very nice man with a kind heart, though, and he says she can take him home again.'

Lily was full of excitement when the story was finished, holding on to the pages as they printed off. She clutched the three pages tight and was still clutching them saying goodbye. 'Can we do another story soon?' she said on the doorstep.

'Suppose you try to think up what it could be about.' Ahmed gave a grin, squatting down to her level. 'Then it would be your very own story.'

Her eyes were starry and she even gave him a little kiss. 'Bye, Dan,' she said, adding, 'thank you,' with a look from her mother. 'I want it to be my very own, I'm so 'cited about that.'

22

Hugo's Return

It was a full plane, going back to London. Hugo shrank deeper into his Club Class seat, relieved to be beside a window and able to look out, look away, and that Brady was at last lost to a complimentary copy of the *Financial Times*. His boss had just delivered the most excruciating pep talk to Hugo while the plane had been stationary on the runway. God, the longing for take-off; bloody Doomsday could have come sooner. Between Brady putting the shits up, his wretchedness, his gargantuan hangover – he'd thrown up last night and felt close to it again now – Hugo longed for oblivion, a pill to knock him out at the least. He was ice cold and clammy, his whole body damp with sweat.

'Don't get on Brady's wrong side,' people in the office often warned. 'He's steel. A fucking JCB fork-lift truck when he chooses, he'll turn you over and dump you in the dung.' Brady had stopped short of that, but the steel had glinted all right.

'I know you've got emotional problems, Hugo,' he'd said, 'they're showing. Don't let them. I gave you a chance when many wouldn't and you pulled through, but don't expect me to do so again. If we win out on Bosphor Air, it'll be no credit to you.

Maybe your opaque glaze passed those guys by yesterday, but it didn't me. You're on borrowed time, I warn you. You need to shape up and sort yourself out.'

Hugo said he was sorry, bad patch and all that, but he'd got the message, and would pull himself up fast. He refrained from saying he could never have pulled through without Nattie. If she let go now, how long would his 'borrowed time' last?

They landed at five-twenty. He had his bag with him and with luck should just be home in time to see the children. He badly wished he'd called Nattie; he hadn't once, felt too devastated the whole time to speak to her. It had also had something to do with Amber and her obsessive come-ons, wrestling with whether a fuck with her would be a release. He was so strung up. If she wanted it that badly, he'd figured, why the hell not?

Last night's dinner, entertaining their contacts in Istanbul who'd helped get them in through the door, had been his undoing. He'd sat brooding, drinking himself into a coma deliberately; he could never have faced Amber without being tanked out of his skull. Such lunacy, imagining she could remotely ease the pain. Hugo sighed. He'd known how fake and false and sordid it would be, as squalid as it got.

Even in his drunken haze he'd been repulsed, even with the room spinning, seeing four flabby boobs instead of two. He hadn't backed off, he'd made it – just – before staggering to the bathroom and throwing up. What kind of sex was that? Had he ever felt dirtier in his life?

Hugo shuffled through Passport Control and joined the taxi queue feeling maggoty and rotten to the core. He climbed into the back of a cab with relief. He was stuck with Amber too now, with her lovey texts and those knowing looks at the airport that had made his innards crawl; he'd never get her off his back. He felt a failure in every direction. Nattie had married him out of affectionate pity, still in love with another man. Was he about to pay the price, for hoping and praying all those years that Ahmed Khan was six feet under the ground?

The taxi made good progress; the traffic was all going the other way. Hugo ached to see Lily and Thomas, dreaded arriving home. His head pounded and bile rose in his throat even as he forced it down. The nausea was stress-induced, he knew; he couldn't shake it off. It hung around like the smell of a dead rat, feeding on his acid terror, welling up at the slightest provocation – and never more so than when he imagined Nattie with her lover.

Ahmed must have returned, she must be seeing him, Victoria had hinted as much. Was she about to tell him so, that very night? Suppose Ahmed was only back for a short time, too worried about the risk to stick around. It would fit with Nattie having a secret affair. She'd want to see Ahmed, no question, be swept up and unable to resist or even be especially discreet, however much she wanted to keep it from her husband. She might have tried to, Hugo told himself bitterly, but she was a useless liar.

Suppose he'd gone along with the 'marital sabbatical' she'd wanted, stood obligingly by, been accommodating and agreed to it all. He groaned out loud in the back of the cab; he couldn't have done it. It had been all he could do to live with Ahmed's ghost.

Couldn't he just try? Wasn't anything better than finality? He knew in his gut, though, that if Ahmed was back for however long, his marriage was in pieces.

He was almost home. He tapped on the partition window. 'Over on the right, just past the lamp-post.' He paid off the cab, fished out his door key and carried his bag up the front path. He hoped the children were still awake and wished so much that he'd called. But to hear Nattie's voice, soft and familiar as the feel of her skin, the lump in his throat would have choked him.

'That you, love?' she called, as he closed the front door. Who did she bloody think it was? 'I'd come down, but I'm giving Tubsy his bottle. Lily's in her pyjamas, all ready for bed. Are you up to reading to her? She'd love it.'

Lily was at the top of the stairs, jumping up and down in her bare feet, calling, 'Daddy, Daddy, come upstairs!' Hugo's legs felt heavy going up. He was shattered, poleaxed, but as he swung her up high for a restoring kiss, the love he felt formed a tight knot in his chest. He set her down again and she tugged at his hand. 'You've got to come and see, Daddy, I've done my very own story and it's got pictures too! It's about a guinea pig called Just William, like Grampsy's called, only it's after a naughty boy in a book! Dan said there's lots of books about him and he's going to get me one. He helped with my story, but I did some myself.'

'I'll come in a minute, Lily love, let me first say hello to Mummy and Thomas. And I've got pressies for you both. I'll get them then you can show me your story.'

He went into Thomas's room, avoiding looking at Nattie, focusing entirely on his son whose chubby little hand was resting loosely on the bottle. He was completely absorbed, toes clenching and unclenching in unalloyed pleasure. It was his last sop to babyhood, the bedtime bottle in his mother's arms.

Hugo bent to kiss the top of his blond head. The smell of warm milk brought a new wave of queasiness and straightening up he brushed against Nattie's gossamer hair, which brought an acute stab of need. He felt dizzy with it. She was wearing an unfamiliar scent; faint, she never put much on, but it wasn't one he'd ever given her, he was sure. 'I'll just go down for the children's presents,' he muttered, and hurried out of the door.

Lily was waiting for him to come back up, sliding her hand along the banister rail with great impatience. He'd bought her a doll in Turkish national dress, which seemed to go down well. 'That's what little girls there wear on special occasions,' he said.

'Lots of faraway countries have that sort of old-fashioned dress.'

'What do you say, Lily?' Nattie prompted, coming out onto the landing holding Thomas. 'And it's high time you were in bed if Daddy's going to read to you. You're getting far too overexcited.'

Lily said thank you in an automatic sort of way. 'She's a very pretty doll. I like the dangly things on her head and her red skirt with all the braid. Now will you come and see my story?'

Hugo had brought Thomas a hand-painted wooden cart that he could pull along on a string. 'We'll play with it in the morning,' he said, giving him a goodnight kiss.

'Say thank you, Tubsy,' Nattie said, jigging him on her hip. 'You know how, you know you do. Say *thank* you and blow Daddy a kiss! One for Lily too.'

'Sank,' Thomas mumbled, which wasn't a bad approximation. He wasn't up for blowing kisses, he was a sleepyhead ready for his bed.

Lily kept tugging on her father's arm. 'Let's see this story then,' he said tiredly, cursing his throbbing head.

She glowed with pride, showing it off. It was much fingered and too professional by half. 'I'm going to do another one,' she said happily, 'next time we see Dan. P'raps about a naughty giraffe who eats leaves from next door's garden.'

'Is Dan one of your teachers at school?' Hugo queried, as lightly as he could manage. 'Don't you usually have Miss Stubbs?'

'Course, Daddy, we have her always, she's our form teacher. Dan is Mummy's friend who we had lunch with today.' Lily hesitated. 'He's very nice,' she added a bit awkwardly, not meeting Hugo's eyes.

He felt quivery looking at the story laid out on her child's table and needed to get to a chair. 'What book do you want, Lily?' he asked, his throat feeling closed over. He pressed on his thighs, trying to steady them.

'Can we have *Amos and Boris*, about the mouse and the whale? It's my best story.' She pulled it out of an untidy pile, handed it to him and climbed into bed.

Hugo moved his very small chair closer and began to read. The hairs at the nape of his neck pricked and the words seemed to elongate and recede like the wavy characters in a website box. Lily hitched up to look at the pictures and follow the story. She reached over him to jab at a page. 'You missed out that whole bit, Daddy. You have to *concentrate*! Miss Stubbs says we mustn't let our thoughts wander.'

'Sounds like you're being a cheeky girl,' Nattie laughed, coming into the room. Hugo kept his eyes trained on the book. 'Don't make Daddy read for long, he's been in an aeroplane, he must be very tired.' She leaned over from the far side of the bed to give Lily a goodnight kiss. 'Sleep tight, angel, sweet dreams – see you in the morning when the sun comes up on your clock.'

Hugo stared after her as she left. She looked back from the door, smiling nervously. Dropping his eyes down he began to read again.

Nattie waited in the kitchen. She felt numb with tension. Having listened to every word of Lily's excitable chatter, she knew there was no putting it off till tomorrow. The decision of when to tell Hugo was out of her hands. Lily had dictated the timing.

The tension was unbearable, the sense of numbness gone, vanished, replaced with tingling shivery adrenalin. What would he say when he came downstairs? How would he react? She went to the glass doors at the far end of the kitchen and stared out; there was no moon, the garden was ink black.

She felt at a terrible loss as to what to do. Did she offer Hugo food? Suggest trying to explain over a meal? Plunge right in and say she was leaving? Her nerve-ends were twitching and waving like so many antennae. She tried to be braced for when they sparked and touched.

'So are you going to tell me what's going on?' Hugo said dully, giving her a startled jolt. She hadn't heard him come in. Seeing him in the brightly lit kitchen jolted her further. He looked shocking, terrible. His eyes were ringed with purple shadow, his hair flattened and dishevelled; his skin was a sickly green.

Her heart pounded. Had he been up all night? 'Hugo, darling, you don't look well. Did you get sick out there? You need to sit down, you really should be in bed by the look of you.'

'I'm not ill. I don't want your sympathy. I'd just like to know what's going on. You owe me some explanation. Where you've been taking my children, who you've brought into their lives. Did it not occur to you that it was something to be discussed? Don't I have a right to be consulted where they're concerned?'

Nattie sat down where she was, at the far end of the kitchen; her legs felt shaky. Somehow she hadn't expected a direct attack, yet what else could he have said? He had hold of the whisky bottle by its neck, he must have been into the sitting room for it, and got a glass out of the cupboard there, which he'd filled almost full. He pulled out a chair at the kitchen table. The whisky gleamed topaz in the chaos of the children's tea; stray peas, streaks of ketchup on plastic plates. She hadn't yet cleared up.

She rose and went over, moving the dirty plates and wiping down the table. 'I suppose you were late back,' Hugo said coldly, alluding to the un-seen-to mess.

'No, we'd been out to lunch, as I think Lily said, but we were home quite early. We weren't sure when to expect you and Lily was hoping you'd be back in time for tea. I wish you'd called, darling. I'd love to have heard how things were going and you could have said hi to Lily, though to be honest I'd probably have waited till you were home before explaining about our lunch today – not something for the phone. I'll give you answers, of course, to everything you ask, and say what I feel would be for the best in the short term, but right now, love, you look really done in. Wouldn't it make sense to have a quick bite and crash out for tonight? We have to talk, but it will be a struggle for both of us, difficult enough without being exhausted and overwrought.'

Nattie felt agonised, watching Hugo for any reaction. He was sipping his Scotch steadily, refusing to look at her. She imagined his thoughts must be mirroring the black anger and desolation written all over his face. It was the wrong time. She'd expected him to be exhausted and hung-over, since there was sure to have been some heavy drinking on the trip, but he looked cadaverous, really unwell. She kept her eyes on him, heart bleeding, aching for a chance to connect.

'No! I want to know now, fuck it – right now, this minute!' he yelled, draining his glass and slamming it down. It was a miracle it didn't smash. 'You're my wife, damn it, though you seem not to have chosen to be for the last six weeks. And it may surprise you, but I happen to care what you've been doing with my children actually, quite a lot.'

He was staring at her savagely now, looking deranged in his rage. 'Where did you take them today? Who have you been seeing? You owe me a few truthful answers for a change.' Hugo gripped the table edge, his eyes glittering, before his body went limp and he slumped back in his chair. He reached for the bottle and refilled his glass with a shaking hand.

Once she said it, once it was done, out in the open . . . Would he be just as viciously angry? Fatalistic? Defeated and crushed? He'd feel bitterly let down whatever. He must know who it was by now, he'd always dreaded Ahmed's return.

She took a breath. 'I heard from Ahmed out of the blue, you see – the day after we were back from Portugal. It seemed astounding after so long, after giving up hope. It was a miracle to know he was alive.'

'But you kept this earth-shattering news to yourself. You chose not to tell me.' Hugo was looking straight at her again, looking coldly into her soul. 'You fell into his arms, told lies. Didn't being married count for one jot? Suppose I'd done that to you? Have you given the slightest thought to what it's like for me, being on the receiving end?'

His eyes were pained and accusing, his forehead clammy and damp. Had he been drinking all night, had no sleep, no food? How had he got himself into this state? When he'd leaned to kiss Tubsy she'd sensed a faint odour of vomit; hardly there, but vomit was like spilt milk on a carpet, a smell that refused to go away.

She held his eyes. 'You can't really believe any of that. It was because of how much I cared and worried for you that I *didn't* tell you. I'd hoped if I saw Ahmed once and heard what had happened, I could explain I was married and that would be that. I wanted to save you from ever knowing he was back. I was sure you'd feel deeply upset and be convinced I was seeing him anyway.'

Nattie kneaded her hands, feeling worried stiff about Hugo and the state he was in. 'I tried, you must believe me, but seeing him again, the emotions it caused ... I'd explain more, tell you what I think would be best – just for now – but you're really not well. Let's talk about it tomorrow, darling, better then.'

'No, we talk tonight. What's with this Dan business anyway? Is that a name you chose just for the children's benefit?' Hugo sneered. 'It's a joke. Hardly suitable for someone of his background, after all.'

Nattie glared. 'His background? Born here? Doing his country a great service?'

'Sorry,' Hugo said decently, looking contrite. 'I'm overwrought.'

She reached out to touch his arm, feeling it was a sign, a softening, but he jerked away with as violent a start as if she'd given him an electric shock. He was trembling badly and his hand round the glass was white-knuckled.

'It was what people called him where he was living,' Nattie said, trying to be conciliatory while giving minimum information. She worried constantly about Ahmed's identity becoming known. 'I'm sure you should eat something,' she urged. 'I'll heat up some soup. I don't believe you've had a thing all day.'

Hugo didn't reject the suggestion. He stared mutely down at the table while she got a tin out of the cupboard and put the contents to heat on the stove. She saw him reach for the whisky bottle and got to it first. 'I'll put some in the soup,' she said, lifting it away. 'It'll be more comforting that way.'

He drank the soup, had a bite or two of a slice of wholemeal bread. She made poached eggs on toast for them both, and sat down with him. They didn't, either of them, make much headway with the eggs, but Hugo looked marginally better, less green.

They didn't speak apart from Nattie urging him to drink water. She wanted him to ask questions. It would help to gauge his mood, how hard he was going to take it, how great the emotional torment. He must have picked up on her talking of what would be for the best, just for now. She was obsessively anxious not to have to say it cold – especially that night – that she was taking Lily, Tubsy and Moppet to live in Lambeth, whatever the obstacles he raised.

'I'll make you a cup of tea,' she said. 'It's the best thing when you're feeling sick.'

He jerked his head up; he'd been lost to his thoughts in the silence. 'I don't want tea,' he snapped. 'What have you done with the whisky bottle?' He looked round half-heartedly, too far gone to focus on trying to find it.

She brought over the bottle. Hugo gave her a look as if to say if he wanted neat whisky she wasn't going to stop him. He poured himself another large glassful and took a swig. 'I suppose he's been here, the last couple of nights, fucking you in this house,' he taunted, the alcohol giving him some fight, 'and in the daytime for weeks.'

'He's never stepped foot in the door. This is your house, *our* house – I stayed in with the children while you were away. Mum came over on Wednesday. I told her about Ahmed, how desperate I felt, and that we couldn't go on as we were.'

'Are you trying to say you want me to move out and leave you here with the children?' Hugo looked ashen, defeated and broken.

'Of course not, how could you think that?' Nattie felt stricken, hating herself, aching to ease the pain that she was inflicting. 'Nothing was further from my mind. I think, though, we need to live separately for a while. A sort of temporary arrangement and see how we go. Ahmed has rented Jake's house for three months – I'll go there with the children. You can have them every other weekend. I'd bring them, stay to help with Tubsy if you wanted it. We could do things together with them too.'

'And after three months?'

'I don't know. Let's not think that far ahead. Everything here will be just as it is, you'll have the car, be in your own home . . .'

'Except that you won't be in it.' Hugo stared at her with his glittering eyes. He looked, if anything, even more demented. Nattie felt a dart of fear. Was he going to fight her, strike her? His hand curled menacingly round the squat whisky glass and she froze.

He had the glass in his hand, swung round and hurled it towards the kitchen sink. It hit the swan neck of the mixer tap, shattered and smashed into the basin. The sound of crashing glass was fearsome, fragments flying, fine shards, large pieces; they both stared transfixed. A potent aroma of whisky was released, as pervasive as a whole spilt bottle. Nattie stayed rooted. Had the noise woken the children? She listened out, praying Lily wouldn't come creeping down, but heard nothing.

She'd sat down again at the end of the table, at right angles to Hugo, and had followed the arc of the glass. Bringing her eyes back, she faced him. He was shaking, staring at his hands, turning them over and back again in a bemused way as if unsure they belonged to him.

'I'll clear up,' she said. 'You go to bed, you're white as chalk; you need to lie down or you could pass out. I'll make some hot lemon and honey and find you one of those sleeping pills we've got somewhere. Things will be—'

'Don't, for Christ's sake, say that, anything but that.' He was visibly shaking; he looked about to break down again or keel over. 'And don't put on this bloody Florence Nightingale act, trying to absolve yourself. I'm not your bloody patient, I'm your husband.' He'd lifted his head, raised his voice. 'However much you'd like to forget it. You just want to get through all this, don't you, be with Ahmed and ruin my life. You can't wait to get away.'

'How can I get across to you that it isn't like that? You know how much I care, how close we've always been. That can never change, never will.' She couldn't blame him for his bitter hysteria, the glass, his wounding words that were all too true – and things *wouldn't* be better in the morning. She knew that, he knew that. 'Please can we talk about this reasonably,' she begged. 'I can't expect you not to hate me for what I'm doing, but for the sake of the children, their stability and happiness, can't we just try to find a way through and stay friends?'

Hugo got to his feet. He looked unsteady, but made it to the cupboard for another glass and sat down heavily on the nearest seat. He poured himself the dregs of the whisky, downed that, and reached for the bottle of red wine on the table.

'I'll sleep on the sofa,' he said, croaking out the words as though they hurt his throat. His shoulders began to heave and he covered his face with both hands. He was sobbing, shaking; he couldn't stop. Nattie went beside him, put her arm round him, held him tight, forced back her own tears. 'I feel so lonely,' he said, taking away his hands and leaning his head on her arm. 'And ashamed.'

'Why? You can't be that! You're wonderful, Hugo, you've got so much going for you.' She didn't know what to say in her infinite sorrowfulness. If only a crisis could be a turning point. She'd hoped for a tiny moment when Hugo had found some fight that he'd recover, get over it, and be able to stand on his own two feet, but that hope was fading fast.

'I'll tell you why I'm ashamed,' he said. 'I behaved badly in Istanbul, drank myself into a stupor, puked up. I couldn't even hack it in the presentation. Brady tore a strip off me on the way back.'

'I'm to blame for all that,' Nattie said, helping him up. She led him to the stairs with her arm around him, feeling indescribable agony and guilt. She had a good idea of what 'behaved badly' meant, and shut her mind to it.

'I couldn't even handle the high moral ground,' Hugo said, looking rueful as they reached the bedroom and she encouraged him to sit down on the bed. 'Slipped up a bit there.'

She helped him undress, taking off his shoes and socks, undoing shirt buttons, peeling off his trousers, persuading him to lie back. She pulled over the duvet, covering him lightly, drew the curtains and crept out. Downstairs she cleared up the chaos of broken glass as quietly as possible and an hour later crept back into the bedroom. Hugo was in a deep, sodden sleep, drugged to oblivion on alcohol, managing at last to blot out the world.

They would get through the weekend, she thought, undressing and climbing in gingerly beside him. What about on Monday when she packed up and left? She had some explaining to do to Lily and Tubsy, and Jasmine to get in touch with – the first moment she could. Nattie felt sure Jasmine would be fine about the situation and wouldn't talk if asked not to. And about coming to the new address; it was nearer for her and she loved the children, knew how much they'd need the continuity.

It was a momentous decision – selfish, that went without saying – but people did up-turn their lives when love got in the way. What people *didn't* do was expose their children to any threat, however remote, from vengeful extremists. It was minimal for now, while they never went out and about with Ahmed, but in the longer term? Living abroad, which still had its risks, was the only way. And where did that leave Hugo?

Nattie lay awake, imagining what it would be like for him, coming home to an empty house. She would call, talk to him, do everything she possibly could to smooth the arrangements. She'd give him all the access he wanted, but suppose the children didn't adapt, felt unsettled and confused, and Hugo couldn't prop himself up. What then?

23

Early Days

On Monday Nattie waited outside the school gates, shivery with nerves and the change in the weather, feeling chilled to the bone in the icy wind. How badly was Lily going to miss her father? She'd enjoyed her afternoon with Ahmed and doing the story, loved all that – bubbled over about it at home, which had caused Hugo such pain – and was excited about seeing Ahmed again, but how was she going to cope with all the upheaval, the strangeness, sleeping in a new bed and no hugging her daddy? Nattie felt riven with guilt.

Lily came running out of the school gates, coated up in her red puffa and woolly hat and clutching an envelope. 'It's a party invitation, Mummy, Jade's birthday. It's soon.' She stared at the Ford car as Nattie opened the passenger door. 'Is this our new car, you said about? I came with Daddy in the other one.'

'We've got two now.' Nattie smiled, strapping the child into her seat beside Tubsy who was having his first ride in the new blue car.

'Hi, Tubsbubs, high-fives!' Lily said exuberantly, pushing at his hand. 'Abcdefg,' she started singing, 'hijklmnop, I'm going to learn it to you all the way home.'

'Teach it to him,' Nattie said automatically. 'We're going to Dan's house now, Lily, and staying for a bit, but back with Daddy at the weekend. Are you going to tell Dan your new idea for a story, the one about the naughty giraffe?'

'But I don't know how it ends,' she wailed, sounding close to crying.

'I'm sure he can help just a little bit with that,' Nattie said, anxious not to trample on any of Lily's creative sensitivities.

'But it will still be my very own story?'

'Of course! It's all your idea. You can write "By Lily Dangerfield" under the title. I took Moppet over this morning, love, in his hutch.'

'Oh, no! He won't know where he is, he might try to escape!'

'I'm quite sure he won't. He's had a nice big carrot and looks very happy and settled. We put his hutch under the apple tree, but you can move it where you like.'

Nattie eyed Tubsy in the driving mirror. He was mumbling to himself, 'Abc, one two see, abc,' and she felt a swathe of maternal adoration, warming as a blush.

'Very good,' she encouraged. 'And the next bit, hijklmnop . . .'

Lily started to sing it too, more than once.

'Is Dan going to be my sort of other daddy?' she asked, with an abrupt and alarmingly unexpected switch. 'Jade has two mummies. Her daddy's married another lady who Jade quite likes, but her big sister hates her. Jade's glad the party's at her own home. Can I have my party at my own home too?'

That touched a nerve – many nerves. Nattie hadn't yet given the party a thought. 'Of course, you can, love, we'd have it on a weekend anyway. We'll do the invitations tomorrow. You can choose the cards and help me with the list.'

'I'm four years and eleven months!' Lily chanted, skittering off difficult territory as fast as she'd switched onto it. 'Nearly everyone's five at school 'cept Jade and me.'

'You could write a story about a little girl who was the youngest in her class.' She glanced back.

'But what *happens* in her life?' Lily said, sounding unconvinced.

Nattie felt quite enough was happening in their lives already.

She drew up in a permit bay and took out her new house key. It was on a ring with the keys to both cars. Ahmed had insisted she had the Mazda key as well – precautionary, he said, you never knew. Opening the door, he was there to greet them. He grinned at Lily, helping her off with her coat. 'Do you know what the hat said to the scarf, Lily?' She shook her head from side to side energetically and her woolly hat fell off. '"You hang around, scarfy," said the hat, "and I'll go on ahead."' Ahmed mimed a scarf being hung round her neck and he put her hat back on to make the point. Lily got it, giggling, but she wasn't to be outdone.

'What happened when the budgie went to the doctor?'

'Dunno. You tell me.'

'The doctor gave him some tweetment.' Ahmed groaned. 'And,' Lily went on excitedly, 'Noah at school told me another one. "Why did the banana go to the doctor?"' Ahmed raised his eyebrows in query. '"Because he wasn't peeling well!"'

'Oh, no, that's even worse,' he laughed. 'I'll try to come up with one or two for you to tell Noah tomorrow if you'd like.'

'Yes please, yes please!' Lily cried, jumping up and down, hair bouncing.

'Are we in for awful corny cracker jokes all afternoon?' Nattie complained.

'What's corny mean?'

'Sort of funny, awful,' Nattie said, 'not funny, clever.'

Ahmed gave her a nudge. 'Don't be so snooty about our funny

jokes. Hey, Tubsy! How're you doing? Was that abc you were singing all to yourself just now?'

Lily sang out loudly. 'Abcdefg – I'm learning him it!' Nattie couldn't face correcting her again. 'Can I go and see Moppet now, Mummy? Can I have something to eat – pleeese?'

'One flapjack or you'll spoil your supper. Okay, Tubsy, you can have a bit too.'

Lily was bursting with impatience to see Moppet, peering through the glass doors to the garden as Ahmed unlocked them, dropping oaty crumbs. She was out like a shot, coatless and as though her life, or Moppet's, depended on it.

They watched her squat down to open the hutch and cuddle her scruffy-haired, black-and-gold guinea pig. Tubsy was occupied, he'd made for the toy box, and Ahmed reached for Nattie's hand. She leaned against him for support. 'You must be exhausted,' he said, 'really done in. And not just with the move.'

Nattie laid her head on his shoulder in silent acknowledgement. He knew what had happened, just how hard Hugo had taken it. She'd told him, talking with her phone tucked under her chin as she packed that morning, throwing everything together in a great rush. She'd helped the man-with-a-van shift the hutch, cases, boxes, her old bicycle – she'd be much nearer the office and planned to bike in – a couple of her favourite pot plants, Lily's pink bike and scooter. She'd left Thomas's buggy behind for Hugo, since Ahmed had bought a new one for her online. It had certainly been a fraught day, even without the worry of how disorientated Lily would feel.

Hugo had wanted to drop her off at school as usual that morning, if for the last time, which with the usual breakfast rush and chaos had helped to slide over the agony of the parting. It had meant having to tell Lily the night before, though, and explain in whispers about going to stay with Dan, hoping Hugo wouldn't overhear and Lily wouldn't instantly relay it back to him.

Watching from the kitchen window, Nattie felt Lily seemed unbothered for now, but there was the new routine to get used to: no more going to school with her daddy and a longer journey too, which meant an earlier start. Nattie didn't know where the nearest park was, for Lily to scoot and Thomas to be pushed on a swing – and she realised with a pang that Ahmed would feel he couldn't come with them. She suppressed a sigh.

Suppressed or not, Ahmed picked up on it and put his arm round her. 'It'll shake down,' he murmured, hugging her close. She turned and saw with amazement that he was crying. He looked shamefaced. 'You're here,' he said, wiping his eyes with the sleeve of his sweatshirt, 'that's all.' He concentrated on watching Lily who was on her haunches, offering Moppet the remains of a dirty carrot. 'It's pretty chilly out there,' he said, 'better bring her in soon. And California's waking up. I guess I should go and do a bit of communicating.'

Nattie went outside and found that Lily was blue with cold. 'Silly thing,' she said, worried, 'you're shivering like a jelly! You must come in. You can watch one of your DVDs and you've got the new doll's house to play with too.' Lily brightened at that, but dragged her feet and looked back at the hutch, as though, so it seemed to Nattie in her guilt, it was the one thing that was homely and familiar to her.

Lily turned back to blow a kiss and she called out, cheerily enough, 'Night, night, Moppet, poppet, I'll bring you some lettuce in the morning.'

'Dan's gone to do some emails,' Nattie said, locking the doors, 'but you can tell him your giraffe story over your supper. I'm sure he'll give a little help.'

Ahmed reappeared in time and listened attentively while Lily, rather shyly for her, told him her idea for a story and registered her concern about how it would end. 'It's a great story,' he said, 'lots of scope for pictures too. A cheeky young giraffe eating leaves off the neighbours' trees – they'd certainly be angry, and the family he lives with would be cross with him too. Now let me see . . .' He held his chin, as though contemplating. 'I wonder what's going to happen next.' Lily gazed at him on such high-wire tenterhooks that he couldn't keep a straight face.

'I think his family would say they couldn't keep him and that he must go away,' Ahmed said, 'which makes him very sad. He roams the streets and finds a job with some tree surgeons – that's the people who cut back trees – and does so well with his long neck, reaching the very far branches, that the family get to hear. They're very proud and want him to come back home, which makes him happy indeed. What do you reckon, Lily? Has your giraffe got a name yet?'

She looked a bit caught out, hadn't thought of that, but came up with one quite smartly. 'Jimmy – Jimmy the giraffe.' Her face was one big smile. 'I love that ending! Can we do it on your computer like before? Can I get down, Mummy?'

'It's a bit late to do it now,' Ahmed said, 'almost your bath time. Let's keep computer work for Fridays when you're home early. We want to do a proper job.'

She wanted that too, while exploding with impatience to see it typed up like last time. 'But I want to show it to Daddy,' she whined, not giving in lightly. 'He liked my other story a lot.' Nattie assured her it would still be done in time.

'Would you like Dan to read you a story?' she asked, when Lily was in her pyjamas and ready for bed. 'Or I can,' she added hesitantly, in an embarrassed way, drawing down the blinds with the stars and moons. She had a great need not to make assumptions; Lily had to feel ready to manage living with two daddies in her life.

'I really want him to read my new *Just William* book, Mummy. It has some big words in it, but I know lots! Will you tell him I do and will he read it then?'

'I expect so if you ask nicely,' Nattie replied. She went into Tubsy's room. Ahmed was leaning over the cot, saying goodnight, and she told him he was needed. 'Lily's in bed waiting,' she said.

He straightened up and gave a grin. 'It's full on, isn't it?'

'Better get used to it,' she said firmly, and went downstairs to do something about supper.

She timed it right, going back up to give Lily a goodnight kiss. Ahmed had just finished reading, was returning the book to the shelf, and Lily's eyes were heavy. She said sleepily that the story wasn't too difficult for her, it was really funny and good. Ahmed rose from the chair beside the bed and bent down to kiss her lightly on her forehead.

'Night, Lily,' he said.

On his way to the door his arm brushed against Nattie's and he locked eyes with a look that shot through her. It was the look she'd pined for and clung to for seven years, the look that frightened her with its force, the force of her need, the look that made her weak-kneed.

She sat down on the bedside chair. 'All well, darling?' she said, smoothing away a strand of Lily's fine hair. 'First night in your new bed!' She regretted saying that immediately, so stupid, talking about the first night, it would make Lily start thinking of her father. Hugo had always rushed back to be in time for the bedtime hug and kiss. Lily minded when he didn't make it, always asking where he was, and she missed seeing him.

'I like this room,' she said, which was comforting to hear. 'I just wish Daddy could come to live with us here. It's my baddest thing in my whole life, not seeing him at my bedtime. Or

Mummy, couldn't Dan come to stay with us in our house, p'raps? Do you think he'd be able to?'

'It really isn't possible either way, darling. Daddy and I need to live separately for a while. But you'll see him on Saturday and all over the weekend; you're his little girl, remember. You'll have to be very grown-up, though, and help with Tubsy if I'm not there or when Jasmine has to go.' The weekend was too distant, it didn't fill the void; Lily had sad, soulful eyes and she was wakeful too, not the sleepy-face she'd been only minutes ago. Nattie ached to make things better, and for her daughter to feel more settled and content.

'Shall we give Daddy a call and then you could blow a kiss down the phone?' she said, reaching into her jeans back pocket for her mobile. She'd planned to call Hugo after a couple of days and hadn't factored in whether Lily should talk to him even then. She hoped her instinct to do it now wasn't simply going to make matters worse.

Hugo's mobile was switched off. Nattie tried the house phone, which rang and rang. He was probably on the tube, on his way home. He could be in a pub, drinking with a gang from the office. She couldn't help worrying a bit, anxiety pricking like a sharp stone in her shoe. Was he all right?

'Daddy's not there,' she said, 'but you could leave a voicemail. He'd love finding a message from you and a goodnight kiss!'

Lily looked very chuffed and spoke excitably into Nattie's mobile. 'Hello, Daddy! Night, night, I'm kissing you down the phone! Mummy says I can have my party for when I'm five at our home.'

He wouldn't know whether Lily meant her new home or old. Nattie fretted about that. She tucked her daughter up and kissed her. 'Time for sleep now, darling. It's getting late and you've got school tomorrow, an earlier start too.'

'Is Dan your boyfriend, Mummy?'

'Sort of, I suppose.' Nattie smiled, feeling fresh pricks of angst. 'Sleep tight now. Your clock's set, everything ready for the morning, time to snuggle down.'

'Jasmine has a boyfriend – you know, Mum, Pete, the nee-naw meccaneec. He wants to marry her but she's not sure. Jade's daddy married his girlfriend who he went to live with, that's why she's Jade's other mummy now.'

'No more talking, love.' Nattie kissed her again and got up to go, extremely keen to avoid the next likely question – was she going to marry Ahmed? She started for the door. 'Sweet dreams, angel. I'm only along the passage. Dan's nearby too, his room is just upstairs.'

Lily's eyes were closing at last. She had her woolly kangaroo and pulled him close, settling into her sleeping position with a little sigh, but whether it was one of sadness or contentment was hard to say. Nattie said a silent prayer for the latter and quietly pulled the door to.

Ahmed heard Nattie's footsteps on the stairs. 'All good?' he asked anxiously, folding her into his arms. 'Lily's not too unsettled?'

'She is a bit. The bedtime hug was something of a ritual with Hugo, but she's hugging Kangy and adjusting. She'll be okay.' Nattie eased herself out of his arms. 'Must do something about supper.' She busied about in the kitchen, needing to unwind, which Ahmed could well understand. He still couldn't believe she'd done it, that she'd put herself through that emotional hell for love of him, and his heart swelled.

He tried to imagine how Lily must feel, the strangeness, not really knowing what was going on, sensing undercurrents that she couldn't comprehend. It would take time to establish a new routine, more time before she was completely used to it and everything felt natural and familiar. He prayed it would be soon.

Their first evening together, he and Nattie had to adjust and settle in as well. He was determined to marry her, have children together, but there were no certainties in life and it was going to be a long hard haul. They could make a life in California, a good life, which would be almost, if not entirely, free of risk. But there was the great big stumbling block of Hugo. Nattie cared deeply about Hugo, always had, which had always been so hard to take. Ahmed cursed inwardly, feeling as obsessed as ever over the pulls on her loyalties; he knew she loved him and that he could make her happy, and yet he'd had to sit it out thousands of miles away, imagining her fond affection for Hugo becoming a habit that was hard to break. A trial separation, three months of uncertainty . . . It was never going to be easy.

Nattie was exhausted, but happy, he could tell. They didn't need to say much, it was enough that they were there, physically there, together. He held her close, going upstairs, then undressed her, made love to her and felt an emotional overload when she fell asleep in his arms. He couldn't lose her now.

The clock was set for six-thirty the next morning. Ahmed reached to kill the alarm, but it was hard to make a move. Nattie said Lily would wait till the sun was up on her bedside clock before coming in, but he still had to scarper fast upstairs to the top-floor bedroom. 'Risky strategy, this need for separate rooms,' he said, lying back and luxuriating in the warmth of her, snug in the crook of his arm. 'I'd have to hide under the bed very fast. How long do we have to keep it up for?'

'Months and years,' Nattie said. 'You should feel jolly lucky I allowed you into your bed at all. And time's marching on.'

Lily's clock did its stuff. Ahmed heard her running along from her room at exactly seven-fifteen. Nattie was up and dressed.

She'd got up with him when he dragged himself out of bed; she was taking no chances with timing on the first morning of the new school run.

Lily's cheerful chatter carried. 'Is Dan having breakfast with us?' he heard her ask in an it's-very-important-to-me sort of tone. 'Will he remember about the jokes for Noah, do you s'pose, Mummy? I reely, reely want him to.'

Ahmed hadn't quite forgotten, but it jogged his memory and it helped to be forearmed. He smiled to himself, dredging up a couple of silly one-liners as he dressed.

Clattering down the uncarpeted single flight he put his head round Lily's open bedroom door. 'Morning, all! Sleep okay, you two? You look very snazzy and bright-eyed, Lily, in your smart red school uniform.' She looked a comic mixture of beaming pride and burning anxiety and was about to speak when Nattie got in first, doing her best to tip him off.

'Lily's hoping you've remembered about the jokes for her to tell her friend, Noah, and I need to get Tubs up and dressed. Can you two head on downstairs? Lily needs to feed Moppet. Can you find her some lettuce and stuff in the fridge? I'll be down in a few minutes to get breakfast on the go.'

Ahmed smiled at her, basking in the warmth of intimacy.

He got the breakfast underway. He made Lily's toast, spreading it with raspberry jam and cutting it into squares. He was telling her his third tame cracker joke, which had Lily in hysterical giggles, when Nattie came into the kitchen. She was jigging Thomas, complaining that he hadn't been at his best, and she raised an eyebrow. 'So what's going on round here? Can I be in on it?'

'Mummy, Mummy, listen!' Lily cried, skipping round and round the kitchen table. 'This is my first joke. What's orange and sounds like a parrot?'

'Can't think.'

'A carrot! And this is my next. Why are owls always invited to the party?'

'You tell me,' Nattie said, strapping Tubsy into his high chair and squishing up a Weetabix. 'Why are they?'

'Because they're such a hoot! I love that one,' Lily said, dancing round. 'And I love this one too. What is a crocodile's favourite game?'

'Let me guess. Could it be Snap?'

Lily sucked on her teeth crossly. 'That's so mean, you're not meant to get it.'

'Breakfast-time now, no more jokes. Let Dan help you wash your hands then sit down, please, we must get on with things. You don't want to be late for school when you've got three whole new jokes to tell Noah.'

Nattie settled into feeding Thomas his cereal, looking a little distant. Ahmed hoped she wasn't thinking of Hugo, alone in the house with no noisy children and no one to wave him away.

'Do you want to stay here with Dan, Tubsy,' she asked, with a glance Ahmed's way, 'or come in the car with Mummy and Lily?'

'Tay.' It was just translatable through his mouthful of milky Weetabix.

'Sure you're okay with that, Dan? Jasmine won't be here for an hour and I won't be back much before. Can you spare the time?'

'Sure thing. Tubs and I are good buddies now, we'll do puzzles and race cars.'

'I'm at work today, Lily,' Nattie said, wiping Tubsy's mouth and turning her way. 'It'll be Jasmine coming this afternoon. It feels a bit funny, after having time off last week, the thought of being back in the office again.' She looked levelly at Ahmed, a look that spoke volumes. 'Getting back into the old routine.'

24

Hugo's Solace

On Saturday morning Hugo forced himself out of a single-frame nightmare. He had been in a straitjacket, physically confined, screaming to be released. The context eluded him, his brain was leaden, not giving a thing, but he still had the sensation of being encased in concrete. Once he was more fully awake, a headache kicked in, the pain like a series of pneumatic drills driving into his skull; he was dripping with sweat and wanted to cry out in agony.

God, it was Saturday too. How could he have done it, got in this state? How could he live with himself? How could he cope? He rolled over, shuddering with the effort, and squinted open his eyes to see the time. Nine o'clock. The bedroom door was ajar, a diagonal of painful light shafting in, shining right into his eyes, while harsh daylight seeped round the window blinds. He closed his eyes again fast.

Nine o'clock. Hugo groaned and drew up his knees. Nattie said she'd bring Lily and Thomas at ten. Staying out late, liquid dinners with drunks from the office, bingeing all week – what single conceivable thing had he hoped to achieve? His children were all he had. Last night was a total blur. He'd been at home, alone and lonely, he knew that much. Feeling released from Amber and her hassling as well.

She had gone to Chertsey to be with her aged mother, which she did most weekends, caring for her and doing her shopping. Amber said her mother really ought to be in a nursing home, but had such a terror of going that it seemed heartless to push it. Better just to help out. It was kind and unselfish and Hugo admired Amber for that – as well as being glad of the weekend respite.

He squinted at the clock again. Ten past already. How was he even going to get out of bed, let alone be in a fit state to look after two noisy demanding kids? He managed to swing down his legs and made it to a sitting position on the side of the bed. Christ, he was still in his work shirt and trousers, must have crashed out in a coma – sweet release from the lousy, unfeeling world. He rubbed at his eyes with the heels of his hands. His mouth felt disgusting, furred up and dry; he felt as repulsively foul-smelling as a pavement drunk.

He got to the bathroom and took three extra-strength codeine. Should he take four? Better not. He cleaned his teeth, overloading the brush with toothpaste, and stepped into the shower, which was effortful, but it helped to feel clean again.

He pulled on a T-shirt, which made him reel, though the freshly laundered check shirt he eased on to wear as an overshirt was a soft fabric and comfortable. He began to feel he had a chance of survival once the painkillers kicked in. They hadn't yet. He slid on his watch; quarter to ten and they could be early. Coffee was what he needed – buckets of it, strong and black.

The kitchen was a mess. He shoved all the empties into a sturdy black refuse sack – bulging guilty evidence, he should have padded the bag with kitchen towel – and made a mug of espresso-machine coffee, double-filled. He lifted it to his lips gratefully with a shaking hand.

He'd made it through a week in the office at least. Amber had seen how much he was struggling, she'd covered for him, been his saviour, but there was a price to pay for that. He'd got by, though, even made it through the opening of Cupcake Corner at Palmers and survived his nemesis, Christine. The A guest-list had been a lost cause, but Amber had rounded up some last-minute glamour and, whether for the freebee and chance of a morning's shopping, a decent number of B-listers had turned up as well.

Better still, a pouting model, one of Amber's fill-ins, riled by the fruity putdowns of a loose-mouthed Press Association photographer, had picked a fight and chucked her glass of cheap champagne at his digital camera. Other cameras had been click-ing: she'd succeeded in carrying Cupcake Corner into all the gossip columns, even the local television news. And with the instant pick-up on social media Christine had a virtual orgasm. She'd told Hugo, sodden, shaking, nauseous, sweating, what a brilliant job he'd done. He was her golden boy, she said – God forbid.

The doorbell rang. Hugo started at the shrill sound and spilled half his coffee; he wiped hurriedly at the spill while his headache raged. He had to lean on the worktop to steady himself, sickened to think of Nattie ringing the bell. She had a key; it was her home. He couldn't stand it. Why couldn't Ahmed have stayed the fuck on the other side of the world, met his end, never been born.

He let out a few curses, took a deep breath, composed his face and went to get the door. He could hear Lily banging the letter-box flap, calling, 'Daddy, Daddy, where are you? Come and open the door!'

'Sorry,' he said, scooping her up and hugging her. 'I was wiping up some spilled coffee, but I bet Mummy will think the kitchen's a bit of a mess anyway!'

Nattie followed in with Thomas attached to her hip and a big canvas bag on her shoulder. She closed the door behind her, turned to face him and he met her eyes. He had to look away. He felt the rush, the swell of his need of her; and an intense rush of bitterness as well. He wanted her, his beautiful wife, his own wife, and she was with another thieving man. She was too beautiful, the pain too great. He'd spent five drunken days trying to blur and obliterate that vision, her beauty; losing his mind, risking his job. Trying to forget her softness, her wonderful dependability before Ahmed's return and the disaster of where they were now.

'You okay, darling?' Nattie said, staring at him, looking full of alarm – which was hardly surprising, after all.

'I'm fine, slight headache, that's all; it's been a long week. How's my Thomas then? Big hug for Daddy?' He held out his arms for his son who clung to her, hurtfully resistant. 'How've they been?' he asked, hiding the hurt.

'I've been reely longing to see you, Daddy,' Lily chipped in, with a what-about-me look on her face; she had to be the centre of attention. 'I got two stars at school, one for writing and one for reading, and I've got a new story to show you! I thought it up all on myself! It's in Mummy's bag where we've packed things for staying. Tubsy's Pampers and stuff like that.'

'Just a few things you might need,' Nattie said, sounding apologetic about it. 'There's plenty of kit in Tubsy's drawers as well. Shall I stay a moment or two to settle them in or would you rather take over right now?'

Hugo sensed her embarrassment. Neither of them knew what to say or do. 'No, stay a while. Have some coffee, don't hurry away.' Hadn't people in this situation mostly fallen out with each other? Nattie wasn't being cold and businesslike, just looking at him with concern. No good reading anything into that caring look. Better stick to needing to curl up and die.

He took Thomas into the kitchen and set him down on his feet. The effort involved in bending, then coming upright again, was bad. Hugo's head throbbed with both physical and emotional pain. He felt giddy; the room was pitching and rolling like being on board ship. Was this the way to enjoy his children? Could he get nothing right in his life?

Nattie had a quick glance round, trying not, he felt, to seem too critical or involved. He'd missed a couple of bottles and the bulging refuse bag was a giveaway; he hadn't had time to sling it into the recycle bin outside the back door. 'I'll just put on the dishwasher,' she said, collecting up mugs and glasses. The machine was mercifully quiet.

'You did really well with Cupcake Corner,' she grinned. 'Christine must have been pleased. That model certainly did you a favour! I read the guy's suing her for more than the cost of his camera, which seems a bit hard.'

She binned some rubbish – used coffee-pods, stray detritus – and asked, a bit pointedly, 'Heidi came to clean okay on Wednesday? I told her to take any laundry down to the cleaner's, by the way, and said you'd collect it. They open at eight, so you can always pick it up on the way to work. Have you been for last week's load yet?'

'I was going to go this morning,' Hugo lied. Laundry hadn't been top of his list.

'Perhaps take the children to the park and get the laundry on the way back? Tubsy does love that little area with the swings.'

'Good idea.' He smiled, trying not to grimace with the pain of arranging his face.

Nattie smiled awkwardly in return. 'I'm sure you've got plans,' she said, 'but they're always happy mooching around at home, if you've nothing special on.'

She knew he hadn't got anywhere near making plans. She

could always see right through him, hardly needed those sur-
reptitious glances at the bottle bag. She knew all right. That was
one thing, but her talk of the children being happy *at home* really
carved him up. They weren't fucking well *at home*; she'd taken
them away from *at home*. They were occasional visitors.

He should have made plans. Other fathers would have. He felt
useless, pathetic; guilty enough to be mordantly angry. Thomas
was clinging to Nattie's leg, his little face pressed against her
skinny black jeans. His son unsettled, needing to get his bearings
in his own home – how could she do that to her children? Ahmed
had let her down too, buggered off, dropped off the face of the
earth – didn't even that give her pause? It was a pointless train
of thought, Hugo knew; he'd never have had five precious years
of marriage if the fucker had kept in touch for a single day more
than a year.

'I'll make the coffee,' he said, pulling himself together. 'How
about playing with your garage, Tomtubs? Let's get it out of the
toy box, shall we? But you must come and help.'

Lily squatted down too, pulling out toys from the muddle in
the deep, low-level kitchen drawer, which made a frightful clatter. Nattie offered to make the coffee while saying it was really
time she left. 'You can't go yet, Mummy!' Lily wailed. 'You've got
my story in your bag and Kangy – and Tubsy's Pampers.'

'Don't be silly, the bag's for here. You're in charge of it now,
Lily, and helping Daddy lots, remember, and doing all we said.'

'I'm going to help you change Tubsy, Daddy,' she said proudly,
'and I'm going to be nice to him too, and not fight.'

'I will need lots of help, angel,' Hugo said. 'It's wonderful to
have you here and . . .' He was distracted. Thomas had unearthed
his favourite police car with the flashing lights and siren; he had
his finger stuck on the siren button and the sound, like the scream
of brakes and clashing steel of a violent car crash, was driving in

daggers of pain. Hugo put his hands to his aching head, feeling close to throwing up. 'Just nipping to the john,' he mumbled and made it to the downstairs loo. He managed a thin dribble of bile and broke out into an all-over cold sweat; his hands trembled as he splashed water onto his face. Dabbing it dry, wincing at the touch, feeling overcome with misery, he flushed the chain for cover and went back.

'I've dug out that percolator Thermos we never remembered to use,' Nattie said, eyeing him. 'The coffee should stay hot and you'll have some on the go for the morning, if you need. I'll have a quick cup then and be off. You'll be okay with them?'

'Sure, why ever not?' he said curtly, resenting her patronising tone, irritated by her knowing how much he needed the coffee. Didn't he really want her to see the state he was in, though? Didn't he want to touch her conscience and trade on her soft heart?

'Jasmine's all set to come to do supper and bath time,' Nattie said. 'She'll babysit too, if you need her to, if she can bring her boyfriend Pete along. I, um, took an executive decision and told her to come about half five, but I can always change that.'

'No, don't, it's fine,' Hugo said, a bit too quickly. He didn't want to seem to be longing for help. He worried about coping with lunch; better go out somewhere.

'I'm sure you'll be glad to have Jasmine around for an hour or two,' Nattie said, pressing down on the plunger and pouring coffee into two bright yellow mugs, 'helping at bath time. And ...' She looked up. 'I hesitate to ask this, but Mum and William are in London tomorrow and they'd love you to bring the children for Sunday tea. Perhaps, if it fits, I could pick them up from over there instead of here at about six? Don't forget Lily's Kangy, though, and the stuff in the bag. Anyway, how does that sound? I'd understand if you'd rather not.'

'Fine, good idea.' Hugo was sipping steaming black coffee, only half absorbing what she said.

Lily screwed up her face. 'I must have Kangy. We can't leave him behind.' She looked close to tears. Hugo tried to sharpen up and concentrate.

'I'll text to remind Daddy, promise,' Nattie said, kissing her. 'Bye, honeybuns, be good children. See you tomorrow at Granny's house.'

He saw her to the door like seeing out a friend, the plumber or electrician. He couldn't bring himself to kiss her cheek, his breath would be so bad. Lily was between them and he was jiggling Thomas too, who was still grizzling, holding out his arms to go to Nattie. It pierced Hugo's heart.

He closed the door behind her and wandered back into the kitchen with Lily, still trying to jolly Thomas into a smile. 'How's my lovely boy then? We're going to have a great day.'

'Now will you look at my story?' Lily demanded, skipping and dancing around. 'Can I have a drink? Tubsy has one too, in the mornings. And we have bits of dry mango or rice biscuits, usually.' Hugo felt panicked, sure there wasn't any of that sort of stuff in the house. He didn't know where to look, it was ages since he'd been left in charge. 'They're in here, on the middle shelf, I think,' Lily said, going to the larder cupboard next to the fridge, 'only I can't reach.'

'I'll get your drinks in a mo,' Hugo said, desperate for more codeine, 'just need to pop upstairs. Keep an eye on your brother for me, my little helper, then we'll sit at the table and you can show me this story of yours. Thomas will need a little attention, of course.'

'You just give him another chew, Daddy – you know that.'

Hugo returned, found the plastic mugs, sorted the drinks and eats. He left Tubsy in his high chair with another piece of mango and faced looking at Lily's Ahmed-inspired story. She laid the pages out in a row. An A4 cover page, two further pages. The title on the cover page, JIMMY THE GIRAFFE, was in big bold multi-coloured capitals, professionally printed in a way that had allowed her to colour in the letters.

BY LILY DANGERFIELD was suitably spaced underneath.

'Dan says having my name on the cover tells everyone it's a story all by my own,' Lily said. 'He helped me a very little bit, but only with the ending, Daddy, only about the tree sur ... people. And I chose the name, Jimmy, on my own too. We do the drawings on Dan's computer with a speshul programme and then I colour them in. Dan said a blue giraffe is very *original* – which means sort of unusual, he said – and he said my brown markings on the blue looked very smart. Do you like them, Daddy, and my colouring-in? Is it a good story?'

Lily was looking at him with huge round honey-brown eyes, her mother's eyes. Hugo swallowed hard and contained his anguish and fast-seeding jealous hatred. 'It's a wonderful story, darling,' he said, with a loving smile, clearing her hair from her eyes, 'and beautifully coloured in, clever girl. I'm a very proud daddy.'

'I haven't thought up another story yet,' she said, getting down to skip round the kitchen table, 'but I will soon. Can we go out now? Our old buggy is still here, Mummy said. We've got a new one at our other house – lots of new things.'

After his struggle through the day, Jasmine couldn't have come sooner. Hugo had just about coped; his seething jealousy had been fortifying. Lily, chatting freely, happily, about Dan this and Dan that – Thomas too, with his 'Dan, Dan, Dan', which sounded like 'Dad, Dad', but wasn't – was a far greater agony than any physical pain, yet the vicious resentment burning him up had helped to lift him out of a defeatist, self-pitying slump. His need to weaken Ahmed's insidious influence was overwhelming. He could think of nothing else.

Jasmine had just left. She'd seen herself out, leaving him to give Thomas the bottle she'd prepared, which wasn't proving an easy task, especially with Hugo's desperate need of a stiff drink. Thomas was restless, missing his mother's arms; she was softer, smelled sweeter, had a more familiar way to hold him. But he smiled up at his father once snugly poppered up in his sleeping bag and settled in his cot.

Hugo read to Lily next and was rewarded with her special arms-round-his-neck goodnight hug. He gazed down at her before leaving; her eyes were closing, she was on her side and so sweetly cuddling her raggedy kangaroo that he felt too emotionally loving to be distracted by bitterness.

The loathing was back again once he was downstairs and fighting to resist a second large neat whisky. He mustn't, couldn't let his children down, couldn't be incapable if they cried in the night. He nursed his misery and hate instead. Ahmed was influencing them, amusing them, manipulating them, but what in hell's name could he do about it? Determination turned into despair. He didn't have Ahmed's quick mind, couldn't draw giraffes on his computer, wasn't a bloody sainted hero. His wife didn't love him enough to stay.

His need of whisky was dementing. He remembered Nattie putting whisky in the soup and found a single tin of consommé in the cupboard. He heated it up in a mug in the microwave and slugged in as much whisky as he dared. He hadn't eaten all day. They'd stayed home, he couldn't face taking the children to a restaurant, and the meaty, oniony smell of the ready-made frozen lasagne heating up had put him off. Feeding Thomas was a full-time job anyway. Amazing Nattie wasn't half starved with the difficulty of ever getting in a mouthful of her own.

She'd cooked him eggs that horrifying night as well ... Hugo made himself an omelette, taking treasured sips of his laced soup while he did, the fiery burn of alcohol reviving him by the minute. He toasted some stale bread and ate hungrily. He decided to do a food shop next day with the children, after a turn in the park; the supermarket was open from eleven o'clock on Sundays if he'd remembered right.

He slept. Hadn't expected to, managing on just one more whisky, and only woke when Lily came running in. He had a faint residual headache, but felt a comparatively new man. It was a better day. Lily and Thomas enjoyed going shopping, Lily telling him what she wanted for lunch, fish fingers and chips. They ate a great many chips smothered in tomato ketchup and very little fish – Nattie wouldn't have approved.

They were excited about going out to tea. 'Can we cook some fairy cakes to take Granny and Gramps?' Lily said, her eyes shining expectantly, tugging on his arm.

'I don't know about that,' Hugo said, playing for time. 'Um, don't you think Granny will have done some baking and be a bit disappointed at being upstaged?'

'What does upstaged mean?'

'Your fairy cakes being better than hers – and when she'll have worked so hard doing tea for us all.'

That saved the day. Lily looked smugly mollified. She didn't even complain when Hugo took the chance to mention going to his parents' one weekend soon. He hadn't faced telling them about the break-up yet, too sodden and lacking the strength to pick up the phone; surviving at work had taken all his energy, staying compos, getting through the week. One day at a time.

He was looking at his watch, about to round up the children and set off for tea when the doorbell rang. Sure to be the Seventh Day Adventists or some ex-inmate thrusting a card, selling dusters and ironing board covers. He would have left it, but Lily was shrieking, 'It's the doorbell, Daddy!' which would have been overheard.

Amber was on the doorstep. He went cold, so surprised that he almost forgot to hide his shock and supreme irritation.

'Don't look so gobsmacked.' She laughed. 'I was on my way back from my mum's and a bit worried how you were managing with the kiddies. It's hard at the best of times, getting through a break-up, and you've taken it bad. I mean, what could be rougher, walking out like that and leaving you in the lurch?' Amber said, with a grimly satisfied expression. 'You look like you're pulling through, though. Mr Handsome again! Aren't you going to ask me in? Any chance of a cuppa then, lover-man?'

Lily had come into the hall; she was hovering behind him, probably staring at Amber wide-eyed. Had she heard that last bit, even about being left in the lurch? She was sure to have got the gist. The damage was done. And he had no out. And Hugo was well aware, after the last week at the office, of just how much he owed Amber. Chances were he'd have lost his job if she hadn't bailed him out.

'Sorry!' he said. 'Come on in. I'm afraid it's a five-minute cuppa, though. We're due at the grandparents' for tea.'

'Nice surprise, though, I hope. Is that your parents? Don't they live out of town?'

'No, it's actually the other lot. Do you mind coming into the kitchen? My young son needs a constant eye.'

'So this is your little girl?' Amber smiled at Lily in a slightly obnoxious way. 'She looks like you, Hugo – a stunner. And this young man too, just a bit chubbier.'

'We call him Tubsy,' Lily said, ''cause he's tubby and eats so much.'

Hugo held on with difficulty, hating every minute with a deep, desperate passion, but he somehow managed to keep his cool and busied himself putting the kettle on.

Thomas didn't seem too happy with the invasion either. He got to his feet to run to his father but tripped, not for the first time, and fell forwards onto his head. He began to scream loudly, which he seldom did after a tumble. Lily went to him, still being the little substitute mother, but Thomas's yells reached such a crescendo that she gave a helpless shrug of her shoulders, imply-ing, a little impatiently, that this was beyond her pay grade. Hugo picked him up and cuddled him.

'There, there, old man,' he soothed, willing Amber – over Thomas's blond head – to just get the message and go. He furi-ously minded her being there, standing so close, touching his arm, giving knowing glances and giving Lily ideas.

He tried to make the tea holding Thomas, who was still screaming. Amber moved to take him over, but Hugo held on tight. 'Can you get two tea bags out of that jar?' he said, with rare firmness. 'He'll settle soon but, I hate to say this, we really need to go in a few minutes. Sorry.' Why hadn't she called, texted – anything but turn up unannounced? She was so thick-skinned.

She plonked herself down at the kitchen table, first clearing away the remains of lunch, and they got through a hurried cup of tea. Hugo sensed Lily taking in every bloody tactile gesture, every word of insinuating chat. He could imagine her reporting back to Nattie, 'A lady came round, I think she's Daddy's new girlfriend!' Shit, shit, shit.

He got Amber to the door, opened it encouragingly, but she stayed her ground. 'Are you on your lonesome tonight, lover-boy? Come round, I'll cook supper. Do you good, a little cosy relaxing after the weekend you've had.' Hugo had a moment's hesitation, dreading the long lonely evening. Parting with the children, facing Nattie, returning to an empty house. Meaningless sex with Amber wouldn't help, wouldn't lessen the agony; it could only make matters worse.

'Thanks, but it's no can do, I'm afraid.' He put on his best rueful face. 'I've fixed to see an old mate, straight on from the in-laws' tea party. Sorry about having to rush. See you.'

Amber had caused tension enough, but his nerves were building again. Tea with Victoria and William, even with the children for cover, would be a concentrated strain. Then came the pain of seeing Nattie. Hugo felt it ever more keenly, even the smallest contact; she'd texted about not forgetting Kangy, which had driven home the stark truth of being separated still more. He should never have bought those two more bottles of whisky out shopping, but he was going to need them that night.

He remembered Shelby calling a while back, phoning out of the blue and making contact. He'd been chatty, easy, charming as ever. 'Give me a bell sometime, when the mood takes you,' he said, signing off. 'Let's have a drink.'

It was typical of Shelby, being so confident that Hugo would be delighted to hear from him again. Shelby's gall had to be experienced to be believed; he always got what he wanted. He'd had a life of being indulged by his rich, entrepreneurial father and glamorous actor mother who was Irish and wild and adored him. Shelby never stuck at anything, he simply used his flashy, black-haired, blue-eyed glamour-pants looks to get out of scrapes and make money in more dubious ways. Dealing in drugs.

Shelby had stolen Nattie from him in those early days, but he hadn't stolen her heart. That had been down to Ahmed. He was about the only man ever to get the better of Shelby, which must rankle deep.

Would it be supping with the devil to share a few shorts with

Shelby? Why not? Hugo could see little harm in it. Shelby had pushed dope at a party, got him onto cannabis, coke and more, though Hugo had to concede that he had only himself to blame for his full-blown addiction. And Shelby had done time for his dealing, after all: he couldn't be back at it, surely?

He'd be company, he was always gossipy and fun. Hugo felt he might even find Shelby in on a Sunday night. He was quite taken with the idea of calling him up – and he'd be honouring what he'd told Amber, which was satisfying in its small way. It was either that or home to black loneliness.

25

Moving On

Ahmed looked at his watch. Nattie would text any minute; it was almost time to collect her. He'd been running her to and from work for the last couple of weeks. *Girl Talk*'s offices were close, but inconveniently placed for public transport. She was going to start cycling in next morning. 'It's crazy, dragging you away from your desk like this,' she said. 'I expect I'll give in if it's pouring, but only then.'

He hadn't argued. She was probably better off biking than being with him in the car, unlikely to be recognised, head down, helmet on.

Nattie was safe enough, out and about, taking the children to the park, especially with her beautiful hair tucked up into that awful woolly beanie, but Ahmed wanted to have a weekend away with her when Hugo took the children to his parents'. The idea of some quality time together had taken hold. She'd be less on edge with her parents-in-law there to keep an eye and Ahmed felt she needed a proper break. He did too, fed up with being cooped up indoors all day, and he'd thought about it a lot.

Could they chance it? If he took every precaution, chose some sleepy seaside town ... It was irresponsible, sure, but the odds on being seen by the wrong pair of eyes while mooching about on the south coast in early November seemed on the whole pretty thin.

Nattie texted and he picked up his coat. Jasmine was back from the school run, sorting the children out with a snack, and he looked in on the kitchen. 'Hi, guys, I'm off for Mum now. How was school, Lily? Good day?'

'We're learning French! *Je m'appelle Lily.*'

'Wow, great stuff,' he said, a bit absently. 'Tell us all when we're back.'

He drove off, enjoying his own domesticated image. He'd felt it was as much a trial run of family life for him as a trial separation for Nattie, and he was managing fine. He'd become used to sharing the house with Jasmine and Thomas on Nattie's workdays; he'd play with Thomas for a bit then potter off with a Thermos of coffee to do a morning's work. He had lunch with Thomas, and Jasmine insisted on cooking him proper meals. It filled her morning, he could see, and he certainly had no complaints, after living on junk food for weeks.

He turned onto the narrow street of warehouses, his waiting place for Nattie, and switched off, grinning to himself, alone in the car. Jake's help, Mrs Cruikshank, who'd looked after them both at the Brixton flat, came on Tuesdays and he'd overheard Jasmine chattering to her the day before.

'He's sweet with the little ones,' Jasmine said, 'he makes them laugh. I must admit I had me doubts, but they're happy and that's what matters. I mind me own business about other people's affairs, but who'd have thought she'd walk out on that hubby of hers? He's a dish, Mary, her hubby. Looks like, you know, that actor, Tim Huddleston. But he's a right mess without her, I can tell you, drinking hisself into the ground.'

'Tom Hiddleston,' Mary Cruikshank had corrected, which Ahmed suspected had passed Jasmine by. 'She and Dan were together before, you know,' Mrs Cruikshank said, 'before she was ever married. She was at the flat, times when I did for Dan. Very in love they were then.'

Mrs Cruikshank was one in a million. She was keeping his cover; however she was old, and it might be easy for her to get muddled. Ahmed hoped she wouldn't slip up.

He waited with the car steaming up in the deserted side street, beginning to worry. Nattie was late. He jumped when the passenger door opened suddenly, his nerves on edge, and his heart started up too, when she leaned over, a bit out of breath, to kiss him.

'Sorry! A late long email came in that I wanted to answer straight off. It was from Sadia Umar and she was waiting on any word from me.' Nattie had told him about the girl – he'd read her novel and been impressed – being out in Pakistan, trying to find a way to save her sister from a forced marriage. 'It's sure to be a doomed mission,' Nattie went on, 'and it upsets me no end.'

'What was she emailing about?'

'Her sister was going to try to steal her own passport from under her stepfather's nose tonight and Sadia was sick with worry, wanting me to be reassuring and tell her that she shouldn't be trying to stop her. I hope I'm right, but I've said all along that it's worth any risk, the chance of having her freedom.'

Ahmed knew the scene only too well, and he tried to prepare the ground. 'It's hard for you and me to understand,' he said, feeling a bit disingenuous, 'but the pressure being put on the sister will be more out of deeply held beliefs than deliberate cruelty. I know family honour is taken to selfish and often horrendous extremes, but to the strictly observant, the whole system depends on conformity, marrying off girls appropriately and keeping them in the fold.'

'To think of the stepfather waking up, it makes me feel faint with horror ... What about your sisters? Did they get to choose their husbands?'

'They didn't test the system, but my parents adjusted anyway, moved with the times, more or less. Arranged marriages still carry on here, of course. I knew people in the community, lawyers, accountants, doctors, whose parents did the choosing and the marriages have worked, in the main.' Ahmed slipped her a grin. 'But it's not for me.' He drew up outside the house. 'We're here now – and Lily's learning French!'

It was Saturday already, one of Nattie's weekends with the children. 'It's such a joy,' she said, nuzzling up, 'seeing you with the children.'

'They're great. Full of surprises, keep me on my toes.'

They really *were* great. He loved watching their characters forming and developing by the day, loved them as his own already, with their unnerving ability to pitch camp in his heart. If only Nattie could relax. He sensed her endless fretting about whether Hugo would survive his weekends without the children – like this one; whether he was drowning in drink or spaced out of his mind.

Nattie's distress was hard to take. When the love was there – and theirs had stood the test over seven years – surely everything else fell into place? They could have a stimulating, fulfilling life together, Ahmed knew, children of their own. Was she going to feel this torn and responsible, worried and beholden to Hugo for ever?

She would be denying him a life's happiness too. Could he push that? He knew her too well; trying to influence her would have the opposite effect. There must be no heavy pressure, no pleading. No whingeing about what it would mean to him to lose her now that they'd found each other again.

Nattie's decision, unlike Sadia's sister's, had to be hers alone. She was strong, serious, responsible, but once she'd decided, whichever way she fell, he knew there'd be no changing her mind.

Suppose she went back to Hugo. There could never be another Nattie. Life without her would be unthinkable, unendurable, and not to have Lily and Thomas around to love and tease and entertain ... Ahmed was confident he could open their young minds to so much. They were receptive, he could bring them on, stretch and encourage them. He was getting morbid. It wouldn't do. But he loved the children, they mattered to him; he wanted them always in his life now.

He could pay for Hugo to come out to California to see them. Should he tell Nattie that? But it would be additional pressure and only draw attention to Hugo's plight.

It was no good, and not in his nature, this defeatist thinking. He loved Nattie and he was right for her. However long it took, however many bumps and twists and disappointments, he had set his heart on marrying her and one day he was going to do so, come what may.

26

A Visit from Jake

Lily's eyes were closing. Nattie kissed her cheek, whispered, 'Sweet dreams,' and tiptoed to the door. She was feeling every sort of emotion: welling love, naturally, and disbelief. It was a constant marvel to her that Ahmed had returned, that he was even alive – and to have been living with him now for almost six weeks seemed unreal. Guilt and anguish about Hugo never left her, but nothing could snuff out the conscious bliss of every hour of every day spent with Ahmed.

It was Saturday. Tom was coming round for supper – alone, since Imogen was on hospital duty – and a happy evening lay ahead with her stepbrother and the man she loved. The children seemed outwardly settled and fine. Lily adored Ahmed, no question. She hung on to his hand, hugged him at bedtime, kept him up to the mark with all her questions. And Thomas too, was pouring out new words at seventeen months, which Ahmed understood even if Nattie didn't. His love of her children was genuine. He was hooked. It was difficult to know how much Lily missed her father. She was always more subdued after seeing him, but that was inevitable, wasn't it?

Nattie knew she and Ahmed were living in a bubble, floating about like fairy people, she thought, as she went along the landing to her bedroom. The realities of life would soon call time. She was under no illusion; bubbles exploded with a silky pop and decisions had to be taken. She went into the bathroom and stared at herself in the mirror, worrying about tired lines on her face. Organising meals, running after toddlers, sorting children's squabbles, was she ageing before her time? She combed her hair, washed in a rush that morning, no blow-drying, and stopped thinking wistfully about all the time her single friends could spend on themselves. She wouldn't swap with them for the world. Ahmed had a knack of smoothing away tired lines.

She sprayed on a splash of scent, turned to go and hesitated; she had things on her mind, Hugo in her thoughts, and didn't feel ready to go downstairs. It was his turn to have the children next weekend, from lunchtime on Friday too, since he was taking them to stay with his parents. For once Nattie didn't mind. Hugo's parents were a comforting safety net and she could ease up – unlike that first terrifying time she'd left the children in his charge.

Her father, Barney, was an alcoholic. Nattie had memories of some violent, frightening scenes, and they'd been in the forefront of her mind when she'd seen the state Hugo was in, arriving at the house for the handover that first morning. She'd been shocked. Hugo had been hardly able to see or speak, let alone look after two small vulnerable children, and she'd almost felt desperate enough to keep them with her, whatever ructions it would cause.

She had phoned Jasmine, begged her to go early in the afternoon and call when she left. Jasmine had clearly been shaken, but after much discussion and cluck-clucking – whether at Nattie for leaving or disapproval of Hugo was hard to say – she'd managed to get across that Hugo was just about surviving and unlikely to drop Tubsy on his head or put whisky in Lily's apple juice.

He'd looked slightly revived next day as well, when she'd collected the children from her mother's. He'd been quite friendly on the doorstep, but then Victoria had been beside him and Nattie had seen beyond the chat, seen the pain and agitation in his eyes. He'd stared at her like a doomed, desperate prisoner-of-war, begging for reprieve. She sensed he'd actually wanted her to see him that way.

It had got better, she told herself. He'd been more in control on later weekends, hadn't seemed quite as abjectly desolate. She imagined – he was certainly showing every sign of it – that extreme jealous hatred for Ahmed had clicked in, which made her sad and distressed. Still that same plaintive wretchedness reflected in his eyes, though, still his trembling hands, the palpable tension whenever she stood near. The tension cut two ways.

Time to go downstairs; she could hear Ahmed busy in the kitchen. He was no cook and she reckoned that the aroma of sautéing onions flooding the house was a cunning ruse to get her to hurry on down and take over. She smiled and went down feeling slightly guilty.

'I've been slaving over a hot stove down here like one of your actual house-husbands,' Ahmed complained. 'Not that I don't enjoy the role, just setting the parameters.'

'That's an induction stove, not hot at all. Okay, what are we doing for Tom, what am I taking over?'

'I wondered about a Spanish omelette? I found some cooked potatoes in the fridge. Or whatever you fancy making with the onions.'

'There are some steaks in the freezer. I'll sauté the potatoes and make some ratatouille – your onions won't go to waste.'

She assembled the cooked potatoes on a chopping board and

Ahmed reached round her for the knife, keeping her trapped in his arms while he chopped. She put her hand over his and stopped him. 'You'll do us both an injury. How about laying the table?'

Tom arrived. He tucked into his steak and spent all evening quizzing Ahmed about the putting together of a television series. He seemed fascinated. 'So what happens? I mean, you're here, battling away at future scripts, but surely, if there's filming going on, you're needed there. Don't scripts need constant tweaking? Don't storylines evolve?'

'Sure they do,' Ahmed said. 'I'm pushing my luck, being here, just about getting away with it, but only because it was all my original idea. There's a writing room out there, with ten bright brains beavering away on the scripts, and I should be in with them. I'll have to show my face sooner or later, but for the moment the moneybags bosses are humouring me. They're keen to keep me sweet.'

Nattie didn't pay much attention; she knew the scene and had private worries. She absorbed Tom's fleeting looks of soulfulness, her intimacy with Ahmed putting Maudie in his thoughts, and she longed for Hugo to be as accepting and resigned. He was far from that, agonised, raw and bleeding.

Tom didn't stay late. Ahmed had been slipping looks that weren't difficult to read.

'You made that a bit obvious,' she remonstrated as Tom left. 'You could have tried harder.'

Ahmed grinned and gave her a kiss. 'I booked our weekend away while you were upstairs. I was saving up telling you – and impatient for a kiss or two.'

'So where are we going? Tell me.'

'Sidmouth. The Victoria Hotel there looks a splendidly stiff-backed sort of place, very jacket-and-tie, more for golfers and colonels than Islamist extremists, and a safe bet, I'd say. I feel dreadfully irresponsible putting you at risk, but it would be good to get away.'

'It's your safety that keeps me awake at night,' Nattie said. 'It'll be fine. And what could be better? Walks on a windy rainy beach in November and you!'

She wanted to get away for a number of reasons, not least the stress factor of Lily's party the following weekend. It made geographical sense to have it in the Queen's Park house, as most of Lily's little schoolfriends lived nearby, but that meant being with Hugo all day. Blowing up balloons, filling goodie bags, sandwich-making, carrot sticks, laying out tea, wrapping prizes. She and Hugo would be meeting and greeting, standing side by side, chatting to the parents for all the world like a happy cohabiting couple. Something was bound to go wrong.

Ahmed made more coffee and put on a CD. He loved cool jazz, Miles Davis, and they settled in, Nattie with her legs up over his on the kitchen sofa. 'Nobody at the office knows I've moved,' she said, worrying about the secrecy. 'I picked up some mail from the house last week. It's just as well I don't get much, I'm sure Hugo would never send any on.'

'Isn't it all circulars? Any office stuff would be on email, surely? I shouldn't give it a thought.'

She did, though. Friends emailed and texted, she had taken Tubsy to tea with those who had babies, but hadn't asked them back, just come up with excuses about work. She hadn't even told Maudie that she was on a trial separation. Oldest friend or not, Maudie couldn't be trusted not to talk. She'd ask way too many questions and want to come round to see Ahmed. No one knew, except Tom, her mother and William, Jasmine and Mrs Cruikshank too, and Hugo of course.

Nattie reached across the table for Ahmed's plate and caught his eye. 'Any news on when Jake might want his house back?'

'He's just emailed, funnily enough. He's coming over, flying in Tuesday, so we'll hear all the low-down – though he says things are going great so I don't think he's about to come back. Can we give him supper? Wednesday perhaps, he's only here the inside of a week.'

'I'll feel quite awkward, treating him like a guest in his own house. Do we have to take down the blinds and rehang Sylvia's curtains? And there's all the toys.'

She looked round the kitchen; the cutlery drawer was hanging open, piles of her work novels sharing the table, one splayed open on top of the fruit in the bowl. They both had iPads charging. Lily's artwork was pinned with a donkey magnet to the enormous silver fridge; there were other magnets too, a cardboard Michelangelo who had a variety of clothes to cover his manhood. They'd dressed him in check shorts and a black leather jacket that day.

'I've shared a flat with Jake, remember,' Ahmed said. 'He knows what to expect.'

Nattie biked to work on the Wednesday when Jake was coming to supper. She enjoyed the ride and they'd had a spell of bright weather, crisp and cold. She should have used the journey to plan that night's meal, only Hugo, or rather Amber, was on her mind.

'Has Daddy got a girlfriend?' Lily had asked, after a weekend with her father.

She'd talked very early on about 'a lady' coming round. Nattie could remember all her chatter exactly. 'We were nearly going to Granny and Gramps and Daddy told the lady that, but she came in for a cup of tea.' It had to be Amber, she was thick-skinned enough to turn up unannounced – and not Lily's favourite person if body language was any guide.

Ahmed was encouraged by the intelligence, but Nattie knew

that Amber wasn't the answer to their prayers. Not after Hugo's confession about Istanbul, his desperate drinking and recent bitter harshness, which had to be an explosion of extreme jealousy. Lily would have talked plenty about Ahmed, she was so full of him, and Tubsy too, with his 'Dan, Dan's' and all the new words. Hugo would be full of loathing.

Amber was good for a leg-over, probably helping him get by at work, with his drinking, protecting him from Brady. She was a top-flight PR executive, after all, and not unattractive.

Nattie parked her bike and went up to the office, dangling her helmet on her arm and pulling off her woolly gloves. 'You're looking a very happy bunny these days,' Ian said, as she reached her desk, 'sunlight shining out of your eyes. All your troubles behind you now?' He was so inquisitive and snoopy.

Nattie grinned. 'Must be my rosy cheeks with all this fresh air. I've taken to biking here.'

'What? Not all the way from Queen's Park? I call that keen.'

'Oh, it's not that bad.' She kicked herself for the stupid slip and moved on fast. 'I'm after a quick bit of cooking help, Ian. An old mate is over from Oz. He lives in Melbourne, which is very trendy and foody, I'm told, and we've got that late meeting today. What can I give him for supper that's classy and quick?'

Ian gave her a mildly suspicious look. 'I'd do a beef stir-fry with mushrooms and greens. Slosh in my favourite sauce – just a mix of oyster and soy sauce, two to one ratio – and some grated ginger, easy! Stir that in and you're done.'

It sounded perfect; Ian knew his stuff. Nattie was thanking him when her desk phone rang. She picked up the receiver grimacing, glad of an excuse to sign off.

It was Sadia. 'I'm back in England now,' she said, 'and just wanted to thank you for all your wonderful support. You kept me strong, I'd have lost my nerve without you.'

'What news? What happened?' Nattie felt embarrassed even to ask when it had been such an impossible mission. She dreaded hearing the worst and found herself holding her breath.

'We did it!' Sadia said shyly, but with an overlay of elation that she couldn't hold in. 'Alesha is here with me now and it feels like we're in one of those romance novels with a happily-ever-after ending. We'd love to see you and thank you in person if you can spare the time. We owe you so much.'

'Of course you don't, and of course I can spare the time. I'm longing to meet your sister and hear all about it. I expect you're in a whirlwind of literary events now you're back and I'm only in the office two days, but let's find a date. How's Tuesday week looking?'

They fixed to meet at a coffee bar near the office.

Nattie sat back, feeling stunned. However had they pulled it off? She remembered her interview with Sadia, the lunch they'd had in Bella Cucina, not least because it had been on the very day she'd found Ahmed's message in Drafts, over two months ago now. She'd blurted out an awkward mention of him at lunch that day and now, with Sadia's extraordinary coup, it was hard not to feel a sort of bond and superstitious connection. Would things go as well for her too?

Nattie had an extended afternoon meeting and by the time she biked home, Jake had already arrived. He was making Lily and Thomas's acquaintance. A lot of raucous giggling was going on.

Jake got up from his haunches and gave her an enveloping hug. 'Get *you*,' he said, standing back. 'Whatever you have to put up with from Ahmed, it suits you. I really hated leaving for Australia without having said goodbye, but you were with Hugo – you know how it is.'

She did. She smiled back at him, gazed happily up at his long lean face, blushing with pleasure. He was tall, lanky, had a good couple of inches on Ahmed. He had a generous mouth, crooked teeth — he'd missed out on an orthodontist, but they were part of the charm. Jake had the softest grey eyes Nattie had ever seen, the colour of a baby rabbit's down, the kindest, most expressive look in them too.

'There's so much I want to ask,' she said, 'but I must first get these two to bed. Have you seen loads of kangaroos?'

'You've seen a real, living kangaroo?' Lily was pink with excitement.

'Lots,' Jake said. 'They lollop across the country roads in Australia. There are road signs saying watch out for crossing kangaroos.'

'Can we go there, Mummy? I'd reely, reely love to see one crossing the road!'

'Australia is a very long way away and it's bath time. We'll have a kangaroo story in bed.'

Over the meal — Nattie took the credit for Ian's stir-fry — Jake got started on Australia. 'You have to come out. Melbourne's a buzzy place, with great food, packed restaurants.'

Ahmed grinned. 'It's California before Australia for us, I'm afraid. We're taking it one step at a time.' Nattie flashed him a look of *if only*.

The clock ticked on. They rehashed old stories and memories till the candles burned down.

Jake had little to say about Sylvia. She still wasn't pregnant. She clung to her mother in Melbourne and wanted to stay there. 'I'm seeing out the year,' Jake said. 'It's all great experience, so feel free to stay on here — the house is yours for another nine months.' He sighed. 'Australia's a terrific place, but my future's here in England. It's where I belong. Sylvia and I have a conundrum to resolve.'

It was good news about the house, but it hardly solved their long-term problems. Jake's were compounded by a floundering relationship, and could Ahmed keep working from afar, even going to and from California? Was he safe? The authorities wouldn't approve of his returning to England. Everything felt balanced on a knife-edge.

Jake had refused their repeated offers of a bed. He'd come over mainly to see his parents and was staying with them. Nattie hid her relief. Jake in the top-floor room that Ahmed was notionally using for appearances' sake would have been complicating.

'I should be going,' Jake said, rising, pressing on the table with his hands.

Nattie and Ahmed stood up too. 'I wish you didn't have to,' Nattie said.

He turned his grey eyes on her. 'I do too, believe me. But—' He broke off, starting a bit with the intrusive sound of Ahmed's mobile. It had very insistent chimes.

'Hank, Hollywood boss,' Ahmed mouthed, and took himself off to deal with the call.

Jake smiled at Nattie, holding out his arms. 'Goodbye hug?'

'I'm feeling quite emotional,' she said, as he enveloped her. 'I'm sad your visit's so short.'

'I'll be back,' he said, separating and holding on to her hands. 'Can't stay away for long.' He stared at her steadily and the expression in his eyes was hard to read.

'What is it?' She felt apprehensive, slight collywobbles.

'I worry about you, Nattie, love. It's a huge decision, cutting ties, all the responsibility you'd have to face. Think very carefully, won't you? Don't be too hasty.' He gave her another quick hug and stepped back, looking slightly abashed. 'I know you won't, though. I'm truly not coming on heavy, don't think that. It's just . . . a need to share the load, I guess.'

She blinked hard, feeling shaken and confused, a little put-upon too, which she knew was unreasonable. She looked down, suddenly brought close to tears, seeing Jake's gentle look of concern.

'You're a wonderful friend,' she mumbled, looking up with a watery smile, 'and sharing the load cuts both ways.' Jake was probably feeling worn down by his depressive wife. 'We're here for you,' she said, adding, hearing Ahmed on the stairs, 'come back soon, won't you.'

27

A Weekend Away

Nattie was early at the school gates. She waited in the car with Tubsy singing 'Tommy Thumb' incessantly, kicking the back of the passenger seat. 'Daddy's coming very soon,' she said, straining round, impatient to have the stressful handover behind her. 'And then you're off to stay with Grandma and Pa.' She had everything ready, Lily's packed 'Hello Kitty' bag, all Tubsy's kit; his travel high chair that bracketed onto a table. She'd prepared food for the journey.

Hugo's car pulled up. He knew the Ford now and came over. She got out, he kissed her cheek, stood back a bit and stared. 'Any decisions?' he muttered. 'Do you know how long it is? How many more weeks do I have to wait.' She didn't answer. A three-month trial separation took them till mid-December, she had little over a month left before telling Hugo her final decision.

Did his pupils look dilated? There was an intensity about him that alarmed her. Was he using? Who was he seeing? She thanked God he was taking the children straight to his parents.

'How's my Thomas,' he said loudly, lifting him out and

swinging him high in the air. 'Whoosh, whoosh!' He was almost chucking him; Nattie felt in panic. 'Can we transfer all the kit?' she said, aware of inquisitive glances from other waiting mums who would be coming to their own conclusions.

The children soon rushed out with Lily dancing about, bouncy as ever. She slowed, seeing both parents, both cars. 'Daddy, Daddy!' she cried then, adjusting: 'Are we going in your car? Must we go to Grandma and Pa?' She made a face. Then she jumped around again, singing, 'It's my party next week, my party!'

Nattie hugged her and told her to be good. She then hugged Tubsy who clung to her and screwed up his face. 'No tears.' She kissed him. 'Be a very good boy for Daddy. See you guys then . . . Have a lovely time! See you Sunday.'

Back in Lambeth, Ahmed had everything ready and they were soon roaring off. The Friday traffic was constraining, but who cared? They'd never had a proper little jaunt together, apart from the time she'd taken him to stay with her grandparents. Ahmed had got on well with her grandfather, John, and Bridget too. Nattie imagined him seeing them again at Christmas, which was only weeks away.

She'd always had Christmas at her grandparents', with her mother and William and, once married, with Hugo and the children too. Would Hugo go to his parents' this year? How wretched would he be, not seeing the children on the day? She tried not to dwell on that, it was too painful to contemplate.

Her mind skittered back seven years. That time she'd taken Ahmed to her grandparents' had been after Shelby, the bastard, had talked to the press and exposed Ahmed to his enemies. She'd felt there were few safer places than staying with her mother's parents in Worcestershire. Thinking about Shelby made Nattie subdued. He'd gone inside for his dealing thanks to Ahmed and the *Post*, but had an ace lawyer and was out in no time. He still had the hefty score of his prison sentence to settle and she had a secret terror of him discovering about Ahmed's return.

They were soon clear of the heavy traffic, though the journey to Sidmouth took over three hours with squally winds and black rainclouds blocking out any moonlight. The vast bulk of the Victoria Hotel finally loomed. It was on high ground with immaculate lawns, Nattie could see in the floodlighting, and looked solidly turn-of-the-century. They were glad to arrive.

The doorman swept them in, eyeing Ahmed's handsome leather bag with interest. 'I can't think what you're doing with that weighty thing without wheels,' Nattie muttered, as a bellboy carried it up a flight of stairs.

'I like it. I like surprising sniffy doormen in smart hotels.'

Room 104 was tucked away at the end of a passage. 'It's perfect,' she said, looking round. The heavy mahogany cupboards and wide oval mirror looked period, from the time the hotel was built, and Nattie discovered a door out to a private balcony. 'But aren't you a bit off beam thinking we can melt into the mahogany furniture? We stick out like sore thumbs or pop stars here. Didn't you see the looks we got from those two old biddies going into dinner? One of the staff could even give a call to the local paper. Isn't that what happens?'

'I took care of that. Said I was writing about West Country hotels for an American publication – I named a Los Angeles rag – mentioned we were on honeymoon as well, and would really appreciate a little privacy. So that I could have you,' he said, scooping her up into his arms, 'on that big high bed, all the hours of the day.'

'Think of everything, don't you?' She relaxed into his kiss, which didn't stop there.

'We'll miss dinner if we don't get a move on now,' Ahmed said, 'and I'm starving.'

'I've just seen the chocolates and champagne. Is that your doing?'

'I tried to order a bottle, but they said it came with the de-luxe room. Not bad, a bit of luxe thrown in.' He popped the cork. 'A quick glass now and the rest later.'

She unpacked their few things, taking a few sips of champagne. It tasted too acid, sharp. Her fault, not that of the champagne. It had affected her that way before.

Ahmed wanted to eat, but she needed a moment of calm and opened the door to the balcony. It let in a wintry blast. She stepped out, the wind taking her hair, and leaned on the rail, buffeted, breathing in the salty air, haunted by the sound and rhythm of the distant waves. It soothed her irrational inner fears, the kind that went with loving too much, that Ahmed would tire of her. Suppose Hugo became a full-on crack-heroin addict again. How would she feel then?

Ahmed came out and stood with her. He captured her hair and held it, smoothed it back, stroked her cheek, her neck, and took her hand. 'You'll share any load?'

She nodded, smiled and went back inside with him. She mustn't be subdued. 'I've found a menu,' he said. 'Have a look. I'm going for quail and duck terrine, shoulder of lamb, and treacle tart with black pepper ice cream.'

'I'll have the trout. You'll have a paunch before you're fifty.'

'But I haven't got one now. Live for the moment, I say!'

It was what they were doing and Nattie smiled. She wanted to have the sort of talk that was best done in bed. Should she wait till Saturday night? Better just to let it happen, she decided, as they were shown to a table in the near deserted dining room. She'd know when it was right. They were the last diners and served speedily; the waiters were already laying up for breakfast.

Ahmed was in an ebullient mood. 'At least I'll be able to get you back to bed quickly,' he said. 'We've got an action-packed day tomorrow, wet windy walks on the Esplanade and dinner out in some cosy bistro where the waiter will be overcome by your beauty and say through a mouthful of gold teeth, "You have beautiful eyes, the eyes are the mirror of the soul."'

Nattie groaned. 'Spare me, please. That's hardly up to the snappy dialogue of *Shorelands*.'

Ahmed was mellow and relaxed as they went back upstairs, but he never drank too much. 'If you'd been brought up like I was,' he said, 'you wouldn't dare.'

He locked the door; they were alone, free of the world, and Nattie wanted to bottle the moment, the wonder of it, the rediscovery, and forget her fears for the future and what lay ahead. Her life was about to change.

In bed she snuggled into the dell of Ahmed's rounded shoulder. They had no need for words. His fingers caressed and began to trail lower, bringing her to a high point, and he buried his head in her breasts.

They made love slowly, beautifully, and as they lay together afterwards, fingers entwined, with a long day and the cares of a long week behind them, Nattie knew they were in perfect harmony. She felt an emotional lurch, all the same, and raised up on an elbow. 'Can I talk or do you want to go to sleep?'

He studied her with his deep dark intelligent eyes. The bedside light was on, there was no escaping that gaze. 'What is it?'

'I'm not sure. It's just that I did a pregnancy test yesterday.'

'And?'

'It seems I'm pregnant, having your baby.'

She lay back and stared ahead, unable to watch for his reaction.

Would he have seen in her face the dread of telling Hugo, her mother, of letting the pregnancy make the decision for her?

'Our child.' His tone was marvelling, without reserve, and he gave into an outburst of passion. 'Don't you see? It's what we're here for. To love, make babies, see parts of us carrying on beyond, the best bits. Our baby will set about civilising the world!'

'Are you always this flowery and highfalutin? We could breed a little monster.'

'You're such a pessimist. Well, maybe our children's babies, it might take a couple of generations.'

'It is past midnight, I think your little bastard seedling needs to get some rest.'

They wouldn't be making any decisions that weekend. Live for the moment. Nattie smiled as they walked hand in hand along the blowy Esplanade next day. She was only too glad to postpone any thoughts of location, practicalities, the extreme emotional upheaval.

The cliff at the end of the bay, a steep sheer fold of rock, was clear of an early-morning mist that had been thick as felt. Now, in the pale sunlight, the cliff was majestic and the pebbles on the beach glistened, washed by the receding tide.

They drove out into the countryside, down tree-lined lanes with the last lovely remnants of autumn leaves; it was a scene to match any New England fall, with chrysanthemum colours, fiery red, yellow and bronze. Over open land, plump clouds dawdled in a soft pink sky, casting shadows over fields of stubble, lemon and ochre brown.

'Our child,' Ahmed kept saying, rolling the words around on his tongue. He was in a state of elation, wonder – the happiest man alive. It was Nattie's dream, just as much as his, but her mood was tempered. There were so many hurdles ahead.

*

On Sunday they planned to take the journey back slowly, leaving at noon when they had to be out of their room. 'Let's stop for a bite at Lyme Regis,' Nattie said. 'It's just up the coast in the right direction and it's a great place. We can have fish and chips on the Cobb, the high historic wall round the harbour, and Lyme's the place for fossils too – remember *The French Lieutenant's Woman*? We can buy one for Lily, and home-made fudge to gorge on all the way home.'

Ahmed was zipping up his leather bag. 'Sounds good,' he said, looking over to her, 'as long as Lyme is as quiet and sleepy as Sidmouth. We're taking too many risks, Nattie darling. We'd have to do any shopping separately.'

'Don't be such an old worry-bags! Lyme's popular, a bit touristy, but it's well out of season and I know you'll love the Cobb. This weekend's going to live on in my mind and it would round it off wonderfully – for all three of us.'

That earned her a grin. 'Okay, you win this time. Lyme Regis it is.'

28

Back to the Past

The car park and the narrow main shopping street were busy. Ahmed felt anxious, crossing to go down some steps to the Cobb. There were few people about, though, as he and Nattie strolled round the harbour in the lee of the famous old wall. The harbour was sheltered and peaceful, dotted with boats laid up for the winter and bathed in a cool blue haze. He felt moved and emotional, wishing he could shake off a slight sense of something about to go wrong.

They had crab sandwiches and chips at a rickety table in one of the many eateries tucked into the wall. The aroma of frying fish mingling with salty seaweed and boating smells was evocative and Ahmed knew, as he held Nattie's hand under the table, that he would never forget this place. He'd never known such a sense of hope and happiness.

'Time we were going,' he said. 'We can't be late back.'

'Pity,' she sighed, 'but you're right. I told Hugo I'd come for the children at half six and I've got to pick up the Ford. Getting across London takes time too.'

Ahmed nodded. He was keen to be off, still feeling an

instinctive wariness, which he supposed was inevitable, given his state of euphoria. Nattie was having his child. He worried about all the Sunday shoppers he'd seen, too many for safety, and they had to cross the busiest area on the way back to the car park. Lyme might be out of season, but it was far from dead. Young marrieds pushing buggies, retirees, loitering youths – the town was doing good business and had a buzz.

'We must do our bit of shopping,' Nattie said, slipping her hand into his.

They were approaching the main street and he broke away with a quick apologetic smile. 'We do need to do it separately,' he said. 'You get the fudge and something for Tubsy,' he pressed a couple of twenties into her hand, 'and I'll find a fossil for Lily. You've got your phone? I'll text when I'm going to the car, but give it time for me to have the engine running and be all set to get straight off. You okay with that?'

'Sure, but isn't this a bit over the top? I understand about room service last night, not taking chances with waiters, but aren't we safe enough, mingling in the Sunday crowd? I want to be with you and we're just doing a bit of shopping.'

'I don't want us seen together, Nattie. Please understand how important it is.'

She wrinkled her nose, muttered ridiculously about the money, saying that he could at least let her buy a bit of fudge, but she set off independently, prepared to accept he was right.

Ahmed waited a few minutes before following. His nerves were working overtime; he had a telepathic scent of danger which was unsettling, making him edgy. He'd had those feelings before.

He went into the first fossil shop he came to and was charmed by the elderly owner who had an obvious love of palaeontology and delight at a genuine customer. A couple of mothers in the shop were hustling out whining children, empty-handed. Ahmed left with two fossils in a brown paper bag and descriptive notes on each. Lily would love them.

Stepping out, he saw a chic sweater in the window of a boutique across the road. He liked the look of the sweater with its dark navy and biscuit stripes – and the tan leather skirt it was teamed with as well. They'd suit Nattie perfectly. He had little chance to shop for her except online and wouldn't be holding her up. He'd spotted her queuing in a busy fudge shop as he hurried by.

As he crossed over to the boutique, instinct caused him to half turn and he knew he'd been seen. He had them in his spatial vision, two men outside a café, one drawing on a cigarette, probably a waiter, and the other, a visiting cousin or brother, he suspected, who looked familiar. Ahmed sensed their cold black eyes focusing, hardening with malevolent intent. He was well aware of them moving away from the café wall, slipping in amongst the shoppers, coming steadily towards him.

A surge of fear overtook him and his thoughts slammed into gear with the speed of a racing driver out of the pits. The boutique was the safest bet. They wouldn't come in, they'd wait just outside, ready to slip a knife into his guts when he reappeared – then melt into the crowd as he slid to the ground. Did he call the police? What could he say? – that two men had looked at him suspiciously? Shit, fuck, why hadn't he worn his glasses, his built-up shoes, his Mr Bashaar button-downs and hideous jacket? Vanity. Being with Nattie . . .

He darted into the shop, its only customer, the prices putting people off. A studious-looking young assistant glanced up hopefully, in need of a sale, and he gave her his most disarming smile.

'That stripy sweater in the window.' He beamed some more. 'I'd love to buy it for my girlfriend – the leather skirt too, if by any chance you had it in a size ten.'

'That one's a ten, I'll get it out of the window,' she responded warmly, flattered by his smiles. He needed her to be on his side.

'And would you, if it's not too much trouble, be able to gift-wrap it, do you think?'

'I'll do my best,' she said. 'We have tissue paper and ribbon, and smart carrier bags.'

Ahmed could see the two men looking in the window, and stepping back out of view he began to text Nattie as fast as his thumbs would fly. *Red alert!!! Go to car park, unhurriedly, and wear beanie u shoved into yr bag. Drive out thru barrier and park on main road u turn onto, going out of Lyme. Keep engine running. Charm any fuzz. Beanie off 4 that!! Moment u see me coming climb over gear stick and curl into little ball where yr feet usually go. Darling, go now!!! Do it now!!!*

He looked up. The girl had the skirt and sweater draped over her arm. Ahmed paid, seeing her relief when his card was accepted, and watched as she began to wrap the clothes in tissue and tie round purple ribbon with meticulous care.

'I don't know how you can make it look so appealing and perfect,' he said, pulling out every charm stop he possessed. 'I wonder, could I ask another favour? My girlfriend's shopping somewhere opposite and it's such a beautifully wrapped present, I'd love to slip it to the car ahead of her and make it a complete surprise. Do you have a back door possibly? Would you mind if I went out that way?'

'Of course not, I'll show you.' She hesitated as two women came into the shop, but then pointed down a passage. 'It's just along there. The key's in the door.'

Ahmed thanked her profusely, dropping his fossil bag into the carrier that he'd tried not to grab with unseemly haste. His adversaries were peering in, clocking what was happening. They'd have a back way out too, through the café – they'd know the back-street geography. He prayed the alley or road behind ran parallel and came out near the car park. If it was a dead end that way, he'd end up dead too.

He opened the back door and legged it. He reckoned he had a 100-metre start. Only one guy was following. Had the other gone for a car? A motorbike? Ahmed pushed past a drunk with a dog and was spat at. Lucky the dog didn't share the same sentiments, he thought, shitloads of fear making him light-headed. He was panting in spasms, his heart feeling about to explode. He kicked at a parked bike, sending it crashing, blocking the alley and gaining himself a few seconds.

He should have told Nattie just to go, drive home. Shit, why hadn't he thought of that? He could have got to a train station, a police station.

If he made it to the car he'd tell her to drive on. But suppose she argued? Suppose he didn't make it? The alley actually came out into the car park. He couldn't believe his luck. He weaved in between the parked cars, ducked under the exit bar and pounded down the short steep lane that led to the main road out of Lyme.

Nattie was there with the car, but a policeman was too, beside the driver's window. Ahmed panicked, trying to imagine explaining to a local copper who was sure to think it an excuse. Shit, would it mean Nattie being seen by the guy chasing? Was he hard behind? Would she have time to duck down unseen?

Racing up to the policeman, he prayed for a lucky break. Nattie was waiting on double red lines. 'Terribly sorry, Officer,' he panted, trying to regain some breath.

'I was just explaining that you'd left something behind,' Nattie said, taking the chance to drop a hint. She was keeping well within the car. Ahmed raised his scrunched-up carrier in confirmation and pleaded with the copper. They'd had their children to collect, been in such a tearing hurry . . .

'So your good wife has been saying. I'll let you off this time, just this once.'

Ahmed thanked him excessively. Glancing back, he saw the copper approach a small white van that had drawn up at a discreet distance behind. He could see the two guys in it; one must have gone for the van. Ahmed memorised the numberplate. He willed the policeman to detain the men for a vital few minutes while Nattie ducked down. He opened the driver's door; she'd already climbed over, she was crouched down in the floorspace, passenger side, and he threw the car into gear. Roaring off, he saw the van doing the same, following, leaving the policeman standing. Would he put the word out? Get the van stopped? But that would take time. It was a wishful thought, Ahmed knew.

He was thinking fast while concentrating on speeding through the outskirts of town. The van would be souped-up. He knew about cars, with his father a minicab driver, knew all the wheezes. 'I'm stepping on it, Nattie, but I'm a good driver. Try not to worry, just stay down out of sight.'

He shot through a traffic light on amber, the van followed on red. He put his foot down, eyes skinned for any child running out between parked cars. He drove faster still on the open road, overtaking on bends, taking crazy risks. The Mazda was up to it, hugging the bends.

He swung right and left with no warning, back onto the main road. He tried to drive in circles, feeling the closer he stayed to Lyme, the more chance of the van being spotted – assuming the policeman had put out the word.

Was the van closing the gap? Shit, shit. He had to get Nattie out of this somehow, somewhere safe while he shook them off; he had to. He saw a big garage in the distance. It would have a shop, a wide turning area. If he went to a pump and Nattie raced out . . .

'I'm turning into a garage,' he said.

'But we filled up in Sidmouth – surely you shouldn't stop?'

'I'm going to a pump, not for petrol, for you to race out and into the shop. Call William, give him the van number, GK10TWL. Tell him to contact MI5 – he'll know how – and say they're after me. Wait in the shop and I'll be back or in contact. Call William again if there's no sign of me in half an hour – but I'll make it somehow. Go, darling. Now!'

She tumbled out and was in the shop with its shoppers and till queues, just as the van turned into the forecourt. Ahmed breathed out; her safety was all. The van drew up hard behind, expecting him to need to fill up, he hoped. He saw the man he recognised open the passenger door – preparing to come and discreetly slip a knife into his heart at the pump? Ahmed tried to time it right, waiting till the guy was out of the car before revving hard, swinging the car full circle in the turning area, and shooting off in the opposite direction.

The van was following, catching up. It would have a small tank. How long before it spluttered and lost speed? Hours? He was on the road back to Sidmouth. If he could make it to the hotel where he was known, he could order a car to pick up Nattie, take her to a station. Ten miles to Sidmouth – not many minutes, the speed he was going. He overtook a lorry on the brow of a hill. The driver flashed furiously and leaned out of his cabin shaking his fist. 'Fuck you! Fucking lunatic!'

The van overtook the lorry too. There was a great screeching of brakes, but it still kept following. They were on an open stretch. Was the van gaining on him?

Then it happened. Ahmed heard the bang. A miracle, too good to be believed; the van had burst a tyre. He saw it slew off the road, braking at such speed, and nosedive into a ditch.

He punched the air and set course for the garage, calling Nattie on the way. He'd done it, shaken them off, and without even a scratch on Jake's precious car.

Nattie felt in a state of nerves on the way back to London, however positive Ahmed was being and jollying her along. He'd been dicing with death and his calmness after such an experience left her in awe. His nerves were steel; he'd protected her, yet she was the one still in shock and wobbly. She was fearful of the chance of a miscarriage too, which would break both their hearts. To be having his baby was a wondrous longed-for dream, but she worried guiltily how it could have happened.

Had she got in a muddle, forgotten to take the pill? She'd had two cards on the go, stupidly, and hadn't been faithfully following the dates. But had that in fact been a kind of subconscious deliberate accident on her part? She genuinely didn't know. Ahmed hadn't asked questions, simply assumed it was an accident, she believed, the fates working in mysterious wondrous ways.

His reaction was her greatest joy, yet it threw what they'd just been through into even sharper focus. He couldn't stay in the country much longer now; they both knew that. And she knew it was time for some serious decision-taking.

As they reached the Chiswick roundabout he turned with a smile. 'Looks like we'll be in plenty of time for you to pick up the Ford and get to Queen's Park. You'll be there before Hugo's back from Oxford. That's not bad going, all things considered!'

29

Lily's Birthday Party

Hugo was on the A40, nearing London. He arched back his shoulders, impatient to be home and feeling badly in need of a drink. After the immense stress of the weekend, his parents' infuriating questions and sighs, he wanted to get home. He felt mentally and physically wiped. The children had worn him out too, but that was just from giving his all when every whoop and grin cracked the mask. His hands had been twitching, he gagged on the smell of the nappies, failed to put the lid of Thomas's spouted mug back on properly while he was feeding him.

'Not far now,' he called back behind him. 'I think Mummy's there already.' He'd glanced at her text at a traffic light. 'She says she's fine waiting, though.'

No response. Lily was bored and grumpy and Thomas was asleep.

It had been impossible to get away with two of his aunts coming to lunch, inquisitive, smothering him with sympathy and cooing over Lily and Thomas. He'd been saved from too many prying questions with the children there, had quite enough of those from his mother, but lunch had taken an age and with all the sidelong commiserating looks he'd almost lost it and let out a few expletives.

He drummed his fingers at another red light, still sore about his mother's inquisition. *She* hadn't been sympathetic like his aunts, no chance; she'd even tried to suggest he was to blame in some way, which was rich. She was never prepared to give him the benefit, always instantly assuming he was the one at fault.

'I just can't believe Nattie would walk out like that for no real reason, Hugo dear. You must have done something to upset her. She's such a good, kind, sensible girl. Some long-ago boyfriend coming back from abroad, she might want to see him and catch up, but to take the children and go? It doesn't make sense.'

The way she'd hesitated then, looking a bit uncomfortable. 'There hasn't been a girl, has there, Hugo? You haven't had an affair?' God, her look of shock, horror at the very idea, he'd had a job not to crack up.

Fucking typical of her all the same. Any truly caring parent would have instinctively taken his side. Why couldn't his parents accept that he was no great achiever and simply love him for what he was? Where was the warmth and spontaneity? He'd never felt more alone and loveless in his life.

Dad at least had been a bit more even-handed. 'It is only a trial separation, you say? I'm sure she'll be back. Stick it out, I would, stiff upper lip and all that.' What did his father know? 'Would you like your mother to talk to her? Tell her the state you're in?' Adam had seen the expression on his son's face, he'd let that drop. 'But for Christ's sake, Hugo, ease up on the bottle. All that wine and you've been at the whisky too, I see. I know this is home, but you could still ask. Take my advice. It's not going to solve anything and it's highly irresponsible too when you're on duty with the children all weekend.'

Hugo gave a sarcastic sniff. He'd hardly had a drop all

weekend; it was surprising his father hadn't locked away the whisky in the safe. He shifted tiredly in his seat, thinking ironically of how desperate he was for a stiff drink.

He wondered about his mother talking to Nattie; it had its attractions. Nattie deserved to be put through it, much as he cringed to imagine the conversation. Nattie would say charmingly it was only a trial separation, though, and for all the embarrassment it would achieve nothing. She knew the state he was in; she'd caused it.

'I need to do a wee wee badly, Daddy. Can we stop?'

'We're only minutes from home. Can you hang on, Lily, there's a good love. Count the days till your party!' He turned to smile and nearly crashed into the car in front. Jamming on the brakes woke up Thomas who started to wail, more loudly by the minute. Hugo tried every cajoling ruse to calm him. The last thing he wanted was Thomas bawling away when they arrived. Nattie would think he hadn't stopped crying since the handover at the school gates.

He turned the corner into the street. 'We're there, Lily, we'll have you inside in no time.' He saw the blue Ford parked outside the house, pretty basic as cars went – Ahmed wasn't making a statement. Was he pushed for cash? Hugo felt mildly cheered by the thought, though Nattie had never been motivated by money.

At that moment, Nattie got out of the car and smiled in his direction, brushing back her hair as the wind caught it. He loved her hair, its sweet-smelling softness, the sensuous feel of it against his cheek when her head rested on his shoulder, when she leaned over his body, hair grazing his stomach . . . it set every nerve in his body alight. And that smile, it was teasing, questioning, sexy, savvy – he'd never known anyone whose smile so exposed the person they were. And it was always focused; she knew how to direct it.

She waited while he parked and opened the car door for Lily, who raced along the pavement to the house. 'She's bursting for a pee. Can you get Thomas out while I let her in? You needn't have waited in the car like that,' he complained. 'You've got a key.'

He opened up for Lily and Nattie soon appeared on the doorstep with Thomas who was still grizzling, despite his father's best efforts. Nattie was carrying him, coaxing him into good humour. 'Who's just woken up then, grumpy old thing! It's nearly your bedtime. You can go back to sleep again just as soon as we're home.'

They were bloody home. Hugo fastened his eyes on her, but she set Thomas down and avoided eye contact. 'I'll leave him with you for a mo, if that's okay, while I transfer over the kit from your car. Then we must scoot off. It's quite late.'

Not his car, *their* car, he wanted to scream at her as he took Thomas's hand, *their* house, *their* home. Lily shot past him, still hitching up her pants. 'Hands,' he yelled angrily. 'You come back here!' She only wanted to run to Nattie and be gone, back to being influenced and indoctrinated by a thieving interloper, slipping off the noose of his love for her, his precious, beautiful child.

Hugo held her up to reach the tap; she splashed water and raced off without drying her hands. 'I want to ask about Moppet,' she yelled back, as he picked up Thomas and went after her, catching up in time to hear her eager questions. 'Is he all right, Mummy? Did you leave him lots to eat when you and Dan were at the seaside?'

'Lots! He's fine; we've been home and his little gold eyes were shining brightly in the dark. We really must go now. School tomorrow. Give Daddy a big goodbye hug.'

Hugo squatted down to Lily's level feeling searing jealousy. Nattie had told him she'd be away, a weekend in the West Country, she'd said, but he'd somehow assumed she was going to see her old friend from university who lived in Exeter. To think of her snuggled up with Ahmed in some seaside resort, a romantic, lovey-dovey weekend ... It was too much to bear. God, he needed that drink.

Lily flinging her arms round his neck and planting a kiss was reassuring. She smelled hot and peachy. His heart was breaking in two. 'Only six sleeps till your party,' he said, smoothing her hair.

'My party, my party,' she chanted, climbing into the car. 'Bye, Daddy, bye, bye!'

He waved after the car, went back indoors and poured himself half a tumbler of neat Scotch. He could do with a joint, he decided – anything to help with the hell of an empty house. Drink and dope were a good combo, relaxing taken together; Shelby's stuff was too high-concentrate without the slowing-up effects of the booze. Concentrated dope was too trippy – and what was the use of feeling hyped, alone in the house?

It was one thing to smoke it with Shelby, easier to pace himself and keep count of the joints. But too much at that potency on top of his black depression and he'd end up with a full-blown paranoia.

Would Shelby show up later? He'd said he would. It would depend on his sex life, probably, who he was seeing, who needed buttering up. Sex for Shelby had to be dual-purpose, a means to an end, pulling pretty girls who opened doors. Hugo wondered at him, being back dealing again, amazed he'd take the risk; mad, dangerous and bad. Shelby had brushed all that aside, saying with that sly appealing grin of his that he knew the scene – all the more so now – who to avoid, how to keep clear of the fuzz. He was only spreading a little pleasure, bringing people together, facilitating and taking a tiny cut.

Spreading a little pleasure. Hugo sighed. It was a whole lot more than that, it was a symphony in bloody space. He wasn't going there again, he'd told Shelby; he had two children and it was almost ten years on, he was old enough to know better. A bit of dope was one thing, he could handle Shelby selling him that, and liked the excuse to have the guy back in his life. They got on. Shelby manned him up, made him feel less of a fucking useless, wifeless wimp.

He quite enjoyed how opposite they were, Shelby with his nimble footwork, charming his way out of scrapes, the daredevil risk-taker; he had all the chutzpah and cheek that Hugo lacked. And Shelby hadn't saddled himself with two children and the millstone of being achingly in love with his wife. Hugo reached for the bottle. He would hold off a while with the spliff, see if Shelby showed up.

He sipped neat whisky, wallowing in misery and an immense sense of impotence while the mobile in his pocket burned a hole. Amber was waiting on a call. She was a bearable weekday fuck, a release of a sort, but it wasn't the night. After the stress of a weekend with his parents, seeing Nattie, handing back the children, all the pain, Amber would grate on his nerves like nails on a blackboard. He owed her a call, though; it had to be done.

'Hi! How're you doing? Mother okay? I hope you don't mind if I duck out tonight, make it tomorrow instead? My old mate Shelby is threatening to show and I'm pretty bushed, to be honest.'

'Hardly surprising after the weekend you've had. Tomorrow it is then, lover-boy, and you could bring some of that weed. We'll need a cheer-up if we haven't won through with Bosphor. We should hear this week, they've taken long enough!' She laughed, that loud, constant, jarring laugh of hers.

'See you tomorrow then,' he said, clicking off before she could prolong things. She was coming on too heavy, acting like she owned him, being excruciating in the office. He'd leaned on her, though, she'd helped him to survive, fuck it, and now he was paying the price. How in hell was he going to find a way out?

If they didn't get that Bosphor account he'd be toast. Winning mattered to Brady, it had got him where he was. He was a sophisticated player, he had the ideas, the breadth of vision. He'd built up Tyler Consulting, persuading clients that perceptions were real, and created an aura of being simply the best. Others had talent and ideas, but it was Brady's will to win that put him out front.

Hugo heard the ting of a text and glanced down. Shelby was minutes away.

He came in bearing a hulking great pizza in a box, which wasn't Hugo's favourite food and was oozing oil through the cardboard. 'I'm starving,' Shelby announced, 'not sure if I can share it with you. It's sex that does it. I'm always famished after sex. Swimming too.'

Hugo snorted. 'Don't tell me you potter along to your local baths. When was the last time you went swimming?'

'I had a nice little dip only last week as it happens – in the Bahamas.'

'How'd you swing that? Tell me in a minute. Come into the kitchen first. That box is dripping all over. Wine? Vodka?'

'Vodka tonic, ice and lemon. You'd better have some pizza, you look like no food has passed your pining lips in weeks.'

'Not sure I run to lemons.' Hugo went to the fridge. The only lemon was furry and blue with mould. How long had it been in the salad drawer? Two months? He held it up. Shelby flipped the swing-bin lid and he aimed it in. Shelby, he could see now, had an expensive-looking tan, quite the gigolo dandy in his uniform black jeans and black sweater. Easy to see why the girls fell for him with those Irish blue eyes and glossy jet-black hair. Ahmed,

Shelby, Nattie went for dark brooding looks. Perhaps, Hugo felt, he could have solved all his problems by dyeing his hair.

'Where did you get that pizza round here?' he said, watching Shelby pick off the pepperoni and put away a huge slice. 'It was still hot when you came.' Shelby had hardly touched his vodka; he always liked to be in control.

'I had it delivered to this girl's flat in Notting Hill, the Bahamas girl. She's a good find. Bit inverted – she likes to slum it, likes rough trade – but her daddy has a string of racehorses and the Bahamas estate. I made some useful contacts out there, all in the inside of a week. People who'll look me up when they're passing through or back from their hols. I know the users, who to approach.'

'Her daddy didn't mind hosting an ex-con boyfriend of hers, out there?'

'Do I look like a jailbird?'

'Amber likes your dope,' Hugo said, rolling a spliff. 'I took some over to her place, it helped blur the edges a bit. You could give her a call, chat her up. She's probably not into more than weed, though, too ambitious.'

He took a drag and passed the spliff over to Shelby. Was he going to buy more? It was only a bit of weed, he could trust himself. And Shelby would have some on him; why else would he come round with his dripping box? They went back a long way, all the same. Shelby may have walked off with Nattie, but they'd both lost out when Ahmed had come along.

'What do you rate the odds on kicking Ahmed off the planet?' Shelby asked, sensing his train of thought, which wasn't difficult. 'A trial separation is as vague as it gets. You didn't agree a time limit, did you? Are you just going to let it drag on?'

Hugo didn't answer. Nattie had said three months and at some stage she'd come to a decision, he knew – much as he dreaded what that would be. Ahmed had his enemies, but she'd never let fear of that stand in the way. She should do, he thought angrily. What about the children? Even her mother wasn't able to talk sense into her about that.

He knew Shelby was watching him, reading him, but so what? He didn't have to pretend or put on an act with Shelby, the relationship was in its own box.

'I suppose Ahmed must have a new name now, a new identity,' Shelby said idly, as though it was a passing thought. 'What's he called these days?'

Some corner of Hugo's addled brain told him to hold back a bit. Shelby had asked for a reason. He wanted to know and it wouldn't be for Hugo's benefit; everything he did was self-motivated. He didn't go in for passing thoughts.

'Nattie keeps his identity close,' Hugo said. 'She calls him Dan, but whether that's simply for the children's benefit, easier to get a handle on, I couldn't say.'

'Something less obvious, I guess. He'd be easy to recognise, of course, by the people who want his guts. Where are he and Nattie living? Is he renting or has he bought a place here, which would be risky, I'd have thought, even if he could get a mortgage. What part of London are they in?'

'He's renting from a friend, I think,' Hugo muttered, feeling uncomfortable. 'I'm not entirely sure where; she always brings and collects the children. The last thing I want is to go there. Weird to think I once rated the man and thought him a halfway decent bloke.' He didn't know what sort of trouble Shelby could make, but couldn't believe it would help. Shelby's hatred of Ahmed wasn't from jealousy, it was visceral; he wanted revenge.

They smoked a bit, exchanged gossip and smut. Hugo described his Cupcake Corner coup; Shelby had seen the mentions in the columns and earmarked the model as possible talent.

Hugo told him to call up Amber, she'd have the contact details, he said eagerly, clinging to a vain hope of Shelby hooking in Amber and getting her off his back. A lost cause, probably; he didn't see her being Shelby's type.

He sensed Shelby tiring of the evening, having extracted out of it what he could. They did the deal over the weed and Hugo walked him to the door, impatient suddenly, for some ill-defined, but Nattie-related reason, to have him out of the house.

Alone again he wrapped himself up in his depression, cuddled it like a comfort blanket and reached for the whisky bottle. Another week, Amber to deflect, the Bosphor Air decision on which his job, his very survival hung. Brady was wise to his drinking, Hugo was sure. He had another chance to see Lily and Thomas on Saturday, there was that to look forward to, but he and Nattie would be side by side, preparing for the party. She'd be there, close, her scent reaching him. How was he going to cope?

They would have to play-act in front of the other parents, yet more stress, and Victoria was coming; she would be anxiously watching for signs. She wanted them back together again almost as much as he did. Some hope. Nattie was living with the fucker, she'd never change course now.

On Wednesday Nattie had her first bout of morning sickness. She had seen a doctor as a temporary patient first thing Monday and had the pregnancy confirmed, Ahmed's baby, their baby. She woke that day feeling queasy and wasn't yet over the terror and horrors of Sunday's drama in Lyme. She was jumpy, worrying about who the two men would have been able to contact. They'd been taken in for questioning, William had ascertained. It seemed both were related to one of Ahmed's enemies who was still inside, and enough incriminating material had been found on their devices to bring charges. That was a relief, but Ahmed was known to be in the country now.

Nattie dragged herself into work feeling rotten. She was tired all day, gagging on the smell of somebody's takeaway, and when the sub-editor came up to her desk, sipping a steaming café latte, she had to make a dash for the loo. In the middle of the afternoon? Morning sickness was a misnomer. It was worse than anything she'd had with Lily and Tubs. Vomiting was one more stress factor to contend with too. Suppose it happened at Lily's birthday party?

Shopping for the party was another small headache, though she'd done most of it online. She'd bought plastic containers for the home-cooked food, cake candles, the goodies for the children's going-home bags; mini packets of love-heart sweets, heart bracelet-making sets for the girls, under £2 online, Rudolph red noses and a car for the boys, a balloon and lollipop for all. Ahmed had thought of Lily doing notes to slip into the bags like *Thanks For Coming To My Party!* or *I Hope You Had A Good Time!* It kept her quiet for hours.

The entertainer was booked – all Lily's friends had one at their parties, it was hard to buck the trend – and Nattie had hired twelve small chairs and a trestle table. She'd resisted delegating anything to Hugo. He wasn't at his most reliable and she was nervous enough as it was.

She felt wretched again on Thursday, and drained. Ahmed clucked round her like an old mother hen. He insisted on doing supper, cooked plain fish, but the aroma put her off. All she wanted was rice, dry toast and Marmite. 'What about my baking session tomorrow?' she wailed. 'I don't want to throw up into the fairy cakes – and in front of Lily. I was going to do a surprise hedgehog birthday cake too, when she'd gone to bed, but I feel sick just thinking about it.'

'I'll sort it,' Ahmed said, reaching for his laptop. 'There are people who make cakes to order. It'll be home-made, your pride'll be intact.'

She gave in weakly. He called Jasmine as well, who agreed to do the school run. It lifted some of the pressure and gave Nattie her first proper night's sleep of the week. She had a lazy Friday morning, feeling better, despite her guilt-ridden fears for the children and the worry of Ahmed's safety, and she managed to make pink-iced cakes with Lily in the afternoon. At eight o'clock there was a ring on the bell and a chocolate-brown hedgehog birthday cake, complete with prickles and a little black-button nose, was delivered. Nattie threw her arms round Ahmed and said if she hadn't loved him before, she did now.

Saturday was Lily's actual birthday. When she came running into her mother's room she found Ahmed there too, dressed, and a pile of presents awaiting her.

'Your main present is downstairs,' Nattie said, leaving Lily, whooping with delight, tearing off wrapping paper under supervision – notes being made of which grandparent had given what – while she got Thomas up and dressed.

Lily could read the label on a huge package beside the breakfast table, almost the height of the table, *Happy Birthday! Love Mummy and Dan*. It was a kitchen cooker range, with all the play kit, frying pans, utensils; not quite in keeping with Jake's state-of-the art kitchen décor, but a friendly addition. Lily loved it and chattered about all the play-dishes she would cook, the friends she wanted to have round to play with her. Lily's need to have schoolfriends to tea was a problem. Nattie told the mothers that they'd be at a friend's house so she would return the child, no need to collect, but Lily must surely talk about Ahmed at school. The rumours must be rife.

Lily didn't know which way to turn she was so excited.

Ahmed had given her a globe too, which the box stated was for eight-year-olds; she pored over that, asked non-stop questions, she was uncontainable. 'I so wish you were coming to my party, Dan,' she said, when it was time to go. 'I'm sure Daddy wouldn't mind.'

He smiled. 'I've got lots of writing to do. Your granny's coming and your godmother, Maudie, you'll be with your friends, helping Mummy and Daddy beforehand too. You'll look after Tubsy? You won't leave him out – promise?'

She hesitated. 'But he's not to start screaming,' she said, and grinned cheekily. Then she ran to Ahmed and gave him a hug and kiss. 'I promise,' she said, 'reely. I was only joking,' before she was dancing all the way out of the door.

Crossing London with Christmas shopping underway was a strain. Nattie swallowed back the nausea that rose in her throat and tried to stay calm. She would say she was getting over a tummy bug if it happened. Her nipples were very painful, the stress building; she passed a hand over her forehead and carried on.

Hugo came out onto the pavement as she parked and set about the unloading with a kind of manic efficiency. There was plenty. Ahmed had given Tubsy a present too, anxious he shouldn't feel left out – a pushcart with bricks that Tubsy wouldn't be parted from. 'For Lily birfday,' he said proudly as it appeared out of the car.

'How's my birthday girl then,' Hugo said, swinging Lily up on high. He set her down with a bump and turned his gaze. 'And her mother?'

'Can we go in and get started?' Nattie said, feeling slightly faint; she loosened her belt a notch. She and Lily were in jeans for the moment; she had a new tunic top from Ahmed, silver grey with a boat neck, to wear with black leggings, and Lily, a pretty, navy-lace skater dress. She was dying to twirl around in it, impatient to get changed, but it seemed best for them to party up later.

'Right, orders, what can I do?' Hugo said, after giving Lily his present, a child's computer that Nattie didn't really approve of. She wished he'd called, discussed it, given her a chance to suggest that all the play games on it were bad for the imagination. 'What can I do?' he repeated, with a staring-eyed, hyperish look on his face.

'Perhaps calm down a little?' Nattie suggested. He was being a bit unnatural and over-keen. Was it stress? He couldn't be on anything, surely?

'I'm not calm,' he said, coming close, taking hold of her hands. 'You're very pale, darling, are you all right?'

'Just a bit stressed like you.' She smiled and extracted her hands.

The trestle table and chairs had arrived; Hugo pushed the kitchen table against the dresser and set them up in its place. Nattie got on with the food, mini sandwiches, bowls of carrots, single grapes, slivers of cucumber that nobody would eat. She gave Lily a sneak preview of the cake, which was met with ecstatic whoops. When she cooked pasta for their lunch and opened a jar of pesto, the sharp smell turned her stomach and she couldn't eat a thing. Hugo didn't seem to notice or didn't comment at least.

The entertainer turned up. He looked remarkably old to be clowning around in a clown's outfit, but he came highly recommended.

Then Victoria arrived. Nattie and Lily had just got changed and with Lily doing her twirls, the centre of attention, Nattie hoped her own pallor would go unnoticed.

She had to wake Tubsy a bit early for the party and he was grouchy, needing to be coaxed out of his post-sleep grumps. Her mother came upstairs and hovered, looking anxious. 'You're not ill, darling? It's not that you look it,' she added hurriedly, 'just a little stressed. I know this isn't the time, but are you any nearer a decision? Hugo's just told me his good news, yet he's acting like the bailiffs are about to walk in the door.'

'What good news? What are you talking about?' Nattie looked down at Thomas on the changing mat. He'd done a poo. She kept her head bent, took deep breaths, couldn't carry on talking, but managed to clean him up and see him into his best dungarees without throwing up. She raised her head weakly. 'Sorry, small smelly interruption. What's this good news, Mum?'

'Only that they got that account, Bosphor Air, and it seems the Turks or whoever have specifically asked for Hugo to handle the account. He can't think why!'

The doorbell rang. 'The first little darling,' Nattie laughed, saved from making any response. 'Half an hour early too – there's always one!'

She and Hugo greeted a steady stream of arrivals. Most of the parents simply dropped off the children, glad of a couple of hours' peace, but two mothers stayed. One, a bland, washed-out-looking girl, who clearly never let her pink-net-petticoated child out of her adoring sight, the other, a dyed-blue-hair grunge queen. She wore a yellow-and-black punk knitted sweater with more holes than fabric, yellow tights, black bovver boots, and had a string of linked safety pins looped round her neck. So that was Star's mum! Nattie liked Lily's little friend, Star, who had a cheery grin and looked fetching in a jeans jacket, shorts and lacy tights.

'You're well prepared with that necklace.' Hugo smiled at Star's mum's safety-pin chain. She stared straight through him.

The entertainer got going, pulling his clown red nose on and off, calling up children, the birthday girl of course, and giving out little prizes. His act was all slapstick and he had them in fits.

Maudie arrived. Hugo kissed her cheek, still holding the bottle of wine he'd been offering. Star's mum had accepted a glass with a sullen glare; the mousy mum, who Victoria was chatting to sociably, had declined. 'Great to see you, Maudie, glad you could make it,' Hugo said, full of bonhomie. 'Glass of wine?'

'Why not.' She eyed Nattie. 'How's you? Where have you been in my life, girl?'

Hugo, about to go for a glass, paused, keen to hear, but Nattie fielded the question. 'Where have *you* been, more like! You were about to go off to New York with the very generous Harold.'

Maudie eyed her. 'This is woman's talk, not for Hugo's innocent male ears. Come into the kitchen. Your mother's doing a good job here, she'll keep an eye.' Nattie followed, electric with tension, and busied herself filling the kettle.

'You're seeing someone, aren't you? The body language is *awful*. But I knew it anyway, way back when you came to dinner.'

The vibrating buzz of Nattie's mobile was well timed. It was swizzling round on a worktop; she picked it up and saw it was a text from Ahmed. *A-okay or B-so-so?*

She couldn't help smiling and texted back: *B-okay, but going on C.*

She looked up. 'Sorry, something silly from a friend. You're right, Maudie, but don't make me talk about it, not yet. It has to come to a head soon.' Another wave of nausea. 'God, sorry – just have to run. Tummy-bug,' she called back. 'I'm not in the best nick!'

Maudie was sympathetic when she returned. She was a good friend underneath. 'That's helped your colour, you looked pale as a ghost. Okay, you win. Tell me when you're ready, but I can keep a secret, you know.'

Victoria came into the kitchen. 'Are you all set out here? I think the clown's winding down. Watch out for the safety-pin lady, Hugo's refilled her glass!'

The noise level reached a cacophony as the children came in and scrambled into seats, the boys making a race of it. A small fierce-looking girl prodded Nattie's thigh. 'I don't do gluten.'

'I'm sure I can find you a rice cake,' Nattie said, hoping the packet she'd had in the cupboard months ago wouldn't be long out of date.

She helped the child into her seat, handed her a couple of the dry round discs and made the mistake of leaving the packet on a worktop. Star's mum picked it up immediately. 'This has been off a whole week!' she said, with a distinct note of triumph.

'It's only a Best Before date,' Nattie smiled. 'Do have one.'

Lily blew out her five multicoloured candles in a single puff; they looked like extra hedgehog spikes, and everyone sang 'Happy Birthday!'. The clown entertainer conducted extravagantly and even Tubsy, in his high chair, joined in.

Nattie took back the cake to cut it into slices. 'You've excelled yourself with this one,' Victoria whispered, coming beside her. 'What a pro job! You'll be setting up in the cake-making business next.' Nattie made a mental note to come clean, but telling her mother she was pregnant had to come first.

There was more entertainment after tea before the doorbell began to ring. Nattie and Hugo saw out the children, handing Josie, Jasper, Noah, Helen their going-home bags, spotty bags for the girls, striped ones for the boys. The Harpers, parents they knew slightly, looked at them curiously, pondering the rumours for sure. Hugo pressed a drink, but Mandy Harper said the baby needed feeding; another time. Nattie hadn't noticed the little pink head, pressed to its mother's chest, peeking out of a baby-sling like a salmon in a fish basket, and the sight of it made her nipples prick. She was dreadfully tired, aching to be home and in Ahmed's arms.

Hugo's arm was round her shoulders as they said the goodbyes.

Star and her mother were the last to leave. 'I don't approve of out-of-date food,' Star's mum said. 'That child had a piece of birthday cake too, which is gluten rich.'

'I'm not her keeper,' Nattie snapped, losing control. 'I think she'll live.'

Hugo saw them out, Star tripping happily down the path. He closed the door and hugged Nattie tight. 'We did it,' he said. 'We made it through the day!'

30

Sadia's Coup

Nattie left the Buckley Building with Hugo on her mind. She was on her way to keep her date with Sadia and her sister and set off for the coffee shop, pleased to be out of the fuggy office and breathing in the crisp still air. It was a rain-free day at last. Heavy drops had clattered onto the car roof on the way home from Lily's party and it had rained all Sunday and Monday.

She was impatient to hear how Sadia had won through and rescued her sister from the forced marriage. It was hard to imagine how she could have pulled it off. Sadia had been tearful and nervous that day at lunch, about to leave for Pakistan on what Nattie had been convinced was a dangerous and doomed mission. But she'd sounded radiantly happy on her return, calling to say she'd succeeded and her sister was with her. It was amazing news. Nattie was thrilled for them and, with Hugo uppermost in her thoughts, it seemed a positive amidst all the negatives.

She was disturbed by her mother's news about Bosphor Air, injured and irritated that when Hugo had every opportunity on the morning of Lily's party to tell her about winning the account, he'd chosen to keep it for Victoria. Nattie knew she was on weak ground to be minding; his keenness to shut her out was understandable and he'd been distressingly hyped-up that day as well – but wouldn't that simply have made him keener to brag a little and talk up his success? It was hurtful. She would have liked to have made a few suggestions and bolster him up.

She worried about him handling the Bosphor account. He may well have seemed thoughtful, deep, good-looking, an elegant Englishman who'd charm the travel writers and be good for Bosphor Air; it was a great new piece of business for Tyler Consulting – but too important to be entrusted to Hugo in his present condition. Nattie feared he'd lose confidence and botch it. He needed warm encouragement at the best of times.

She imagined he was just about getting by with his regular clients; they were familiar, comparatively easy-going, and Christine must be in a rare accommodating mood after Cupcake Corner's glory moment in the sun. Not Brady. Hugo's bleary eyes and hyper mood-swings can't have passed his chairman by. The least slip and Brady would be merciless; it was surprising he hadn't kicked him out already. There was no shortage of ambitious back-stabbers in the firm either. Nattie sighed. She had her own problems.

Arriving at the coffee shop, she found that Sadia and Alesha were there already, seated at a table in the window. They jumped up to welcome her and Sadia gave her a hug.

'This is Alesha,' she said with fond sisterly pride. 'I'm so glad you can meet.'

'It's your great triumph that we can do,' Nattie said, with a wide smile.

The girls were as alike as twins, despite the six-year age gap, the same oval-shaped face and small-boned slenderness, although Alesha was taller and looked the more spirited of the two – as though she had more of a sense of fun. She was wearing Western clothes, a safe black skirt, light blue sweater and no head covering; her thick, dark, shoulder-length hair was loose, tucked behind her ears. It was hard to believe she'd been living in a strictly religious household so recently, policed and confined, about to be forced into marriage.

'Your father must be incredibly relieved to have you both safely home,' Nattie said, as they settled in. 'He'll have been worried sick these past weeks, I'm sure. I suppose you could only get a visitor's visa?' she wondered, struck by the thought and worrying suddenly that their euphoria could only be short-lived.

'No,' Sadia said, gleefully, 'Alesha's able to stay. I can't believe we did it and are really here!'

'So tell all.' Nattie looked from one happy girl to the other.

'I stayed in a hotel, but visited the house often,' Sadia said. 'I was terrified the first time, expecting our mother to be difficult, but it was nearly ten years since she'd seen me and I'd hoped she might actually give me a hug. She didn't, she was just really cold and suspicious. Even the house was unwelcoming, a two-storey block with a high white wall, nothing like our lovely old home in Lahore. I needed to persuade her that I hadn't come to make trouble, though, so I put on a show of going along with everything and said I'd really wanted to have a little time with Alesha, a few sisterly moments before the big day.'

'Your mother must have known how Alesha felt about the marriage, which I can see would have made it more credible that you'd want to be there,' Nattie remarked, 'as a shoulder for her to cry on.'

Alesha nodded eagerly. 'Sadia was brilliant. Like they say here, she played a blinder – she should be in Bollywood. She criticised arranged marriages, just to be believable, and argued with our mother, sticking out her chin and saying why shouldn't the girl have an equal say in a decision that was for life?'

'And how did your mother react to that?' Nattie asked wryly.

'She flew into a furious rage, pouring out venom and screaming that Sadia should be punished for daring to question what was pure and good.'

'It was okay, more or less,' Sadia said. 'I wasn't given a beating. I'd often wondered, though, whether she'd ever regretted leaving Dad, given our stepfather's views, but Alesha says not.'

'No, she's as radical and judgemental as he is, a leading light in a community that spends all its time gossiping, stigmatising and forcing girls into loveless marriages.'

'Things are improving,' Sadia said in a lawyerly way, trying to flag up the positive. 'Our mother and stepfather live in Rawalpindi, which is huge and modern – historical too, it was an important base in the British Raj – and the majority of people living there have a more enlightened and rational outlook on life these days.'

'Go on.' Nattie sneaked a look at her watch. She was only on a coffee break. 'However did you win through with the passport and visa?'

'I've never been more frightened in my life,' Alesha said. 'Our stepfather kept my passport in a locked cabinet, thankfully not in a safe with a code, but he put his keys in a bowl on his bedside table at night, right beside him, and I had to creep into the bedroom, take the whole bunch and find the key to the cabinet . . .' She shuddered, remembering.

'I was in such a panicky sweat, I left damp toe-prints on the lino in the hall. The bedroom was carpeted, though, and so was the room with the cabinet. That helped, but I had to return the bunch too, which was an even worse agony really.'

'I dread to think what they'd have done to you if they'd woken up,' Nattie said, feeling a shiver pass through her, and Sadia reached across the table for her sister's hand.

She turned then with a smile. 'We have you to thank for the visa, Nattie. It was your fantastic help, telling me about the forced marriage unit that allowed me to win through with the visa. Without that, Alesha's bravery would have been in vain. She was due to be married this week.

'I'd needed Alesha to smuggle out her passport, but I still had to get it to the British High Commission in Islamabad, which is only half an hour from Rawalpindi – the airport is too – and do what I could about the visa.

'I called the unit with little hope. It was set up to help rescue British citizen girls, after all, and Alesha didn't qualify. I asked to speak to the man whose name you'd given me, but they said he wasn't there. I begged them to pass on my mobile number, but didn't hear anything more. I was really despondent. Then just as I was setting off miserably for the British High Commission, he called! He said he was in Islamabad and would be happy to accompany me and press my case.

'He even queued with me for hours. He carried clout and my father being a British citizen and having a good job helped too; the officials eventually agreed to grant Alesha a visa with exceptional leave to remain. I was crying tears of joy. We were able to get the application expedited as well, and I collected the passport the very next day.'

'But however did you manage to get Alesha to the airport and out of the country?'

'I'd thought the Mehndi ceremony would be our best chance to make our escape,' Sadia said. 'I had it all planned.'

'Tell me about the Mehndi ceremony.'

'In Pakistan an arranged marriage is a long-drawn-out process. There's the proposal party when the groom's parents and family elders formally ask the girl's parents for her hand and rings are exchanged. The groom's mother or sister puts the ring on the girl's finger and vice versa, never any contact between the couple. There's a sort of musical celebration called the Dholki, when a whole lot of women come to the bride's house and sing and dance, then just before the wedding day there's the henna ceremony, which is called the Mehndi.

'It's a women's event and the concept of the beauty parlour is pretty big in Pakistan so Alesha's henna party was being held in town. The women bring along sweets and gifts and put henna on the bride's hands and feet – it's often done by professionals using beautiful decorative designs. Traditionally the bride's mother and family don't attend, the groom's side arrange it all, but the Mehndi has become more elastic and I'd been allowed to go. I was under strict instructions to order a cab and see that Alesha arrived home by the appointed time.'

'And the cab was your chance, when you were going to make a run for it? You had the passports, airline tickets?'

'Yes, secreted in my underwear just in case someone snooped in my bag. I had two small online cases waiting at the hotel where I'd been staying, mine and one for Alesha – I'd worried that travelling with no bags at all could have drawn attention. We left as soon as we could, picked up the cases and taxied on to the airport. Our combined adrenalin would have fuelled that cab all the way there!'

'Waiting for take-off was like anticipating an axe falling on our necks,' Alesha said. 'We couldn't believe the plane would leave on time; it was a night flight and they're more often delayed than not. And once our mother and stepfather discovered the missing passport – well, that would have been it! They'd have seen Sadia into jail for attempted kidnap or something, I'd have been beaten or worse and married off. It was truly like waiting for the torturer to arrive.'

Alesha's hand, loosely looped round her cappuccino cup, still bore the faint remains of the henna designs and Nattie wondered if they'd caused comment at the airport.

'I was anxious about them being a giveaway,' Sadia said, 'but Alesha kept her hands covered with floaty veils as far as possible. I prayed that our mother and stepfather would imagine an accident or street attack or something, and wouldn't think of checking on the passport right away. I told Alesha that, but only half believed it myself. The tension was unbearable, showing our passports, waiting for alarms to be raised. I still can't really believe we're here!'

'Our dad is seriously worried about repercussions,' Alesha said, 'with all the wedding preparations, the shock and outrage, loss of honour. He's had abusive calls, terrible threats; the police even visited, saying complaints had been made. Dad told them I hadn't taken anything and he couldn't see anything criminal in a girl changing her mind before the wedding. It happened. They had to agree.'

'He's made us rent a flat on this side of London,' said Sadia, 'and he's going to move too. We'd rather be here all the same, watching our backs, than see Alesha forced to be the wife of a cousin on our mother's side.'

'Sadia's even more at risk than I am,' her sister said, 'because of her book.'

Nattie congratulated her on how well it was doing and Sadia looked delighted. 'I told Alesha about pouring out all my private troubles that day you interviewed me about it,' she said. 'You were so warm and sympathetic and we'd only just met.'

'You were sympathetic too,' Nattie smiled, 'when I embarrassingly mentioned the man I'd loved – talking about myself, the very last thing an interviewer should do. It was your lowered eyelashes: they made me think of him.'

Sadia didn't know where to look.

'I really felt for you,' she said. 'You were married and had a family, but to have been in love with a man who'd disappeared, it was easy to see you still cared. So hard for you, not knowing what had happened, even if he was still alive.'

Nattie felt ashamed. 'I should get back,' she mumbled, making a show of looking at her watch. She sat up straighter and let it out. 'But I *do* know what happened now. You see, I heard from him, that very same day, right after we'd had lunch. He's here, seven years on, back in the country and safe. I'm with him now, ruining my husband's life.'

She stared from one girl to the other; they still had their problems, but they weren't tied, they were free to live their lives. Tears welled. She felt more ashamed than ever, and angry with herself. It was the pregnancy, her hormones playing up.

Both girls put out a hand to hers, a simultaneous gesture; Nattie was kneading her hands, elbows on the table.

'Sorry,' she said, recovering. 'I'm in rather an overwrought state, and late too. I have to go. It's just that everything's coming to a head in my life. I have to make an impossible decision and there's nothing worse than hurting someone you love. One I love too much, the other, not quite enough.'

She stood up hurriedly and managed a wan grin. 'This is awful, baring my soul when I should be back at my desk. You must please forgive me. I'm so happy for you both. Call any time if I can ever be of help.'

Sadia and Alesha came out with her. They stood on the pavement saying their goodbyes and offering encouragement.

'It's hard, isn't it,' Sadia said, giving her another hug, 'the pull of duties and ties?'

'I'd just go with your heart,' Alesha said, seventeen and free as air.

Sadia gave her a firm elder-sister's look. 'Nattie will do what is right; we should let her make her own decisions – and get back to the office. We mustn't hold her up a minute longer.'

Nattie smiled, nodded in a vague sort of way, and set off down the street at a clop. Her back was turned, her eyes brimming over again, but when she thought of all the girls less lucky than Alesha, denied rights, distressed, dominated, she felt humble. Was there anything more precious in life than the freedom to make one's own decisions?

31

Mother and Daughter

Victoria looked down at her phone again and re-read Nattie's text.

Can I see you, Mum? I need to talk. What's best for you in next couple of days? Around five tomorrow, after work, or Friday's good, except for picking up Lily. Ahmed will look after Tubsy, then both of them in the afternoon.

Victoria clicked off and went to stand at the kitchen window. She was tired, just in from a long busy day, and stared out through the glass. The garden was cloaked in blackness, but with the bright light from the kitchen she could make out shape and form. Was it crunch time? Had Nattie made her decision?

Five o'clock tomorrow would be best. Victoria didn't feel especially happy about Ahmed looking after the children – not that he wasn't responsible, probably more so than Hugo as things were; it was just a feeling they were getting too close to him. It must be so painful for their father. She sighed. They were into December already, with the whole business of Christmas coming up – and what was Nattie going to do about that?

She texted Nattie back.

Sorry, busy Friday, let's go for five tomorrow? Hope nothing too serious. Be lovely to see you, darling.

She got on with the evening, cooked, did a few chores, tried to still her mind. William called. 'On my way, sorry!' He never made it by the appointed time.

'A bit less late than usual,' Victoria said, trying to be cheerful when he came in. 'I'm glad I factored in an extra twenty minutes' cooking time.'

He kissed her. 'Perfect synchronisation then.'

They sat down to supper and she mentioned Nattie's text.

'I don't want to worry you,' William said, pouring her a glass of wine, 'I'm sure Ahmed isn't really in much danger, but a couple of the lesser players, Iqbal and Haroon, are up for release. He was at school with these guys and Harehills may be part of Leeds, but it's as tight-closed as any small village community you'll get. It will hardly have been popular there that Ahmed broke rank. He's a hero with us, but back there, it's not like he's an old boy who made good. There's the honour thing too. It's not great, those two snivelling shitholes coming out.

'Remember Yazid, the thicko ringleader of that small cell?' William carried on. 'He's still inside, but there's also Shelby, of course, that little cunt, who's got a score or two to settle and he's been throwing his weight around again for some time now, weaselling his way into the clubs and doing the social scene.'

'God, Shelby,' Victoria said. William was doing a poor job of not worrying her. 'I had enough stress over Nattie's fling with him. He had it in for Ahmed back then all right. Remember the time he came to the house trying to persuade me that Ahmed was in with the terrorists? I saw him off with a flea in his ear, though Nattie would never believe it. I can hardly blame her, it was just at the time when the

Home Office and MI5 were checking Ahmed out.' Victoria felt sorrowful, remembering the pulls of loyalty and immense stressfulness of the job.

'I've often wondered,' she said, 'whether it was Shelby who fed Hugo his drugs. I expect you know, don't you? You, the *Post*, set Shelby up pretty successfully with that entrapment ring, after all, and got him put away.'

She raised her eyebrows, but William wasn't letting on; he never did about anything connected with the paper. He answered about Hugo tangentially, though.

'Nattie's right to be terrified of Hugo reverting. Addiction is an illness in many ways, which people forget. Anyone with an addictive personality is always at risk. It's rough, the bind she's in. She'd never forgive herself if he slipped back; she can only pray that having the children around will help him to hold off.'

William reached across the table for Victoria's hand then rose to make the coffee. 'You'll know soon enough what she's decided,' he said, over his shoulder. 'I don't know what she'll do. Ahmed's keeping his head down, but it's not much of a life. He'd be better off living on the other side of America. Certainly, if Nattie was with him, they'd have to.'

'That's what I dread most of all. If I say a word about it to her, though, I'll only push her straight onto a plane. I worry about the children too, getting so fond of Ahmed. It seems terribly hard on Hugo.'

'They adore their father – you're making a bit too much of that. Children are very adaptable. I have great faith in Nattie. She's not a wimp, she'll sort out her life soon.'

'She looked terribly pale at Lily's party . . .'

William's phone shrilled before he could comment. He listened a minute. 'Shit. Change the front page – now, fast! Send it over.' He clicked off. 'A plane's come down in the Aegean. It's grim.

Sure to be another fucking bomb. Sorry, darling, I'll be a bit busy. You're seeing Nattie in hours; try not to worry.'

That, Victoria thought miserably, brought down by the news, all the frightening world events and pressure points, the legions of dead, the millions of lives affected, was easier said than done.

Nattie banged the knocker and called through the letterbox: 'It's me!'

She came in along with a blast of icy air and turned to push the door shut. Dumping down her bags, she gave her mother a proper, meaningful hug. Victoria could feel her daughter's need of her and of her support, however nervous she might be about saying whatever it was she wanted to unload.

'How are you, Mum?' Nattie said, lifting off her bike helmet and letting her hair tumble. Her cheeks were pink, her breath steaming. She looked lovely, really beautiful.

'All good,' Victoria said, smiling. 'I like seeing this colour in your cheeks. You look very rosy and healthy – unlike the other day.'

'It's riding my bike, it's cold out there! I've locked it to the railings, okay?'

'Sure. You're straight from work?' She hated Nattie riding her bike after dark.

'Yup – and before you ask, I've got great new bike lights. Ahmed insisted. He's got me these really fancy ones.' Nattie was stuffing her mitts into the pockets of her black puffa coat, which she shrugged off and left draped on the hall chair.

'I'll get the kettle on,' Victoria said, making for the kitchen.

'Can I have water? I'm a bit off tea and coffee.'

Surely she'd want something nice and warming, coming in from the cold? Was that some new caffeine scare or other? William said all the health fads, whether good, alarmist or bad, always sold papers. 'You're looking so much better, darling,' she said. 'I worried at Lily's party. I know what a strain those things are.'

'I was struggling rather,' Nattie admitted, taking a glass out of the cupboard and holding it under the tap, 'feeling pretty rotten in fact. It's why I've come.' She smiled nervously. 'There's something I need to tell you.'

What could she mean? Victoria felt chill shivers down the length of her spine as in a split second she imagined every possible black-winged carrier of doom. It couldn't be some sort of cancer, surely? Please God not that. It had to be something serious, wouldn't she otherwise have simply picked up the phone?

Nattie perched on the sofa arm, sipping her water thoughtfully.

'Come and sit down properly, love, and tell me.' Victoria's eyes were beginning to smart. She'd had a sleepless night, which wasn't helping, set off by William's talk of the two terrorist plotters coming out of jail, as well as her private fears about Nattie and California. 'I hope it isn't anything too serious. You're not ill or anything – it's nothing like that?' She gave a light laugh, an instinctive masking of her feelings. 'Or is it about your decision? Hugo's in such agony, you must tell him soon.'

'I know that, Mum. What I've come about is sort of related, though, but I'd hate you to think that it's something that would ever affect my decision. It hasn't and it won't, I promise.'

Victoria stared steadily at her daughter, more confused than ever.

'You see, I'm pregnant, Mum. I'm having Ahmed's baby.'

The slow dawning of how wide of the mark she'd been caused a hot flush of embarrassment. Victoria felt the heat, the blood-rush, suffuse her from the neck up. 'I don't know how I didn't get there,' she said. 'With the sickness, how could I have been so dense!' She deposited her mug of tea and stared down, linking and fingering her hands. She was battling with a fluttering in her stomach, a sense of her compass being awry, lost bearings, a slight, impossible-to-articulate moral discomfort that shouldn't come into it.

She looked up again. 'Sorry, love, it's just taking me a while to get my head round it. There are a lot of ramifications ... It's such beastly luck, the morning sickness, and having it all day too, if Saturday was typical. I understand completely now how much you were struggling. You're still in the early stages then? I really should have guessed.'

'Can't you look a little bit more happy about it, Mum? It's another grandchild, God willing. Aren't you pleased?' Nattie looked hurt and questioning. 'It's very much wanted – isn't that what it should all be about?' She stuck out her jaw, going on the attack, longing for a wholehearted seal of maternal approval. Victoria felt emotionally protective, but desperately worried and confused.

Nattie got up abruptly and went to refill her glass from the tap over the sink and Victoria realised how much she must have dreaded coming to tell her; it was a precious piece of news and she would naturally have longed for it to be joyfully received. Had she automatically expected her mother to be shocked and distressed? How awful to have been so typically less than spontaneous, so predictably cautious and reserved. It was in her nature, though, the way she was built.

She jumped up and put her arm round Nattie's shoulders, feeling her heart soar as her daughter turned into her arms for a hug. They stood clinging together by the sink, Victoria stroking Nattie's hair, feeling her heartbeat competing with her own. 'I just needed a little time to adjust,' she said as they separated and she lifted a strand of hair away from Nattie's eyes. 'It's a new life and I'm thrilled for you. It's wonderful, but it does make for complications, as I'm sure you know.'

She stopped herself from saying that she couldn't see how it could fail to affect Nattie's decision; it had to. She couldn't get beyond all the obvious worries. Even if Nattie went back to him, how could Hugo possibly handle her having Ahmed's child? It would be a continuous reminder, a connection with Ahmed.

'It's going to hit Hugo dreadfully hard, of course,' Victoria said, as they went to sit down again. 'I was really worried about him on Saturday, even wondered if he could have taken something. It would be too awful if he went down that road.'

'Don't, Mum, that's such heavy pressure. And can't you ever think of it from Ahmed's side, how much this baby must mean to him? Take yourself back; he risked his life, gave evidence, gave up the freedom to come and go. I think all that makes our baby the more extra special somehow. I know I can't expect Hugo to understand that. I know all the problems. I've pulled Hugo back from the brink in my time. There's Lily and Tubsy too . . .'

Nattie rose. 'I should be getting back. Try not to worry too much, Mum. I'll sort out my life – just as long as this stinky morning sickness doesn't last a whole nine months.'

'When's the baby due?' Victoria felt quite light-headed, feeling the load lifting, sensing that she and Nattie were in a good place again, the precious mother and daughter relationship restored.

'Late June – a summer baby. It won't need to be all bundled up against the cold.'

Victoria watched Nattie bike down the road, back light winking furiously, went in again and closed the door, shutting out the December cold. The hall was warm and filled with the smell of her daughter's light scent; she'd squirted some on from a mini spray-bottle in her bag before leaving. She was going home to be kissed by Ahmed. The lingering scent set Victoria back again. Her qualms hadn't gone away; she couldn't think about the good in her mixed feelings, only the downside. She wanted Nattie's happiness, but it was a mess.

If Nattie stayed with Ahmed, Hugo would see his children less and less. It was the way things went. And suppose she ended it with Ahmed for whatever reason, it was hard to see Hugo gladly accepting her back. A tall ask, after all he'd been living through, surely, to expect him to look after and love Ahmed's child as his own. Ahmed visiting regularly, it would be an impossible strain. Wasn't Hugo going to buckle under with all the stress and pressure anyway, whatever happened?

32

Decision

Nattie was back in minutes, Jake's house was no distance from her mother's. She humped her bike up the front steps and in through the door; she'd had a wheel nicked leaving it padlocked out front.

'You still here, Jasmine?' she called. 'Thanks. I'd popped in to see my mother, but don't feel you need to stay if Dan's here. He is halfway capable, you know.'

Jasmine came into the hall. 'I thought he'd like help with their tea. Lily can be such a cheeky little miss, laying down the law about what she wants to eat.'

Nattie opened the back door to lock up her bike outside and Jasmine had something to say about it. 'Brrr, blimey, it's colder than a witch's tit out there. Any babysitting needed tomorrow?' she added hopefully. She didn't work Fridays and she and Pete were getting married – a year next April, and already trying to save.

'Sorry, no plans,' Nattie said, but as it was one of Hugo's weekends with the children, Jasmine would have extra hours then.

She saw Jasmine out and closed the front door with a sense of relief. She needed to be alone with Ahmed and to have the house to themselves.

He was in the kitchen, giving Thomas his supper, spooning in yoghurt. He put down the pot and plastic spoon to come to give her a kiss. 'Mmm, you smell good – but you've taken off all the gear. Done me out of seeing you shake out your hair in that sexy way.'

'Sexy's a naughty word,' Lily said with authority, turning from the dishwasher, which she loved to fill.

'It's not very naughty.' Ahmed gave her hair a tweak as she came bouncing up. 'I've heard a certain little girl say much naughtier things.'

'What? What has she said?' Nattie asked, instantly worried about the words Lily could pick up at school.

'That's just between Lily and me, and she's not going to say it again, are you, Lily? Remember your promise?' She narrowed her eyes at him, cross at being reminded.

Tubsy was trying to aim spoonfuls of yoghurt into his mouth with limited success. He quickly tired of the task, maximum effort for minimum reward, and started hammering at his high-chair table, sending spatters of yoghurt flying.

'Oh, Tubsy, darling, we hadn't forgotten you.' Nattie wiped his hands and face and lifted him out of his high chair. She hugged him, feeling emotionally fragile and beginning to worry already about Hugo's ability to cope at the weekend.

She played games with the children, allowed a little DVD viewing, lost herself in the agony of what lay ahead. There was no going back. She'd done it, plunged into the gully, told her mother she knew the way forward, and now she had to face up to telling Hugo and Ahmed what it was.

'Bedtime, you two, up we go!' The three of them trooped upstairs. 'Into the bath with you and then I'll call Dan to read a story.'

Wrapping up Tubsy in his towel, rubbing him dry, she could

tell her breath was juddery; she held her cuddly boy close, trying to calm her thumping heart, if not her nerves. She had to do it, had to tell Ahmed before anything else. From that all else flowed – or became silted up, or sucked her down into the abyss. She had to do it now – well, soon, over the weekend. When – Friday night? No, not when she was seeing Hugo next morning; even with the children as cover she'd be feeling dangerously overwrought. It would have to be after taking them, as soon as she returned here.

She got Tubsy's bottle and called Ahmed to read to Lily. It was the right time to tell him; they'd be alone in the house, no distractions. And it was just far enough away to give her the space she badly needed, time to formulate arguments, to plan, to prepare herself mentally – as if that were possible. They would have the rest of the day, Saturday night, Sunday, precious time together. How would they cope?

Thursday night, Friday, the hours of daylight and darkness moved on inexorably; they blurred into each other, fading and fast disappearing. Nattie laughed and smiled, fed the children, fed Ahmed, she shopped, functioned thanks to the weird phenomenon of autopilot, which carried her through the school run, her daily routine. The hardest part was the car ride home alone.

Ahmed must have some sort of idea; he had X-ray eyes and could see into her as clearly as if she were transparent, like an old-fashioned ticking clock with its workings exposed. He must be seeing her pumping blood, the lift and fall of her lungs, the manic whirring of her brain; perhaps even the infinitesimal growth of his embryo child. He'd have an idea all right, with his sensitivity, but was he aware of the indescribable pain?

The hours slipped by as fast as the countryside out of a train window. At some stage, Nattie couldn't remember when, Ahmed had voiced the unwanted truth, speaking it softly into her mouth, a question in a kiss. 'It's time for us to talk? But not now, not tonight?' She'd pulled back, looked at him and he'd known it would be soon.

Friday night came, the train speeding up. The children were in bed, asleep, she and Ahmed had a quiet evening together. They turned in early and Nattie was silent as they went upstairs. In bed Ahmed was passionate, loving her with a particular intensity; she had no need to talk. They lay holding hands as they usually did after lovemaking, a time when they often shared ideas, jokes, media putdowns, racy chat about personalities, private little bitches. It didn't seem the night for talking, though; they lay with their fingers entwined and hardly spoke at all.

Ahmed lifted their linked hands to his lips, sucking gently on one of her fingers. 'Do you want to talk now? California comes into it, doesn't it?'

'Yes. But I'd rather tomorrow, when I'm back from taking the children and we have the house to ourselves. You don't mind waiting till then?'

He put his mouth to her finger again, which seemed as good an answer as any.

'I had a plan for this weekend,' he said, after a bit, 'going to see your grandparents. I long to see them again, but that's out of the window now. No more pottering round the countryside – I can't bear to think of what you went through in Lyme, Nattie darling. They'd have got me without you, those two guys. You were a rock, helping and spurring me on.' He pulled her close. 'I don't want any space between us tonight, I want to sleep with you in my arms.'

Hugo looked limp and haggard, standing in the doorway, kind of unshielded; he had a frailty about him, as though even opening the door had taken all the energy in his possession. Was he starving himself? He looked, Nattie realised with a sudden shock and sinking feeling, as if he was in the throes of a harrowing comedown from some substance, some dreaded chemical prop. Would the children be safe? Was it irresponsible of her to leave them with him? What could she say? 'I can't leave you in charge; you look too washed out'?

She'd hate to row in front of Lily and Tubsy; even if it were out of earshot they'd sense the tension, which would be so bad for them, and Hugo had looked almost as close to the edge on other weekends. He'd probably manage somehow. The children were all he had.

He came down the path to greet them, blinking several times in the crisp bright daylight and covering his eyes with the spread of his hand before squatting down when Lily ran towards him. He gathered her up in his arms. 'Hello, my lovely, my wonderful girl.' He stroked her hair while looking up at Nattie over Lily's silky blonde head. It was more than a look, it was a piercing, gaunt-eyed stare. He was a dying man, his look said, sinking beneath the ice.

He blinked and dropped his eyes, turned his attention to Tubsy. 'How's my Thomas Tubs then? Come and give Daddy a hug!' Tubsy held back; he needed adjustment time, which Hugo understood. He didn't push it and struggled up onto his feet. Lily took his hand in a daughterly way and they went on ahead indoors. Nattie followed slowly; she was walking at Tubsy's pace which, on his short chubby legs, was unhurried.

She refused Hugo's offer of coffee with as much kindly softness as she could manage.

'You'll be okay with them?' she said, trying to keep her voice light. 'Any problems, just give a buzz. I may be out of London,' she said untruthfully, worrying what sort of wretched state she could be in herself, 'but Mum's around this weekend and I know she'd love to help.'

'Daddy's got me to help,' Lily said, looked up at him proudly for confirmation, 'and I do, don't I, Daddy? I'm your good little helper – and Tubsy's mummy just for now.' She was her bouncy self, skipping round the kitchen, jumping up and down.

'You've seen the canvas bag with the usual guff?' Nattie said, desperate to go.

Hugo was staring again. 'I can bring them over to your mother's on Sunday if you like,' he said, 'save you coming all this way.' It was more an attempt to slow her up than genuine keenness to be accommodating, she felt. His hurt at her need to get away was palpable. Or was he worried about Amber dropping in? Perhaps she was a regular Sunday fixture.

It would be a help, though, to meet at her mother's, particularly this Sunday, and Nattie thanked him. 'Be brill of you,' she said. 'Six o'clock?'

Hugo walked with her to the door. 'When will you let me know? It is three months.' Those staring eyes again, and when he rested a hand on her lower arm she could feel how badly it was shaking.

'I'll tell you soon,' she said. 'Very soon.'

It was a peak Saturday before Christmas. The crowds were ten deep and the traffic stationary half the time. It took Nattie over an hour to get back to Lambeth and it was almost noon when she finally drew up and parked. After the supreme tension she'd felt in the car she went up the front steps feeling unnaturally calm.

Ahmed heard her key and sprinted down from his study.

He kissed her and it was a proper kiss, they took their time over it.

He led her by the hand into the sitting room. 'I've been

marking time,' he said. 'I wasn't exactly concentrating on *Shorelands*.'

He'd put a jug of water ready on the coffee table, two glasses, and took her to sit with him on the sofa. She had a flashback – no, wrong word, it wasn't a hauled-back memory, that day they'd met by the Millennium Bridge was too recent and vividly etched. The day when Ahmed had hailed a cab and brought her to Jake's house, when he'd asked her not to sit in the straight-backed chair, but to be beside him while he talked. He'd drawn her down with him on this same sofa just as now, except that this time she was the one with painfully difficult things to say.

She would never regret coming to Jake's house that afternoon; to have resisted and walked away would have meant being half a person for the rest of her life. Some things transcended the wrongness, they had a purity and rightness that couldn't be denied. Love was about many things, discovery, constancy, mirrored senses, making sacrifices, but more than anything, a universe of understanding – and that was what she had to draw on now, test Ahmed's understanding to its limits.

'Who goes first?' he said, pouring her water. 'I'd rather you did. My side is simple: I want to be with you, love and protect you, marry you, but I come with baggage as we both know.'

Ahmed had a lump in his throat, he felt it there as he swallowed. He longed for any glimmer of hope; he couldn't look at Nattie without having to muzzle a howl of agony. It had to be contained. He thought of the beauty of what they had, unchanged feelings since the days when they were both so young and shyly discovering they were in love. They'd lived through enormous dramas then, more dramas now and Nattie had stood by him, loving, strong and constant. She'd never wavered.

She was pregnant with his child; didn't that change everything fundamentally? Didn't it override the great weight of Hugo? Did she have to be a martyr and slave to Hugo's helplessness for the rest of her life?

Ahmed knew where his own duty lay. Now that his cover was blown and he was known to be in the country, every day he lingered, even behind closed doors in Jake's barred and bolted house, spelled greater risk.

Nattie's eyes, amber gold, glistening, were studying him, looking liquidly close to tears. He wanted to fight the will she was finding, beg her to come with him to California. The children were young enough; she could bring them to England to see their father. But he knew the pent-up frustration he was feeling was about to be released, about to explode like a glorious firework all over his brain – all his exultant feelings of hope and expectation over the past three months lit up in splendour for a last second before being lost to the night. Could he be reading the signs wrong? Was there any hope?

'Tell me what you're thinking, Nattie. Tell me where we're at.'

Nattie played with her hands, feeling her wedding ring under her fingers. She didn't want to start, wanted to run from her decision, but to where?

She drew a breath. 'We're on borrowed time. We both know we've been living in a bubble – so intensely happy, in my case, that I've hardly dared breathe for fear of blowing us off course, but our time's run out. We have to be responsible and talk now, while we're alone in the house, just the two of us and little no-name who's a few months off taking part.'

She was grateful when Ahmed refilled her water glass; her throat was dry. She felt drained, shrivelled and withered, dreading with every fibre saying what had to be said. Ahmed was holding her eyes and she stared back.

'You can't stay in England beyond this weekend, darling,' she began, finally finding the will to speak. 'Another person recognises you, another of your enemies with a brother or cousin in Leeds, whose best mate lives in Harehills, whose best mate you put inside. You put Shelby inside indirectly too, and he's not one of life's natural forgivers.'

Ahmed picked up her hand. 'Shelby's been my greatest worry all along.'

'You have to go back to California, but I can't come too.' Nattie brought up their hands to her cheek. 'These last months have been perfect happiness, so much so that I've felt frightened; I've lived in terror of losing you, terror of you turning to another woman. I love you with all my heart, which is now about to shatter into a thousand pieces, but there's no other way. You have to go without me and we have to live apart. I can't take Hugo's children to California, it would be the end of him. They're all he has, he'd lose his will to survive.'

Ahmed took back his hand. He clenched both hands into tight fists; white-knuckled. When he looked up with a direct unflinching gaze, her tears spilled.

'That's only one side of the story,' he said, keeping up his unwavering look and not reacting to her tears. 'I have a say in this too. We love each other and you're having my baby. Aren't you leaving that out of account? Where am I in all this? What about the birth and seeing our child grow up? It is our child, Nattie, and in case you've forgotten, I'm going to marry you, that's a given. It's just a question of when.' He turned away and looked down the room. She had an embryo life inside her and had never felt emptier. Without Ahmed she was a shell.

'You're everywhere in this, and our child is too, but I can't come with you and bring the children. You'd always be more conspicuous with me tagging along, more at risk – even in

California. There was that interview Shelby gave to the press when he tried to link you to terrorists. There wasn't a lot of publicity about us at the time, but enough to stir memories and trigger people's minds. And Shelby's out there, biding his time; he needs to get even again, six times over. He'll find a way to expose you. He'll talk, paint you as a wife-snatcher, say nasty things – and you wouldn't only be risking your reputation. You must see all this.'

Ahmed rose abruptly from the sofa and walked to the far window. He stood looking out. Nattie had said what she had to; stayed calm, kept control. Now the tears rolled freely down her cheeks. She let them. He came back looking drawn and unyielding; didn't sit down again, didn't soften and wipe away her tears, and she felt the cold draught of the distance he'd set up with a sense of desperation. Without his quick, light teasing, his loving, everything was blackness. It was an eternal eclipse on a sunny day.

He stared at her from where he stood. 'You'd go back to Hugo? You miss him at heart, you care about him – perhaps more than me.'

'Is that a statement? Because, question or statement, it's wrong. I love you completely, which leaves no room for Hugo. I have feelings for him, they're sincere, a kind of loving, but incomparable – a pleasant drink, not the nectar that's you. I have to make this impossible decision. Hugo's addictive weakness is an illness, he's fighting it for the sake of his children and I can't let him give up the fight. I married him, I lost trust eventually, when you cut off contact, and took that fateful step. It was in the depths of my bitter hurt and despair and now I have to bear the consequences.' She was barely holding on, close to hysteria, on the verge of losing her resolve.

'You want to go back to him – right now? Go back and live with him again, just as before? You could do that?' Nattie sensed Ahmed was transmitting a plea for reassurance – she knew him so well. He was questioning her coldly, stiff and unrelenting, but bleeding freely inside. The thought of her slipping straight back into Hugo's bed was too much for him to bear.

'I've no intention of going straight back to Hugo,' she said, keeping her calm. 'There's no chance of that, even if I wanted to. When I tell him I'm having your baby – which is inevitably going to be an incredible shock and hit him unbearably hard, what he'll say or do, how he'll handle it, is impossible to guess. No, I'd stay here for a while, as long as I can come to some arrangement with Jake. It would be a temporary stopgap; he'd need to get a decent rent, far more than I could afford. Then after that I could always live in Mum and William's basement till I work something out. There's room for the children there.'

To be talking in bland, businesslike, practical terms when her heart was rent in pieces was making her feel as if she was in a play, rehearsing a role. But it was a real-time tragedy – another one, seven years on from the last.

The room was scented, a vase of freesias on a side table, lilies on the mantelpiece. Ahmed bought fresh flowers regularly online. She wanted him beside her, wanted his special smell, to hear the rhythm of his breathing. She'd faced saying what she had to, been braced for the bitter hurt – she believed he'd known her decision the moment she'd made it, almost before she'd felt sure of it – but to have him standing there, questioning, still distant, not in the same place, was a greater agony than she'd ever known.

'I may in time go back to live with Hugo, assuming he wanted it, but only with a whole set of conditions in place, arrangements about the baby and you. This is our baby, conceived in love, ours to share and bring up in harmony. There's no way I'd ever let you be a stranger to your own child.'

'So what are the conditions? Do I get any say in those?' Ahmed sounded so plaintive and pushed out that she could bear it no longer. She sprang to her feet and went up close, forcing him to look at her, desperate to be held.

'Oh, darling, hold me, don't stop loving me. We're not going to lose contact, even living apart most of the time. We'll never lose contact, please not that, never again. I just know I have to do this thing.'

He kissed her then, with a fierce, ardent passion, and she knew the bonds still held firm. When they separated and she was visibly shaking, her lip bleeding, he kept hold of her so tightly that she couldn't breathe. She eased out of his grasp, leaned forward and dropped her head onto his chest, regaining her breath and feeling flooded with warmth. She'd felt close to fainting minutes before.

There were questions, untied ends, and it was her turn to lead him to the sofa where they sat in silence, needing nothing more than to be close. Nattie felt cocooned, immune from harm with his arm round her, keeping her tight-held, but she needed him to speak his thoughts. She touched his lips. 'I'm done talking, it's your turn now.'

He smoothed her hair. 'It pains me to say this and I'm not functioning properly, but Lyme was the writing on the wall. I should have left the very next day. I feel wretchedly irresponsible, still being here. I keep my eye in – I'm a reporter before scriptwriter – and remember those two sidekicks, Iqbal and Haroon? I saw they were up for release a while back, they're probably out by now. And Shelby's in the columns daily with some society bird or other on his arm; he's certainly around and in a position to do me. He's talked about as the heart-throb jailbird son of an entrepreneur, he has a huge Twitter following and I'd bet quite a lot that he's pushing dope again. If he's back in touch with Hugo, he'll know I'm in the country and be plotting for sure.'

Nattie shivered.

Ahmed looked at her. 'What really cuts so deep is that it's not the risks: this is all about Hugo, isn't it? Admit it. I want to hear you say it. This is all about Hugo – but what about my state of mind? My misery and loneliness? My feelings don't stand a chance.' Nattie could see how rigid he'd gone. He'd separated again and his eyes locked on hers were glittering with pain.

'Nor do my feelings,' she said. 'You don't have a monopoly on "misery and loneliness". But you must see that the risks and Hugo are intertwined. If you hadn't been at risk you wouldn't have gone to America and I wouldn't have married him. Who knows, you and I might have had three yawling kiddos by now, and you'd still be working at the *Post*. But as it is, what we have and feel for each other is unique. For my part certainly, it's the entirety of my life. I'll never let go of this perfect happiness – but nor can I tarnish it by taking Hugo's children and escaping. I couldn't live with the guilt, the constant fear that he couldn't survive and his life was draining away.'

Ahmed didn't comment. 'I'm still waiting to hear what these "conditions" are that are supposed to keep us in contact,' he said instead.

'Hugo's going to have to accept that you must be able to see your child whenever you want and can manage to do so. I'd bring him or her out to see you too, as often as possible – and to fit in with what's going on in your life, of course.' Nattie felt tears pricking again. Suppose he was living with someone, even married? 'I want us to be in regular touch – very regular,' she said, feeling privately determined and holding in the fear.

There was a long silence. She sat looking down, chewing on her still bleeding lip, until Ahmed finally parcelled up her hand.

'Well, that shut me up for a bit, didn't it?' He gave a grudging but wonderfully heartening grin. 'There's one glaring unanswered question in all this,' he said. 'What happens if Hugo won't have you back, pregnant with my baby, and wants nothing to do with you?'

'You would still be at risk and I'd still feel I couldn't take his children out of the country. And if he ever found somebody to love him more and circumstances changed,' she hesitated a moment, 'you'd probably have moved on by then and be married.' She sighed, wishing she hadn't voiced those fears.

'I won't marry anyone else. I'd send anyone worth having over here for Hugo.' Ahmed grinned again, yet Nattie knew his lightness was a defence, his way of masking the depth of his hurt and wretchedness. Then his expression softened and he wiped at her teary eyes. 'Why's that making you look so sad?'

He reached for his glass of water, handed Nattie hers. 'I'm going to drink to Amber, just in case.'

'I'd rather drink to us,' she said, clinking glasses, 'to our future, whenever it comes, and to this precious last weekend. Better make the most of me.'

'Oh, I will, don't you worry. You'll be on your knees by the time you push me, kicking and screaming, onto that plane.'

33

Sunday Night with Shelby

Hugo went to his car and stood by it, waiting a moment before getting in, watching Nattie drive off with the children. He saw her reach the traffic lights that soon changed to green, take a right turn and drive on out of sight. The blue Ford, Ahmed's car, had been parked right outside her mother's house when he'd arrived half an hour ago with the children. 'Boo car, boo car!' Thomas had shrieked, fidgeting excitedly in his seat while Hugo was swinging round to park behind it.

'You won't tell about Mummy's present, will you?' Lily said, for the umpteenth time. Hugo had promised he wouldn't, again, and told her not to worry.

He couldn't have got by without his daughter's enthusiastic productivity. She'd decided to make biscuits as Christmas presents – her teacher at school had suggested it – and asked him to find a recipe online. 'Please, will you look, Daddy? Mummy finds them, and it shows you step by step.' By some miracle – he'd felt like a husband packed off by his wife on a cookery course, except that he didn't have a wife as things were – they had actually managed to cook a batch of misshapen biscuits. 'Can we buy a pretty tin for them in a shop?' That next bright idea of Lily's had usefully filled up more hanging-loose time. He had made it through the weekend.

He sighed and got into his car. The handover had been quick and uneventful, William not around, just Victoria and Nattie. They looked as if they'd been in quite deep conversation. No chance of pinning Nattie down on when exactly 'soon' meant with Lily and Thomas and his mother-in-law around, but he'd tried to communicate in looks. Saying his goodbyes, Thomas had turned away when he'd asked him for a kiss, and buried his face in his mother's jeans. It meant nothing, it was more of a game to Thomas, but Hugo yearned for demonstrative love and felt cut to pieces.

'So the waiting goes on,' he said out loud, as he set off down the road. Another hateful week beginning, another long lonely night ahead; he'd earned his bit of release, he told himself, gripping the wheel as his craving took over. He needed a line. He'd been holding out all weekend, lasting till Sunday night when he could have his reward.

He'd felt emotionally loving all weekend, overcome, his eyes blurring any time he looked at his children while cursing himself for ruining what precious minutes he had with them. Fighting a climb-down on Saturday, steadying himself against chairbacks, table-tops, praying the Valium would kick in and calm him. It had been just what he'd sworn to himself he wouldn't do. It wasn't so easy, though, when being with Amber only made him yearn still more acutely for Nattie, and his week was spent stumbling from one crisis to another, actual, imagined or impending.

Saturday night had been unendurable, containing his desperate crying need, knowing the one small near-empty ziplock packet he had left, nestling behind an ancient box of macaroni on the top shelf of the food cupboard, was within reach. He'd thought of Lily's sleeping face and resisted.

They'd told him in rehab often enough that coke and crack weren't physically addictive like heroin, it was more a psychological need, his mind convincing him that he had to keep coming back for more and more. The drug over-stimulated his central nervous system, they said, so the more he used, the more nerved-up and on edge he'd feel. Well, that was as may be, but either way, body or brain, all he knew was that his craving need was extreme.

Shelby would pitch up later, he was sure. To be feeling such impatience was disturbing – anyone would think he fancied him, Hugo sneered to himself. In reality he was far less enamoured of Shelby these days; the laid-on charm, the way he had seemed to light up the place, had worn thin. Old memories had surfaced. He remembered once seeing Shelby whispering into a man's ear, brushing cheeks while his forefinger had been drawing sensuous circles on the man's hand. He could glide between the sexes with ease, he'd sleep with anyone if the banknotes flowed. Hugo shuddered to think of Shelby's elegant fingers resting on his arm the previous Sunday, as they negotiated terms; he felt revolted recalling the light pressure of those fingers, yet the deal had been vital to him, the only way he could get by.

His feeling of queasiness was always close to the surface, ever since Nattie's rejection on a night that was branded on his mind. When she'd shrunk from his touch he'd known it had been nothing to do with her need of a few nights off, he had sensed even then that his life could be falling apart. And he was right, it had done, God how it had. He was finished, fucked, crawling from one day to the next, feeling like a mollusc without a shell, easy meat for an arch predator like Shelby.

That was the grimness of where he was at, being bled dry and degraded. His association with Shelby wasn't just a pathetic bit of risk-taking; Shelby had him where he wanted him, dangling, screaming for ever more stuff. Hugo loathed being so dependent, feeling like a prostitute in thrall to a pimp.

What about other sources? There was that girl, that messed-up kid, who sold coke and crack in packets of Walkers crisps. He'd had sex with her years ago, he remembered. They'd got high together in the days before Nattie had helped him get clean. That girl had been a full-on crack-addict. God knew where she was now, though, or what kind of a state she'd be in.

Would Shelby bring crack as well as coke? He'd have a supply tucked away in an inner pocket or some orifice of his, no doubt, and he wouldn't be light on coke. 'Just a line,' he always said. 'One line never did anyone any harm.'

That was true in a sense. Not on a weekend when he had the children to care for, but a line wasn't harming him during the week. A line or two had helped him survive the stress and his terror of ballsing up Bosphor Air. It had helped him win over that skinny travel editor, Melanie, on the *Courier*. Spiky Melanie was a goer; she would have guessed with all his exhilarated chatter and flirting that he was pepped up, but whether from curiosity, fascination or approval, she'd signed up for the Bosphor Air press junket, which was all that mattered. Brady seemed surprised and pleased with how things were going, but he'd probably sussed out the Amber situation and given her the credit.

Three hours at least to kill before there was any chance of Shelby showing. The coffee-spoon remains of the coke wouldn't last long. Would Amber help to pass the time? She'd be home from seeing her mother and expecting a call. They could smoke a joint or two. She wouldn't be out of dope now that he'd put her in touch with Shelby. Hugo sensed she wasn't a smoker, too cautious and keen to climb the Tyler's pole. She did it for him, to get closer. He felt bad about that; he wasn't treating her right.

She minded about Melanie, who'd already done a positive

piece on Bosphor in the *Courier*. Amber liked to be his fucking saviour, not have him managing on his own. She nagged on about the need to make a clean break with Nattie. It was coming anyway, she pressed, and surely his pride was at stake? What pride? He loved Nattie. Hugo thought of Amber saying he should be first in, telling Nattie to fuck on off and let him get on with his life. 'Think what a better place you'd be in, free of the strain. You owe it to me,' Amber had said, turning soulful eyes on him. 'This is no way for any of us to live, even your bloody wife.'

Hugo reached home. He snorted the last of his supply, waited a minute or two till the potent, good-mood effect gave him all the energy he needed to make his call to Amber.

Home again three hours later, his spirits were winding down, the fading effects of Amber's dope making him nervy and introspective. Christ, she'd said she loved him – that wasn't in the script. Shit, shit, what was he going to do? He'd set too much store on the thickness of her pale, freckled skin. Amber was hardly sensitive, never seemed to twig that he saw her out of desperation, guilt-driven thanks for keeping him afloat. How the fuck was he going to get her off his back? God, what a mess.

Shelby texted. He'd be half an hour, no more. Hugo poured himself a whisky.

His phone tinged again. It was a text from Nattie. *Can we meet? We need to talk. Tuesday, five-thirty, if you can manage it, while Jasmine's there?*

He stared at his phone till the screen went blank. He brought up the message again. He'd been waiting, marking time for three months, but the next forty-eight hours would be harder than all that time put together. How was he going to survive? And for what – the death blow? Nietzsche said hope was the worst of all evils; it prolonged torment. But if he stopped hoping, his torment wouldn't just be prolonged, it would be unending.

Leaving early on Tuesday was going to be tricky; he'd have to switch a Palmers department store general meeting. Christine wouldn't be pleased, but he'd have put off the Queen, Prime Minister or American President if need be. He wasn't giving Nattie any chance of an out, nor waiting a moment longer to hear his fate.

He texted her back, pulse racing as he jabbed at his phone. *Tuesday's fine. Make it nearer six. Let yourself in. It's your home.*

The doorbell rang.

Hugo walked slowly to the front door. He was suddenly less desperately impatient than usual for Shelby's arrival; only Nattie could have managed to distract him from his hungering need. But Shelby was a Pavlovian trigger and Hugo's heart pumped fast; he needed fresh supplies and Shelby's mantra was ringing in his ears: 'One line never did anyone any harm.' But a single line wasn't going to last him an unconscionable forty-eight hours. He craved the crack experience, laying his hands on a few of those precious stones, 'jujube babies', the crisp-packet girl used to call them; he ached for the sweet, violent shock of being thrown back in his chair.

Shelby breezed in with a bottle of Scotch in one hand, champagne in the other and smelling of rich soft leather along with some discreet scent that was too ferny. He was looking very, very pleased with himself, and Hugo wondered why, feeling disturbed.

He held out the whisky bottle, which Hugo snaffled gratefully, and put the other bottle down on the hall table, taking off his jacket and patting it proudly.

'How do you like my new Givenchy bomber jacket? Cost nearly two grand.'

'Who'd have guessed?'

'Now, now!' Shelby draped the jacket with appropriate reverence on the banister post, retrieved his bottle and made for the kitchen, calling back, 'I'll stick with champagne.' Hugo followed and found suitable glasses, pouring his whisky while Shelby popped the cork. It hit the ceiling, causing Hugo to jerk his hand and spill precious Scotch, but he grabbed a glass in time to catch the fizzing champagne.

Shelby took a few sips, looking round. 'Bit of a mess this place, isn't it?' He was being quite restrained, in fact. The Christmas biscuit cooking had left a trail in the already mucky kitchen. 'You've got a cleaner, I hope,' Shelby went on. 'You need one.' He picked up his bottle. 'I'm taking this to the sitting room. I've eaten – since you're never much of a host. I've got a supper circuit going, I know which daddies have sent their girls to Leiths cookery school and where's best to get fed. What about you, Hugo, old darling,' he said, as an afterthought, 'you eaten? Has the sylph-like Amber done her stuff in the kitchen and wherever else?'

'I'm fine,' Hugo said, clunking some ice into his whisky and following with his bottle, 'except that Amber's got too keen. Trouble is, she covers for me at Tyler's. She could make life pretty good hell there and do me in if I told it to her straight. A woman scorned and all that.' Should he be opening up to Shelby? It was risky enough on a good day, but the Amber problem was much on his mind.

'We can't have you losing your source of income,' Shelby laughed. 'Better keep Amber sweet then. No point being wimpish and coming clean. I'd use her for all she's worth. Keep the relationship like your kitchen, a nice dirty mess. And a line or two will help things along, of course, it never—'

'I know,' Hugo snapped, irritated, 'never did anybody any harm.' Shelby would always come out with it. 'You seem in high spirits tonight,' he said more amenably. 'Done some good trade? How good a deal can we cut on some coke and a bit of crack?'

Shelby was settled in an armchair. He rested his glass and gave a wide grin. He had very white teeth, extraordinarily blue eyes. 'That's my boy!' He laughed, chucking back a hank of his black hair. 'That'll do you a power of good – or bad. You like a bit of bad, though, don't you?'

'Not much, but a lump or two of crack would help me along.'

'How'd it be if we settle for fifty quid a gram for the coke and twenty a rock of crack? I've got a few rocks on me, you're in luck.'

It didn't sound too harsh a deal. Hugo sorted his cash, always had to be cash, and by the time he looked up, Shelby had produced a few twists of white paper and five loose stones from some unknown safe haven about his person.

He sat back and picked up his glass. 'So, want to know why I'm in such a good mood?'

'Well, you're going to tell me, aren't you?'

'I've just ensured that Ahmed Khan will be getting a nice stream of hate publicity in a few days or so. I've been setting it up, should get off the ground by about Tuesday and build fast. By the end of the week the little turd, his name, and a photo too, with any luck, will be emblazoned and exposed. That's the joy of social media – you drop a match ... that's all it takes. He'll be ashes, charred remains, the fucking bastard.' Shelby grinned again. 'So you should be pleased with me all round tonight,' he said.

Hugo knew he was serious and it sounded bad. However violent his jealousy, he was horrified, shocked to the core; it could clearly put Ahmed at risk of his life.

His pulse raced and his stomach contracted while instinct told him to play it cool, to keep stringing Shelby along and keep him boasting. 'I can see you've got scores to settle and I detest the man for what he's done, coming back with a single aim to prise Nattie away now he's ready to settle down or whatever, but—'

'But what? Don't you want him out of the way?'

'Shit, Shelby, of course I do, but if you've made it impossible for him to live here Nattie will go after him, take my children and run.' Hugo felt sick. She might even have been deciding to stay married ... What had Shelby done? 'You don't even know his name or where they're living,' he said, praying Shelby hadn't found out. 'Even I don't know his actual new identity.'

'I know where they live – in his old flatmate's house. I remember meeting Jack Wright at parties way back, before that alien piece of rancid shit your wife's so keen on set me up, he and his tame rag, the *Post*. Nothing dirtier than entrapment.'

'Of course you're bitter,' Hugo said tightly, beginning to lose his bravura, appalled to think Shelby knew where Nattie lived, 'but you'd painted him as a terrorist and put his life in imminent danger with that interview you gave – I know all about it, Nattie's told me – so Ahmed was bound to have axes to grind.

'However did you find out where they're living?' he asked, trying to cool the criticism and adopt a marvelling tone. He wanted to keep up a façade, sound awed and impressed, not in a panic; even in his woozy, wound-down state he knew he had to find out everything he could and not let Shelby dry up.

'Piece o' cake! I saw the name of Lily's school on one of her books in your kitchen. I simply followed Nattie back from her school run one day and checked out the owner of the house.'

Hugo stared; he felt invaded and abused. Was all of it his fault? The smug look on Shelby's self-absorbed face was more than he could bear.

'Gosh, private dick stuff,' he said flippantly, while the words stuck in his throat. 'But I can't imagine how you can have just set up a media storm, just like that.'

'That's easy. I've followed a bunch of Muslims on Twitter who sound like they're hard-line extremists, given myself a nicely appropriate Twitter name, and I'm getting a couple of hash tags going too, *#Traitor* and *#wifesnatcher*. I can tailor comments to *#Traitor* that will give some of those charming guys a neat lead to Lambeth. Word soon spreads.' Shelby had an even greater beam of complacency on his face.

Hugo felt shivering horror as a slow dawning of the enormity of the risk overtook him. Nattie could be knifed along with Ahmed, kidnapped ... And terrorists didn't play by the Queensberry Rules, even the children's lives could be on the line. What could he do? She had to be warned.

'And,' Shelby went on, 'once the fact of him being back here is known, skulking into the country when even the fucking authorities told him to stay away; once people are Tweeting, attaching photos – there aren't many, but one's enough – and Facebooking about it, then the papers may pick it up too. They couldn't before when they were expected to honour the code and not use his name, but now, if his name was out there ... A media storm, even a little one, is news.' Shelby's grin held pure malice. 'It's his turn to be set up now, the cunt. Let him see what it's like.'

'No one could call him my favourite guy,' Hugo said desperately, wishing his head was clearer, 'but Christ, Shelby, you could get the man killed, Nattie put at risk too. Ahmed saved her life, for God's sake, and her mother's, the lives of thousands. Imagine if that bomb had gone off. You want to be responsible for his death?'

'Calm down, dearie, you've gone quite white. The bugger will scarper off fast, back to whatever shithole part of the world he came from, you can be sure. Serve him right anyway, if one of those Brit-haters took a pot shot at him. He's one of their kind and he's had it coming. It's payback time.'

Hugo stood up, clenching his fists. 'I think you should leave now,' he said. He had to get Shelby out of the house; he felt cold hatred such as he'd never known before.

'Don't mess with me,' Shelby said easily, without moving. 'I can always get you too, any day.'

'I shouldn't try.' Hugo felt giddiness coming in waves, the room was shifting, shivers travelling down his spine, but he hung on and found some grit. 'It would do you no good at all. What you're setting up sounds like incitement to kill. So will you go now? Or do I have to call the police? I don't mind being done for drugs if it brings some protection for Nattie and our children, but it puts you in a bit of a spot.'

Shelby rose and stretched back his shoulders lazily. He ambled into the hall, picked up his Givenchy leather bomber jacket and strolled to the front door, where he turned with a sneer. 'You're a failure, Hugo, and you know it, a wimp. Get a life. Get shot of Nattie, she's bringing you down. Call me if you need anything, of course, any nuggets. No hard feelings, old man.'

He left with a swagger, though Hugo sensed he'd been taken aback; brought up a bit sharp, he felt, from the set of those black-bomber shoulders as Shelby turned out of the gate. He realised then how violently he was trembling. He'd been within a whisker of lashing out; his fists were still clenched.

He shut and bolted the door. He had Victoria's mobile number in his phone, which he pulled out of his pocket, calling her impulsively without giving any thought to what to say. Nor had he looked at the time and cursed, seeing it was almost midnight. There was no answer, which was unsurprising – no less frustrating, though.

He left a message. 'Sorry about this late call, but can you tell William rather urgently that I believe Shelby Tait has started a Twitter campaign against Ahmed, and it could be dangerous. I don't know if there's anything that can be done?'

For all his discomfort and awkwardness in William's company Hugo respected his powerhouse qualities; he edited a huge-circulation newspaper and if anyone could spike Shelby's evil doings, William was best placed.

He sent a text as well. He debated contacting Nattie, but her mother would tell her and Nattie would ask awkward questions about Shelby, which he couldn't face. She would never forgive him. He leaned against the wall in the hall, shaking, praying to God that there was a way. By now the drugs in his system had lost their effect, leaving him quivering, dry-mouthed and craving more.

A fresh wave of nausea swept in and erupted, he just made it to the downstairs loo, kneeling in front of the pan and retching up everything in his stomach. Cold sweat sprang out on his brow. His hands were clammy and his shoulders still heaved with con-vulsive jerks.

He staggered back to the sitting room, legs hardly supporting him, and collapsed into the armchair where his glass and the inroaded bottle of Scotch were within reach. Hugo poured him-self half a tumbler, releasing the unmistakable, irresistible aroma. The rich, gold-brown liquid glinted in the glass and burned comfortingly as he took sips. His mind felt clearer. Shelby had made a rare misjudgement, he felt, telling him what he'd done in that cocky, bragging way. He'd been so sure that spaced-out Hugo, eaten up with jealous hatred, would be pleased as Punch, delighted to think of Ahmed being forced out of the country. Shelby must have expected to have a load of praise poured on his glossy, devious head.

Hugo stared at the twists of paper and crack. The feeling that everything was his fault was lodged deep. He'd let Shelby into his life again, let himself be befriended; he'd become one of Shelby's dependent flock, those well-heeled suckers all over London, help-lessly shelling out.

His mind kept churning as he tried to think more rationally. Had he overreacted? Was the threat really that great? Surely a few Tweets weren't going to lead Ahmed's enemies right to his rented door. It was no good, didn't wash; he couldn't minimise the dangers nor lessen his despairing sense of guilt.

There was his release, right there, the rocks of crack on the table. Just one of those sweet babes would blast away the misery in a blinding flash. He had the pipe hidden in his clothes cupboard and now he had the stones. But the supply had to last him. He wouldn't be seeing Shelby again, he'd have to find a new source.

His phone ringing made him start backwards like being caught in the act.

'What's all this about?' William asked sharply. 'How do you know what Shelby's up to? What are you doing, being back in touch with him anyway – or can I guess?'

'I hardly am,' Hugo pleaded, instantly on the defensive. 'Shelby suggested a drink, for old times' sake; it was madness to see him, I know.'

'Let's have it then,' William said. 'Tell me everything you can.'

Hugo spelled it all out, including Shelby following Nattie on the school run. From the silence down the line William was lis-tening intently.

'We must see the house is protected before anything else,' he said finally. 'I know a security firm; they'll round up a few heavies, get them over there right away.

'There's not much we can do about this Twitter campaign, though. Twitter is all about anonymity. We can monitor the hash tags; I'll set up a team. We'll probably guess which is Shelby's Twitter name from the content and may be able to get it closed down, others too. Twitter will act when it's bad enough. There won't be any recent pics of Ahmed, maybe just some from university or his year at the BBC. None saw the light at the time of the bomb and his giving evidence. The media may have wanted to do spreads on him, the hero of the hour, all that stuff, but we all held off.'

William was in charge and taking instant action. Hugo felt overwhelmed and poured out his stumbling thanks. 'It's about as disgusting as it gets,' he said, feeling blistering hatred of Shelby. 'I feel to blame. I'm very sorry.'

'Yes, well ... We'll leave it at that, shall we?' William hung up abruptly.

Were security guards really enough protection? William must feel it was a better course than upheaving the family in the middle of the night, Hugo supposed, which could possibly draw attention. His head was spinning. He looked at the drugs on the coffee table. He'd been spending a couple of hundred pounds weekly. Nattie was coming on Tuesday, assuming they got through all this. Could he hold out till then? No crack, no snorting? Better try. After Tuesday a few crack jujubes might be all the solace he could ever hope for.

Victoria had been straining to hear both sides of the conversation; she was in her nightdress, sitting on the bed, while William was talking, feeling terrified for Nattie and the children's safety.

Nattie had phoned only that evening and when she heard of her decision, a great weight had lifted, Victoria's whole body had tingled with the relief and intense happiness she felt.

Now she rose and paced the bedroom, close to tears. She'd seen the flashing light on her phone while reading in bed, listened to the message and immediately called out to William in panic.

She stood looking at him. He was speaking rapidly into his phone, making arrangements, giving instructions about calling

999 – himself as well – at the first sign of anything suspicious. 'Best leave the kids to sleep in peace,' he advised. 'These guards are tough, they'll do the business if need be.'

'I couldn't hear all of what Hugo was saying,' Victoria said. 'Was he suggesting that Shelby knew where Nattie and Ahmed lived? How on earth could he have found that out?' She felt steadily more horrified as William explained, as well as absorbing the full significance of Hugo being in contact with Shelby.

'Thank God Ahmed's off to the airport in the morning.' She sighed. 'I can't tell you how relieved I feel about Nattie's decision. Not only for her safety, but I've lived with the dread of losing her and the children, being all that distance away.'

'It was a cruelly painful choice for her,' William said. 'I think she's shown great strength of will, but it was certainly timely with this hideous scam of Shelby's.'

'Is there nothing more to be done about him?' Victoria asked, feeling filled with an even greater loathing. She'd seen through him when he'd come to see her, trying to spread lies about Ahmed.

'I wish there was. Shelby's a rat. I can tell my mates in the Met that he could be dealing again and worth keeping an eye on, but he's sharp, he'll know he's made an error of judgement, bragging to Hugo, especially if his Twitter account gets closed. He'll take good care to cover his tracks.'

Victoria sat down heavily on the bed before climbing in wearily. 'It's hard to imagine that Shelby can be as mad as to be back dealing again. It's sheer lunacy. And to think of him pushing drugs, manipulating poor Hugo when he's at his most vulnerable – surely even Shelby's better than that.'

'Are you kidding? You can't seriously believe he'd give a brass fart about "poor Hugo's" vulnerability? He'll have been rubbing his hands in glee. Dealers thrive on insecure losers, as well as the socialite druggies with the bucks and time to fill. I hope very much that Nattie can sort Hugo out if he's using again, but it gets harder when people are older. There's the drain on the family funds, the worry of the children ...' William climbed into bed beside her and nestled up close. 'I hope I'm wrong, and I probably shouldn't be laying it on, distressing you like this, but Hugo was definitely on the back foot about Shelby. It's better you're forewarned.'

She felt the draught of a chill wind. She'd been anxious enough about Hugo's condition at Lily's party, though knowing Nattie's decision, had begun to relax a little. But the fact of Shelby, there on a Sunday night ... Why else would he be there but to push drugs? She was beginning to realise that her soft spot for Hugo had been formed through rather rose-tinted glasses.

She reached for William's hand. 'I'm not questioning what you say, it all sounds frighteningly possible, but Hugo's a good father, a kind-hearted man and he loves Nattie very much. He lives for her and the children, so I really believe he could find the will.' Her heart was thudding, she could feel it against her ribs, hear it; she thought of his having an addictive personality and said a prayer.

William held on to the hand she'd slipped into his then leapt up and reached for his phone. 'I haven't done the most important thing of all! I haven't told Ahmed about all this. Not for him so much – he's off in the morning and from what Hugo said it sounds as if Shelby has yet to set all his Twitter balls in motion, but it'll be a very brief lull before the storm. Nattie certainly shouldn't go to the airport with Ahmed tomorrow.'

'I'll call her first thing,' Victoria interrupted, panicking. 'I only hope she'll listen.'

'She'll fight any suggestion of not going. I need to text Ahmed sharpish. Nattie will have to be hyper-alert and on her guard, and he's the best person to impress on her that she and the children obviously can't stay on in that house and say what she needs to watch out for. He cares, he'll know all the precautions she should take. He's a quick thinker, my protégé,' William said dryly.

He was being lightly sardonic with that last remark, but he'd looked away, having some inward thought, and Victoria felt excluded. 'What is it?' she asked, a bit hurt.

William was sitting beside her on the bed, phone in his hand, and he turned. 'I know it has to be, but I just feel very sad they can't be together. Sorry, but I just do.'

She looked down. They didn't see entirely eye to eye, where Hugo and the marriage was concerned.

William put his arm round her, which meant a lot, then texted his urgent message.

34

Parting

Ahmed reached out to switch off the alarm clock, set for six o'clock, much less sleepily than usual, and Nattie moved closer. 'Don't go, not yet.' He must have been lying awake too, she sensed.

'I wasn't going to. I was going to wake you up in the best possible way I know. Remember, years ago, when we were into poetry? *Once did I breathe another's breath, and in my mistress move . . .*' He took her into his arms.

'*Once was I not mine own at all,*' Nattie finished for him, drawing him in, '*and then I was in love.*' She clung to the feeling of his need of her; it had to last.

'I want you to feel me, love me, no hair of distance,' he was mumbling as they kissed. For now, she thought, naked and joined – but what about later? There would be thousands of miles between them in hours.

They lay for a while, a bundle of limbs. Nattie thought of what it was to love, the gift of it, to live in another's emotions, take on that person's pain, sweet ecstasy, their trauma . . . She would feel Ahmed's highs, his moods, distance no bar, and he would know hers. He'd send unspoken support by pigeon carrier, Hurricane Matilda or whatever, thoughts racing across oceans, cadging lifts on westerly winds.

She laid a hand on his stomach, feeling the rise and fall of his quickened breath, then, lifting her face to look at him, she said with forced lightness, 'If I'd known you were as awake as I was we could have been here earlier.'

'Now you tell me!'

He left her to get dressed half an hour later than usual, picking up his phone and eyeing it as he went. 'Someone texted after midnight,' he said, 'not California – and hardly anyone has this number. I'll check it out upstairs.'

Nattie showered and dressed in the clothes he'd bought her in Lyme Regis that had a tale to tell, the tan leather skirt and soft stripy sweater. Not what she would normally wear for the school run on a Monday morning, but it wasn't a normal Monday – nor a normal any other day. But for the baby she'd have felt that all the life in her was draining away as the minutes ticked by.

Lily was still fast asleep. She slept more heavily of late, less often watching for the sun to come up on her clock, her signal to invade her mother's room. Nattie had put out her school clothes and Tubsy's things, and laid the breakfast table the night before; she wanted no faffing about, hunting for clean socks, when it was their last hour or so of being all together in the house.

She went in to Lily. 'Wake-up time, lovely! School today – and Dan's going to America, remember? You must give him a big hug.' She'd told the children the night before, coming back from her mother's.

Lily yawned and rubbed her eyes. 'When's he back, Mummy? He must be here in time for Christmas as I'm making him a calendar at school. I've got lots to bring home on my last day.' Nattie had almost forgotten how close to the end of term it was.

'Better get up now, darling, while I see to Tubs; your clothes are all there, all ready, and I'll be with you in a minute.'

As she went out of the room Ahmed was coming downstairs. He put his cheek to hers. 'That text I had was from William. I need to talk to you about it – quite urgently.'

'Why? What's up?' She stared. William must know something and it had to be bad.

'You can't come to the airport, Nattie darling, it's not safe.'

'Are you mad? I'm coming and there's nothing that you, William, or anyone else could do or say that would stop me. If it's not safe to drive we can get a cab – I'll get my own if necessary.' Then she calmed down. 'It's Shelby, isn't it. What's he done?'

'Better not now. You've got to get Lily to school. I'll call you in the car on your way home.'

Nattie's phone was buzzing. She saw the message on the screen and looked up. 'Text from Mum, saying it's urgent.'

'She'll want to tell you the same thing,' Ahmed muttered, 'that it's not safe for you to come to the airport.'

Nattie glared at him. She texted her mother. *Can't talk now, Mum, usual breakfast rush. Call after school run.*

Breakfast was typical chatter and clatter. Tubsy upturned his bowl of squidged-up Weetabix, which dripped down the side of his high chair; the normality of everything that morning had an eerily surreal feel.

'I wish you weren't going to America, Dan,' Lily said. 'Do you reely have to?'

''Fraid so. Not sure when I'll be back either, but you're reading so well now, I'll write you letters with American stamps on them that you'll be able to read yourself. Will you write me one back?'

'I'll write lots!' She got down from the table, dancing up to him while he put another pod in the coffee machine, jumping about in high spirits. 'Will Mummy know where to send them?'

'Sure thing – but she's giving us looks, Lily love, she thinks I'm making you late. Off you go, I'll feed Moppet for you, but I would like one last hug.'

Lily ran into his arms and he hugged her tight, smoothing her hair and pushing her head to his chest. She pulled back and looked at him.

'You're crying. Don't cry! You will be back in time for Christmas? I've got to give you my present.'

'It wasn't proper crying, just I so hate saying goodbye. Very exciting, this talk of a present. And who knows? I might just have something for you.'

He stayed in the kitchen with Tubsy while Nattie hustled Lily out of the door.

Lily was talkative on the way to school. 'I wish Dan wasn't going, Mummy. Will we have to move out of his house? Will we be with Daddy while he's away?'

'I'm not sure. We'll probably stay here – in Dan's house – for a while. He may get back before too long, but he'll have to be in America quite a lot of the time now.' She gave a quick backwards glance to Lily, strapped into her seat. 'You've got tea with Jade today, darling, remember. Her mummy is picking you up from school. I'll come there for you later.'

'I'm going to finish the calendar in school today, so he's got to come back for Christmas. He's my other daddy, isn't he? I told my teacher that.'

They were at the school. Nattie parked and they got out – Lily could undo her own seatbelt now, and she started off at a run. 'Lunch box!' Nattie called, smiling and handing it over as Lily rushed back. 'And a kiss before you go.' She watched Lily in through the gates, golden hair flying, saw her link up with her friend, Noah, and go into school, chattering non-stop. Then she drove away, tears flowing freely down her cheeks.

The Ford had Bluetooth and when Ahmed phoned from home as promised, his voice filled the car; it was the essence of him, male, light, strong, full of warmth. It was hard to bear; her heart was bleeding. But she listened as carefully as he pleaded that she should, and soon knew the worst.

'What Shelby's done is like hiring a contract killer,' she exclaimed. He'd take his revenge that far? How low could anyone get? And how thankful she felt about William's security guards. They owed him a lot. She had to grip the wheel hard, shaking with fear for Ahmed's safety, and violent outrage.

'You do see now how serious it is, Nattie? You can't come to the airport. Shelby's probably Tweeting his mischief as we speak. I can't let you anywhere near me on the way or at the airport. You mustn't come.'

She felt such furious determination that it dried her tears. 'My turn now,' she said forcefully. 'You listen to me! We go to the airport together in a licensed black cab. We have our wits about us there and have the protection of the crowds. I'm with you till you're through that departure gate, whether you like it or not. Shelby doesn't mess with us like this, no way. If there could be any crumb of comfort in all this, it's that he'll have missed the bloody boat with you flying out ahead of time. I'll still have to bring Tubsy with us to the airport, though. Mum's probably tied up and anyway, she'd only try to stop me going. Pity Jasmine looks after that other baby on Mondays.'

'I anticipated you'd make this sort of fuss,' Ahmed said, sounding almost amused. 'I called Tom to say goodbye, told him a bit of what's happened, and he offered to help out with Tubsy. "Quality time with my nephew," he said – though he's worried he might put the Pampers on wrong side up.'

'I'm sure even Tom can work out the right side,' Nattie said, relieved.

'He'll be okay. I've taken out one of your little frozen pots for Tubsy's lunch, which should help. William called and confirmed that the house is still being guarded. I spoke to your mother while he was on, and tried to reassure her, but you must phone her as soon as you're back, darling, she's really distressed.'

'I'm home, now,' Nattie said, frustrated with her mother while feeling more scared than she was letting on. 'Just drawing up.' She peered round, getting out of the car, heart fluttering, but saw no one loitering in the street, nothing untoward.

Tom arrived minutes after her. He came into the hall holding out his arms and she folded into them, glad of the hug. He drew back and looked at her with huge understanding in his eyes. 'I'm not keen on Ahmed pushing off like this – it's certainly come as a bit of a shock. I don't know about you, Nattie, but I'm going to miss him a lot.'

'Well, he has his good points . . .' She smiled, but time was short: she had to call her mother and Ahmed had a plane to catch. Tom would be there when she was back from the airport; they could talk then. Talk? How would she cope and manage to speak, even to him? Perhaps it was as well he'd be there, she could cry in front of Tom.

She swiftly took him through Tubsy's routine, including his midday nap. 'You'll be glad of a bit of peace by then and he's always ready for it, goes down like a lamb.'

'That's a blessing! You'd better go, Nattie. A taxi was drawing up as I arrived, I expect it's yours. And don't you worry, Tubs and I will be fine.'

Tom hung back in the kitchen with his typical sensitivity. Nattie had flung off her coat, coming in, and Ahmed was holding it ready. He kissed the back of her neck as he helped her into it and she turned in to him, heart pressed to heart, but they had to go.

He went into the kitchen, ruffled Tubsy's curly blond hair and kissed him. He had a last look round, storing snatches of memory, then went into the sitting room and looked out of the back window at the garden and Moppet's hutch. Then he walked purposefully out of the room, picked up his bags and called good-bye to Tom.

Tom came into the hall. 'Safe flight, you old sod, and mind you come back sooner than the last time,' he said, his voice gruff with emotion, before he opened the front door for them and they hurried out to the waiting taxi.

It was a gloomy, overcast day, reassuringly dark in the cab; they needed anonymity. Ahmed tucked Nattie's arm under his and held her hand. 'Well, we made it into the cab in one piece,' he smiled. 'One down, but a few more hurdles at the airport. When we get there I want you to make for a different entrance, Nattie. We can link up again by phone. You must think risk and take constant precautions the whole time now. Promise me you will? It's essential.'

'Ease up on me a bit, can't you? I've just had a basinful from Mum, as you predicted, and I had a job to stop her from coming round tonight, but I think she realised how badly I'd need to be alone. You haven't told me how William discovered about Shelby. Had he been on to the press? Don't spare me the details.'

'It was from Hugo – he got in touch with William late last night. He'd just had Shelby round who'd bragged about his plans – obviously hadn't bargained on Hugo's decent reaction. But from the gossip columns, the people Shelby's in with, he's back showering snow around London like confetti, and I hate to say it, Nattie, but it looks like Hugo's back using the stuff.'

'So that's how Shelby knew which school to follow me home from.' Her heart sank to her boots; she felt sickened to think of Shelby manipulating poor Hugo for his own evil ends. And confirmation of Hugo using again was a disaster. She'd seen the signs, though, known the awful inevitability. Was it crack as well as coke? Hugo needed the lift and sense of euphoria coke gave, not for the kicks, simply to help him function at all. He must be hanging on to his job by a thread. But crack . . .

'Twitter's fast,' she said, pulling her mind back, and realising, as she said it, what a huge understatement that was. There could be spotters at the airport already.

She shivered and pressed closer to Ahmed. 'I can't believe I'm saying this, but thank God you were flying out this very day. It's spiking Shelby's guns at the least. He gets to you over my dead body.'

'Don't say that! But I'm not the problem, Nattie darling – it's you. You must take the risk you're under more seriously. There could be people out there who'll try to get to me through you. Shelby knows where we've been living, that's the real fear. I haven't had time to see what Tweets are out there, whether he's got going yet, but he will.' Nattie was surprised, she'd been gone a good hour on the school run. 'Nowhere's really safe for you now – except California.' Ahmed gave a wry smile and kissed her lips. 'Jake's house least of all. You can't stay there a day longer. I'll talk you through my plans for that, but we're almost there. Tell you over coffee.'

'But William's storming into action, you say, putting a team onto monitoring and countering Tweets, even getting Twitter addresses removed; surely the whole thing will fizzle out like a failed firework?' They were in the underpass tunnel at Heathrow, soon to go in through different doors, wheel his cases to be checked in, have a last few moments over coffee before the final goodbye. People everywhere, time running out, and there was so much more to say. She wanted to be having a lifetime's conversation, talking about love and connection, not Shelby and Islamist terrorists.

'You're being a bit extreme,' she said.

'I'm not. I'm telling it like it is. William's a different generation; he knows a lot, has power, all the power of the press at his elbow, but even he doesn't know the full reach of social media. It's an unstoppable, unkillable beast. The terrorists are at war with us. And however long ago it was I thwarted a plot almost on the scale of nine-eleven, they want my head.'

Ahmed was travelling Business Class and was spared a long queue. Nattie had lagged well behind and as he turned to leave the check-in desk he phoned her. 'Keep me in sight and I'll find somewhere we can sit and talk.'

He feared for them both, but he was the one whose life was in danger. The risk to her, she still believed, was minimal.

He made for a small café and got the last available table. There was noise, a bulky family at the next table whose piled-up kit was in everyone's way, whose children kept running off, the father stumbling over the luggage, going after them. There were open packets of crisps, cheese-and-onion-flavoured; the smell was bringing bile into Nattie's throat, but it was containable.

Ahmed talked in hushed undertones. 'You can't stay in Jake's house, nor your mother's basement. She and William live too close, it's too great a risk. I did some fast phoning while you were taking Lily to school. I talked to Jake in Australia. It was evening, a good time, and I told him all. He's coming over to sort out a new rental. He's got keys, you can leave all yours in the hall. Jake says you needn't rehang those curtains of Sylvia's we took down so don't fret about that! And good news, Sylvia's pregnant, so he's not worried about our fiddles in Lily's room.' He lifted Nattie's hand to his lips, looking at her so movingly over it that she burst into tears.

'Sorry,' she said, recovering, 'I know you've got more to say. There's no one I can descend on, though, with two children and a guinea pig. I'll have to go to Mum's for a while.'

'No, you won't. First on cars. The Ford is yours, in your name, not easily traced to me. Shelby knows it, but I'd like to think he's done his damnedest now. He'll be watching his own back too. Hugo saw him off apparently, and Shelby's on weak ground. But you can't stay in Jake's house a day longer, so I've rented you a furnished flat in Notting Hill. It's paid up, all sorted, you won't have water and electricity bills, they'll come to me. It looks good online, a maisonette with enough garden for Moppet. Go and see it this afternoon with Tubsy. You must move tomorrow, darling, that's most important of all.' Ahmed had hold of her hand so tightly, she felt he was trying to press that home even harder.

'Don't go to work tomorrow, have a sickie,' he said. 'You'll have Jasmine there to help and be with Tubs while you do the move – I've given her the gist of this on the phone – and I've left you a long note with all the details. The flat keys are with the estate agents who'll show you round and explain everything. Call me if you need to; always call. I'm going to look after you, Nattie. I have money, it's not a problem – so don't start protesting – and it's somewhere I can come to when the baby is born. I'm going to buy the flat as an investment; it's for sale.'

'What about Hugo?' Nattie asked in a small voice, her head swimming. 'What if he wants me back?'

'I'll understand. I will have bought the flat soon enough; I may do short-term lets if you're with Hugo, make the flat earn its keep – and hope to use it myself, once or twice of course.'

He looked at his watch then back up into her face. 'I'm going to marry you, Nattie darling, however long it takes – though I hope that won't be as long as it took Captain Corelli. We'll walk on beaches holding hands and puff ourselves up with pride about our genius child. Who knows, maybe we'll have had another by then.' He put his hand to her stomach and kissed her eyes.

'It will be hard for you with Hugo. He could lose his job and he'll be full of blame for ever having let Shelby cross the threshold. But I very much doubt now, with your decision,' Ahmed said, 'that he'll be checking out other sources; he'll try to stay clean. And if I'm really honest, and saying it makes me feel like I'm signing my own death warrant, you'd probably be safest back in Queen's Park. A better man than I would have said that earlier.'

'Don't,' she said, 'just bloody don't.' She pulled free and buried her head in her hands.

Ahmed lifted them away, held on to them and fastened his eyes on hers. She felt her blood drain away like sand in a timer; the minutes were ticking by. 'I feel a bit faint,' she said. 'It's only partly the baby, more just an excuse, but don't let go of me, not quite yet.' She found some control and blinked away a tear, heart swelling to bursting.

'How am I going to bear to watch *Shorelands*?' she said. 'And it's spoilt for me anyway now. I know the plot, I'll know what's coming . . .'

'I'll put in a twist or two that you'll work out are just for you. They'll have special meaning.'

Nattie kept on holding his hands; she couldn't prepare for the emptiness, couldn't let go.

Ahmed held her eyes. 'It's getting late – I'd better go. I'll walk ahead of you.'

There was no distance between them when they linked up at Departures. They didn't care who saw them as they clung, wet-eyed, each storing the feel, the shape and warmth and heart-beat of the other. 'You'll keep me close out there?' she whispered, before he separated. He wiped his eyes, and hers, picked up his bag and walked up to the barrier. She watched him through, not expecting him to turn, but he did, with a soft, sad smile, then was lost to the other side.

35

Emptiness

Nattie walked woodenly away from the departure gates, her senses numbed, her head empty of thought. She was dry-eyed waiting in the queue for a taxi and for most of the way back into London, but reaching the Hammersmith flyover, she broke down completely, sobbing out loud in the back of the taxi, her shoulders shaking violently. She was convulsed, overcome with desolation. Tears blurring her vision, streaming down her cheeks. When the taxi drew up outside Jake's house, the driver got out looking concerned, and asked if she'd be okay. He even insisted on walking her right to her door. She didn't protest.

She went in, worrying about Tom seeing her ravaged face, but he wasn't about, probably getting Thomas up from his rest, and it gave her a few minutes to recover. She began to feel calmer then, better able to face him and think more clearly.

Was she really going to move the very next day? It seemed impossible to imagine, the way she felt, limp from emotional exhaustion and too little sleep, but from the moment she turned her key and set foot inside she'd known that even without the dangers, her fears for the children, Jake's house without Ahmed in it was the very last place she wanted to be.

The house was so still and quiet. She called upstairs. 'Hi, Tom! All okay?'

'I'm just on the phone – in the upstairs study. Be there in a tick. Tubs is still sleeping, but stirring, I think.'

'No rush, finish your call. I'll get him up.'

Nattie shed her coat and went up, taking the stairs very slowly; her legs felt heavy, as in a nightmarish dream where she had somewhere to get to, but thwarted in her every attempt to reach it.

She leaned over the cot. Tubsy, unsure whether he wanted to wake up, undecided whether to smile or cry, gave a token wail, but he soon adjusted. Nattie got him up and he said, excitedly, trotting out of the door, 'Dan, Dan do train?' She chased after him and caught up with him at the stairs.

'Dan's gone to America, he's on a woosh, woosh plane, and Uncle Tom is about to go back to his painting. It's just you and me, Tubsy. We'll go out in the blue car this afternoon, to see a new house.'

The kitchen was an impenetrable jungle. Tom and Tubsy seemed to have upturned toys she never knew they owned. The floor was a spaghetti junction of half-linked rail-track; it was a farmyard, it was garaging ambulances, fire engines, JCB diggers and as many cars as you'd see on the M25. Tubsy was soon happily distracted.

'Hi, Sis,' Tom called, zooming downstairs and doing a slight double take, seeing Nattie's swollen, piggy eyes. 'I've been on two long calls. You okay to talk?' he said. 'I'm, um, sorry.'

'It's all right, Tom, I've done my tears. Thanks for coming, being there for us.' She smiled, but it wasn't "us" any more and a great lump came back into her throat. 'All well, I hope, with your calls?'

'Sure, but they kind of involve you. Maudie called, just out of the blue, which came as something of a shock. That was her I was talking to. It was really all about you, but she was chatty and said we must get together sometime. She's worried about you, Nattie, and a tad miffed that you hadn't confided in her. I hadn't realised how little she knew, so I'm afraid I've spilled a few beans. Sorry, but she is trustworthy, Nattie. I think you ought to see her and let some of it out. It's helped me, being able to unload onto you.'

'I will. I've missed her in my life, but you know the risks, we had to be so careful. I just felt . . .' Nattie tailed off, distracted by a huge temptation to tell Tom about the baby. 'And the other call?'

'It was from Ahmed, actually; he was about to take off. He wants me to help you move house tomorrow and as a thank-you he wants to send me a return ticket to LA. He says he's got bags of room and I should come out for a few days after Christmas. Do you think I should accept?'

'Yes, definitely! You're the one person he can trust to know where he lives. Take a few paintings – you could pick up some terrific clients. You've got your work on Instagram; plenty more you can show. Will you keep in touch with Maudie now?'

'I'll think about it . . . Will you see her, though? And Nattie, I'm not sure if I should tell you, but Ahmed let on to me about the baby. I'm so happy for you. Share that with Maudie too, won't you? She'd love it.'

Nattie felt nervous, strapping Thomas into his car seat later; Shelby wouldn't know Ahmed was gone yet, and she couldn't see any guards as she looked over her shoulder, up and down the street. It was a grey wintry afternoon, three o'clock and still full daylight. There were few passing cars and no one much about, just a teenager on a skateboard, an elderly man wheeling a tartan shopping bag.

She drove across London and found the flat, which was in a street off Ladbroke Grove, the Harrow Road end, and easier for the school run by far. The guy from the estate agent, a sharp dresser in a double-breasted suit, seemed very intrigued with her friend, with whom he'd done pretty good business, first thing that morning. 'We only took instructions on the flat last week, and the photographs only went online last night. Will he be back from his travels soon and able to see the property for himself?'

'He's on a big job,' Nattie said obliquely. 'Did he mention I'd like to move in tomorrow?'

'Oh, yes, and he suggested we put the heating on today, have it nice and warm for you and this little chappie by then.' Harvey, he said his name was, chucked Tubsy under his chin.

It was a three-bedroom flat with a lovely big through room, living, kitchen and dining all in one, on the ground floor, and the bedrooms one floor up. The décor was neutral, fine, and she marvelled that Ahmed could have found something as attractive and presentably furnished as this, in half an hour on a Monday morning. She could see why he hadn't had time to look for Shelby's Tweets.

He had even hired a van for Tom, who was going to do the heavy lifting. Jasmine would be looking after Tubsy while it was all going on and would bring him with her when she collected Lily from school. Nattie was going to meet up with them at the school and lead the way to the new flat. It was another new address for Jasmine, but she seemed very philosophical about it all, taking it in her stride. Nattie felt relieved and intensely grateful, especially since after seeing them sorted and settled she had to drive the short distance to Queen's Park to tell Hugo her decision.

That was tomorrow, though. Tonight was for sobbing herself to sleep in the bed she had shared with Ahmed.

She locked up the new flat, leaving the heating on, and drove with Tubsy to Jade's house, where Lily was having tea. Lily looked very ready to come home – was that just because it was a tiring time of year with so much going on?

'Jade's mummy was crying about something to do with Jade's daddy,' Lily said, once they were in the car. 'He wants to take some table or other, and Jade's mummy kept saying, "And just before Christmas too!" Are you getting a divorce like them, Mummy? Are you going to marry Dan?'

'No, Lily, I'm married to Daddy. Dan's a sort of distant daddy. He loves you and Tubsy very much, and me, and we'll see him on the times he can come over from America. I'm going to miss him!'

'I am too.' Lily seemed okay with that, though, and about the new flat she had yet to see – which was very near school, Nattie said, and no distance from Daddy either.

Nattie still had to call in sick; she would do it first thing in the morning. Moving house would have been a legitimate excuse except that no one at the office knew about the various upheavals in her life and they might have taken some explaining.

She gave the children their supper, got them into the bath, Tubsy had his bottle then she went into Lily's room to read her a story.

Lily was crying. 'I don't like it here without Dan. The house feels funny, sort of empty. I won't be able to do any more stories with him. I wish he hadn't gone.'

'So do I, darling, but you can write to him about any ideas you have, I'll help you.'

'Will he do them like a book just the same and send them back?'

'I expect so, darling. He may be very busy – he'll be working very hard out there – but I'm sure he'll try. And you'll be busy with your schoolwork. Are you making something for Daddy in school as well?' Nattie held her breath. She felt desperately sad for Hugo; a hand-made present from Lily would mean so much.

'It's a sort of folder for him to keep his papers in. I hope he likes it.'

'Daddy will love that! I'll read you one of the *Just William* stories, shall I? But I think you're very sleepy ... Lily soon dropped off, pulling round the duvet and snuggling into her usual sleeping position with Kangy. Nattie crept out of the room.

She hadn't been downstairs long when the doorbell rang. She froze, hearing the shrill intrusive sound, feeling numb with fear. She went, terrified, to peer at the security screen. It could be a delivery. Ahmed was always having things arrive – how could she tell a delivery boy from a terrorist?

The screen was lit up and it was a relief to see it was a woman. A partial relief, since it was Maudie, her oldest friend, but it wasn't the night for it. Even chatting to Maudie was going to take all of Nattie's reserves of energy and willpower. She couldn't cope.

Nattie went wearily to get the door and Maudie breezed in, chic as ever in jeans, high-heeled boots and a poncho. 'I wasn't having you crying into your Cup a Soup tonight,' she said cheerfully, lifting the poncho off over her neat head. 'You're going to open a decent bottle and we're going to get stuck in. I'm sure Ahmed keeps this place well stocked.'

'Kept,' Nattie corrected. 'He's gone, he's halfway across the world by now.' She stared at Maudie miserably, yet found herself feeling a shaft of gratitude, imagining the long hours, the intense loneliness of being in Jake's house without Ahmed.

'Come into the kitchen, it's stuffed with food and drink, all of which I've got to move out of here tomorrow. Thank God, Tom's going to set to and help. I'd have been lost without him – he's been a rock. I gather he's filled you in a bit?' She looked at Maudie anxiously, unsure how much she knew.

'Yep, I've got the picture and I won't talk. Have no worries there. You've seen these hashtags – #traitor? #AhmedKhan?' Nattie shook her head. 'Well, if you haven't, don't look! Now what's in the fridge . . .' Maudie opened the vast heavy door and pounced on a bottle of Sancerre. 'This'll hit the spot. And we need eggs – I'll make us omelettes. You can slice up some tomatoes and lay a knife and fork.'

'Nothing like taking over,' Nattie said, managing a smile.

She talked for hours when she got started.

Maudie was astounded about the baby. 'Shit, you're not on your third already! You're giving me a real old complex. I'll have to get going one of these days. Now,' she said briskly, 'I want to tell you a story about a friend of mine, then I'll let you get to bed and have that good long cry.'

'What friend?'

'She's a client, but a very nice one. We got talking once and she told me about her situation that's not a million miles from yours. She had this husband who was a mild old cove, a good sort, very introverted and into rare books and booze. She fell in love with a bright, witty man in television one day, but couldn't leave the helpless one – he depended on her for everything, you see, and they had a load of children too. So they had a sort of compromise *ménage à trois* scene, until one day, the husband announced out of nowhere that he was leaving her. He upped and married a tough businesswoman with a successful catering firm and my friend's life began anew.

'So there you are, you never know what's down the line,' Maudie said with a big grin on her face. 'Keep your pecker up, won't you? And now you're looking all forlorn again.'

'Yes, well – "down the line" is a long way away. But thanks for coming tonight, Maudie, really. You saved me from sinking and it's meant a lot.'

36

Resolution

'Who would ever move house?' Nattie grimaced at Tom. He was being stoic, even as she produced yet another overloaded packing case for him to take to the van. Amazon had delivered a quantity of double-walled flat-pack removal cartons early that morning, Ahmed must have thought of that too, in his extraordinarily productive hour before leaving. It was just as well. She kept finding more stuffed drawers, more toys, books, things they'd accumulated; belongings of his that he'd forgotten, though those were no problem now that they had the flat – nor was storage of the case he'd left behind with a spare set of kit for future visits. That wouldn't be soon.

There were the clothes Ahmed had bought her, jewellery too, chosen sensitively, especially a thin gold necklace she adored. She'd remonstrated with him every time, but not over the Ford; that was theirs, she said, he'd be glad of a car when he came. There was no chance of seeing him before the baby was born, she knew. No snatched weekends, Shelby had seen to that. But nor should there be if she were honest with herself – if she was determined to do everything in her power to help Hugo and to try to settle into a relationship that would work.

Lily's cooking stove, her blackboard, plants in pots, a television, Ahmed's music kit, Moppet's hutch, so much to fit into the van. 'Keep it coming,' Tom said. 'We'll get there!'

Jasmine was helping too, as well as looking after Tubsy. 'What about his cot, the little lamb?' she said. 'He needs his midday sleepies.'

'I think it best,' Nattie said, looking hopefully at Tom, 'if we put Tubsy down early for a short rest, then either Tom or I will come back in the van for the cot.'

'I guess that's one for me,' Tom said. He was certainly earning his ticket to California.

Jasmine was a wonderful repository for anything going begging, thrilled with the clothes Ahmed had said he didn't want. She did a good job on the food cupboards too, clearing and cleaning them efficiently, and was delighted to take the half-used packets, putting them separately in a neat pile. She told Nattie to wrap the frozen food in thick layers of newspaper. 'It's insulation, keeps it frozen for hours so it'll be fine when you get there.'

'Sounds brilliant,' Nattie said, with a smile.

She and Tom made it away by half twelve. The unloading was much simpler, the van soon emptied, and she sent out for pizzas while Tom extracted bottles of beer from the stash of drink he'd just carted in. Ahmed hadn't stinted with supplies. Then, beers in hand, they flopped down on chairs and patted themselves on the back.

'Thanks for everything, Tom, for being there for us. You've been more than a friend to Ahmed. And how could I have managed without you today?'

'It's been fun – kind of! No, really. I like the flat too. Ahmed didn't hang about, did he?'

'He never does,' Nattie said, opening cupboard doors, swigging her beer. 'There's excellent storage space here – good for my lonely nights, unpacking all those boxes.'

'I still think you should have gone with him.'

'I couldn't. It would have felt like leaving Hugo to kill himself. I married him, Tom, I have to cherish him, even if the love isn't quite as it should be.'

'He's back on cocaine?'

'Yep. And crack most likely, but not heroin, I'm sure. I take a crumb of comfort from how he's got by on his weekends with the children. He must have found some inner will. They mean so much to him, he'd have disintegrated if I'd taken them to California.'

The pizzas arrived; they ate hungrily. Nattie made coffee then Tom went off for the cot. It gave her a window of privacy. She wanted to text Ahmed before Tom was back and it was time to get Lily and show Jasmine the ropes at the flat.

Six in the morning in California. Ahmed would still be asleep; no noisy children now, his life changing pace.

She texted him and said she'd love a call before she had to face Hugo. It was for the comfort of hearing his voice; he couldn't help her, couldn't stiffen her backbone, no one could. She had to strip away Amber, Tyler Consultancy, money worries, even Ahmed. She and Hugo had to get through the thicket unaided, just them alone.

Ahmed called – conveniently when she was in the car on her way to Queen's Park. He wished her luck with Hugo, saying fervently how hard that was for him to do. He chatted, told her about the hectic time he had coming up with the filming, all the arguments, changes to the scripts, said he loved her and she should never forget that. Ending the call was awful. It only served to make facing Hugo harder; it hadn't helped at all.

*

Nattie was first at the house. The key was on her key ring where it had always been and she let herself in. The place smelled vile. It truly stank. Heidi came on a Thursday, so it was five days since she'd been, but even so . . . The smell could be rotten food, Nattie decided, making straight for the kitchen. Looking round, she could see signs of Hugo's vain attempt to clear up, but the sad, unloved feel of the place was heartrending. It wasn't a sort of bachelor squalor, dirty plates piled high and saucepans with congealed remains, it was more the lack of any sign of eating at all. It had the look of a family kitchen let go, barren, non-functioning; Lily's drawings were under magnets on the fridge, a sit-on blue plastic car was pushed into a corner, but the dead pots of herbs on the windowsill, a black sack that clinked as she touched it told a wretched tale.

She found the source of the smell – sour yoghurt pots and assorted veg, all black with mould – in the swing bin. She reckoned Heidi must have had a clear-out of the fridge and assumed quite reasonably that Hugo would take out the rubbish. Nattie dealt with it, taking it to the bin outside. As she came back in, the smell was still there. It hit her then: it was vomit. She sniffed her way to the downstairs loo where she discovered the source and set to. Her long day was beginning to feel even longer.

It was six o'clock now – how late was he going to be? She went into the sitting room where Hugo hadn't cleared away a quarter-full wine bottle and a wine glass with a lipsticked rim. There was a tumbler and empty whisky bottle on the floor beside his favourite armchair.

She heard his key in the door and glanced in the mirror over the fireplace. It was instinctive, a female thing, but it helped her confidence to feel her hair wasn't flat and she wasn't looking too washed-out; the next hour would be draining enough.

'I'm here,' she called, 'in the sitting room.'

Hugo came in looking slightly demonic. His suit was hanging off him, he'd lost so much weight. He sniffed the air a bit, lifting his head, adjusting, she imagined, to the odour of disinfectant in the house.

'Well, hi there, stranger,' he said, being overtly breezy and glint-eyed, 'welcome to your own home! What's it to be? Glass of the old Sauve? Or are you going to be dead boring and want a cup of tea?' He stretched out the word *tea*, cocking his head from side to side and being unnaturally brash.

He was confirming her worst fears. She'd visualised him snorting in the washroom at Tyler's before leaving or the Gents in some pub on the way home.

'Let's have some tea. It's soothing; it'll help,' she said, ignoring his glowering reaction. 'I'll put the kettle on. We've got a lot to talk about.'

'Tea? God! It'll be cucumber sandwiches and Rich Tea biscuits next, and cream buns.'

'I didn't go to the shops on the way, just cleaned up your downstairs loo.'

'*Our* loo, damn you! I suppose you're about to tell me you're leaving old Blighty, your home and me? Better put me out of my misery then and get back to your packing.'

'*Un*packing actually. I've had to move – today. Your new old friend Shelby has put my life in enough danger, and the children's lives. Jake's house isn't a safe place for us to be.'

Hugo slumped down in an armchair. His face was grey, sunken, he had huge under-eye shadows; his hair, when he was fit, was a feature of his good looks, mousy, but shiny and clean, floppy and forward-hanging in an appealing way. It was never, as now, flat to his head, lank and straggly. Nattie saw him notice the empty bottle on the floor; it caused him to glance at the lipsticky wine glass. He let out a low groan and buried his head in his hands.

She left him to go to make mugs of tea and phone Jasmine. 'Hugo doesn't seem very well,' she said. 'I think I could be here a couple of hours. Are you good to put the children in the bath and do a bottle? I'll be back as soon as I can, but just reassure me, Jasmine. It's the first night there for them – are they okay, do you think?'

'I'll tell them you're with their daddy, I'm sure they'll be fine. Lily's been fixing her new room and Tubsy's very settled in, like he knows the place already.' He did, he'd had the previous afternoon there. And Lily, seeing the flat for the first time, had seemed happy enough, exploring and clucking over Moppet. 'No worries about time for me,' Jasmine went on. 'I'm getting Pete over, if that's okay? He can give me a ride home.'

Nattie thanked her and relaxed a bit. The single carton of milk in the fridge was well and truly off; she remembered a tin of powdered milk on the top shelf in the food cupboard, climbed on a chair and moved two tins of flageolet beans, a hangover from a craze for a particular lamb recipe, to reach it. She shifted an ancient packet of macaroni to tidy away the tins and saw twists of paper that took her back to another decade, another place. She was in Hugo's Hammersmith flat, coaxing him up from the filthy floor, holding him tight while he clung wildly, screaming of demons. She left his supply where it was. Removing it wouldn't help. Hugo had to find the resistance, the will to lick his habit; he had to get there himself.

She mixed spoonfuls of powdered milk with water and poured some into the tea; she found, to her amazement, an unopened packet of Rich Tea biscuits then remembered once buying them when one of Hugo's aunts had been coming.

Hugo was still bent low with his head in his hands; no more bravado, he was a sagging bag of bones. 'Please sit up properly,' she said, feeling like a starched nurse with a patient, 'and have a few sips of this. It's good and hot – and don't laugh, but I've found some biscuits. It's powdered milk, though, I'm afraid. I found a tin of it behind a packet of macaroni on the top shelf of the food cupboard.'

He looked up then, stared like a man coming out of a trance. 'Oh, you did? Right up there? Do I have to drink this? I might be sick, can't keep much down just now.'

'Try it. I put some sugar in, it's settling. And dip in a biscuit too.'

'I'm not a child. And if I don't have a bit of Scotch I'll pass out. I've got some in the hall, bought a couple of bottles on the way home. I'll just get one.'

She could see the sweat break out as he tried to stand. 'I'll get it,' she said, 'but drink the tea.' He stared at her, stared down at the tea, then lifted the mug to his lips with both hands.

'I've got a glass here,' he called after her as she went out into the hall.

She stayed silently in the doorway, coming back, relieved to see he was still sipping the tea. He sensed her there and lifted his eyes, putting down the mug and spilling some, holding out a hand for the bottle like a supplicant.

Nattie handed it over and sat down in the other armchair. 'Ahmed left the country yesterday,' she said. 'He was on a plane before Shelby's Twitter feed had time to have caused people to be skulking around at Jake's or at the airport. He'd have been an easy target otherwise, probably knifed or axed in the street before he ever made it to Heathrow. It's as well I'd made my decision in time. He knew about Shelby's doings before leaving, of course. William had called.'

Hugo had a tormented look in his eyes. Nattie forestalled him as he tried to speak. 'I know how you must feel about the Shelby business. It makes me shivery even to think of being followed, but let's draw a veil over it all, shall we?' She smiled. Hugo stayed mute, sipping whisky, his eyes in their sunken sockets constantly staring.

'Shall I go first?' she suggested. It was what she'd said to Ahmed only a couple of days ago. It felt like a lifetime already. 'I'm going to try to explain what I think is the best way forward, but stop me any time you want. I'm sorry I've taken so long about it, but it's been such a huge emotional upheaval. Ahmed alive and home again, the shock and bolt from the blue. He's gone now.' She swallowed. 'I know it's been hard for you, Hugo, with all the stresses and strains. I hope you understand.'

'Oh, God,' he mumbled. He was focusing, raw. 'How long has Ahmed gone for? For good? What a lousy fucking mess.' The chemicals in his system were draining and she dreaded to think how addicted he could have become. He looked ghastly. Was he going to have to go into rehab again? It would be the end of his job.

'Yes, he's left now, gone abroad. He's far away. But there's something I have to tell you, which, if you do still want me back at some stage, might make you want to change your mind. I'll still be here in London with the children, though, either way. We had to move out of Jake's house today, because of Shelby, but we're in a flat that's quite near here. You'll be able to see plenty of them.'

He took a long gulp of whisky. 'What is it you have to tell me? Just say it.'

'I'm having Ahmed's baby. I'd want to be with him from time to time – like at the birth and when he's able to come on a visit to enjoy his child. I may go out to where he is once in a while as well. Probably take the children, but I'll always come back, unless you'd started a new life. That's it, Hugo. I'm sorry, I've let you down very badly. I love you in my way – I always will, that hasn't changed – but I'm afraid that seeing Ahmed again, I wasn't able to keep control.'

'But you haven't gone with him. Why not?'

'I wanted to help you where I can and you're a loving father. I can't take your children away and deprive you of seeing them – I couldn't do that.'

'You'd be prepared to have his child and live here with me – with his child?'

'Yes, if you wanted it and felt able to cope. Not straight away. In due time, if you'd got clean. You managed to, all those years ago when you were in a far worse state, so you can do it. I'd stay in the flat for a while, a couple of months, maybe. I can be there indefinitely and I have a car.'

'Who's paying for the flat, the car? William and your mother?'

'No, Ahmed is. The car is his really, to use when he's over.'

'Where does he get the money?'

'He's done pretty well, actually.' It was hard to keep the pride out of her voice.

'Bloody man.'

'You'll need plenty of time to think all this through,' Nattie said, looking at him anxiously, wondering if he was going to have enough incentive this time to find the will, 'to know whether the very idea is beyond you or something you could bear. It's for you to decide.'

Hugo drained his whisky glass, poured more and struggled to his feet. He walked to the window, keeping his back to her. Returning to his seat, he was crying. He sat hunched, shoulders rounded, his head bent low.

She didn't speak.

'I don't need time,' he said, looking up. 'To have you with me again, living here, is the only thing that can give my life any meaning. I've loved you since I was nineteen, that's always been my trouble.'

'And you could find the will? No rehab? Chuck away what's behind the macaroni packet? Silly place, people do clean shelves once in a while, you know. Better inside the packet.'

'I was going to get on top of it, but ...' Hugo had been about to carry on, but dried up. He'd seen how meaningless that was; saying it wasn't enough.

'How do you feel about Ahmed's child as part of our family, though?' Nattie pressed. 'You've only talked about me. It's not as though he and I have gone our separate ways like people divorcing, remarrying, combining their offspring or whatever. He'd have an active role, be a full-on father – and I'd want him to be. I really need you to think very hard about that over the next few days. It's so important if we're going to work anything out.'

'But it's your baby, Nattie, part of you; living with a child of yours wouldn't be the problem, it's you keeping in touch with Ahmed that's the hard part. I've lived in constant secret fear of his return, since before we were married. He's been a ghost in the room, a hungry-eyed gremlin on my shoulder. It's almost better to know where I am, in some ways, painful as the knowledge of you seeing him would be.

'And as to that stash you saw ... I'd been so determined to hold out and be sober for when you came, still holding on to a thread of hope. The trouble was that Amber appeared last night. She'd picked up on some of the Tweets. Shelby's campaign is off the ground, but it hasn't gone viral, you'll be glad to know – I'd kept looking all yesterday. I was clear-headed enough for that, still lasting out at that stage.'

'What set you back then? Something Amber said?'

'She convinced me that you'd fly the coop, as she put it, now that Shelby had ensured Ahmed had to get out fast. She's got keen, you see, and believed the way was clear ... She's kept me afloat at Tyler's, found reasons for my absences, covered when I've been hung out. But being halfway sober last night I found the guts to tell her I couldn't go on seeing her. I should have said it before. Now, though, far from bailing me out, she'll do the opposite. I'm very likely to lose my job, Nattie – I think you should know that.'

'I doubt she really will. Brady likes you, you've got that going for you, and if you've got clean and are on top of things, he's not going to be swayed by Amber making a bit of trouble. People do bitch in workplaces, Brady's wise to all that. Anyway, I don't think Amber would do it for long. She isn't like that. She's a fun-loving person, the sort to cut her losses; she'll get over you before too long. And Amber's not so thick-skinned that she won't have known, deep down, that you didn't have the right feelings for her. I don't think she'll do you in.'

Hugo was looking dumbstruck. Nattie left him and went to check out the freezer. She found a lasagne she'd made months ago, but it should be okay. She stuck it in the microwave to cook from frozen, hoping that wasn't breaking any rules, and went back in to him. 'Can you go to the supermarket for bread, milk and eggs, and some soup too, while you're at it, and a packet of spinach. You must have something green.'

He wasn't taking any of that in. 'Shall I tell you something mildly funny?' he said.

'Go on then.'

'Remember Brian from SleepSweet, who you said we should have to supper? You really took agin him on the night, though you'd mellowed when he showed an interest in Tom's paintings.'

'Yes, I remember,' she said. 'He was a weedy womaniser. I can't believe he has much success, and it was a waste of space for any leads to new business.'

'It wasn't. He called me yesterday and said he'd recommended me to his new boss. The firm they've got isn't cutting it. I nearly fell off my chair. He wants me to come in and meet them and discuss when and whether Tyler's would pitch.'

'That's not funny; it's great! How's Bosphor going? I've been worried about that. Have you been scuppering yourself there?'

'Nearly, but I had some luck. You'll do your full prude look, but snorting a line can be a lifeline once in a while. I was full of oomph, chatting up the travel editor of the *Courier*, and she was curious. She's a user, I think – it takes one to know one – and anyway, I made a hit. She's written a good piece since.'

'That's such a rag, that paper.'

'No credit where it's due?'

'None. Go and get the shopping, get some air, work up an appetite.'

'I'm not into food,' Hugo said, watching while she found a notepad and wrote a list. He was thinner than a reed, unsteady as he went out of the door, but he went.

'Wear a coat!' Nattie shouted after him, before texting Jasmine with an even later ETA.

She felt bloodied, nakedly guilty. The last three months had been unimaginably happy, love and joy distilled to their purest essence with the inevitability of their time being finite – as she'd known in her heart. The trouble with love, feeling that nothing more exists than breathing the same air, touching and belonging, was that more did exist, a world beyond, the lives of others.

To have to face up to the sure knowledge that she'd driven Hugo to such a state of black, destructive desolation that he'd kept company with a snake like Shelby was a heavy penance. *She*, not Hugo, had caused Shelby to gather his ammunition; *her* actions, not Hugo's, had started the rot.

Now she had to patch together the fabric of family life. She had to hope and pray, try to put Hugo back on track. She would hold off moving in again for as long as possible, while her heart was so raw, then do her best to make him feel loved.

He had to live with her pregnancy, see her change shape, suffer the constant reminders, accept the fault lines and settle for what she could give.

Could they find a way through? Lily and Tubsy would glue them together, they'd adjust to the new baby too, and all that went with it. They'd enjoy seeing Ahmed, their distant daddy, once in a while; he would always be special in their lives.

He was more than that to Nattie. Somewhere out there, a pinpoint of light shone bright in the dark of an unknown future. She would never stop hoping. Life could take many different turns.

Epilogue

Christmas came and went. Hugo joined Nattie, her mother and William at Nattie's grandparents'. It was the usual tight squash, but Bridget cooked a magnificent Christmas dinner and they had a traditional family time.

Ahmed loved Lily's handmade calendar and she loved the books and American clothes he'd sent. He had Christmas Day with his eccentric Californian neighbour, a cricket-obsessed Englishman who wrote songs and smoked cheroots. They barbecued steaks in the garden.

Hugo hung on to his job. Brady was impressed that he'd had the guts to come and apologise for a bad patch, and congratulated him on his handling of Bosphor Air. Tyler's won the furniture account too, that Brian had put their way. They lost Palmers department store. Hugo got his Christmas bonus all the same, which tided him over. He wasn't in good financial shape after his dealings with Shelby.

Amber was not a happy bunny, but she moved on and began a relationship with a cosmetics client who showered her with the product. Not ideal, fraternising with the client, but she had a new glow and mended fences with Hugo – 'No hard feelings, lover-boy' – and a rumour went round the office that wedding bells were on the cards with her new man.

Shelby didn't get his comeuppance, he was far too canny for that, but his campaign fizzled out quickly with the William-orchestrated counter Tweets asserting that Ahmed was on the other side of the world and it was all a got-up scam. Nattie's safety caused constant anxiety, but the risk had been minimised as far as possible.

Jasmine went on a diet, worrying about fitting into her wedding dress, though there was nearly a year to go.

Ian at the office was very snoopy about Nattie's pregnancy. He asked, with a finger to the side of his nose, if it had anything to do with all those extra-long lunch hours she'd taken a few months back. She told him he had a fertile imagination.

Moppet pegged out unexpectedly. Ahmed sent an 'In Memoriam' poem and they had a tearful burial in the back garden at Queen's Park. Nattie and Hugo bought Lily a silvery-grey replacement that they called Poppet.

Nattie had stayed on at the flat for a couple of months, surviving on memories, but she was round with Hugo quite a bit, feeding him up and keeping him on the straight. Jasmine appreciated the extra hours.

Lily told her teacher and all her schoolfriends that her mummy and her distant daddy were having a baby.

Tubsy was out of nappies and at nursery school in time for the birth.

Nattie's baby was born on the first of June, a little prematurely, but Ahmed made it over in time and was with her at the birth. It was a boy, six pounds five ounces. They named him William Jake John Bashaar. Ahmed felt sure he would be Bill Bashaar when he was older; it had a good ring. Ahmed said his newborn son was the ugliest, most perfect little bugger he'd ever seen in the whole of his existence. He was a very proud dad.

Acknowledgements

The writing is only a part of the whole, few books would happen without the incalculable help and experience of many professionals and friends.

My warmest thanks to John Sullivan, Stephen Sherbourne, Sayeeda Warsi, Louette Harding, Luke Alkin, Tim and Jenny Hamilton, Paul O'Louglhan, Dominic Ruffy of the Amy Winehouse Foundation and all at Addaction, a charity dedicated to helping people manage their drug and alcohol addictions; they have helped many in need to regain their lives.

I would be floundering in the wilderness without my wonderful editor at Simon & Schuster, Suzanne Baboneau, whose wisdom and instinct I treasure and my agent, Michael Sissons, with his mastery of all things bookish, unerring judgement and firm guiding hand; and Fiona Petheram at PFD, always so terrifically supportive and wise. They have my heartfelt thanks. As do all the team at Simon & Schuster, Ian Chapman, Sue Stephens, Emma Capron, Sara-Jade Virtue, Maisie Lawrence and many more.

Warm thanks too, to Carola Godman Irvine who bid at an

auction to have a character named in this book. She chose to have her two sons named, Matthew and Charley, who have their part to play. And where would I be without my loyal readers? To know that anyone has read and enjoyed one of my books is a very special privilege.

I depend on my husband, Michael, in all things and my wonderful children and grandchildren; you are all my rock and I love you.

*Turn the page to find out where Nattie
and Ahmed's story first began . . .*

A Matter of Loyalty

CHAPTER 1

A gale was blowing. The last tenacious leaves were being torn from the copper beech and maples in the garden, from the horse chestnuts in the lane, the cherry trees over the yew hedge in the church car park. Leaves everywhere, floating, whirling past the kitchen window. They made Victoria think for a moment of a wartime sky filled with parachuting soldiers and she felt almost tearful. But the house was comfortingly snug and warm.

It was in the village of Ferndale, near Southampton. A small mellowed 1830s house that would have creaked and let in draughts had William not modernized and insulated it, extended and stretched it outwards and upwards to its rafters. Just as cars revealed much about their owners, Plumstead House spoke eloquently of his passion for space and light.

She had married him knowing his innermost thoughts and feelings, but not his living habits. Two people in the public eye, she, a government minister and Member of Parliament for Southampton East, he, editor of *The Post,* a national newspaper; they'd hardly met more than a dozen times in the nine long months of their love affair. It had been a constant media cat and mouse game before everything was explosively blown apart. Then had come the immense emotional upheaval, the private pain of finally extricating themselves from other loyalties.

Two years on, with all her new responsibilities, life was quite frightening but William was in it now, happily, tenderly, sparringly, combatively – in it full time.

He looked up from the Sunday newspapers. 'You're deep in thought. What is it?'

'Oh, nothing much; you, the gale. I know you won't be going into the office for high-sided vehicle dramas and upended trees, but there is all this stuff about Peter Barnes in the papers . . . It isn't going anywhere, he'll stay Foreign Secretary, he and the PM are intertwined. Can't you be more original and stay above it all?'

'The paper can handle fallen trees.' William grinned, making clear that while he wasn't going into the office he had every intention of zapping Peter Barnes – who deserved all he got, the disloyal shit – in thick black headlines in tomorrow's *Post*.

There was always a government Cassius, Victoria thought, feeling as irritated by the Foreign Secretary as if with an itchy rash. He took out his fury with *The Post* on her.

William seldom went into the office on Sundays now. He had done so quite often during his first marriage and it was hard not to feel a little smug about his changed routine. Strange to think he'd edited the paper for just on a decade; that was quite a landmark achievement, a triumph even, in the fast-moving dog-eating-dog media world.

She thought about his lunch on Friday with his South African proprietor, Oscar Bluemont. There had been a venture capitalist along whom Oscar was keen to impress and William had suddenly found himself elevated to editor-in-chief. 'First I'd heard of it,' he said dryly. 'You'd think he'd have got round to sharing that with me.'

His proprietor was an eccentric with a keen business head, a cool couple of billion, a svelte blonde wife and several ex-ones, too. Victoria was fond of him. He was a quirky little gnome-like character who pranced about on spindly legs like a puppet and he had a definite soft spot for her. He had been loyally supportive all through the painful publicity over the affair – when William was making news instead of reporting it. But then he hadn't wanted to lose a first-rate editor.

Oscar had just won a bidding war for a failing Sunday newspaper, *The Dispatch*, and she hoped William's new title didn't mean he'd be overseeing that as well. He already did a weekly current-affairs programme on television, *The Firing Line*, on top of editing *The Post*. It was more than enough.

'Is Oscar going to do something to mark your ten years?' she asked, knowing how much the proprietor loved lavish parties. 'He's here all this month, isn't he, till December?'

'Don't! He's talked of nothing else. I've insisted any sort of bash has to be at the office, though, and kept internal and contained or he'd ask a thousand or so of his closest chums along and ensure it was in every diary column – and all saying it's been ten years too long already.' William grinned and went back to his paper.

He was concentrating intently on an article and it reminded her of first meeting him only three years ago, a tall, dishevelled editor with a fearsome reputation whose arresting stare had been entirely focused on her. It had thrown her completely off course. He'd been forty-eight then and looked his age; his face deeply grooved, the careless unhealthy newspaper hours carved deep. He seemed no older now, though; he had taken all the knocks and professional strain and done all the hard living going.

It was time to get on. Breakfast needed clearing and nothing would be further from William's mind. He wasn't domesticated or a first-class cook like her ex-husband Barney, but there was a load to be shared – and never more so than now.

Three months of being Home Secretary and it didn't get any easier. There were policemen in the garden. They had installed two huts, one with high-tech equipment and another for resting up. Being guarded night and day, weekends as well, was a huge hideous intrusion, but she had to accept the need. A Special Branch detective was with her at all times when she was out and about. It was as much for the safety of others, they said: if she was a target then everyone round her was at risk as well.

With privacy in such short supply Sundays were to be treasured. On Saturdays she was busy with her constituency surgery and William was often off to collect his two just-teenage girls. He returned them on Sunday nights, on the way to London, trailing back for the long hours of the working week.

He had left Ursula, his wife of twenty years, walked out on his three children, Tom, Emma and Jessie. Victoria had felt consumed with guilt while never quite seeing herself as the other woman. Her feelings for William had been too powerful and deep. She had fought against them, broken off all contact, yet all the while been waiting, hoping, willing him to leave.

Who could say now, she thought with wry relief, that it had been so wrong? Ursula was living with Julian, a writer and antiquarian bookseller, whom she seemed to love with a far greater passion than anything she'd felt for William – for all the bitter hurt and accusations. There was even Martha too, now, their wonderful pink peaceable baby with a solemn steady gaze who was adored by all.

Ursula was forty-five, three years older than Victoria, yet she was the one with a new child. It seemed rough justice – although Victoria knew that was an unjust thought even as it came to her.

Having a miscarriage, losing William's baby in the thick of their affair, had gouged so great a hole in her that nothing could fill it. No warm earth of passing time, no grass had grown over.

Victoria carried her loss, she wore it like a baby-sling. It had been late in the pregnancy, the sex already determined, a boy. She thought of him being sucked out of her in all that warm wet blood, the tourniquet-like contractions. The lasting pain, though, had been emotional. At a stage when it had seemed too much to hope that William would leave Ursula, the baby had felt a part of him and uniquely theirs.

Her only other child, Nattie, had been sixteen at the time. Nattie had known about the affair, the pregnancy, the particular stresses with her father, Barney, and coped with it all. Nattie was a golden doted-on daughter and beautiful; everyone said so. Her face was open, gentle, smiling, trusting; men were a constant worry. Long fine hair, fair like her father's – Victoria's was dark – and wide amber eyes that glowed.

She was good friends with William's son, Tom, who was in his early twenties. They often came to Hampshire on the same weekend. Julian's 18-year-old son, James – who lived with his father now, together with Ursula and the girls – came too, occasionally. James's childhood had been in Africa; his mother was a Ugandan doctor whom Julian had always supported but never married. She had let her son come to England while doing his A-levels and he'd just got into Cambridge.

They were all in each other's slipstreams now, Victoria thought. Her life, like a fast flowing river, had hit rocks and thrashed about, but miraculously found its smooth new path. An unhappy marriage, Nattie her only child, and suddenly there were five offspring around at times, all variously connected and getting on fine. The constituency house had certainly needed to be stretched.

The roads were quite traffic-free on that filthy night, driving back to London. They talked little. Travelling with a police driver and a detective made it hard, but on the flipside it put pay to any marital eruptions and full-throated rows.

Rodney was on duty. Victoria liked him the best of the 'tecs, as they were called, the three detectives on the protection team. He was good-looking in a Kevin Spacey sort of a way and never tried too hard to be unobtrusive. Asked to join in a conversation he was always cheerfully forthright in his views.

A story running in all the Sunday papers about a trouble-making Islamist cleric got William going and he broke into the subdued atmosphere of the car. 'They use religion like a web, like flypaper, these fundamentalists,' he declared. 'Luring in susceptible students, distorting their faith. It's serious. We'll be demanding this guy's removal in the paper tomorrow and getting plenty of support, you can be sure.' Victoria shot him an impatient look; that stance could only make life harder and add to her workload.

'And they can always beat the system,' Rodney chipped in airily. 'They stand on their soapboxes stirring it up, seeking the destruction of the very country that gives them the freedoms they enjoy. They'd wipe out democracy, yet we're not allowed to infringe their so-called rights,' he finished, letting slip a very non-PC sneer.

Victoria fought back, feeling got at. 'But isn't that as it should be? We fought wars for freedom of speech; millions gave their lives. You've got extremists, sure, but don't forget the silent peaceful majority, Rodney; a lot more sympathizing Muslims might become militant if we start clamping down. It's a delicate balance.'

William, the police, they all wanted a tough-talking Home Secretary, but they should know by now she was no softy. After all those painful decisions taken in her last job at Health, all the bad press . . . They could give her a little credit for that.

A policeman was on guard as usual at their South London

house, standing patiently in the paved front garden, half-hidden by two huge sentry-like camellia bushes. He was at the bottom of the front steps – still with the original Georgian black and white tiles that Victoria loved – that led up to the wide Oxford-blue front door.

They had bought the house in squatters' condition when William was still supporting Ursula. Polish builders and double-glazing had transformed it. On a busy main road, but shielded by a front garden wall and trellis, the house itself had symmetry, space and light. It was close to Parliament and *The Post* too, located in its tall tower, tight to the river on the South Bank. William's twelfth-floor office had a sensational view.

Rodney said his goodnights and the two armoured cars drove off, one of them the usual backup car. Victoria had work to finish and William set about making tea for the policeman on duty.

He would take up the morning's first editions then, always delivered to the door, and read in bed till she came upstairs. Climbing in beside him she would lift away the papers, lean across to turn off his light. He would intercept her hand and pull her on top of him, talking of love. He knew her needs, knew when to hurt, bite, scratch, pull, when to be gentle. He'd once said she had incredibly sensitive nipples and she had queried how he was such an authority on the subject and the extent of his research.

If he rolled her over, as he mostly did, he'd stretch out for the light so that neither had to do it later. It was a comfortingly physical end-of-weekend routine.

At something like five the next morning she felt William's toe. It brushed her calf, a cautious exploratory touch, and she sleepily took his outstretched hand.

'Did I wake you?'

Victoria considered that. 'No, it's okay.' She was already

half-awake, thinking of the week ahead, one marathon after another, fraught meetings, questions in Parliament, even a state banquet at Buckingham Palace.

She turned and looked at William in the semi-dark. The clocks had only just gone back and despite the heavy cream curtains, the lifting sky outside was giving a hint and promise of morning. 'It's a bit rough,' she said, yawning, 'when a state banquet at the Palace is about my only chance of seeing you all week.'

'We were asked to a royal film premiere too, on Wednesday – the Countess of Wessex is going.' William squeezed her hand. 'It's the new Kidman film—'

'Same night? I suppose the Royals don't all have to show up at every banquet.'

'Are you deliberately missing the Kidman point? I've always wanted to meet her. A temp had accepted for us without a call to your office. I despair.' William paused a moment. 'How awake are you? Can I talk?'

'Sure.' She wondered what was coming.

'We're breeding terrorists, MI5 can only scratch the surface. I've just taken on an impressive young Muslim reporter – his stuff's sensitive and sharp, but twats like George are so suspicious they think he could be an activist mole. That's typical fucking George, but, from the tip-offs we get, the stories I could print, it's bad out there. People resent communities turning in on themselves. It's a grim scene.'

'British born, your new reporter?'

'Yes. Leeds, I think. I like him, Ahmed Khan. He's going places. He'll be editing *The Post* one of these days.'

'George is right to be cautious,' she said, thinking of the insidious infiltration of the universities, the turning of those bright young minds.

'George? Right? Give us a break.' William never let up on his poor deputy. 'I'm getting up,' he whispered, squeezing her hand again. 'It's thinking time. And you need some more sleep.'

She had an hour or so more in bed and dressing for the office felt much readier for the day ahead. Fit for department cock-ups, jealous colleagues, media snares − all the invisible wires that would be strung across her path through the week.

'Morning, Minister − good weekend?'

'Wonderfully quiet! And you, Tony?' Victoria asked, coming in through the outer office on the way to her own. 'Yours too, I hope?'

Her principal private secretary smiled. He was competent, pleasant, dutifully hardworking, though no match for Marty who'd filled that role in her very first job in government, three years ago, as Minister of Housing and Planning at DEFRA.

Victoria still had feelings of awe, walking into her vast ballroom of an office. With its red slub sofa and chairs, oval mahogany conference table and cheering paintings the trappings were impressive enough, but it was really a strategic war room where she fought her corner and life-affecting decisions could be made.

The morning newspapers were all laid out and *The Post*'s predictable headline, 'Sack The Man!' brought a small smile. Peter Barnes, the 'Snake-in-the-grass Foreign Secretary', was accused of openly briefing against Number Ten and, in *The Post*'s eyes, should be shown the door.

No chance, Victoria thought. The Prime Minister was a believer in the better-inside-the-tent principle, he wasn't having any Cassiuses on the backbenches hurtling killer-darts. She wished he would sack Barnes. The Foreign Secretary was out to get her and knew his way round Westminster, all the subtlest ways of doing her down.

*

They were late for the state banquet. Victoria's long white gloves had gone missing, her fake diamond necklace wouldn't do up and she couldn't wear her favourite dress because of an archaic code about not wearing black in front of the Queen. And William wasn't even home.

He came panting upstairs then and said all the right things about her second-best burgundy dress. 'Can't we skip the whole thing and be ill?' he grinned, wasting precious minutes kissing her. She waggled her watch arm and tried to hurry him up with the whole fiddly rigmarole of dressing in white tie.

William succeeded with her necklace clasp, she gave up the hunt for the gloves and they shot out of the house. Rodney had the car doors standing open and the two heavy vehicles sped away. Over Lambeth Bridge, down Horseferry Road, along Grosvenor Gardens: Victoria was aware of a discreet rear blue light being on and suspected it was professional pride. It mattered, getting them there on time.

They swept in through the imposing Palace gates – no searching of her police-driven government car – and drew up at a more leisurely pace alongside the red-carpeted stone entrance steps under cover of the drive-in porch.

Hurrying up the palatial Grand Staircase past handsome ornate portraits of George III and Queen Charlotte, she whispered they were the last King and Queen of America; it was impossible, in that rarefied atmosphere, not to speak in a hush.

Footmen directed them along wide passages into the Picture Gallery where the paintings were by Rembrandt, Van Dyck, Rubens, Vermeer. The hundred and fifty or so guests were gathered there for drinks. A scattering of tiaras shimmered and more white-gloved footmen were circulating with trays. She and William took flutes of champagne and turned to speak to whoever was nearest, and in that long length of elegant hall it happened to be the Foreign Secretary, Peter Barnes.

His smile was sophisticated and easy. 'Short of copy this week, I see, William. Although a bit rich, don't you think, calling our excellent Prime Minister wet.' He was alluding slickly to *The Post*'s continued personal attacks while twisting the slant.

'On the contrary,' William said, smiling just as smoothly. 'These are important matters that have to be aired.' Victoria imagined the recharging of Barnes's vitriolic feelings and inwardly sighed.

A senior Palace dignitary touched her arm. The banquet was in honour of the Chinese President and as Foreign and Home Secretaries, she and Barnes, along with their spouses, were being invited into the Music Room to meet the royal party.

A military string band, the Welsh Guards, was playing in the Minstrel's Gallery as they joined the other guests in the State Ballroom. The long tables were sumptuously bedecked with gold plate and immense silver-gilt epergne centrepieces piled with pyramids of fruit. The flowers were spectacular, vast arrangements of deep-red velvety roses set in branching foliage of golds and browns.

They had been seated well apart. William stayed with her for a moment as they stood waiting for the royal party, chatting to the Chinese diplomat she would be next to.

'Better get to my place now,' William said, touching her arm.

As he turned to go Victoria saw him feel in his trouser pocket for a vibrating mobile. It shouldn't have been on; a couple of people gave very sniffy looks as he took it out. The paper would only call in an emergency, she thought, stiffening, imagining some new Home Office horror, before being distracted and filled with alarm by the sight of a white-faced official hurrying towards her.

They moved to a corner where they could talk more privately. 'There's been a bomb explosion in the West End, Minister,' he whispered, his face panic-stricken. He looked helpless without precedent or protocol. 'Eleven dead, I'm afraid. You may, um, want to leave now . . .?'

Eleven people dead . . . her stomach was lurching. There was a strange ringing sensation in her head. The scale of the injured didn't bear thinking about. It was her duty, her responsibility, to keep the public safe from terrorist bombs and she had failed.

'You'll explain?' Victoria said to the agonized official, outwardly calm as she looked round urgently for the nearest exit. Then, grabbing her bag from the table, she and William made a conspicuous dash, aware of the rustling disapproval, everyone's eyes following their path. The murmurings about bad form would be very short-lived.

The bomb had exploded in Leicester Square, in the cinema entrance where the royal premiere was taking place, right by the barriers with the pressed-up crowds.

Where were Nattie, Tom, James? Any one of them could have been out in the West End. Had they wandered by to glimpse the stars arriving for a premiere? Oh, God.

William had his mobile clamped to his ear and was relaying all he was being told. 'Seems the Countess was only seconds away. The film stars were all up on the first floor, though, waiting in the receiving line. They're in shock, but okay. It was the people at the barriers, photographers, police, and the suicide bomber, of course.'

Victoria was soon on her own mobile, listening as her Permanent Secretary, Sir Adam Childs, methodically, unflappably, gave her the same sickening details.

'Just leaving the Palace now, Adam,' she said breathlessly. 'I must get home quickly and change – you'll keep in constant

touch?' They could have been just arriving at that cinema themselves. Had their names been on an acceptance list? William's
office had said they were coming at first.

They called Nattie and Tom who were fine. James was, too.

In the car Victoria found it hard to speak for the lump in her
throat. She pulled herself together and, turning to William, said
flatly, 'I'm doing the television statement, the PM's leaving it to
me. I'll need to get to a studio fast.'

'You'll have time, you'll be fine,' he assured, trying to give
comfort.

The feeling of gagging stayed with her as she worked out what
to say: inadequate words, but the only ones. She had a terror of
crumpling weakly in front of the cameras, although the adrena-
line was ripping through her like wildfire.

William, who was brilliant at expressing things, knew better
than to offer help. He was staring out of the window, thinking
professionally she could tell. It still gave her a start when he suddenly turned and started to quiz Rodney.

'Suicide bomber for definite, do we know? The cinema will
have been searched, won't it, with a royal coming? The dogs
brought in, full-blown security?'

'Yes, all of that,' Rodney replied, 'and our chaps will have been
scrutinizing the crowd. It's more difficult in the colder weather
with all the anoraks and bulky clothes. Seems the guy was wearing a bomb vest. That's new here. The 7/7 and 21/7 bombers'
explosives were packed in rucksacks, peroxide-based stuff. With a
vest it has to be a much smaller volume, far more sophisticated—'
He dried up then, probably remembering William's role as editor
and the need for more restraint.

Images swirled in her mind, looming and receding like a
fairground hall of horrors, distorted and obscene – only these
were real: flying bodies, severed limbs. Victoria could hear the

pulverizing sound of the explosion, the screams. She thought of the unsuspecting happy crowd; parents and loved ones glued to their televisions at home.

The royal car had been so close. The bomber seemed to have panicked and hurled himself at the barrier, instantly flinging his own and the lives of ten others away. And the toll was sure to rise. His exploding bomb vest had showered lethally detonated shrapnel everywhere, like omni-directional shotgun fire, like the blasting of a mine.

The attacker's personal details were likely to be known soon; suicide bombers seldom bothered to strip themselves of all clues to their identity since they were going to die anyway. But who had masterminded the whole plan? That would be harder to uncover.

Keeping the country safe from terrorists, Victoria thought, was her job, the task she'd been given. Protecting ordinary decent people, guarding the nation's borders. 'We're breeding terrorists,' William had said. The threat was constant, in cities and quiet provincial streets, in attitudes and prejudice. She had done her utmost and more, but it hadn't been enough.